Novena

Jack Hopkins

DEDICATION

For my grandchildren

Patrick, Tom, Mikey, Teddy, Charlie, and Harry

CONTENTS

Contents

Continued

ACKNOWLEDGEMENTS

Thank you for the feedback: Dermot Muldowney, Michael Doyle, Terry Turner, Eileen Timms, Rita Cott, and John Jessup.

PROLOGUE

Dublin: May 1959

The shoe repair trade was slow at this time of year, probably because, Cobbler Maguire supposed, people were buying sandals or just buying new shoes after a cold wet and miserable winter. So, when the well-dressed gentleman calling himself Mr Smith, with the refined country accent arrived to collect his repaired quality brogues, Maguire, the proprietor of the small shop in Dublin's Trinity Street, felt his spirits lift. The gentleman's face was difficult to see as his black hair and dark hat came down almost to his eyebrows, while his dark horned rimmed glasses and heavy black moustache obscured the remainder of his face.

"May I see that leather briefcase displayed in your window?" The gentleman asked, having received his shoes in a paper bag and paid his bill.

"Most certainly, Sir," replied Maguire, at the same time feeling a ray of hope for a sale. "That soft calf leather case," he continued, as he handed it to the customer, "was handcrafted by me and has a six-inch-wide bottom while opening at the top. In addition, it has side pockets on the inside and another pocket on the right outside. As well, you can see there is a flap-over cover for the brass close and key lock. And I'll give a five-year guarantee on it."

The gentleman looked straight at Maguire and said, "Yes, I can see the quality of your craftsmanship, but I wonder is your discretion up to the same standard?" Maguire, just for a second, hesitated but then answered, "I certainly hope so Sir, but.... How?"

"Well, Mr Maguire, I would like to purchase this briefcase, but I would like you to add within it a discrete false bottom. For this additional work, no questions asked, I am willing to pay you twice the price of the case. So, Mr Maguire, what do you think of that?"

1

Maguire pondered this notion, not because he could not or would not do the job, but because he wondered if he could extract a higher fee for his services. The gentleman, however, broke the silence by saying.

"You seem a little hesitant, Mr Maguire, so let me first assure you that what I intend to use the secret compartment for is simply to hide a present for a relative. Secondly, I will give you a deposit of £5 now and should your work be satisfactory I will give you a bonus of another £5. Now, Mr Maguire, I would like your decision, Yes, or No?"

"Certainly, Yes Mr Smith," replied Maguire, all hesitation gone, "what exactly is it you want? And when do you want it?"

New York: July 1959

In a rundown area in the 'not so nice' New York neighbourhood of the Bronx, a man with a refined Irish country accent, entered a store selling all types of guns and ammunition. He placed a hand-crafted leather briefcase with a false bottom on the floor beside him and asked the clerk behind the counter to show him some handguns.

Having made his selection, he purchased a product that felt comfortable in his hand, together with a silencer and two boxes of the required bullets. He secured the lot within the secret compartment of the briefcase before he left the store.

Three days later, he had returned to his home in Ireland and hid the gun and ammunition in a place to which only he had access.

Dublin: September 1959

Almost immediately, the Cobbler Maguire recognised the gentleman who entered his shop on that cold, wet and windy autumn day. It couldn't be a complaint, he thought, as he had been quite methodical and scrupulous in the workmanship of the case itself and its false bottom.

"Mr Maguire, a very good day to you!" The gentleman said with a smile and continued. "You did a special job for me last May, and I have another item I would like your skill with. You see, I will be going abroad soon, and I will require a suitcase made of the same soft leather as the briefcase I purchased. Is that something with which you could help me?"

"Most certainly. You are Mr Smith, isn't that correct?" "Yes, that is correct, Mr Maguire. Now I will not require this suitcase until the end of October. Is that enough time to complete the task?"

"It is Mr Smith, and may I ask, will you be requiring a false bottom in it?"

Smith smiled. "Not this time Mr Maguire, I will, however, require its inside measurements to be four feet long, two feet wide, and two feet deep. As apart from my apparel it will also need to accommodate a special heavy work of art."

"Let me write those measurements down and if you give me a few minutes Mr Smith I'll work out a price for you!"

The price was agreed upon.

Dublin: November 1959

Small Article appearing in the 'Irish Times' Friday 13th November.

Tragic Canal Accident: The body of a well-known Irish leatherworker and cobbler, Timothy Maguire, was taken from the Grand Canal yesterday. It seems that when walking home from his local pub, Mr Maguire, a non-swimmer, tripped and fell into deep water near his home in Baggot Street. He is survived by his wife Annie, two children under 10 and one brother. Mr Maguire's business in the city's Trinity Street will continue to be operated by his brother Michael, also a leather craftsman.

Dublin: December 1959

The black-haired gentleman with a large black moustache to match adjusted his dark horn-rimmed spectacles, in a gesture, that gave the impression he was interested in a particular book on the bookshelf nearest the Ballsbridge Library's check-out desk. He was not interested in any book, but was, from the corner of his eye, extremely interested in the process the Librarian followed to register a new Library member.

The Librarian, having checked the potential member's application form together with identification, address etc. took a bundle of membership cards secured with an elastic band from the desk drawer. She then filled in the card, added her signature, and handed it to the new member saying. "You may borrow up to four books for two weeks, and should you not return them by their due date, you will incur a fine." The new member took the card, thanked the issuer, and went off to select her books. The Librarian placed the bundle of blank membership cards back in the drawer.

The black-haired man with glasses and moustache went quickly to the far end from the check-out desk and then looked back to ensure the Librarian was alone. Having confirmed this, he then rushed back to the desk and in an excited state said to her.

"Quickly, there are some children ripping pages out of the books down at the back!"

"What?" She asked, registering what he said but wishing confirmation.

"Kids," he said, "tearing up perfectly good books. You need to stop them!"

She shot up from her chair and almost ran toward the back. Once she had started her quest, he leaned over the desk, opened the drawer, and slipped a blank Library card from beneath the elastic band and casually pocketed it. He then turned around and walked out the exit.

THE CHURCH

Dublin 1960

The 'Star of the Sea' church, in Sandymount, dates from the 1850s. In 1960, it consisted of its central nave facing the 'High altar' with its main aisle separating rows of pews left and right. In addition, apart from the nave, there were also left and right sections each with its aisle and a single row of pews. The left or 'Irishtown side' faced a small altar to 'St Joseph 'with one confession box fitted against the sidewall. Inside the altar rail to the left of St Joseph's altar was the 'sacristy' door, allowing access to and from all altars. The right or 'Sandymount side' also with an aisle and pews, faced a small altar to 'The Blessed Virgin.' Against the wall on the right were three more evenly spaced Confession boxes.

The pulpit stood a little down from the high altar on the left.

Most of the congregation could see, and certainly hear, the ceremonies and lessons from the High Altar and pulpit. There were small sections around the church dedicated to e.g., St Anthony, St Patrick, The Sacred Heart, The Blessed Virgin, and The Head of Jesus with a Crown of Thorns. Some of these have the facility to light a candle or donate a monetary gift.

CHAPTER 1

Sunday 28ᵗʰ February (8.00 AM Mass)

It was five minutes to seven in the morning, and 42-year-old Peg O'Connell could stand the pain no longer. She manoeuvred herself out of bed and had a quick shower with the make-shift contraption her husband Richard had attached to the bath taps. The heat of the water undoubtedly gave her some relief from the pain, which seemed particularly bad on this morning.

Once dressed, she decided on an early Mass as she was up and about. Richard was playing with the two younger children, who had jumped on top of him in the bed while she was in the shower. The two older ones, John 16 and Monica 14 were still stuck to their beds. So, at 7.45 AM precisely, she left her house on Strand Road for the church.

Within a few minutes, Peg had turned onto Newgrove Avenue, out of the wind and spray from Dublin Bay. A little further on, she stopped at Miss Milligan's hardware shop on the Green to glance at the notices posted on the board in the window. One caught her eye.

DRAMA

With a view to form a **'Sandymount Amateur Dramatic Society'**

A meeting will be held for all those interested.

AT

The Lecture Hall

Sandymount Methodist Church

9 Sandymount Green

Shrove Tuesday 1/3/60 at 8 PM

Note: Apart from budding Thespians, we will also need help with production, direction, stage management, lighting & sound, costume, make-up and general help with tea-making, cleaning, clerical and administration.

Initiators in the spirit of ecumenism: Miss Evelyn Roberts, Mrs Cecilia Lombardi, Fr Joseph McKenna 'Star of the Sea' and Rev Roger Shillitoe 'Methodist Church.'

Just drop in for a cup of tea and a chat

Contact: Miss Roberts on 692561, should you have any questions?

Now there is something, Peg thought, which could get your mind off run-of-the-mill living, as she continued down Sandymount Road to fulfil her Sunday obligation.

As part of the celebration of 8 o'clock morning mass in the 'Star of the Sea', Canon Skeffington moved to 'the book of the gospels' on the high altar's left side. At the same time, the congregation all stood to face the priest's back, while simultaneously with their thumbs, crossing themselves on their forehead, lips, and breast, as he began to read the word of God.

Located halfway up in the nave's right-hand pews was Eileen Hannigan, an attractive woman who was 37 years old but looked five years younger. She wore a darkish green coat which complimented her natural wavy auburn hair that was only slightly covered with a black lace mantilla. Eileen followed not a word of the Latin text muttered by the priest. Instead, she was miles away, thinking of her husband James and their relationship, which had lost its buzz and now become listless. Moreover, she thought of her three children and their various needs, new clothes for her youngest five-year-old Paul and the eleven-year-old twins Thomas and Tilly and then Seamus aged 14, just had to have new football boots. Then she focused on her Sunday routine. This consisted of buying the Sunday papers on the way home, getting the children's breakfast, and readying them for the 10 o'clock children's mass, while at the same time preparing the Sunday fry-up for Himself. With breakfast finished, he would read the papers while she cleaned up and prepared the Sunday roast dinner.

At around 12.30, Eileen's husband would head off to the pub for a couple of pints, returning for dinner ready on the table by 1.30 PM. Once the family had finished their meal, she again cleaned up while he dozed in his armchair. Finally, she would get herself ready to visit her mother at Grangegorman District mental hospital, located on the other side of the city. The visiting times were from 3 PM to 5.30 PM, and mostly she arrived there before 3.30. To her husband's credit, and despite their strained relationship, he looked after the twins and little Paul for the afternoon bringing them to 'Herbert Park,' the 'Strand,' or the afternoon picture show in the Ritz cinema, locally called the 'Shack.' Seamus, her fourteen-year-old, would go off with his pals for the afternoon, usually to play or watch football.

Eileen continued with these thoughts, as best she could, knowing, however, she was just using them to camouflage another thought that kept pushing itself for dominance in her head. This wondrous thing that was seeking attention was nothing less than her great, great, beautiful secret, and the fear and joy it brought to her life. Today, though, she intended, with God's help, to remove it once and for all. Though the physical and mental excitement as well as the pleasure she derived from it was something she had never, ever, experienced in her life before. But this Sunday, she told herself once more it would be different because once she received the blessed sacrament in 'holy communion' the strength received from it would help her to finally do what was right. But, interrupting her daydreams suddenly then, the gospel concluded and she, together with the rest of the congregation, resumed their seats, while the Canon made his way to the pulpit for the day's homily.

"My dear brethren," he began. "As you are aware, this Wednesday marks the beginning of Lent with the crossing of ash on the forehead to remind us that we will surely die, and our earthy remains will turn to ashes of dust. It is a period of penance and sacrifices we all make for the death on Good Friday and resurrection Easter Sunday of our Lord and Saviour Jesus Christ. Remember, Jesus died on the cross to redeem you from 'original sin' and so open the gates of heaven to all those deserving.

Because Jesus did this, we need to show our appreciation for his great gesture by contributing our sacrifices. The Church has set out the minimum of such, which, under the pain of sin, each adult should live out. I am, of course, referring to the schedule of 'fast' and 'abstinence' as detailed in the pamphlets available at the church doors. However, each catholic should also make their own contribution, such as, giving up various pleasures like, cigarettes, alcoholic drink, or sweet cakes.

Now such little sacrifices are all well and good, but as an addition, I wish to announce that this parish will have a special holy activity to assist its parishioners to make a special sacrifice to the glory of God. What I am referring to, my Dear Brethren, is the 'Novena of Grace' in honour of St. Francis Xavier. This novena will run over nine days, commencing in this church at 8. PM on next Friday the 4th of March and continuing each night at the same time with the final prayers and offerings on Saturday 12th of March. In addition, the novena sessions for Saturday 5th and Saturday 12th will also be held at 9.30 AM on those days for the novena prayers, the rosary, and sermon, followed by the 10.00 AM mass and benediction. These extra sessions are for the convenience of the participants who may not be able to attend the Saturday evening sessions.

I am also delighted to advise you that Father John Horgan SJ, from The Jesuit house in Gardiner Street, will conduct the novena.

Now, as your parish priest, I strongly urge you to participate in this religious event, firstly, as a sacrifice for Lent and secondly, for any special 'intention' you have for yourself or someone else. There is no doubt that when you complete this novena, participating in its prayers and lessons, together with receiving the 'blessed sacrament' in holy communion God will grant your requests, through the intersession of St. Francis. Of course, should your intentions not be for your own or the good of others, they will not be granted.

Apart from confessions being held at the usual times on Saturdays, Fr Horgan and another priest of the parish will hear them for an hour immediately following benediction each night throughout the novena. With this in mind, I would advise you that as the novena finishes on Saturday the 12th of March and as I have said a requirement is to receive the 'blessed sacrament', at some point throughout, you may also receive it on the Sunday the 13th, to fulfil the 'Novena obligation' once you have completed the previous nine days of prayers and lessons."

The Canon continued speaking, but Eileen Hannigan had stopped paying attention as she realised, that what she had heard was a sign from above to put her intention to the test and remove her secret, wonderful as it was, from her life forever even though it would probably tear her apart.

As Eileen was thinking about the novena to achieve her 'intention,'

Mrs Mary Murphy, an acquaintance of Eileen, sitting just two pews up, and was thinking something similar. In Mary's case, however, her life was a complete shamble. She knew that she alone was to blame for the mess she was in and sure enough from the outside it all looks, not great, but basically all right. However, inside her head, together with inside her house, with Stephen her husband and children, life was disastrous. Moreover, the thing she was doing to keep everything looking all right could only end in a catastrophe of embarrassment if she was caught and maybe even see her end up in jail. She knew she was the reason her husband had taken to the drink, and if not already there, he was certainly heading for alcoholism. The result was every spare penny was going to Powers whiskey, with little left for the household and the children's needs.

Mary's problems began inside her head following one of the 'fire and brimstone' sermon's given by a Redemptorist Missionary, at the previous September women's retreat in this very church. She knew beforehand the church's teaching on baptism and still born infants before hearing it preached, in no uncertain terms, from the pulpit. But it still shocked her to the core with sadness as she had herself given birth to such a baby. So, on her way home that evening, she accompanied by another acquaintance, one Vera O'Brien, an expert on the saints and all things catholic, Mary asked two questions of Vera, with the answer to the first being:

Limbo is not the hell of the dammed, but a place of state or rest. And the answer to the second: *Baptism is necessary for salvation because our Divine Lord has said: Unless a man is born again of water and the Holy Ghost, he cannot enter into the kingdom of God.*

That night, following the retreat sermon, while in bed with her husband, Mary refused his intimate advances, and such refusals continued up to the present time. She was aware that she was obligated to accommodate his needs but could not find it in her head or her heart to participate. She had previously admitted to herself that she was not at all fond of the sexual side of her marriage but had indulged in it for Stephen's sake as well as fulfilling her catholic duty. Her refusal in this matter had led to Stephen taking to the bottle and this, in turn, was causing major difficulties for her three children. It resulted with herself breaking one of God's great Ten Commandments. She would, therefore, surely do the novena in hope of getting some peace but also, she would visit the doctor tomorrow and talk to him about her problems in the marriage bed.

As the congregation stood for the 'creed,' Dr James McNulty, who was situated halfway up the Irishtown side, saw many of his patients throughout the attendees. McNulty was fondly known as 'Robin' (Hood) due to only charging the wealthy for his services, while providing free care for those struggling. Robin had been a gifted student throughout his time in the College of Surgeons in Dublin and then in the Foundation programme at St. Mary's Hospital, London, and indeed following his time there as 'Senior House Officer' Robin was offered and accepted a full-time surgical position. Two months later, however, on September 3rd, 1939, Neville Chamberlain made the historical radio broadcast announcing that Britain was at war with the Germans.

Robin had no hesitation in volunteering his services, and upon receiving his commission was sent to Scotland for training in medical-military structures, processes, and hierarchical command procedures. When this was completed, he received orders to report, directly, for duty on the south coast of Kent.

On the day before leaving on the train for Dover, however, he called into St Mary's to pick up a 'reference,' as to his skills, character etc., from his old boss Chief Surgeon Sir Reginald Stanford. Collecting this testimonial from the reception desk, he heard some distinctive Irish accents across the foyer at the Accounts hatch. He glanced around to see only the backs of two young ladies accompanied by an older woman. Beside them, on the floor, was a suitcase labelled 'British Rail- Euston/Holyhead/ Dun Laoghaire.' The older lady was then speaking to the cashier, relating how she appreciated the successful treatment one of her accompanying daughters had received. At the same time, while writing out a cheque, she said she was returning home today to participate in a ladies' 'bridge tournament' but her daughters, now both of an age to make their own decisions, were staying on in London for an extra night to attend the show at the Palladium as, despite the war, everything in the city appeared safe. The cashier agreed that she had seen no real changes since Chamberlain's announcement, except for numerous uniformed personnel rushing about on foot or transported around in trucks.

Robin turned back quickly not wishing to appear rude but wondered why the young woman had been admitted, perhaps, he thought, for an operation not performed in Ireland either due to religion, state laws, or medical reluctance. He pocketed his reference and headed off to spend the best part of the next 5 years practicing his skills in various theatres of war in Europe and North Africa. Then, when his services were no longer required, he resigned his commission and was discharged from his duties with a string of honours.

On his return to Dublin, he secured a surgical position in Hollis Street maternity hospital and remained there until he resigned in 1951 at which time, he moved into general Practice in Sandymount. The reason for this move was his frustration with the prevailing restrictions, practices, and attitudes on women's health issues by the medical association, the state, and the church. Indeed, this frustration reached a peak with their opposition to a proposed, excellent social, 'Mother and Child' health scheme. This insightful proposal, by the then Health Minister Dr Noel Brown, subsequently failed to be implemented, resulting in the resignation of the Minister. This last straw for Robin prompted his move from his immersion in women's health at Hollis Street to a less restrictive and wider medical practice.

Many of Robin's colleagues, as scientists, particularly in Britain, did not believe in a deity, but he did believe in the spiritual side of life. Indeed, such had been enforced when he saw, first-hand, the faith of those slowly dying of wounds from the madness of war. However, while not practicing much of catholic teaching, he used catholic practices to connect to the spiritual entity he believed was God. Nonetheless, he believed the Catholic Church had many philosophical questions that, as far as he was concerned, needed to be answered.

Most of all, however, Robin, unbeknown to everyone in the parish, had an enormous need and desire he wished to fulfil but could not. To do so would provoke the wrath of the Catholic Church and likely have a detrimental effect on his livelihood. He was so desperate in this desire though that consideration of participation in the novena of ritual prayer might, with Spiritual help, assist him in realising his aspiration. In fact, he decided, he would even make his confession before the obligatory 'receiving of communion' to enact the process exactly.

He was actually of the opinion, regarding 'confession,' that for him, it was both intrusive and valueless in his relationship with the Spirit. However, he did understand that it was therapeutic for many penitents. Today, therefore, just like every Sunday, he would receive communion without confessing church designated sins to church officials. But, in consideration of his enormous desire, he would take up his cross and bear his soul, probably to the visiting Fr Horgan, next Saturday morning.

Yes, Robin confirmed in his mind, he would participate fully and at 10 AM on Saturday he would leave his bachelor residence and surgery, on Tritonville Road, and take the three-minute walk through the Crescent directly to the church for confession. It had to be at least 20 years since he had sought absolution from a cleric. But better to get it over with, in the morning, as he intended to drive to nearby Elm Park to play golf for the afternoon. Not that he held out much hope for his chances. But it would be good to spend the time in the company of his close friend with whom he shared his golf and many other interests like theatre, rugby, rare meals out and intimate liaisons, and someday, he hoped, they would get to holiday together. In fact, his friend often laughingly admonished him when Robin told people he lived alone, pointing out that the widow Mrs Byrne, took the positions of housekeeper, cook, and receptionist, and was practically residing with him six days of the week.

With the 'Creed' finished, everyone resumed their seats, and the 'Collection' was taken up while the priest got on with the 'Offertory.' The 'Collection' itself yielded a substantial sum, as Sandymount was considered one of the more opulent parishes in the archdiocese. Once complete, the money offerings for this, as with all Sunday masses, was taken into the 'sacristy,' placed in white money bags, and locked in a cupboard, until, following the last mass of the day, the clerk, Dermot Shaw, would count and prepare it to be put into the bank's 'night lodgement safe.'

As the 'Consecration' was about to begin, Robin noticed one of his patients up near the top of the nave. The lady was easily recognisable from the back by her, large, never without, bright red beret. Vera O'Brien, Robin thought, was certainly eccentric and undoubtedly bordering on religious insanity.

Seated four pews down from the high Altar and close to the pulpit, Vera was bracing herself for the greatest miracle ever given to her, namely, the transubstantiation of bread and wine into the body and blood of Jesus himself. She had many problems in her life, but she also had many saints to consult about each one. In addition, she knew her catechism off by heart. This resulted in her usually being able to find answers from God for all anxieties, ills, or mysteries that came her way. For example, when she had a sore throat last week, St Blaise had it cleared up in no time at all. Prayer, she knew, was her great strength, and as with every Sunday, she would attend a second mass at 11.30 for more prayer, as there could never be enough of that in the world. In fact, she was convinced that God had probably arranged to have the novena to solve the great dilemma she had with her husband Raymond and their marital vows. On the one hand, she couldn't refuse him his marital rights, but on the other, she couldn't assist him committing sin. Throughout the consecration, she continuously thanked God for sending her this great 'Novena of Grace' to show her the way. Perhaps, at the completion of the novena she thought, she would at last understand why Jesus mostly, and sometimes St Veronica, appeared to her in her bedroom. Of course, Vera was not stupid enough to let anyone know of her visions. To do so, would only give evidential justification to those who considered she was religious mad. Oh yes, Vera was well aware of what people thought of her dedication to God and his holy church, but she was also, in no doubt of her own rationality.

The dilemma with her husband though was not going to be easy to resolve, as her Raymond did not have her faith. Like recently, when he was in great pain with his piles, she asked him to say a prayer every night to St Fiacre and his reply was.

"Is he the patron saint of arses?"

Oh Jesus, forgive me, she thought, for even thinking such a crude word in the church. St Jude, then came into her mind as she thought he might have to be considered, being the saint of help for the hopeless, but he should only be used as a last resort.

As the 'Consecration' began she concentrated with all her being in muttering to herself, Jesus, Jesus, Jesus over and over as the priest said the words in Latin for 'This is my body' over the host of bread which was then held high at which point the altar boy rang a little bell and the priest genuflected. The priest then, over the chalice of wine, said 'This is my blood' again this was held on high accompanied by the bell ringing.

Probably the quietest moment of the whole mass was the genuflection in between the consecration of the bread and wine. But then once it was completed with the genuflection after the chalice was held up it seemed as if the whole congregation had been holding their breath and everyone suddenly exhaled and cleared their throats in a unity of relief.

Holding her head low then, Vera continued in deep prayer, and thought of her visions and what they meant, until the 'Communion' was about to be distributed. The people receiving, began to move up and kneel at the altar rails, while others, awaiting their turn, formed queues behind.

As Robin waited, those who had received walked back, passing him on his right. One woman's gait caught his attention, yet another patient, Mrs Peg O'Connell. Seeing her awkward movements immediately triggered in him a sudden, but controlled rage. Here was a woman who had consulted him just a few months ago, having recently moved to Sandymount from the close by suburb of Ballsbridge. She had asked him if there was anything he could for her back and pelvic pain, together with her ongoing incontinence? He had immediately asked what had caused her walking disability, which he'd noticed as she entered his office. Her reply was that she did not know, but it had stemmed from the time she had had her second child. With further investigation and examination, he discovered that she had been given, unbeknown to herself, a 'Symphysiotomy.' He had explained to her that it was an operation to widen the pelvis when there is a problem with the mechanics of having babies. He didn't tell her that it was encouraged by the Catholic Church because giving birth by Caesarean Section was considered unsafe after three such operations. And, following such, sterilisation was recommended by non-Catholic doctors while a sympathetic hysterectomy would be recommended by those of a catholic persuasion. Indeed, as of today, in his opinion, she also needed some expert gynaecological work together with a hysterectomy but trying to have one performed, in an Irish catholic hospital, on a semi-functioning womb, was most improbable. Nonetheless, he was in a position to deal with her surgery.

So, Peg O'Connell to be sure, had her own physical intentions she would like addressed in a novena, but she was much more hoping to have an 'intention' for her son John granted. The poor child, although at sixteen he wouldn't like that label, tried to act like everything was fine, but he had confided in her of his fear and dread that each day brought, at the same time making her promise not to tell Da, as both knew Da would run riot about the situation to the extent that John's life would be completely upended. For the remainder of the 'mass,' however, Peg wondered if she should take the bull by the horns and confront the situation for John herself, but the nagging gripping pain below her waist would not allow her to make a firm decision. She needed to take some of those Panadol Dr McNulty had prescribed, but she didn't like to take anything, up to three hours, before receiving the blessed sacrament.

*

Throughout the mass, standing at the back near a small altar to St Patrick, was a big man, Mikey O'Rourke, who projected great physical strength, yet his gentle blue laughing eyes suggested a kindness behind the physique. While Mikey stood at the back, he was keeping an eye on another character standing close by. This was a local tramp known as Johnny Rags because of his ragged dress. Johnny, a man very fond of the drink and lacking much of his mental faculties, was prone to make noises and speak out loud during mass should the fancy take him. And indeed, the mention of the word 'Grace' by the parish priest, had already triggered Johnny to say aloud. "Graceland man and I'm all shuck up."

Johnny's outburst prompted reluctant smiles from all within close range, and Mikey O'Rourke was no exception. Mikey, or 'Big Mickey,' as he was nicknamed when growing up on a large farm in County Galway, had an older brother and three younger sisters. His brother did, of course, inherit the farm and was already in control, with the father and mother still living in the farmhouse in retirement. Two of his sisters were married, while the youngest was in college in the US. Mikey's parents, however, had invested in all their children's education, as well as gifting them each a sizeable nest egg for their future. So, following his graduation, with an engineering degree from UCD, Mikey saw no future in returning to Galway and instead procured a secure job with Dublin Corporation, bought a small terrace house on Claremont Road, and settled into a bachelor life in Sandymount. His attendance at mass was more out of habit than obligation or duty and once the communion was over, he would slip out, drive to Kingsbridge Station, and catch the 9.30 AM train to Limerick to watch the soccer in Thomond Park where the team he followed, Shamrock Rovers, would play Limerick in a 'Shield' game. A Gaelic Athletic Association (GAA) player and follower when growing up, Mikey developed a love of soccer and rugby during his time at UCD and so on this day he would enjoy hopefully watching his premier Dublin team win. The game would be finished before 5.00 PM, and he would catch a taxi from the grounds for the ten-minute ride to the railway station and the 5.30 PM back to Dublin. Even though he was thirty years of age, he would not allow his father to know of his love for soccer and rugby, as the old man was a staunch GAA lover and believed in the 'ban on foreign games.'

Mikey was due to visit his parents quite soon, but he kept putting it off as while he wished to see them, visiting the farm was heart-breaking. The reason being that he had fallen in love with Thelma, a Dublin girl, while doing his degree and even brought her home to meet his parents. However, something between his brother and Thelma clicked and ignited a passionate flame that resulted in the love of his life becoming his sister-in-law. He was mending well at present but seeing her was never easy.

His life, therefore, apart from his let-down in love, seemed to be charmed. He did, however, have a serious antisocial addiction that, if exposed, would put him to shame to all who held him in high regard. He knew his addiction had to be overcome, but until he had heard about the novena, it had not occurred to him that a focus on prayer might just be the catalyst to stop the weakness.

*

As Eileen Hannigan came out the church door, she removed the mantilla from her head and replaced it with a green scarf she had in her handbag. She smiled to herself as she moved towards the church gates, thinking of the way dress customs change over the years. In church, many younger women now just covered their heads with mantillas, while men were all bareheaded. As she neared the gate, she noticed most men had donned fedoras, but the older ones still preferred caps. Unlike the various colours available in scarfs and hats for women, fedoras were rather dull, seeming to come in only browns, greys and black. The black, usually for priests or religious brothers.

As she moved through the front gate to the paper vendor stall facing the church, Eileen noticed, on her left, the poor unfortunate Johnny Rags sitting on the footpath with a begging bowl on his lap. She bought the 'Sunday mail' and the 'Sunday Independent' noticing the independent's headline stating "34 confirmed dead" in the aeroplane crash in Shannon on Friday. Underneath was a photograph of Mr de Valera, the president, visiting the crash site. She muttered a quick prayer for the souls of the diseased and recovery of the injured, as she folded the papers, and walked over to Johnny Rags where she dropped the change from the papers into his bowl. Indeed, Eileen was just one of many who contributed a little help to the man, whom many knew, had seen much better days.

CHAPTER 2

Sunday 28th February (10.00 AM Children's Mass)

Joan Lawlor, a non-practicing registered nurse, but better known in Sandymount as the Butcher's wife, entered the church at the same time as one of her young neighbours Seamus Hannigan, son of Eileen. He was accompanied as usual by his pal Pat, she smiled to herself knowing their age to be around 13 or 14, and both were rarely seen apart.

"Hello Mrs Lawlor," they said in unison, to which she replied, "Hello Lads," before she headed for the centre aisle and the boys went to the right. Joan liked to get into the church before mass started and take the opportunity to say some special prayers for one special person. Every day of her life, over many years, she carried a massive ache in her heart which was only temporarily lifted when she took such time in contemplation. She knew well, she was blessed with a loving family, a comfortable home and practically no money worries, yet, over the years, the ache had persisted.

The two young lads were about to move into the last pew on the Sandymount side, when Pat pulled his pal back, whispering, "Not there!" at the same time indicating with his eyes who was seated further along, none other than the 'Queer' Patrick (Pansy) Foley. They quickly moved up another two rows and sat and waited. They had positioned themselves there for two important reasons, firstly, being 14, they couldn't possibly sit with the children, up-front in the centre, and secondly, a lot of the girls around their age, from Roslyn Park School, would usually pass by and sit further up. Seamus had a huge crush on one such 'angel' named Sinéad Martin. Of course, nobody was aware of his great passion, not even Pat. They had come to 'Mass' a little early, so they could watch the girls parade along, whispering to each other with giggles and little gasps as each 'mot' walked by.

Then, closely coming behind the extremely attractive Rosie O'Neill, another more imposing figure shuffled by. It was none other than 'Johnny Rags,' the local 'Tramp,' whom by all reports was not only an alcoholic but also 'mad as a meat axe.' It was known that Johnny grew up in a 'well-to-do' family in the house next door to Dr McNulty, on Tritonville Road, where his two spinster sisters continue to live. These women themselves were considered an oddity, as they kept very much to themselves and when Robin's housekeeper, Mrs Byrne, once asked if they were Catholics, the reply she received was that they were practicing atheists. Johnny himself had studied Law at UCD, followed by a 'Masters' at Oxford. He practiced as a barrister for some years, but then lost the battle with the drink, which finally drove him mad. There were numerous urban legends pertaining to Johnny O'Keefe, as was his real name, not the least being, that he had once been an altar boy in this very church. Now, however, much to the fascination of Seamus and Pat, Johnny Rags moved into a pew two up from them and slid right along to be up against the church wall. Once there, he gave out one of his elephants 'brrrrrrr' hoots, not very loud, but quite audible to those in his immediate surround. The boys looked at each other and burst into a stifled fit of shaking giggles. This they continued at pace, getting more and more intense, until a middle-aged man in the seat directly in front of them turned around and whispered firmly.

"Show some respect in the house of God! Will you?"

Immediately, they subsided and were afraid to even glance at each other in case they would start again.

Patrick Foley saw the whole episode and felt sorry for Johnny Rags. Also, he felt sorry for himself as, although he pretended not to have noticed the two boys avoiding his pew, he knew many people, men in particular, found him disgusting. This of course he fully understood as he found himself disgusting, particularly since a year before when in 'confession,' in another parish, he had told the priest of his feelings for other men and indeed the bad thoughts of intimacies he had contemplated to perform with them. The priest had said such things were an abomination of disgust and that he was to blame solely for wanting such loathsome things and unless he changed his attitude of mind, and promised God never to sin as such again, he would surely be dammed to the fires of hell for all eternity.

Well, Patrick had tried with all his being to change those yearnings but had no success at all. The result was that he felt worthless and, whilst avoiding confession since, he continued to pray that his feelings would change to those of a 'normal' man. A man like Mr Masterson, for example, the man who had told the boys off for giggling. Mr Masterson, a married man with children, was a well-known and respected pillar of the parish, being a member of the 'The Saint Vincent De Paul' society and the altar society, as well as a being a church 'collector.' By far, though, Mr Masterson was known for his job as supervisor in the 'religious department' of Shaws department store in O'Connell Street in the city. Shaws, was a competitor of the larger Clerys, and located close to it but Shaws had a very exclusive and loyal clientele. Mr Masterson's whole life, Patrick thought, was surrounded by God what with firstly, being a dedicated catholic family man, secondly, his church and charity work and finally being surrounded by and selling holy pictures, statues, rosary beads, crucifixes, scapulars, relic holders, medals to the Father, Son and Holy Ghost, The Blessed Virgin, and all the saints, not to mention Holy communion and Confirmation medals and rosettes. In addition, there were on sale in Mr Masterson's department numerous church and religious sacred vessels and ornaments.

But unbeknown to Patrick Foley, Mr Thomas Masterson had, lurking in his head, a plan. An ambitious plan that could well jeopardise his entry, not alone to this very church, but also into heaven itself.

Suddenly, a bell pinged to signal the beginning of mass and while two altar boys and young Fr McKenna made their way to the high altar the congregation all stood except for Johnny Rags who remained seated and gave out another, even louder, elephant hoot, 'Brrrr.' Most of the sound, however, was muffled with everyone rising to their feet. Again, the boys got the giggles, but quickly controlled them before another rebuke came from Mr Masterson.

With the gospel of the mass finished, Fr McKenna took a seat on the altar as the Canon appeared from the sacristy and went to the pulpit. He first said a few words to the children regarding Lent and having to make sacrifices during the holy period. Then, he repeated the same sermon he had delivered at the 8 o'clock.

Throughout the 'Offertory' Joan Lawlor and Patrick Foley continued their thoughts regarding the benefits the novena might bring to their lives. At the same time, Patrick couldn't help noticing how well the priest's vestments hung on his attractive body. By contrast though, Thomas Masterson was not thinking about how the novena could solve his situation, rather, he was thinking of a seductive transformation. A transformation that would be enhanced by his looks. Not that he ever thought about his looks, as he was my nature a modest man. However, his wife, and girlfriends before he married, as well as aunts and relatives had on numerous occasions commented on his good looks. These looks, nonetheless, did have one blemish and that occurred when he was twelve years of age. He had been playing a hurley match when he took the full swing of an opposition stick to the mouth. He required six stitches, and it was fixed except for the slightest but visible scar. But that could be hidden, he thought. So, as he sat preparing for the consecration, the novena came to mind, not in the hope of it putting a stop to his transformational plans but maybe helping him to deal with it.

With the whole congregation on their knees and heads bowed in total silence and reverence, Fr McKenna whispered the consecration words over the host and as he held it on high the bell tingled but then as he was halfway down to genuflect, Johnny Rags screamed out, at the top of his voice.

"DEV-A-FUCKING-LERA. Bastard. Bastard." He followed this immediately by an extremely loud elephant "Brrrrrrrrr," The complete silence given for the consecration continued it seemed for seconds but not in reverence, rather, it was as if the entire church had been struck dumb by the blast of blasphemy. To his credit, Fr McKenna wavered only momentarily before he genuflected completely and then continued with the words for the prescribed ritual over the chalice. Then came the usual congregational exhaling and coughing breaths, accompanied, on this occasion, however, due to Johnny's outburst, by whispers and mumbles of outrage from adults and giddy laughter from kids. Indeed, most of the adults had scowls of resentment, astonishment, and abhorrence.

Seamus and Pat were elevated to a delightful state of shock as the parishioners positioned around Johnny Rags, firstly, requested him to come out of his seat. The request was met with a loud refusal accompanied by a string of profanities. Then several men attempted to drag him out. The whole congregation by then had forgotten about mass and were concentrated instead on the developing drama. The more parishioners tried to drag Johnny along the seat from the wall, the more he screamed elephant's hoots while referring to his would-be captors as arseholes and shites. However, when he had a go at the Archbishop of Dublin by screaming, "John Charles Mac Fucking Quaid," Mr Masterson, the pillar of the church, grabbed Rags in a headlock muffling his screams and along with five other men literally carried him out of the church into the grounds. Throughout the fracas, Fr McKenna had gone quietly about his business, and all was calm again for the distribution of communion.

When Thomas Masterson returned, having dealt with the disruptive Johnny Rags, he slipped into the pew once more beside his wife of many years, Nora. She looked over at Thomas and smiled. My hero, she thought, feeling a burst of pride run through her veins. He was the type of man any woman would be delighted to have by her side, what with his good looks, respectable job, and his ongoing charitable work for the St Vincent de Paul society. Indeed, Nora had often thought that their lives were blessed due to Thomas' good works. Not least of these was his organisation of the Sandymount Christmas raffle in aid of the Society, for the poor, homeless and destitute.

In his capacity as the raffle organiser and coordinator, Thomas went to every business venture in the area and begged a contribution from them for the various prizes. For example, 'Lawlor's' the butcher shop gave a turkey and ham, the two pubs each gave dozens of bottles of stout and a several bottles of whiskey. The 'Ritz cinema' gave complimentary tickets for the pictures, 'Maypotters' newsagent gave a complimentary newspaper for a month as well as arranging the raffle tickets to be printed. In addition, there were boxes of vegetables, books, garden tools, holy pictures etc. etc. Then, with the money raised, Thomas would seek out those in need, not only in Sandymount, but beyond, where a need could be met.

*

As Eileen Hannigan was preparing the dinner and singing along with Bridie Gallagher on the radio '*It's my own Irish home-far across the foam-although I've often left it-in foreign lands to roam*'…. The twins, Thomas, and Tilly, dragging young Paul with them, burst through the back-door shouting. "Ma!" "Ma!"

"Whatever is the matter?" asked Eileen, a little alarmed. "Is Seamus alright?"

"Yes, but Johnny Rags had to be pulled out of the church! He was shouting bad words when the priest was holding up Jesus" said Tilly, gaining the chance to speak before Thomas, who tended to stutter slightly when excited.

"Oh, my goodness!" said Eileen, who by then was joined by her husband. "What did Johnny do?" He asked, laughing, "make the elephant noise?"

"No, no", put in six-year-old Paul, he said. "Fuck fucking, Charles"!

"Oh, my God," said Eileen, bending to put her arms around him, at the same time saying.

"They are terrible bad words, and you must never say them again." The three others couldn't help but crack up in raptures of laughter, quickly joined by Eileen and finally by Paul himself, who was at a loss in knowing what was so funny?

CHAPTER 3

Sunday 28th February (11.30 AM Mass)

Detective Inspector Richard O'Connell, husband of Peg, slipped in early to the end seat on the right side of the centre pews for the 'half past eleven' mass. Richard liked to get in early for two reasons. The first was his interest in watching the people as they arrived. This liking of observation of people, no doubt, came from his detective work. It was essential, he believed, when interviewing people, as he might be able to tell, by their actions, if they were telling the truth. The second reason for his early arrival was to balance out his guilt for always leaving early, usually after the communion. Because, as far as Richard was concerned, the mass had three main components, the offertory, the consecration, and the communion. So, once the communion was finished, so was Richard.

Fr Peter Crampton celebrated this Mass, the pious, but abrupt 59-year-old second curate in the parish. He was extremely popular as a confessor, as it was rumoured that he was quite deaf. Also, as far as anyone knew he never questioned a penitent on their sins but just gave absolution and a penance of one 'Our Father' and seven 'Hail Marys' to everyone, no matter what they confessed. This universal penance could be confirmed by anyone within 15 yards of the box, as Fr Crampton tended to shout out the penance and the absolution after it. But confession notwithstanding, today, following the gospel, he also took a seat on the altar as the Canon made his way to the pulpit.

*

When Miss Evelyn Roberts, seated in a left middle pew, heard about the novena she felt a hope for some contentment, specifically a contentment she had not had since before her best friend Bridget got married and went off to America with her new husband in October of last year. With her friend gone, Eve, as she liked to be called, realised she had no other friends. Certainly, she was no social outcast and had plenty of acquaintances, but she longed for another female friend and companion like Bridget. She and Bridget had done so much together, like going on tours, outings, holidays and especially to the pictures. They both loved the same kind of films, which were usually the romantic ones with a bit of comedy. Thinking about the pictures reminded her she still had two complimentary passes for the Shack. The two passes, which she had won, in the Christmas 'Vincent de Paul' raffle, were only valid to the end of March, but since

Bridget's departure she literally had no one to go with; she was certainly not going to go alone, as such she thought would make her look pathetic.

So, not only did Eve miss Bridget, but she really longed to have her friend back. In fact, her longing had been so intense that she had concluded that she must be a Lesbian. She was also convinced of her sexual status because, when growing up, two males, both family members, had violated her girlhood. This she had found completely abhorrent and upon reporting it to her mother had been told to keep quiet, and it would be dealt with. Her mother then told her that all men were like that, and she would be well advised to keep clear of them. Eve followed her mother's advice. All her family were deceased now except for her only sibling, a married sister, Edwina, eleven years her senior, with one child, Samantha, who lived in London. Apart from that, she had only her dog, Bonzo, an English cocker spaniel, with which, she was very much attached. She loved animals but was not overboard in this. However today, after mass, she was going straight to the Zoo to visit her Giraffe, whom she partly sponsored. But also, it gave her the opportunity for social intercourse, and there was always the chance she might make a special friend there.

Coming to terms though with her believed Lesbian life status, Eve decided that while she would not ever practice a homosexual act with another female, she'd seek a friendship like that she had enjoyed with Bridget. Her efforts so far, however, had met with little success.

As chance would have it though, with living on Serpentine Avenue, Eve had noticed many numbers of females coming and going to their employment in the close-by Irish Hospital Sweepstake headquarters. Here, she'd thought, was an opportunity, where she could leave her current position as the secretary in an all-male Chartered accountant's office, to a work in an environment full of women. In such an environment, she believed, she was bound to meet a nice female companion. So, she had applied seeking a position there, in line with her qualifications, and was delighted to have received a letter in return stating that they would be recruiting again at the end of April, had liked her C V, and would be in touch in six weeks to arrange an interview.

Eve had been reasonably popular at school and had loved involvement in the production of school plays and musicals, and therefore came up with the idea of organising a local Drama society. This, she reasoned, would be another way to make friends. She had approached Fr McKenna and the Rev Shillitoe for their assistance in this regard. Then, following much preparation, plus an additional committee member, one Cecilia Lombardi, proposed by Rev Shillitoe, the first public meeting for interest would be held this Tuesday evening. These two practical approaches, i.e., a new job and the Drama society, together with participation in the 'Novena of Grace' should procure the friend she craved, only of course, if it was for her good!

*

Bronwyn Williams, née Sheridan of 'Howth Sheridan Antiques,' and her husband David were seated in the front seat before the high altar They had arrived about two minutes before the mass started, so the church was quite full as they walked straight up the centre aisle to the front seat. Bronwyn, a convinced atheist, liked people to notice her, and she would expect most of the women in the church to envy her. As a couple, though, they certainly stood out. David, being over six feet tall, while she was a petite four feet eight inches in her Amalfi high heels. The women, she thought, would love to have her 'Harrods of London' coat and hat, as well as, she supposed, the rest of her clothes purchased in 'Brown Thomas' in Dublin. In addition, she knew they all envied her having such a good-looking and debonair husband. Oh yes, he charmed all the women and even some men, but to her, he was a useless infertile shit, whom she only really married because she thought he would inherit millions, which he did not. Instead, he was a travel clerk in Thomas Cook in Grafton Street. Jesus Christ, she thought, what a let own? And to think, everything had looked so good, as she remembered their first meeting in London. It was now a little over twenty years since she and her older sister Bethany had met David and his friend Charles in the England capital. Preferring now not to dwell on the reasons she was there, she remembered instead the two young handsome lads who, at the interval of a show they were attending, began to talk and flirt with them. Following the show, they had accompanied them, at their invitation, to a very posh tearoom for refreshments.

Of the two, obviously upper-class English lads, Bronwyn found David the most attractive. Standing approximately six feet two inches tall, he was a mixture of the screen actors Cary Grant and Errol Flynn in voice, accent, and charm. He was also great fun, to the extent that shortly after they had ordered the tea and cakes, he had said.

"Tá na cácaí álainn milis ar feadh dhá chailíní milis." The two girls looked at him with open mouths, knowing that in Gaelic he had said something like, 'These are lovely, sweet cakes for two sweet girls. Then, in English, he suddenly broke into a full Cork accent, which the girls immediately recognised. Suddenly, he had changed again to a broad Dublin accent, saying.

"Does your mammy know yous young ones is out tonite?" The four went into fits of laughter at this, after which they found out that David, an only child, was actually Irish, and in London for a few days to visit his old-school friend Charles, and while being a fluent Irish speaker, he also had a great interest in regional accents and historical events. His upper-class English accent had been acquired while boarding, together with his friend, at 'Harrow' Public school in northwest London. David's father, a widower, Bronwyn further gleaned, was a stockbroker in Dublin with a very successful investment company which funded his passion for racehorses.

Following school, David didn't go up to Oxford like his friend Charles. Instead, his father, David senior, insisted he come straight home and learn, from the ground up, the investment business. However, once there, his dad kept him away from the real business to concentrate only on administration and office management. David had requested his father, on numerous occasions, to allow him greater access to the real business activities, but with no success. His salary though was extremely generous, and he soon tired of trying to do more and settled into a comfortable playboy lifestyle until, of course, he met Bronwyn. He had proposed marriage in Dublin four months after they had met and agreed to convert from 'The Church of Ireland' to 'Roman Catholicism.' Her request for this conversion was not based on a religious devotion, rather, it was about exercising control in their relationship from the start.

Upon being married, they were given the house in Marine drive as a wedding present from David's father, and it was basically furnished by Bronwyn's parents. This was all Bronwyn would receive from her parents as their house and the business, upon the death of her parent's, reverted to her uncle and his son.

Disaster had then struck, however, as within two months of them taking their vows, David's father committed suicide when it became public, he had been taking investor's money to fund enormous gambling wagers which did not pay off. The business folded, and David, luckily through a friend, got a job with travel agent Thomas Cook. In addition, Bronwyn felt that their house in Marine Drive Sandymount, was a major come down from the big, detached house, in which she and her sister were raised, on the hill of Howth. And indeed, just before she and David married, when told his father was giving them the Sandymount house, she had reacted strongly, saying such a location was uncouth, being so close to the city dump. Her reason was because she had set her heart on a much bigger property on Shrewsbury Road in Ballsbridge. When David told his father of Bronwyn's preference, he was basically told to take the house offered or get no house, so Bronwyn had to concede, thinking that when the old shit died, with David the only heir, she could live where she wanted. But now, with the old shit's suicide, there was nothing left. So, they were even lucky to be where they were, despite being next door to the O'Brien clan with a menagerie of kids.

The Williams discovered, however, following David's father's death, that the Marine Drive house had belonged to David for nearly a year before they were married. It transpired that the father knew he was in trouble and intended to declare himself bankrupt. Beforehand though, with client funds, he purchased the house, and in order for it not to be counted as his asset, he put David's name on the deeds.

The loss of the great inheritance was the first major blow to Bronwyn. The second was that David had no ambition to improve his career and so give her greater prestige as his wife. But the worst thing of all, regarding her marriage, was that her sterile husband was incapable of making her pregnant. They had tried for three years before she went to a 'Specialist' in Fitzwilliam Square. It turned out that she appeared to be fine. When David had been told this news, he pointed out that it couldn't possibly be him, as his equipment was in perfect working order. She knew, of course, that it had to be him, but his manhood would not allow him to have such confirmed. She, of course, was convinced that everyone assumed it was her fault. 'Barren,' the ignorant would label her. When in fact it was 'Debonair David' who was endowed, she viciously thought, with a mere bicycle pump. Such concentration of thoughts had as usual raised such rage in her that she wanted to shout from the altar that David was responsible for their childlessness. In fact, what made it even worse was that she knew, most certainly, that she was fertile. Adoption was not an option she considered, as the thoughts of raising someone else's bastard made her feel sick. She had even thought of taking a stud lover but could never find a man suitable for the task.

David would have preferred to be sitting closer to the back of the church but was, nonetheless, contented to be part of a catholic congregation. Growing up as a Protestant in Dublin, he had always felt slightly sectioned off from the dominant catholic community, but now he was much more at home. Not that he had the slightest interest in the religion itself, but it suited him much better from a social perspective. He also liked being in this church, as he was a great lover of historical expositions and facts. For example, this very 'church' in December 1852, while in the process of being built, had the front and rear gable walls blown down in major storms. Also, James Joyce, before writing Episode 13 of his famous book 'Ulysses', wrote to his Aunt Josephine to send him details of the Star of the Sea church and the area surrounding it. This, being the same

Episode where Bloom pleasures himself on the strand, with the church behind him, while Gertie McDowell lifts her skirt. David smiled to himself and wondered if many in the congregation were aware of this. He supposed probably not, as while the book was not banned in Ireland, it certainly was not available for sale. He had bought his copy in London on the recommendation of his English tutor at Harrow. Catholicism, however, for David had one extremely attractive feature, 'Confession,' not that he was one of its great practitioners. However, since converting, he had confessed via the catholic rite three times and felt a profound sense of unburdening and relief from its absolution. In fact, when he had gone to confession, during his lunch hour three months ago, in Clarendon Street church, close to where he worked, he had felt an enormous unburdening. Certainly, the Church of Ireland had a confessional process in a general way, together with a process like that of Catholicism, namely, confessing directly to a cleric, but it was not something he, or his lukewarm protestant family members put much emphasis on.

Notwithstanding all of that, David was well aware his marriage was a failure, but divorce in Ireland was not an option either by state or church. So, being fully au fait with these inflexible statutes he now, more than ever, showed an indulgent attendance to his wife's needs because he had a remedy, one that would eventually sort out all their marital problems. He also had a secret stash of cash, to which Bronwyn was not privy. He had come by this when going through his father's clothes to arrange for them to go to a charity. One coat appeared to be excessively heavy and upon investigation by ripping its lining, he discovered wads of cash. Cash in American dollars and English pounds. In all it had converted to £4,850, a princely sum for sure. In a state of great excitement, upon this discovery, he immediately thought to tell Bronwyn but relented when remembering her frivolous attitude to spending for appearance's sake. Instead, he made some investments in his name only and put another sum into a private bank account, with correspondence for all going to a different address than Marine Drive. He rationalised that this money was after all his, but he would not see Bronwyn go short, as such would make him look bad.

When the Canon, during his homily, made the announcement, regarding the novena, Bronwyn considered it to be nothing less than an exercise to make ignorant idiots feel good and further empower the Catholic Church over them. David, however, wondered what a 'Novena of Grace' was all about? It sounded quite interesting!

CHAPTER 4

Sunday "28th February (Afternoon)

Detective Inspector Richard O'Connell exited the church on the Irishtown side following the communion. He was first out and satisfied he had completed his weekly duty, he walked down Leahy Terrace towards the sea and turned right for home onto the strand side of Beach Road. A native of Dingle Co. Kerry, he loved the smell of the sea and all things to do with it. He was delighted therefore when he got his transfer, from reasonably close Donnybrook Garda station to Irishtown, as it prompted his moving to live facing Sandymount strand with little upset for the family. Apart from his dedication to the wife and her constant pain together with her concern for their son John. Richard had one great passion, namely, fishing. However, due to the strand's topography, he had concluded that the only real fishing to be had there would be 'longline.'

Longline fishing basically entailed stretching a line between two stakes, preferably strong iron, or steel, and flagged on top for markers. The line itself would have several smaller lines with attached baited hooks. The line would be set well out on the strand just as the tide was incoming and should be watched until well covered to avoid seagulls pilfering the baits. The tide would then come completely in, right up to the strand wall, subsequently covering the whole fishing apparatus several hundred yards out. Then as the tide receded it would be followed out and guided by the markers, the catch collected before such was exposed for gull temptation. Longline fishing as such though was a much more summer pursuit. However, knowing the tide for next Sunday, Richard thought, would be ideal, weather permitting as high tide was set for 12.30 PM. This would allow for the process to be completed in daylight. Richard also was rostered off for that day and had acquired all the tackle required from the 'Fishing' shop in the city's Capel Street, so his only requirement was the bait. He might get the opportunity to dig some on the strand, but if not, he knew there was an ample supply of lug and rag worms available in the store where the tackle was purchased.

*

Having bought the papers at 12.10 PM David and Bronwyn Williams commenced their short walk up Sandymount Road and were soon joined by their neighbour Vera O'Brien. They all exchanged the customary comments on the weather, after which Vera said.

"I have been meaning to tell you Mrs Williams that I love your coat, it's beautiful, and it looks so smart on you."

"Oh, thank you, yes, I do rather like it. My sister Bethany brought the coat and hat over from Harrods in London when she came for Christmas."

"Yes, said Vera, "I can see the fur on the hat matches the fur on the collar, it is really lovely."

"Well of course," added Bronwyn, "I do like the feel of mink, there is something luxurious about it."

While Bronwyn was reveling in the accolades, David, wishing to change the subject, interjected.

"So, Mrs O'Brien, you, being a feast of catholic information, what is this 'Novena of Grace' all about?" Vera was only too delighted to oblige an answer to this very attractive man and gave him the full chapter and verse on a 'Novena process' together with the catechism quote, *'Grace is a special help given to us by God to do good acts and avoid sin.'*

*

"You should not encourage that bloody cow, especially about religion!" said Bronwyn once she had closed their front door. David just laughed it off and said, "Sure, poor Veronica is harmless, and you'd have to admit she knows her Catholicism." Bronwyn just grunted, taking The Times into the sitting room where she lit the fire which David had set before they headed off for mass. To be sure, Bronwyn had insisted they had gas central heating installed; however, she did like an open fire but made sure David understood it was his job to set it, clean it out, and look after the fuel ordering.

While Bronwyn was making herself a cup of tea, David told her he was having trouble with the car, saying he thought it was the carburetor and would go out to the garage to see if he could find the problem. She in turn told him not to be making noises out there that the neighbours could hear, as it was Sunday, and it was frowned on to work on the Sabbath. David just smiled to himself as he went, thinking that she could never be accused of that! He did, in fact, leave the door between the Kitchen and garage open, so his wife could hear sufficient sounds of engine tinkering.

Bronwyn herself took the notion of the Sabbath quite literally and refused to do any form of household chore including cooking on Sundays, so David cooked at weekends. Her mid-morning cuppa now sat on the coffee table beside the 'Times' and the 'Irish Independent.' The headline on the plane crash in Shannon on Friday 26th, screamed out from the front page of the 'Independent' bringing with it for Bronwyn a sadness, stress, and fear, she had deep within her. The reason being that her favourite aunt Clare had been killed three years previously in an aeroplane crash in Manchester. Both Bronwyn and her sister had been devastated by the accident and made a pact promising each other they would never, no matter what the circumstance, board an airliner. This latest disaster served only to cement Bronwyn's resolve.

Having reported to his wife that he believed he had temporarily repaired the car fault, David then, complete with grey tweed overcoat and light grey fedora, headed up to O'Reilly's for his Sunday pint. Before going into the pub, though, he had a quick glance at the notices in Miss Milligan's window. A broad smile crossed his face upon reading the 'Drama' notice. After entering the pub, he placed his hat on the bar, sat up on a stool and ordered a pint. He looked quickly around and noted many of the usual Sunday afternoon patrons had already arrived. These included Mr Masterson who was seated in his secluded spot at the far end of the pub with his half pint, small Jamison and copy of 'The Sunday Press.' David knew his name because, coming out of mass several weeks ago, Vera O'Brien had asked Masterson by name when the next meeting was to be held for the 'alter society and church wardens.'

As David was waiting for his pint to settle, he pretended to read the headlines in the 'Sunday Telegraph' but was really thinking of the many reasons to look forward to when involved in that little 'Dramatic society' and its meeting due to take place on Tuesday. Firstly, he would meet new friends and neighbours. Secondly, he would have an excuse to be out of the house and away from Bronwyn. And thirdly, his love of theatre, shows, plays, and musicals could once again be satisfied. This love of the stage and performance had been honed, before he met Bronwyn, while he was a young member of the 'Rathmines and Rathgar Musical Society.' Once married, however, Bronwyn had claimed he loved the old Society more than her and nagged until he eventually resigned.

*

His pint arrived, and he took a big swig as another man sat up beside him. David recognised him as James Hannigan from across the 'Drive' and they both just nodded to each other while David picked up his hat and pint and moved to a small table near the window at the front for solitude, reflection, and observation. His observation was of James Hannigan a small thin man approximately 5 feet 6 inches in height and weighing no more than about 8 stone. Certainly, he was not bad looking and seemed to have a good personality with a fast attractive way of speaking, but how could such a beautiful woman as his wife Eileen have married such a weed. This was an enigma to David, but then he thought, thinking of his own predicament, marriage is a bit of a gamble for many.

Meanwhile, Bronwyn had just put the phone down from her weekly three-minute chat with her, England based sister Bethany, who worked in the Foreign Office in London's Whitehall. Bethany lived in a lovely two bedroomed flat in Charing Cross, a short walk to her office, with the result, she lunched at home every day in her own surrounds.

Bethany was the most athletic of the two sisters, and she had been so excited, telling Bronwyn that the following Tuesday evening she's been picked to umpire a 'Netball' championship game. Bronwyn was happy for her in that Bethany no longer played competition games but, still, loved to participate physically. Bron and Beth had grown up very close and Bron missed not having Beth here, but Beth was now a career woman in the 'Foreign Office' in the capital of England, and who would expect her to give that up and come back to dull Dublin?

It had been Bethany, two years Bronwyn's senior, who had discovered, even before Bronwyn herself, that at the tender age of sixteen Bronwyn had become pregnant by the gorgeous twenty-one-year-old Jimmy Smith, who lived even further up the hill of Howth, in an even bigger house than theirs. Bethany took charge, and while their mother was away in Belfast at a three day 'bridge tournament,' Beth arranged for Bron's problem to be got rid of. So, on a beautiful spring morning in April 1938, Bethany accompanied her younger sister to Nurse Madden's nursing home in Rathmines. The abortion, a bloody painful affair, left Bronwyn physically ill and extremely depressed. But she did have three days bed rest before her mother returned. Her father being told she simply had women's problems. She had struggled through school for a few days and gradually got back to an almost a normal life, but she continued each menstrual period to suffer agonising pain. Her mother finally, with much quizzing of both young women, got to the truth of the trouble and brought Bronwyn to see a top Dublin gynaecologist. He recommended specific surgery by Sir Reginald Stanford at St Mary's in London. So, shortly afterwards, she made the trip accompanied by her sister and mother.

Her operation was a complete success, and indeed it also afforded her the opportunity to meet her future husband. Going back over it all in her head again it still made her depressed and although it was never an option, she often fantasied that she had had the baby, married Jimmy, and lived happily ever after. Instead, she had lost her chance at motherhood and ended up in a disastrous marriage. The relationship between Bethany and Charles had come to nothing but Beth had remained in England and made a prestigious career for herself. Every summer though Bronwyn took the mail boat from Dun Laoghaire and visit Bethany in London for a week and then at Christmas Bethany would come to Marine Drive for the holiday. This recent Christmas Bethany had brought her the coat and hat she had just worn to mass. Her present to Bethany was a trip this summer to Paris for herself and Bethany staying in a 5-star hotel off the Champs-Elysées. That was one good thing David's job provided, 'highly discounted' travel and hotel rates.

*

With Stephen Murphy sleeping off the Sunday dinner and several pints plus, Mary Murphy left the house. She left her eldest, Catherine 17, in charge of the other kids. Only for Catherine, Mary could never leave the house outside school hours, as she could not trust her husband's lack of sobriety should there be an emergency. Catherine was a smart, studious girl, who had sailed through her Leaving Certificate last year with seven honours and was currently studying Hotel Management at Rathmines Technical College.

Once out of the house Mary felt an anticipation of relaxation as she walked the five minutes to visit Mrs Emily Jones in Claremont Park. Two months earlier, when Mary was finding it extremely difficult to manage on the ever-decreasing housekeeping money she received from Stephen, she saw an advertisement in Miss Milligan's window for light work, house-cleaning, and invalid assistance, at a house in Claremont Park. Mary called and thankfully was given the job by a very glamorous and obviously well-educated English widow, Mrs Jones. Mary's duties included house cleaning three times a week and general help to her employer.

It turned out that while Mary had seen Mrs Jones around the village and noticed she had a slight limp, she had not been aware that Mrs Jones wore a prosthetic left leg, having lost her leg some 20 years earlier in the London Blitz. Her prosthetic limb enabled her to walk short distances and generally move about, however, heavier tasks such as vacuuming, dusting, and clothes washing were extremely difficult. She had explained to Mary that her and her sister had moved from London to Cork to work after the war, with her sister getting a position in a bank, while Mrs Jones herself got transferred to a branch of the Insurance Company she had worked for in London. They came to Ireland for a new life, as they both had lost their husbands within one month of each other in the 'Battle of Britain.' During their time in Cork, they had invested wisely and then were surprised with a non-expected inheritance. So, they decided to take early retirement only last year and moved from Cork to Sandymount. But tragically, soon after the move her sister was diagnosed with breast cancer and within three months she had passed away.

Mary had noticed that there were several photographs around the house of the two sisters, but there was none of their husbands. So, shortly after they had become good friends Mary asked Mrs Jones did, she have any photos of her husband, and was told that she did, but the sisters had mutually decided not to display them as being constantly reminded of their deaths was heart-breaking.

More and more, however, Mary was finding Mrs Jones' home a refuge from her difficult and sometimes maddening life with her own husband. Despite this, she had proved herself repeatedly to be unworthy of this extremely nice Mrs Jones. This unworthiness was due to Mary stealing money from her benevolent employer, who had given her a lifeline and trusted her to even handle much of her household finances. The original official work schedule had been for two hours work, each Monday, Wednesday, and Friday, for which Mary received one guinea per week. It was paid in seven-shilling lots at the end of each workday. However, following the second week, instead of giving Mary the money, Mrs Jones asked her to fetch it from a shoebox she had at the bottom of her wardrobe, in her bedroom. To Mary's amazement, the box was full almost to the top with silver coins, 'Half grown' pieces and 'Two-Shilling pieces. She estimated the total to be over 6- or 7-pounds worth, or maybe even as much as 10 pounds or more. Quickly then, so as not to seem inquisitive, Mary took two 'Half-crowns' and a 'two-bob bit' to make her 7 shillings. Upon coming back down, she showed Mrs Jones what she had taken and then asked her why she did not put that money into the bank or Post Office? Her employer just laughed, saying it was just a habit herself and sister developed over the years, in that at the end of each day they put whatever they had of those coins in the box to save for something special.

"But there must be at least 10 pounds there!" Said Mary, still agog at the treasure chest.

"Oh, I suppose," replied Mrs Jones, but I really have no idea of the actual amount, and I'm certainly not going to sit down and count it. Besides, I like the surprise when I bring it to the bank."

Even though, from then on, it was the process to take her pay from the shoebox Mary took only her due. But then when Stephen came home one Friday and said that someone had stolen all his wages in the pub, Mary got desperate. As apart from the rent and the electricity bill, she also had to think about coal for the fire and food for the poor innocent children. So, out of absolute necessity, the following Monday she took an extra 2 shillings from the shoebox. She worried about it all of Tuesday and when she went to work on Wednesday, she expected Mrs Jones to fire her straight away or even worse have the Gardaí waiting. But Mrs Jones was as lovely and welcoming as ever.

Nonetheless, on Stephen's next pay day Mary and the three kids were standing outside the front door of Bolton Street Tech, where he worked as a teacher, and embarrassed him into giving her half his wage pack before he went to the pub. She also promised to do the same every Friday unless he came home first and gave her half before he started drinking. This, he complied with until he began to take money from her purse and if she went out, he would turn the house upside down to find the wage she got from Mrs Jones. Next came the disappearance of the few decent items they had received as wedding presents together with her gold bracelet which, undoubtedly, she knew he had hocked. Finally, at her wits end, she began to take extra from the Jones' treasure chest each day she worked, but never more than two half crowns in one go. At one point, she worried that the shoebox would run dry, but it never seemed to be any less full than when she first saw it.

It was all her own fault of course because she would not give in to Stephen's bed demands and so he turned into an alcoholic, a condition that required money. This money he took from the housekeeping, which Mary had to compensate by stealing from her lovely friend and employer.

*

3.40 PM, Eileen Hannigan left the nursing home after only a 10 minutes' visit to her mother. This had been her shortest visit yet, but she felt little guilt as there had been practically no conversation and what there was made little sense. The thing however that did make her feel guilty, was the fact that within a few minutes, she would be putting herself into the 'occasion of sin' but on this occasion, she would resist the temptation and ensure it never happened again.

Two minutes later as she walked along North Circular Road, a car pulled alongside her, the passenger door opened, and she sat in. The driver leaned over and kissed her on the lips. Her immediate response was hesitant, but then she gave in to her inner want. A short time later, Eileen and her companion entered a flat on the same road, closing the door tightly behind them.

*

Returning from her visit with Gerry the Giraffe at the zoo, Evelyn Roberts sat upstairs on the bus smoking a 'Carroll's No.1' cigarette not for enjoyment but for the sophisticated 'look' she believed it gave her. She looked out the window as the bus, travelling along North Circular Road, made its way towards town. She was envious of all the couples and numerous groups of people laughing and enjoying each other's company. In fact, one man with a female companion looked like someone she had seen somewhere before! But then she thought, that upon completion of the novena her own wish for a female companion might soon come true.

Later, that evening as Eve made her way to the final committee meeting before the grand public affair on Tuesday, she knew she would be five minutes late. She should have been on time but as she was leaving the house 'Bonzo' had started to whine. Her canine companion did this occasionally when he felt she was neglecting his attention and walks. He had missed his Sunday afternoon walk today due to her visit to the Zoo, but she felt she had made up for this with a quick outing and some of his favourite biscuits. Initially, though, tonight she had ignored the whining and left her house near the railway line but by the time she reached the 'Shack' her guilt got the better of her, and she returned to find the beautiful long-eared mutt with the saddest face imaginable. So, she organised the lead onto his collar and put the small blanket from his basket into a shopping bag and set off a second time.

Regarding this whole 'Drama' exercise she had one little concern and one big concern. The little concern was with Mrs Cecilia Lombardi. Pastor Shillitoe had recommended her, or in fact almost insisted, on her input to the venture. He explained that she was by profession a 'radiographer' in Baggot Street hospital and a member of his 'Merrion Gates' book club. He extolled her prowess on the theatre and indeed the arts in general. So, due to this introduction, Eve and Fr McKenna felt obliged to accept her onto the committee. In fact, both Eve and the priest originally thought she must be a Protestant and the Pastor wanted her to balance the sides so to speak. But she was, in fact, a catholic who was married to an Italian, and she lived in the close-by parish of Merrion where she attended church.

From her interaction at the previous meetings Mrs Lombardi, was certainly knowledgeable in theatre production which she demonstrated most beneficially at the first committee meeting. But when Eve tried to engage her socially, by asking her if her husband liked living in Dublin, she had been evasive to the point of rudeness and so Eve kept the social chatter to a minimum.

The second concern Eve had regarding the whole venture was the worry that no-one or just a few would turn up on Tuesday to participate. That outcome would certainly be embarrassing, what with her being the original driving force. Nonetheless, 'Nothing ventured…' she thought as she walked into the hall.

The agenda for the Tuesday public meeting was finalised and it was decided Eve would open the proceedings and take each agenda item in order, with the other committee members leading the discussion on the items they had been allotted. Throughout the discussions Bonzo had slept on his blanket beside his mistress who occasionally leaned down and scratched him behind his ears. As they were tidying up around 9.15 Mrs Lombardi said she was being picked up by a friend at 9.30 and asked if Eve or Fr McKenna wanted to be dropped home. Eve immediately declined, saying she appreciated the offer but needed to give Bonzo the walk. Fr McKenna looked at his watch, thanked her, but said he'd be home by the time her lift arrived.

Following their 'Goodnight' the priest and Eve left together and within minutes Eve and the dog turned left at the Green for Claremont Road enroute to Serpentine Ave. The good father continued on down Sandymount Road.

As Eve and Bonzo were less than fifteen yards along Claremont Road, however, a man got out of a car that had parked just in front of them. He waited by the kerb for them to pass before attempting to enter his gate. However, Bonzo pulled on the lead and started to sniff around the man's feet.

"Well now! Hello there, fella," the man said, bending down and patting the dog on the back and sides, "I'm Mikey O'Rourke and who might you be?"

"His name is Bonzo," said Eve, "and he's pleased to meet you." She then gently pulled the dog along on their way.

"And I am pleased to meet you too Mr Bonzo, and have a very good night," Mikey replied. Eve raised her hand in a little wave of acknowledgement, thinking, what a very nice man was he.

CHAPTER 5

Monday 29th February

At a quarter to nine in the morning, after finding his bicycle punctured, John O'Connell, nicknamed 'Copper' because his father was a Garda, was sitting upstairs on a stopped number 3 bus at Ringsend church. He, like most of the other passengers, blessed himself in respect to the church and its spiritual resident. He was on his way to Westland Row Christian brother's school, where he was preparing for his Intermediate Certificate. He preferred to go to school on his bike, even though it was colder, wetter, and windier because he could pass the house of Rosie O'Neill the crush of his life. He felt completely unable to even speak to this beauty, such was the impression she had on him. Yet, he would often see her walking along Beach Road to Roslyn Park School, and this sighting alone would brighten at least the start of the day. Usually, however, after that, things got shittier and shittier until classes finished, and he made his way home with the hope of another sighting.

The Intermediate Certificate exam, a milestone in his life, would be held in the school at the beginning of June this year. The school itself, together with all 'Christian' brother's schools, was renowned for the use of the 'leather strap' punishment instrument as a teaching aid. The 'leather' consisting of a few lengths of hard leather, approximately 9 inches long by 1 ½ inches wide were pressed together to about ¾ of an inch thickness. Apart from its use as a teaching aid, by way of a threat the 'Christian' brothers also use the 'leather' to inflict pain on young boys who talked to each other in class or acted in any way like children. It was used specifically, they had been informed, for pupils to learn respect for and obedience to the brothers, the Catholic Church, their Irish heritage and of course God himself.

Copper hated school, and most of all he hated Brother Spencer because 'Spence' was a sadist. Copper's fourth year school pal 'Steeler' had told him all about sadists and how they got sexy pleasure by inflicting pain on others. The two boys both agreed between themselves that from then on, these 'Christian' brothers should be known as the SS (Savage Sadists). In addition, apart from the constant use of the leather for any reason and/or no reason 'Spence,' in Copper's mind, was just like the cruel Nazi camp boss in the picture 'Stalag 17. Spence though, Copper was convinced, felt the same power about his position over the Irish class as the camp commandant did over the prisoners. Holy Brother Spencer, Copper decided, was probably the worst prick he had ever come in contact with. But then he thought back to another sleazy prick he had in third class 'Primary School' and realised there was not much between them.

Kavo, the brother in charge of 3B Primary, taught all subjects in a room that also housed 3A boys being taught by a lay teacher. Kavo was not only a 'sadist prick' like Spence, but also a 'pervert prick.' This 'Christian' deviant developed a particular teaching process that seemed to feed his perverse pleasure of inflecting pain on 10-year-old boys, as well as delighting in their terror. His methodology followed the same pattern for each lesson. At the beginning of, say, the 'Irish' language class, he would instruct the 40 odd pupils to move into a circle around the desks. Then he would sit at the front and would ask the first boy a question. Should the answer be correct, or the boy was one of his 'pets,' the boy would move onto the back of the line as it would go anti-clockwise round the desks. Should the answer be incorrect, the punishment was at least two hard slaps of the leather on open palms, and then move onto the back of the line for the next round. Sometimes, Kavo kept going until he managed to slap everyone at least once, which unfortunately meant that the unfortunate and most ignorant gobshites were multi slapped! Should there be any talking or other major infringement, additional leather would be given. Kavo however, did not confine himself to the leather, he also had a bamboo cane and this he used by smacking the kids on the top of the head. Copper remembered once arriving home with a broken skin scar on his head. Upon seeing it, his mother asked how he got it and when he told her she was, of course, extremely annoyed. However, they didn't tell Da or there would have been ructions. The next day, Copper's mother knocked on the class door and had a word with Kavo. She was just one of a string of many to complain about not just Kavo's physical abuse but also for his abuse with strange and secret conversations. These strange conversations would commence when at some point Kavo would pick out a kid and sit down with them for a long one-to-one talk. Once he had finished with one kid, he would then call up another. This practice went on for days, with the chosen ones never divulging what it was all about? In fact, they were even terrified to be asked.

Then one day Sammy who sat beside Copper got the call. Kavo and Sammy talked for about 20 minutes. Sammy was awfully quiet when he came back and said not a word. Even when they went out to the yard at break, Sammy said he was not allowed to talk about it. Finally, Copper got the call.

"I can see up along and between the desks," said Kavo, "you and

your friend Sammy touching each other up the legs of your trousers."
When he said this, Kavo had a smarmy grin on his face. Copper was literally
speechless for a second on hearing this downright lie. But hesitantly, he
spluttered.

"No Sir, No Brother I…We never do anything like that, no…"

"But I see you doing it, and Sammy said you do it." Replied the
accuser.

"No…………… We do not. Honestly, sir, we never did that."

"But I see you do it. I can see it all the time." Copper's face had
turned red with shame, and he was trembling. He felt weak and his head
was all fuzzy. But in his head, he quickly thought maybe him, and Sammy
had been messin about and pushin and hittin each other and maybe the
'brother' thought they were touchin each other over their trousers. Yes,
maybe that was what he saw, as they had never touched each other at all
either over or under their trousers. Maybe it looked like it though when
they were fightin or scrappin or messin and only pullin their jackets or
jumpers. Why? Oh, why would Sammy say such a big lie that they were
doing under trouser messin?

Sitting in the bus and thinking back, but now sixteen, Copper knew
it was because Kavo had made him say it out of fear. Literally, Kavo had
frightened him so much, he made him lie. Copper, though, stuck to his
guns and was only frightened into the lie that they had touched each other
over their clothes in a wrong place. So, when Kavo got the admission lie the
conversation continued with Kavo asking him, among other things, what
his special name was, for his boy thing? And did he touch other boys or
girls? Copper had been completely embarrassed and humiliated by having
to tell the 'Christian' brother his secret desires and little things only he or
his mother knew. In fact, in the school yard after the 'conversation' Copper
was so mad he asked Sammy why he had lied. Sammy had said that Kavo
made him. Copper punched Sammy a few times anyway, and they sort of
kept away from each other from then on.

The bus had then reached Pearse Street National School when
Copper remembered another SS member, Brother Delaney. Delaney took
the combined '4th year' A and B classes for religion from 12.00 to 12.30 PM
each day. Etched in John's memory was the punishment Fred Fingleton
took at the hands of Delaney. It was nothing short of cruel and cowardly
viciousness with Delaney, over what seemed like ten to fifteen minutes but
was probably only three to four, to savagely beat with hands and leather a

passive Fingleton. The victim had to be passive and certainly unresponsive, as any attempt at a verbal or physical response would have resulted in further beating or probable expulsion from the 'Christian' school. Copper could not even remember the reason for the savage attack but as he had looked on, with the rest of the petrified class, he knew in his heart that the smacks to the face and head and punches to the body together with the leather whacks simply was not right. In fact, at one-point Copper thought that Fred would be a hospital case if it continued, and it crossed his mind to stand up and shout, 'Enough,' but of course, he chickened out, and it did continue until Fred was thrown out of the class. He did return two days later, and nothing was said by Delaney as Fred took his seat.

But today 'Spence' had to be faced and would no doubt end up giving Copper, at least four hard leather whacks hopefully only on the hands. Definitely, though, there was something else going on in Spence's head regarding Copper, as he would try to humiliate him whenever possible. This was brought home only last week when the 'Secondary School' Football Juniors were playing a championship match against Christian Brothers School, Marino. Copper had been an established team member in all 'Row' football jerseys both in Primary and Secondary school so as usual he togged out for the game against Marino but just as they were about to take to the pitch, Spence announced that O'Connell was not to play, and a substitute would take his place. Copper felt completely humiliated, and this was even exacerbated when several of the other players asked Spence why a player of Copper's ability was not playing. Such was Copper's embarrassment that he did not even hear the reason. Yet, on reflection, it must have been something to the effect that he was not good enough.

Nonetheless, his homework, to the best of his ability, was completed on his Irish Reader 'Scéal Séadna' so he got off the bus and headed for another day at 'Stalag 17'.

*

9 AM Shaws Department store: Thomas Masterson had spent his life suppressing the urge for temporary transformation to his alluring desire. However, one Saturday evening over a year ago, he was exposed to a solution by way of a 'picture' he attended, with his wife Nora, at the 'Shack.' The picture, 'The three faces of Eve' about a woman with multiple personalities, and indeed where one personality knew everything about another struck Thomas like a lightning bolt. Indeed, it struck his interest so much he researched the 20th Century Fox film to discover it was based on a book by two psychiatrists. With such credentials, then, he concluded that his great urge for temporary transformation probably meant that two

different people were existing in his single body. So, following much inner debate with his Catholic conscience, he reached a satisfactory conclusion that neither one of his personalities was responsible for the actions of the other. This in turn then encouraged him to prepare to make the metamorphosis firstly, as a test, and if it all worked out, he could then transform whenever he desired and of course it was safe to do so. As part of this preparation, the first thing Thomas did was to buy a wig. In fact, this had sat for nearly a year in his shed in a waterproof rag-covered bag at the bottom of a locked toolbox. He had purchased the blond female wig on one of his Wednesday afternoon half days. The wig shop was up some flights of stairs over a shoe shop on Exchequer Street, almost directly opposite 'The Old Stand' pub. Thomas had had the fright of his life on that occasion because as he was about to cross the Street from 'The old Stand' side to enter the shop when who should he see, coming from the George's Street direction, but that tall English chap who drank in O'Reilly's on Sundays. Thomas stopped dead and turned around to follow the Englishman's movements reflected in the shop window he was facing. In astonishment, Thomas watched as his Sandymount neighbour turned into the doorway and proceeded up the stairs to the wig shop. Thomas could only rush into 'The Old Stand' order a large Jamison and sit by the window in relief at not been caught making an indiscrete purchase. Twenty minutes later, the Englishman emerged with a packet under his arm and headed off towards Grafton Street. Thomas gave it another fifteen minutes and another Jamison before he ventured over to the shop himself. Once inside, the male sales assistant who was very feminine in his demeanour and actions smiled when Thomas told him he wished to buy a blond wig for his wife's birthday. Then, when Thomas said his wife's head-size was the same as his own assistant smiled even more, giving Thomas the impression, he knew exactly why Thomas wanted the wig.

"Why don't I get Sir a wig cap and a selection of some suitable hair pieces for Sir to try on?" said the assistant. Thomas nodded his acceptance and the assistant pranced off.

"Now," said the assistant, on his return, "Place the wig cap on first, and it will hold down your own hair, and then I can assist, or Sir may go into the 'try-on' room in privacy to select. Thomas opted for the privacy and thought he looked good as a blond. He then handed over cash for the purchase, and the assistant asked for his name and address for his records and the receipt. Thomas, in his perplexed state, and without thinking, gave his right name but managed to give his address as being on Sandymount Road instead of Beach Road with a different house number. He then sheepishly exited the shop with speed.

Following the wig episode, it had taken months for Thomas to get the courage to continue with his goal. The result was that over the previous few months he had purchased, in his own store, some cosmetics as well as ladies' shoes and clothes. He did this at a rate not to cause any raised eyebrows, as employees were given a discount on purchases in all departments. Of course, purchasing ladies' underwear and nylon stockings was another matter! It could be done of course, but it would leave a male purchaser open to mild whispered gossip and this, at all costs, was to be avoided. Regarding the clothes, Thomas also had access to some second-hand coats, dresses, and blouses which people gave to him for distribution to the poor, in his capacity as parish representative for the St Vincent de Paul society. This, Thomas dismissed immediately from his plan as firstly, he wanted to avoid wearing clothing from people he knew and secondly, in most cases the garments were too small. The first big commitment he made though was to take a short-term lease on a bed-sit in Ranelagh, a three-month sub-let, money up front, and no documentation. It was made last Friday with a country tradesman, Mick McDonnell, who generally worked in Dublin but had secured a three-month contract on a building site in London.

So, on Saturday last, telling Nora he was going to the 'Wood hobby' shop in Ranelagh to get some special woodworking tools for his hobby, he took the clothes and cosmetics he had secreted in his garden work-shed, and transferred them to the bed-sit. Later on, today, however, he would have to procure the underwear. But he had a plan for that. Nonetheless, he hoped he would be home early enough to have his tea and make it to 'The Miraculous Medal,' an ongoing ritual ceremony to the blessed virgin at the church. It was held every Monday night and commenced at eight o'clock.

With this thought in mind then at around 9.30 AM returning from the toilet to the department, Thomas saw one of his biggest customers, Rev Mother Josephus, Provincial of the sisters of Mercy in Ireland accompanied by a younger nun. They were talking to trainee salesman Paddy O'Dowd. Twenty-year-old O'Dowd had only recently been transferred from the receiving dock, to train as a salesman and join the other department salesman, Matt Brophy, both under Thomas' supervision. With his 'teddy-boy' look, O'Dowd would not have been Thomas' choice, as the cut of the young man, together with his cocky attitude, was not in keeping with a religious environment. In fact, only recently upon Thomas giving him instruction to separate a muddle of eighteen-inch religious statues, he had heard O'Dowd, in a broad Dublin accent, say to Brophy, "Masterson says those fuckin St Anthony's and St Christopher's are to be kept well away from the Virgin Mary's, an also the bleedin Sacred hearts are too close to the workers St Josephs!"

And this, thought Thomas, is the person currently talking to a holy nun customer. It was imperative therefore for him to rescue the quite rotund Rev Mother.

"Good morning, Mother Josephus," he said, moving over to the animated O'Dowd and subdued nuns. The nun looked up at Thomas and a shy smile of recognition ran across her flushed red cheeks. "Hello Mr Masterson, I'm glad to see you are on duty today. This is Sister Stanislaus." The young sister and Thomas exchanged a nodded greeting, and The Reverend Mother continued.

"We are looking for some candle sticks! But this young man was trying to interest me in some statues of the 'Infant of Prague' in fact, he said if I bought 12, he would give me two crucifixes free and if I bought 24, I would receive five crucifixes free, and he'd throw in three framed photographs of his Holiness Pope John!"

Thomas' face flushed with embarrassment.

"I'm so sorry Rev Mother, Mr O'Dowd is new and a little enthusiastic." He then turned to O'Dowd and said, "Thank you, Mr O'Dowd, I'll look after the Rev Mother. Oh, and you might sort out, and with a little reverence please, those new rosary beads that have just arrived."

O'Dowd made a face that indicated he was unaware that he had done something wrong and walked off. Thomas then asked the nun how he could help her. She replied that she was looking for two brass candle sticks for a new altar in their mother house. Thomas advised her that a new batch of numerous sizes was arriving tomorrow and would be available from 10 AM, he could arrange to have them delivered. She said she had to attend a mass in the pro-cathedral tomorrow and would call in at 11.30 to select the ones she wanted.

As she was leaving Thomas wished her "God Bless," to which she replied.

"God and his Holy Mother bless you too, Mr Masterson."

Thomas then walked to what he referred to as his supervisory station that resembled a lectern-stand with a drawer. It stood a little apart from the serving and cash counter and had no stool to go with it, as Thomas was obliged to stand behind it to keep an eye on the staff or deal with stock dockets, delivery notes, and sales sheets. Arriving at his base, he discovered that someone, probably O'Dowd, had placed some three dozen, 18-inch statues of St Teresa on the floor, virtually against and around the left side of his workstation. He would, he thought, have words with the culprit later, but first he had to make plans for that evening.

As a very honest man, Supervisor Masterson over the previous few weeks he had added up, not the discounted value, but the full retail value of the ladies' underwear he intended to, in a manner of speaking, purchase. He would secure the items when the store was relatively empty, and he was supposedly working late. He then would make out sales dockets for statues, rosaries, or other religious items to the same value as the underwear and put this cash into the cash register during business tomorrow. In this way, the store would not be at a loss and as he cashed up at the end of every working day, it was a straightforward process to complete. All going well, he should make it to 'The Miraculous Medal' by 8.00 PM. But Thomas was not going there directly, in fact, he intended to take the underwear to his bed-sit in Ranelagh and then take the number 18 bus from Ranelagh to Sandymount and slip into the church just in time for 'benediction'. Then he would meet Nora on the way out, and they would walk home together.

*

6.00 PM Stephen Murphy, husband of Mary, left Bolton Street Technical College, where he was just about hanging onto his teaching position. He headed for Donovan's public house. The pub, only a few minutes' walk from the Tech, is located almost on the corner where Bolton and Capel streets meet. On this same corner, on the other side of the road, is located an establishment called Dolly Fossett's, a house of pleasure and entertainment for men. Over the many months of his marital deprivation, resulting in the need for inebriation, Stephen has been a regular at O'Donovan's and while entering and leaving, via the pub door, he has seen many men with collars up and hats down, enter and exit the house of ill repute. On several occasions, he has felt the need and indeed entitlement to be one of them. However, the one time he was going to actually follow through he decided he needed a drink first and the drink won out over the lust.

By 8.30 PM Stephen, quietly pissed, emerged from his home away from home to head for home. As he steadied himself against the door to tie up his scarf against the cold wind and drizzle, he noticed through the haze and rain a man come out of Dolly's. He immediately felt he recognised the client and began to root around for his glasses. But by the time he had finally located them, his target was off up Capel Street at pace.

The Novena

*

6.30 PM Thomas Masterson was at his workstation, faking work by moving sales dockets about. He was waiting for Willie Byrne, the night watchman, to make his first security check around. When Willie eventually arrived, he asked Masterson how long he thought he might be working on late, in order to let him out the back door. Thomas had replied he'd be no more than an hour at most. Willie, much to Thomas' annoyance, was on for a chat.

"So, Mr Masterson what will you be giving up for Lent? But I suppose a man surrounded by all dem statues wouldn't have many vices!" he said, looking down at the three dozen St Teresa's nearly on top of the workstation.

"Oh," said Thomas, quoting from the bible "Does a righteous man not fall seven times a day?"

"Jaysis," replied Willie, "in dat case I'm bollicks, and to tink I was goin to give up the smokes, but now I tink it won't make one shite of a difference."

"Oh," replied Thomas, "sure Jesus accepts every little sacrifice!"

"Rite, I'm sure he'd love my ten woodbines!" chuckled Willie and continued, "In any way, I'm off and if I'm not at the door, ring the bell, and I'll come and let you out."

At last, Thomas was alone and decided this was his best opportunity to head up the stairs to the lady's department. Knowing exactly where to go, from previous reconnaissance, Thomas firstly took a Shaws paper carry bag from under the serving counter, and then quickly going to the Brassiere drawer smoothly retrieved two garments the sizes he had estimated, based on try-ons of Nora's. Next, he got two pink slips, thinking the colour was quite feminine. Two suspender belts were his next procurements. He ignored the corsets and latest 'Roll-ons' thinking he did not need such 'pull-ins.' However, while going through the 'Knickers;' drawer he was alerted by the singing voice of Willie Byrne getting closer:

Pardon me if I'm sentimental when I say goodbye

Don't be angry with me should I cry

I'm a fool, but I love you dear until the day I die

The Novena

Now and then there's a fool such as I

Thomas quickly grabbed a handful of knickers and stuffed them into his bag and speedily made his way down the stairs to his workstation. He'd only just got there when, from across the floor, coming through the 'Delph and China' section came Willie with another song:

I want to walk you home

Please let me walk you home

Da, da, da, da

I'm not tryin to smart

I'm not tryin to break your heart

Then Willie shouted from a good bit across the floor, "I was just thinkin Mr Masterson, I could give up bleedin workin! How would that be for the Lord Jaysis?" and with that, he went into raptures of laughter.

Thomas was not amused and only just about listening as he was much more concerned about the bag of underwear at his feet. So, just before Willie closed in, and without even thinking or looking down, he kicked the bag over and away from his desk behind the St Teresa statues.

Willie was suddenly there and smiling.

"Do you like Fats Domino, Mr Masterson? I think that's a great bleedin song! In any way, I'll hang on here till you're ready to go and '*walk you home*' he mimicked laughing, or else you'll have to wait for an hour because I have to do a full store check that'll take about an hour. "Okay," replied Thomas, "I'll be with you in a minute," at the same time wondering how he could get the bag of underwear into his briefcase. But Thomas was nothing if not resourceful, when in a tight corner. "Willie," he said, could you please do me a big favour? Over there by the back wall there are pictures of St Patrick, would you go and give then a count, I think there are ten, but I'm not certain?"

"No bother," replied Willie, "at least I know there'll be no bleedin snakes near them! He laughed, moving off. Thomas then without taking his eyes off the watchman leaned down behind the desk, unclasped his briefcase with his right hand while simultaneously with his left and simply by feel, grabbed the bag, and stuffed it quickly into the case. At this point, Willie was on his way back, "Ten St Patrick's and not a snake in sight," he reported. Thomas wrote the number 10 in a scribble on the piece of paper in front of him, folded it in two, picked up his briefcase and placed the paper inside before securing the clasp. "Ready to go when you are, my good man," he said, with much relief.

*

6.45 PM, having finished their tea, Mary Murphy prepared the two younger children for bed and left her seventeen-year-old, Catherine, in charge. As Mary was going out the door however, she met her neighbour Mrs Ryan.

"I'm just popping down to the doctor," Mary told her. "Catherine is keeping an eye on the kids till Stephen gets home."

"Oh, I hope it's nothing serious?"

"Not really, Mrs Ryan. Just a bit of 'trouble down below'."

"Oh, sure don't I know all about that, Mrs Murphy. Sure, it's a woman's lot! So, himself will be in later?"

"I suppose, after 'closing time'," Mary answered, at the same time putting her eyes up to heaven. Mary well knew that Mrs Ryan was very much aware of her Stephen's relationship with alcohol, so there was no point in trying to hide it.

Ten minutes later Mary knocked at Dr McNulty's house surgery and Mrs Byrne opened the door and showed her to the waiting room. There were two others before her, but she was happy to have the opportunity for a quiet read of the magazines there she could not herself afford.

"Ah, good evening, Mrs Murphy," said Robin with a smile, "please take a seat and tell me, how are all the family? Your eldest, the girl Catherine. The last time she was here, she was waiting for her Leaving results. How did she get on?"

"Seven honours," said Mary, with pride. "She's now doing Hotel Management up in Rathmines."

"Well, isn't that just dandy." Said Robin, broadening a smile.

"So, why you have come to see me today?" He inquired with the niceties over.

"Well, I suppose its two things really," she said, making herself comfortable in her chair opposite him, "and to be honest, they are a bit embarrassing to talk about."

"Well, Mrs Murphy, I've seen all kinds of bodies, ugly, twisted, maimed, and broken, both male and female, I have also heard probably more about human goings-on than even the priests in the 'Star of the Sea' so you will not embarrass me in any way and can be assured whatever you wish to tell me will remain within this room!"

Mary took a deep breath.

"Well, it has to do with me not wanting marriage relations with my husband,"

"Ah, right I see," said Robin, and he continued.

"Now Mrs Murphy, I am pleased to talk about this subject and examine you physically regarding it, but if you would feel more comfortable with Mrs Byrne, present I can call her in. She is a retired Nurse, you know!"

"Oh no, I'd rather just talk to you alone."

"Fine, so, do you know the reason yourself for not participating sexually with Mr Murphy?

"Well, I was never thrilled with it, but I knew my duty to him and to God. But you see I have three lovely children who I thank God for every day, but I also had two still-born babies and at the last retreat in the church, the 'Missioner' made it clear, speaking from the pulpit, that babies born dead would never see the face of God as they had not been baptised!" Robin nodded, experience, telling him to let her keep going till she wished to stop. "It was really after that, I decided in my head I could not take the chance of condemning another innocent baby to Limbo for all eternity. The result is that Stephen took to the drink, and I suppose is now an alcoholic. I do intend to do the 'Novena of Grace' to ask God to help me want to do the sex thing again, but I was wondering could there be something else that's stopping me?"

"Alright," said Robin when he was sure she had finished. "The first thing you need to understand is that I am not a priest and therefore cannot advise you on Limbo or the likes. But it seems to be that we Catholics are always being told that God is all loving, and He even said, 'suffer the little children to come unto me.' So, as far as I'm concerned, those babies are probably bouncing in the arms of Our Lady as we speak." But I emphasise this is my opinion and may not be what some clergy believe."

"Thank you, doctor, I understand what you are saying and really appreciate it. But do you think it is the cause of my problem?"

"Well, it certainly is a reason you have concluded to be a big part of the cause. But is it the whole or even fundamental cause? I would have to ask many questions before I could really try to make a stab at a diagnosis. So, are you happy to answer my questions as truthfully as you can?"

"Yes doctor."

"Very well then, Mrs Murphy. Firstly, from as far back as you can remember when growing up, how strong was your feeling for boys, like getting crushes on them? Before you answer, let's pretend we have a measuring tape for measuring feelings. One inch on the tape is very little or low feelings and ten inches on the tape very high or intense feelings like big crushes on boys. Now, I should tell you that anywhere from 1 to 10 is a natural result. So, where were you on the scale growing up regarding your feelings for boys?

"I suppose I was below the halfway about four. No, now that I think about it, I was not boy mad at all like some girls! Actually, I suppose I was more likely a two."

"Now, that is good, Mrs Murphy. Just keep your answers honest, as they won't go outside this office. Now the next question is. When girls are at school, they also get crushes on other girls in their class or in higher classes. What number on the scale were you in that category, Mrs Murphy, remembering 1 for low and 10 for intense?"

Laughing, Mary said. "I think I was a nine and a half at the convent, for Una Brophy in the year above me. She was beautiful, everything I wanted to be. In truth, whenever she looked at me, I blushed from head to toe and the other girls teased me."

"Excellent, Mrs Murphy. Now when you got through puberty with all the differences occurring in your body, not to mention the dreadful pimples, once all that was over and you had grown into a healthy young woman, did your feelings for boys and girls remain at the same crush levels on the scale? That is low for the boys and high for the girls."

"Doctor, now that you put it that way, I suppose they did. But sure, two women couldn't produce a family or marry, that wouldn't be normal. So, like everyone else, I made it my business to get on with what was expected. I fell in love with Stephen, and for years I did my duty. But it was definitely the still-born babies that made me stop the marital relations with

Stephen and God forgive me, I suppose if I'm honest, I'm glad I did. But I know it's wrong and causing all sorts of trouble." With that, she burst into tears.

Robin handed her a paper handkerchief and when the tears had stopped, he slowly began to explain some important aspects of life that she might think about. When he finished, he told her the world of people was made up of many variations. Differences in colour, race, height, religion, language, political leanings, rich, poor, and even people with different preferences as to whom they wished to have an intimate sexual relationship. For example, in general, most people want this relationship to be with a member of the opposite sex. Others, like priests, decide to be celibate. But there are also many who wish to have a sexual relationship with a member of their own sex. Having told her this, he then said.

"Mary, it is not my place as a doctor to judge whether any of these differences are right or wrong, correct, or incorrect or even good or evil. I am just advising you that we are all different in our looks, outlook, needs and desires, and we all have to find the best place for ourselves. So now Mary, I need you to think carefully before you answer the next question, and you don't have to answer it if you would rather not, it's up to you. This question is, since you have been married, Mary, have you at any time had thoughts of a loving physical relationship with another woman?" Mary's jaw dropped, but then she composed herself and answered as truthfully as she could. Robin then sat back and talked to her for a further ten minutes telling her to consider what they had discussed, and to seek further counselling from a particular source he recommended, but only if she felt she needed it.

She left the surgery feeling a great weight lifted from her shoulders but also facing a future of extreme uncertainty.

*

At 8.00 PM Joe McKenna, one of the curates in The Star of the Sea church, entered the private club in Bray Co. Wicklow. He was not dressed in his clerical black or white reversed priestly collar. Rather, Joe McKenna wore ordinary casual clothes, which he had changed into in his sister's house on Morehampton Road in Donnybrook. It was from the bus stop outside her house that Joe had taken the bus straight to Bray. The club was open almost every night of the year and Joe, a life member, liked to visit it at least twice a week or more often if possible. When he was studying at the seminary in Rome, he visited a similar club and found the activities practiced there released his pent-up frustration and allowed him to continue with his study for the service of the church. He was aware that if the parishioners in Sandymount knew of his membership of this club, they would be horrified. But he had in conscience justified these practices in order to pursue his greater quest for the glory of God.

The only time Joe communicated with other club members was when he was participating in the club activities. Before and after, however, should he be using the bathing or shower area, he'd keep strictly to himself. In this way, he hoped to avoid anyone getting too close and therefore discovering his priestly identity.

CHAPTER 6

Tuesday 1st March

Mrs Cecilia Lombardi awoke with the sound of her alarm clock at 7.00 AM. She was annoyed at it ringing as she was having a beautiful dream about a wonderful man whom she loved dearly but might never have as a husband. The reason for this was of course that she already had a husband, Antonio, who was living in Italy. Estranged, was the word that was used to describe their relationship. And this estrangement was caused by Antonio's idea of a woman's duty to her husband. This duty, Cecilia soon realised within six months of their wedding day, was bordering on being his slave. It would not be unkind to say he abused her, but non-physical abuse was not really taken seriously.

It all started soon after their marriage when he would go off to work leaving her a written list of different things, he required her to complete before his return. These chores were in addition to the general housewife housekeeping activities. When items on the list were not carried out and/or not carried out to his standard, which was unknown until his inspection, then he would initially become bad humoured. As time passed, however, the bad humour turned to verbal abuse. Then there were the instructions on what, where and when household requirements were purchased. Finally, and the last straw, was when he began to tell her how to be dressed and how to act when he returned home from work. From the beginning, she tried to fight back and keep her dignity, but the more she protested, the more he shouted verbal abuse. Then one day almost two years ago, she simply packed her cases while he was at work and left him a letter saying she had had enough and was returning home to Dublin where he could contact her at her brother's address. In all that time, she had not heard one word from him as she made a new life for herself, having secured a position as radiographer in Baggot Street hospital.

Following Secondary School Cecilia had trained as a radiographer and later worked using her skills at Hollis Street Maternity and St Vincent's General hospitals. In fact, during her time at St Vincent's, Cecilia and her friend Kate went for a week's holiday in Rome, and it was there that she met Antonio. She along with Kate had been having difficulties with the fast and furious traffic trying to cross 'Via Celio Vibenna' to get to the Colosseum when Antonio came along and stood beside them. He smiled his handsome smile at Cecilia and spoke.

"Inglese?" Cecilia was momentarily dumb but Kate who was on her other side answered.

"No Irlandese."

"Oh, bella," he said, and continued, "You speak English?"

"Yes, of course," said Cecilia, having regained control.

"May I assist you both to cross, please?" he asked.

"Yes, that would be good," the girls said, almost in unison.

"Very well, now I am Antonio, and you are?" He looked at Cecilia, who was hesitant to give her name out to a stranger, until she got a poke in the back from Kate.

"I'm Cecilia and this is Kate." She replied.

"Bella," he said and continued, "now to cross this fast traffic, you must also move fast. So, Cecilia, you take the hand of Kate, please." Kate grabbed Cecilia's hand, and suddenly Antonio had Cecilia's other hand in his and was pulling the two girls quickly through the cars and busses until they reached their goal. He didn't let go her hand when they arrived at the other side, and she was also reluctant to let go. Eventually, however, when she finally released him, he asked if he might act as a guide for them in the Colosseum. They were charmed, and he educated them on everything imaginable about the old and wonderful theatre, after which he brought them for coffee, where they discovered he was a bureaucrat for Italy's State tourist department. He, in turn, found out from them the name of their Rome hotel, and the next day he telephoned Cecilia to tell her he found her beauty irresistible and wished for her to have dinner with him. Within three months they were married and his parents, slightly dubious of their son marrying a foreigner, were nonetheless delighted that that foreigner was a Catholic. However, the glamour and romance soon dissipated with the required subservience he expected from her.

*

At a few minutes after eight in the morning David Williams slammed the telephone back on its stand. He made sure it was loud enough for Bronwyn to hear in the upstairs bedroom.

"Feck that bloody phone." He then said, also loudly.

"What's the matter?" came his wife's voice from above?"

"The bloody telephone line is dead," he answered, "I was just trying to check with Amiens Street station to make sure my train for Belfast was still on schedule. Anyway, it's usually on time. But I'll ring the Posts and Telegraphs from the station and report the telephone line break. And, my dear, you do remember what we discussed going to bed, no dinner for me tonight, I'll get something on the train and be in around 7.00 PM. Bronwyn just grunted and turned over, delighted he'd be gone for the day.

*

Copper O'Connell left his house on Strand Road at 8.40 AM. Having fixed the puncture on his bicycle the previous evening, he was happy to see it had held up overnight. He had two good reasons for wanting to cycle to school, the first being the freedom of not waiting for busses, and the second was Rosie O'Neill. Rosie lived on Beach Road, which was the road continuing towards town from Strand Road. Rosie's school, Roslyn Part, was also on Beach Road so, as Copper cycled down Beach Road, he would often see her on her way to classes. Usually, they just smiled as they went past each other, but once or twice their eyes met and there were blushes from both. However, on the mornings Copper encountered Rosie, his day was literally rosy. It didn't even matter when Spence inflicted pain on him, he just thought good thoughts of Rosie. Such were the good reasons for cycling to school. Nonetheless, he also hated the cycling journey, firstly, because of the cold which seemed to get through whatever clothes he put on. And when it rained, which was almost every day it seemed, he would arrive in school wet through.

Bad as the cold and wet were though, the worst thing he hated about cycling down Beach Road was the savage mongrel dog. This mongrel was half Alsatian and half Terrier. It kind of looked like an Alsatian but about half the size. This savage fleabag went by the name of Henry and chased cars, busses, trucks, and vans, but by far, cyclists were its favourite game. Not a day went by that this animal would fail to attack Copper should he travel down Beach Road. It would charge at his left foot barking, growling, snapping, and yelping in a frenzied assault attempt. On every occasion, Copper tried to act as if he didn't care, but he was, in fact, petrified. This fear though was temporarily put on hold by his desire to see a smile from Rosie.

Unfortunately, the last time he went to school on the bike, before he got the puncture, he saw Rosie coming up towards him when suddenly 'Henry the hurricane' charged at his foot. Copper tried desperately to be cool and tried to semi-kick the mutt away, saying in his best accent. "Get away, doggy, there's a good dog!" But thinking, the fuckin bastard, I hope I don't fall. Jaysis, she'll think I'm afraid of dogs! I am! I'm fuckin shakin! But worse was to come because as he had put his foot out to push the dog away, it grabbed onto his shoe and hung on for what seemed like minutes but was probably only a second. At the same time, Rosie was in line with him and Henry in tow or perhaps toe, literally. Copper kept shaking his foot until the dog let go and slumped off as he and the bike continued at speed. All Copper could do was feel completely embarrassed and disappointed, as he had missed her smile. But on reflection, he was convinced he saw Rosie break into a grin at his dog-attack predicament, and this made him even more embarrassed.

As he cycled along today, however, the dog went for him once more, but he avoided putting his foot out in case it would grab him again. In addition, he missed seeing Rosie and when in school he ended up receiving in total four slaps of the leather on each hand, six of which had been administered by Spence because he could not answer some question on 'Scéal Séadna". As it turned out, he did know the answer, but just didn't understand the way Spence had put the question in Gaelic.

*

Following 10.00 o'clock mass and some after prayers at the Pro-Cathedral, in close-by Marlborough Street, Rev Mother Josephus and Sister Stanislaus made their way to Shaws to pick out the candlesticks. The Rev Mother, immediately upon seeing Mr Masterson conversing with Mr O'Dowd near the counter, made straight over to them. The four exchanged greetings, and then Thomas asked O'Dowd to find Mr Brophy and then attend to the statues stacked near his workstation. He then asked the nuns to accompany him over to the workstation where he would, hopefully, find a delivery docket for the candlesticks. To his relief, the docket was there, and he then asked the nuns to give him a few minutes while he went to retrieve them from the stockroom.

The reverend ladies said they were in no hurry and would wait right there by the station and St Theresa statues until his return. A minute later, Sister Stanislaus picked up one effigy of the saint and began to discuss it with her colleague. As they were commenting on the statue's colours, O'Dowd and Brophy arrived.

"Could ya just excuse us a minute Sister," said O'Dowd, "I need to get at the back of them St Theresa's and hand them out to Mr Brophy there, so they won't be too near Mr Masterson, I tink he's getting a bit claustrophobic with so many women around him." Brophy laughed and so also did the young nun, but she soon stopped with the stern look she got from her superior. The two nuns nonetheless obliged and moved out of the way to the front of the workstation. O'Dowd moved to the back of the statue group bent down picked one up and handed it across to Brophy, who in turn placed it in a box on a hand truck. Then O'Dowd bent down to retrieve a second but discovered instead what appeared to be a pair of bright blue women's knickers. He picked them up and hooking an index finger into each side of the waist band opened them out and held them up for the three others to see.

"You didn't drop these, by any chance, Rev Mother? He asked, trying desperately to keep a straight.

The Rev Mother turned purple, the young sister turned scarlet, and Brophy turned away in a fit of uncontrolled laughter.

"Certainly, not Mr O'Dowd! Please show some respect and put those away immediately."

"Ah jaysssss, I'm sorry Mother, but I thought you might have dropped them while you were lookin at the statues! Look, eh…. I didn't mean that like ya dropped them off yourself, but that you bought them in the shop here and then dropped them out of a bag or somethin? Cause, like they are big, so I thought there was more chance of them bein yours, instead of Sister Santaclauses' there?"

Brophy was by then in complete bits and lost in raptures of hysterical laughter as Thomas arrived back.

"What is it you find so funny, Mr Brophy?" he asked with concern, looking at the shocked faces of the nuns.

"I'm sorry Mr Masterson, but Mr O'Dowd just found a pair of knickers behind the statues and…."

"Right!" was all Masterson could reply, while his head bit by bit worked out what had happened the previous night. He just stood there saying nothing and wondering in desperation how to proceed.

Luckily, the Rev Mother broke the silence.

"Do you have the candlesticks, Mr Masterson?"

"Eh…yes, of course, Rev Mother," he said, leaning down and taking the top pair from the carton he had brought. Mother Josephus practically snatched them from his hand, saying.

"They will be fine, please put them on our account and I wish you God Bless Mr Masterson and suggest you have a word with Mr O'Dowd about showing respect for the habit!"

With that, she took off at high speed, with her companion having difficulty keeping up.

"What in God's name did you say to her?" Thomas asked O'Dowd.

"Ah Jaysis Mr Masterson," he said holding up the knickers again, "I only asked her if she dropped these?" And once again, Brophy broke into fits.

"Please grow up, Mr Brophy," Thomas chided, and then to O'Dowd. "Where did they come from?"

"They were just in front of the back row of the St Theresa's. I've no idea how the Jaysis they got there?"

"Look firstly, mind your language Mr O'Dowd and secondly, the both of you have a lot to learn working in this department and later, I will give you some of the etiquette required. Meanwhile, I want you both to go to the stockroom and check today's stock arrivals and then bring them up here. Before you do that, Mr O'Dowd leave that undergarment on my workstation and when you have completed the stock task, you or Mr Brophy will return the garment to the Ladies Department."

With the blue knickers dropped on top of the sales and stock dockets the two assistants headed off for the stockroom, but not before Thomas heard O'Dowd say to Brophy, "They must be St Theresa's knickers, it's a bleedin miracle!" They both then roared with laughter as they continued on their way. Then, when no one was looking, Thomas slid the undergarment into the pocket of his trousers beneath his handkerchief.

*

5.10 PM. Detective Inspector O'Connell along with two accompanying Gardaí were at Collinstown airport awaiting the arrival of a flight from London. Earlier in the day they had received a 'Trunk' call to the station, from the London Metropolitan police, with a tip off that Tony Turner, the renowned and dangerous Bath Avenue criminal, was booked on the 6.30 PM flight to Dublin under the name of Peter Kenny. Turner was wanted under two warrants, one for assault and battery and the other for armed robbery. They did not expect trouble but were prepared, with O'Connell himself armed with a concealed handgun and the Gardaí with their batons. When the passengers eventually began to emerge from the customs area, they scrutinised each male for a match to the photograph of Turner each was holding. Also, they were aware that Turner was small in stature and sported a small scar on his right cheek from a knife fight he had had as a youth.

The sixth male passenger to emerge, while much bigger than Turner, somehow caught Inspector O'Connell's attention. He certainly did not recognise the black haired, heavily moustached, and spectacled man, in the dark brown overcoat and grey hat, but there was something about the way he walked that was familiar. Suddenly, however, just behind the stranger, Turner appeared. His head was bowed, and he was moving quickly. In response, the three were on to him, with O'Connell saying.

"Excuse me Sir, we are from the Gardaí could we have your name please?" Turner looked frantically at the exit, but then decided to face it out.

"Peter Kenny, and why do you ask, officer?" he said, in a heavy cockney accent. "And I'm Harold Macmillan, I don't think," replied the Inspector, and continued, "We believe your real name is Tony Turner, and we would like you to accompany us quietly to a custom's room where you will be searched, and following this, be brought to Irishtown police station for questioning. If you, in any way, try to resist, you will be forcefully subdued and restrained."

Turner just shrugged his shoulders and went along with them without any resistance.

*

6.15 PM Thomas Masterson arrived home and just before he sat down for his tea, he went out to his shed to hide the controversial pair of knickers. He had a dark green crock vase his wife had given him, in which he kept small wooden plugs to cover screw holes in his wood working hobby. It was half full, so he emptied them out onto his workbench, pushed the knickers to the bottom of the non-transparent vessel and covered them over with the plugs. He then placed the vase on the top shelf at the back, where it was impossible for Nora to reach. Then, locking the shed door, he went back inside for his tea.

*

David Williams arrived home around 7.00 that evening to find Bronwyn all fussed and bothered. "Whatever is the matter, darling?" he asked.

"It's Beth," she replied, "about ten minutes ago, I got a telegram from her to say she had had an accident, and I need to go and look after her for a few weeks," she continued, as tears welled up in her eyes, "and our bloody phone is not working! "And trying to make a trunk call from the phone box on the Green is a nightmare with all the coins necessary. Then, most probably, it is broken anyway! Did you report our phone to the P and T?"

"Oh darling," replied David, "this is terrible. Please show me the telegram?"

Bronwyn handed him the message from the hall table.

Telegram

Have broken leg (stop) Home help visits here but need you (stop) Sail Wednesday night for London Thursday AM (stop). Do not call (stop) cannot reach phone (stop) Till Thursday Love Bethany (stop)

"Oh, my god," said David, after reading the message. "Please my love, you are very understandably upset. But I wonder, how she could have broken her leg?"

"Probably, umpiring one of those stupid Netball games."

"Please don't fret darling Bron! I'll arrange a first-class trip on the mail boat for you tomorrow evening, so just pack your case and whatever else you need. Oh yes, and I did report the phone, but they said they could not get to us till Friday. Anyway, it appears you might only frustrate poor Bethany if you telephoned as she can probably hear it, but cannot reach it, and that would be very upsetting for her. But first thing in the morning, I'll telegram her to let her know you will be there on Thursday morning."

"Typical of the bloody Post and Telegraphs," chimed in Bronwyn, "inefficiency, as with everything else in this bloody country, we were far better off under British rule!"

"Oh, don't fret darling I'm getting Freddie Peters from work, an expert, it seems on telephone repairs, to come around tomorrow evening to have a look, it is probably just the connection. Oh, and be careful about British rule, I think O'Brien next door might be a bit of a rebel!"

"Right, as if I care! And you can see to your own dinner. I certainly cannot now." She said, storming off up the stairs.

"Of course, darling," he replied, "and by the way, I'm just putting my head into that Drama meeting in the Methodist church tonight for an hour. Would you like to come along and meet some of our neighbours?"

"Certainly not, but it's probably good to have you out of my hair, as I have so much to prepare between now and tomorrow evening," she replied, before he heard the bathroom door slam shut.

*

Following a family meal of the best steak, onions, carrots and spuds, Joan Lawlor, one-time nurse but now the butcher's wife and mother was in her bedroom getting ready to go out to the Drama meeting at the Methodist church hall. Her youngest, Jack, was bathed and tucked up asleep while the two older ones were in their pajamas to be sent to bed at their father's behest but certainly before 9.00 PM.

As Joan applied her make-up, she could hear someone on 'Radio Éireann' talking about the preparation for the St Patrick's Day parade due to take place on March 17th in just over two weeks' time. St Patrick's Day was exceptional to her, not just for the celebration of Ireland's patron saint, but it was also the birthdate of her first child. She had given birth to her illegitimate daughter in London almost thirteen years ago, and the day following the birth she had lost her baby to an adoption to which she had agreed but regretted since. She had held her daughter for only about three minutes but to this day, cannot forget the dimple in her chin, the blond fuzzy hair, and the small birthmark under her inside left ankle. She also remembered quite vividly the baby's little fingers and toes, and her left ear sticking out a bit more than the right. Not only did she remember everything about her baby, but she also never lost the guilt from giving her up.

The whole episode now seemed like a dream as she once again went over the details in her mind of that heart-breaking time.

Joan's nursing training at Great Ormond Street hospital in London had been almost complete when she had found herself pregnant. She had taken up with a young Houseman, Richard Snow, three months previously, and believed he was the one for her. Of course, she had been wrong, as he had no intention of settling down at that point. He had been perfect to the extent that he was willing to pay for an abortion even though it was illegal. But with him in the medical fraternity, he had the inside track on the best and safest available. She, however, would not consider this even as an option, and so Richard's family had paid all her costs for confinement and the delivery of the child in an exclusive nursing home in Hampstead. They had also arranged for the child to be adopted by a Catholic family, probably from the United States she had been told, when she had signed her baby's life away to strangers whom, it was emphasised, she could never know. On the day after the child was taken away, Richard visited her with an offer of more money to pay for her fare home. This she flatly refused, and so they said their goodbyes, each knowing they would never meet again.

She had finished her nurse's training and a year later, when home on holiday, she met Joseph at a ceilidh in Dublin. He was great fun, loved Irish music and played the fiddle when he was not running the butcher's shop in Sandymount, recently inherited from his deceased father. Soon they fell in love and were married, but not before Joan had told Joseph of her plight in London. He was very understanding and told her that what had happened before they met was gone, and they should not talk of it again. They had not talked of it again, and with her giving birth to three children within her marriage it all seemed to fade away. But it didn't fade away for her, as never did a day pass without her thinking of her first child, whom she had named Patricia. This St Patrick's Day the baby she gave away would be thirteen, and it would be another year of heartache with her precious angel turning into a teenager and her real mother not there to see her.

*

From 7.45 PM, Rev Shillitoe welcomed everyone to the Methodist Hall and as they arrived, he handed each a sheet of paper with the programme for the meeting:

Sandymount Amateur Dramatic Society

Inaugural Meeting 1/3/60

1. Greeting/Opening

2. Production Choice

(a) The Righteous are bold (Frank Carney)

(b) Murder on the Nile (Agatha Christie)

(c) An Inspector calls (J B Priestly)

(d) The Well of the Saints (J M Synge)

3. Direction

4. Actors/Parts

5. Stage Management/Production

6. Prompt

7. Costumes/Wardrobe

8. Sound/Lighting

9. Scenes

10. Refreshments

11. Production assistants

As Vera O'Brien was entering the hall, she met David Williams arriving at the same time. She grinned and asked him.

"Is Mrs Williams not interested in Drama, Mr Williams?"

He gave her his charming smile in return while answering.

"No, not in the formal sense anyway, but unfortunately, she is packing her case tonight as she is going abroad for a few weeks." Vera and husband often talked about the travel perks the Williams' got from his travel clerk job, so, it was not in the least strange for Bronwyn to be off some place.

"Off somewhere nice, is she?" Pushed Vera, as she made her way to the left, but only got a straight, "Yes." In reply, as he, turned right.

Shortly after, Peg O'Connell eased herself into a chair beside the then seated Vera O'Brien who smiled and spoke to Peg.

"Are you alright Mrs, you sound as if you strained your back?"

"Oh, thank you for asking, it is just an arthritis like compliant, mostly in my back today."

"Oh, what you need," replied Vera, "is a few prayers to St James, the Great patron saint of rheumatism. Or even maybe better still, a few to St Gemma Galgani for back pain. And sure, I'll say a few myself for you, Mrs eh………?"

"O'Connell, Peg O'Connell."

"Nice to meet you, Mrs O'Connell, and I'm Mrs Vera O'Brien."

"Nice to meet you too Mrs O'Brien, although I wonder why I'm here as I can't act or anything like that but…."

"I know exactly what you mean," said Vera, interrupting her, "sure it's somewhere to go and get you out of the house."

"Yes, you're so right, Mrs O'Brien, and I'm glad I met someone here like myself, as I've only recently moved to Sandymount."

"Ah, don't worry about that, sure the people around here are lovely, and we'll all look after you."

"Oh, that's nice," replied Peg, "and tell me Mrs O'Brien, do you have any children?" The conversation continued on until the committee took their seats, and all quietened down.

Evelyn Roberts, the social companion seeker, was happy and relieved with the 43 people who had turned up. She had counted each as they entered. She then sat with the other committee members, behind a table on a raised platform at the top of the hall. She waited another minute for everyone to settle down and then stood to make the opening address. She recognised many of the faces but did not know their names. There were two people whom for some reason she thought were married, but they had arrived separately and sat quite a distance apart. Others she recognised, she thought, probably from around the village or had seen them at mass. But then she smiled to herself when she did recognise someone. It was that nice man with the green and white scarf she's met on Sunday night when walking home with 'Bonzo,' and this then in turn reminded her how glad she was she had no need to bring the dog along tonight.

Finally, she cleared her throat, welcomed, and thanked everyone for coming, saying she was delighted to see so many interested in the project. She then introduced the committee members, stating that each would lead the meeting with a different item on the agenda, but that all in the audience were welcome to interrupt at any time should they wish to make a point or give some input. It was after all, she emphasised, their Drama society, so their contribution was essential.

She then told the audience she had been selected to lead the agenda item number 2, which was 'Production Choice'.

"Now, regarding this choice" she stated, "we the committee discussed as a team, the four plays as listed on the agenda sheet under (a), (b), (c) and (d). It was decided that each of the first three, that is (a), (b) and (c) were either too difficult to produce as a beginning play for a new group and in addition, each of these plays requires at least 8 actors, plus the other important production needs. What that means is that simply the first three were going to be too hard to do, and we were not convinced that we'd get enough people to go the journey, from preparation and first rehearsal to actual performance. So, for our first production, we put it to you, that 'The Well of the Saints' a comedy by John Millington Singe requiring five actors three males and two females, should be our first effort. Now, has anyone any objections to that?"

There were no objections, so Eve then handed out a sheet briefly explaining what the play was about and its required cast:

The Well of the saints

(By John Millington Synge)

Synopsis: *Two blind married beggars Martin and Mary Doul are old and ugly looking, but think they are, in fact, beautiful. The people of the town have given them to believe this lie. Then, the holy man arrives and performs a miracle, with the help of the water from a holy well, to make them see again. Upon seeing again, they don't like the look of each other, so Martin takes a job working for Timmy the Smith. Martin cannot resist the beauty of Timmy's fiancée, Molly Byrne, and makes advances towards her. Molly rejects these advances and big strong Timmy sends Martin off. The result then is that Martin and Mary lose their sight again.*

When the holy man comes back to marry Timmy and Molly, he offers to give them their sight again, but this offer is refused. The holy man is insulted by the refusal and the local people cast the Douls from their village and the blind couple move off to look for more sympathetic folk.

Cast: Martin Doul, an elderly blind beggar, Mary Doul, his wife, also blind, Timmy, a young blacksmith, Molly Byrne, Timmy's lovely fiancée, and the Saint, a wandering holy man. Others to play extras in the village.

When everyone had an opportunity to read the leaflet, Eve began to attempt to find people for the cast and other jobs.

No one felt confident enough to direct, so Cecilia Lombardi took on that roll.

Eve Roberts got the job as producer and stage manager with the assistance of the butcher's wife, Joan Lawlor and the Garda's wife, Peg O'Connor. Then someone from the audience shouted that they should get the cast sorted out first and then allocate the other jobs later. Everyone agreed and Eve was happy to go along but stated that each part would require the prospective cast member to read a piece of that character from the play itself.

Following this procedure, Mr and Mrs Cummins from Lea Road secured the parts of the blind Martin and Mary Doul. David Williams sought the part of the holy man, but someone announced from the back that he didn't look holy enough, which got a great laugh, and the part went to Patrick Foley, who became quite animated and moved by his selection. Eileen Hannigan was nominated by someone for the part of Molly Byrne. Eileen protested that she was too old for the part, but with further urging, she went up to do the reading. Eve pointed out the required section, which Eileen briefly read through to herself and then began aloud.

"This is Molly speaking to Martin Doul in Act II:"

"I'll tell your wife if you talk to me like that…. You've heard, maybe, she's below picking nettles for the widow O'Flinn, who took great pity on her when she seen the two of you fighting, and yourself putting shame on her at the crossing of the roads."

When Eileen stopped, there was silence for a second and then everyone burst into applause as she had spoken as a young country girl with gusto and confidence. Eve looked at Cecilia, and they smiled at each other, knowing they had a probable star on their hands. Eileen got the part, while a young man probably ten years her junior was to be the blacksmith.

Two other important jobs were also allotted, the first to David Williams was that of Costume and Wardrobe procurement due to his experience in the Rathmines and Rathgar musical society. The second was that of Lighting and Sound going to Mikey O'Rourke. When Mikey volunteered for this job, Eve asked him if he was an electrician, to which he replied that he was, to a certain extent, and left it at that.

"Well, what does that mean?" She asked. "We are delighted for you to take on that job, but we wouldn't want someone to electrocute themselves or someone else." Mikey smiled at Eve and replied quietly, so only a few could hear. "Okay, I'll come clean," he said, in an American gangster accent, "I'm not an electrician, I'm an electrical engineer. Will that do, Ma'am?"

"Certainly," she replied, a little sorry for asking but happy to have gained additional information on the big man.

With all the agenda items covered and great enthusiasm for the production, it was decided that due to many of those present attending the novena, there would be two half-meetings for development updates together with progress reports from those who could make it to either. The first short meeting would be this coming Thursday 3rd at 7.00 PM and the second on Friday 11th at 7.00 PM.

Mary Murphy had volunteered to make the tea and run the refreshments side of the operation, but it was agreed that there would be no refreshments for the two upcoming short meetings.

As Mary was leaving the hall, however, she noticed her own neighbour Mrs Ryan sitting beside her employer Mrs Jones, with both in deep conversation. She pretended not to see them and walked on, but not before she noticed Mrs Jones hand a piece of paper to Mrs Ryan. Another worry she thought, maybe Mrs Jones was offering the cleaning job to Mrs Ryan! But she couldn't think about that then, as she had much more to occupy her mind.

However, just as she was about to leave, her friend Mrs Lawlor, the butcher's wife, who was talking to Mrs Hannigan and some other woman she didn't know, called her over to stay for a while and have a cup of tea. She didn't take much convincing, as her daughter Catherine was baby-sitting. Also, she was not worried about Stephen arriving home drunk because that wouldn't happen till the pubs closed way after 11.00 PM. What she was worried about though was Mrs Jones finding out about her drunken husband from Mrs Ryan.

So, with a cup and saucer in her hand Mary was introduced to the stranger who turned out to be Mrs Peg O'Connell a recent arrival in Sandymount.

"So then," said Joan Lawlor, "are we all attending the novena starting on Friday? She asked, generally, by way of getting the chat started. Her three companions all nodded and answered yes but then Mrs O'Connell said.

"I'm doing it mainly for my son John, who is having a really tough time with his 'Irish' for the 'Inter cert.'

"Oh, God help him," said Vera. But Eileen asked, "Which school is he at?"

"The Christian brothers in Westland Row," Peg answered. "He is having particular difficulties with the Irish teacher, Brother Spencer, who seems to get pleasure from the constant use of the strap.

"Yes," said Joan, "those brothers are very hard, but they're supposed to get the results."

"Well," said Eileen, "being a teacher myself, I believe it should not be necessary to beat knowledge into children."

"I know," said Peg, "but it's the 'reader' they are doing that seems to be causing all the problems. Brother Spenser believes it should be read and gone through, like any book, so the full story is not known until the end. But I think, if, young John only knew what it was about in English, he would be able to follow it better."

"Well, I'm afraid I can't help you there," said Eileen, "I taught History and English and was never much use, at the Irish." The others nodded in agreement, indicating their own lack of ability in the language.

"Ah, sure even his father," said Peg, "who is a Garda, with better Irish than me can't help him with this Scéal Séadna book!

"Oh, I know, you're right," said Joan, "about our ability with the Irish sure it's an awful state of affairs altogether. Sure, didn't I read recently that that playwright, Brendan Behan, says that the education system in this country has ended up with most of us being ignorant in two languages."

They all tittered at this, only to be interrupted by a sophisticated English accent asking.

"Did I hear someone mention Scéal Séadna?" They all looked around to see that the voice belonged to the tall, blond, and handsome David Williams.

"Yes, Mr Williams, "said Joan, smiling at the handsome face, "Mrs O'Connell here needs someone to explain the story to her, so her son can understand it better, but with your accent, I suppose you'd have less chance than even us poor Gaelic scholars."

"Well, Mrs Lawlor," replied David, perhaps you might be wrong there, as I am quite familiar with the story!"

Eileen smiled at him, expecting Mr Williams would probably give them chapter and verse, but the others looked extremely surprised.

"Now, let me see," he began. "Well, firstly, Scéal Séadna itself simply means 'The story of Séadna.' Now, then, this story is told to children as they sit by the fire. It's about a 'cobbler' who makes a bargain with the devil. The bargain being his soul in exchange for money!"

"Oh, holy Jesus protect us," said Vera. David ignored her and went on.

"So, one day as Séadna, the cobbler, was working in his shop, he realised he was running out of leather to make shoes so he would have to go and buy some. Upon checking his cash then, he realised he only just had enough, in the three shillings he had left, to cover the required purchase. So, he set off with the money in his pocket to visit Diarmaid Marley, who had the leather shop in the town of Macroom.

On the road Séadna meets a child, a bare-footed woman, and a man all of whom are poor. He buys bread with one shilling for the child and gives the two adults a shilling each."

"Oh," said Vera, "it was probably Jesus, Mary and Joseph!"

"Will you let him tell the story," Said Joan rather sternly, "and we might find out!"

"Sorry, Mr Williams," Vera said, and made a face at Joan.

"Well," continued David, "an angel then appeared to Séadna and said that because he was so kind to the poor, he could have three wishes. But the angel then cautioned Séadna that the smart thing to do would be to firstly ask for God's mercy to make sure he got the heaven when he died.

Séadna, however, ignored the angel's advice and wished, firstly, that the next person who sat in his favourite roped chair, except for himself, would stick to it. His second wish was for the next person, except for himself, who took oatmeal from his little bag would have their hand stuck in it. And thirdly, the next person, again except for himself, who climbed his apple tree to get its lovely fruit, would stick to it. The angel immediately vanished, and only then did Séadna realise how foolish he had been with his wishes.

Feeling depressed about the whole thing he decided to continue on to Macroom and see if he could get some leather on credit from Diarmaid. But suddenly a 'dark man' who was the devil appears to him in full costume, with horns, tail, and cloven feet."

"Oh, Jesus protect us," said Vera, and then, "sorry Mr Williams."

"Okay," said David and continued.

"Now the devil offered Séadna a purse of money to buy leather, as much as he liked, for the next thirteen years but after that period Séadna had to accompany the devil, presumably to hell.

As Séadna had never seen so much money, and he was tired walking the road, he thought he could well do with buying a horse with the money and still have plenty left. So, there, and then, he made the bargain with the Devil. The same bargain also, I believe, caused the 'sticking wishes,' to the chair, the meal-bag, and the apple tree to be lifted. After this, the devil vanished in flames.

Séadna then headed on to town with the purse of money to buy the horse. At the fair, he picked out a nice animal, but when he went to pay, he found the money was gone from his pocket. So, there was nothing to do but get the leather on credit from Diarmaid.

Later on, at home he found the money had mysteriously returned to his pocket and he wondered why such a thing happened. Anyway, over the next thirteen years Séadna's business thrived, and he employed many more cobblers to work producing his superior quality shoes. With all this wealth, Séadna was wonderful to those in need and to his employees.

There was then much talk that he would marry soon, but nobody knew who it was he would marry. There was one woman he was probably in love with, but because of the bargain with the devil, he felt he could not commit under those circumstances.

At one point, however, the original bare-footed woman came to him again and gave him a jewel to wear to protect him from evil. She also came once more shortly before his 13 years were up and told him that she had removed the purse of money from him at the fair, for a short period, so he couldn't buy the horse or else he would have broken the bargain, to buy only leather, with the devil. She then gave him back the shilling, he had originally given her, and told him to place it under his roped chair before the devil returned. This he did, and some hours before the thirteen years were up the devil appeared in all his evil.

Séadna told the devil he was too early and while he was finishing off a pair of shoes, he told the devil to take a seat in his chair until the exact departure time came. The devil sat down and despite the 'sticking' curse being lifted off the chair the devil found he could not move and Séadna went to him and blessed him with the jewel the bare-footed woman had given him. The devil, immediately, burst into an explosion of flames and disappeared through the chair, and it seems gone forever from Séadna, who took up the last years of his life working for the king of the land."

With that, David lifted his open-palmed hands to show he was finished.

"Oh, my Lord! Thank you for that Mr Williams." Sad Peg. "That will be a great help."

Then Joan piped in.

"Well, talk about never really knowing people! Or what they can do! Mr Williams, you certainly seem to have many strings to your bow!"

He certainly does, thought Eileen, and you only know the half of it!

Vera was mesmerised by this beautiful man and thought, not alone is he good-looking and smart, but probably the best thing about him overall is that he is a convert from being a protestant.

David left the meeting alone and as he walked home it occurred to him that, in a strange sort of way, his own situation and the solution processes he had to take had many similarities with those of the story of Séadna.

*

Fr McKenna and Patrick Foley, together, left the meeting on their bicycles, both going in the same direction. Patrick was still full up with getting the part and asked the priest to give him some hints on how to act holy as he was only a simple hairdresser.

"In there," Patrick said, pointing at the hair salon on his left called 'Sandymount Waves.'

"I don't think there's anything simple about you, Patrick. I think you are a most interesting person and probably extremely smart once you open yourself to others. You know you got that part because of your ability to articulate that particular scene you read, precisely?"

"Oh, my Lord," said Patrick, "I think I've come on with an embarrassed flush."

They both laughed, and the priest said he needed to get a haircut himself. Patrick said he'd be delighted to cut the priest's hair but thought he might be embarrassed having it clipped in a Ladies salon. The priest agreed, but also said that they should get together to talk further about Patrick's part. To arrange this, he'd telephone Patrick at the salon tomorrow. He said they could meet in 'Wynns' hotel in Abbey Street in Dublin, as it was a place where a lot of the clergy were known to frequent for a drink.

As they both cycled on down Sandymount Road Patrick said he thought he had seen the priest the previous night in Ballsbridge.

"Oh, you did," replied the priest, thinking you could do nothing in this town without someone seeing you. "I was on my way to Donnybrook to visit my sister, she lives on Morehampton Road.

"Oh, your sister, right. Sorry, it's just that people forget that priests have families. It's like they are always on their own!"

"Well, mostly, that is the life we lay out for ourselves, no ties. But I'm lucky that my sister lives near enough to visit."

"Yes, that is true. So, do you have many brothers and sisters?

"Well, would you believe, no brothers but one other sister, and she's a nun, in South America, Columbia?"

"Just one sister living here then, but I suppose being on your own, you must get lonely. Oh, I'm sorry Father, I'm so inquisitive. Tell me to mind my own business. Anyway, this is where we branch off. Telephone when you know you're free and we can arrange to meet."

"Okay Patrick and yes, I do get very lonely, so I'll look forward to our get together. Good night and God Bless."

"Goodnight Father."

Patrick cycled on past the Protestant church on his left and thought to himself, now there is a very attractive, astute, and mysterious man. He was attractive in his good looks and the manner in which he carried himself. Even to the extent of looking good in all that back gear. There was certainly few who could carry that off. He was astute in that Patrick knew he was smart himself, but constantly held himself back in displaying his abilities and knowledge because it was bad enough being a Queer without being a smart arsed Queer. Patrick fed his smartness with a voracious appetite for knowledge, which he satisfied with the help of the Ballsbridge library. Fr McKenna, though, was also mysterious because he had told Patrick categorically that he had no brothers, yet Patrick had seen with his own eyes the night before, Fr McKenna's brother come out of the sister's house in Donnybrook and catch a bus.

It had been after Patrick left the library with his weekly procurement of at least four books that he crossed the bridge to get a packet of Alpine before he headed home on his bicycle. But just as he was about to enter the shop, he saw the figure of the priest cycling out of Beatty's Avenue, cross the bridge and head up Herbert Park towards Donnybrook. Patrick being curious, interested, and unable to stop himself, checked his books were secure on his back carrier, jumped on his own cycle and took off after the priest. He soon caught up but kept a good distance and followed watching and wondering as the priest turned onto Morehampton Road and went into a house.

Surely, thought Patrick, this is not part of his parish but then maybe it's just someone he knows and is visiting them. With no more to observe he then went into a shop, further on, on the far side of the road, to purchase his cigarettes. There were about three people in front of him and each one took an age to make their purchases. Then when his turn came the proprietor did not have enough change and had to go out the back to get it. This again took an age. Finally, he got his Alpine twenty pack and decided to have a smoke before he started for home as he could never enjoy smoking while cycling. But as usual as his mother often said, '*When things go wrong, they can often get worser!*' And they did, as his 'Ronson lighter' appeared to be out of fuel and the thoughts of going into that shop again was not an option he liked to consider. So, shaking it a bit and waiting another minute he clicked it and got a small but sufficient flame to light up. The first drag was heaven sent and he then, over the next few minutes he took his time, until his craving was satisfied. He flicked the 'but' onto the path, squashed it with his foot and mounted the bike to head back the way he had come. Then, just as he was passing the door Fr McKenna had entered, he saw a man kiss a woman on the cheek, say goodbye and walk to the bus stop directly outside the house. Getting a clear view of the man while holding his own head down there was no doubt in Patrick's mind that the man was Fr McKenna's brother. Then upon reaching Herbert Park. Patrick stopped and watched as the man got on a bus going to Bray or somewhere between Donnybrook and Bray.

*

Following some tea and biscuits Mikey O'Rourke waited until Eve was leaving the Drama meeting and dropped in beside her as she walked out the church gate onto Newgrove Ave by the green.

"So, how is the great 'Bonzo' today? He asked.

"Very well, when I left him tonight?" she said, with a wide smiling face. She then explained the dog was home and minding her house.

"A dog's duty," he said, and continued. "I'm Mikey O'Rourke, as I told Bonzo on Sunday night. I live in Sandymount but am originally from Galway! And, you'd be Miss Evelyn Roberts, the 'Drama Queen." Eve smiled not sure quite how to take that remark but opting for it to be a sort of compliment.

"Eve," she said, please call me Eve."

"Oh right," he said, "Eve it will be then, and I'm Mikey." They continued walking and talking along Claremont Road until they got to the 'Farney Park' and Eve, completely caught up in their conversation only then realised they had gone well past where his car had been parked on Sunday.

"I thought you lived way back nearer the green?" She said, interrupting his explanation for his green and white "Shamrock Rovers' scarf.

"Oh, yes I do Eve, but a Galway gentleman always walks a lady home, especially at night and when he knows her."

"Well," she replied, "that is very gallant of you Sir, but this lady is quite capable of making her own way home and besides," she teased with a little lie, "I live about two and a quarter mile away, in Milltown."

"What?" He said, stopping dead with a slight shock on his face, because he knew exactly how far it was to Milltown as his team 'Rovers' had their home ground there at 'Glenmalure Park.' But then, he quickly relaxed and spoke.

"What may I ask, is two and a quarter mile when one is in the company of an intelligent and articulate conversationalist?"

"Oh, you have a bit of way with words yourself, even if they're lacking in truth! Intelligent and articulate conversationalist, I don't think! But to be honest I'm only codding you; I actually just live up near the Railway gates on Serpentine Ave. So, you can go back now as I'll be home in five minutes."

"Oh, no Mademoiselle," he ventured, "even five minutes with the queen of drama is not to be missed."

They laughed and joked on until they arrived at her house.

"This is it," she said. "Thank you, and goodnight."

"Yes, and a very goodnight to you Eve," he replied, but waited till the door had closed behind her and she was safe inside.

Once Eve had got into bed that night, she tried to remember the last time someone had seen her home. Mr O'Rourke, or I should say Mikey, she thought, was so very friendly and funny. She felt really good as it looked like she had hit gold on the friendship trail from her Drama plan. Because, while she had not clicked with any single women, she had gotten on famously with Joan Lawlor, Mary Murphy, and Peg O'Connell all of whom were married, but also, she had met that big, yet gentle Galway-man. She smiled to herself thinking, yes, a gentleman and then turned over and went to a contented sleep.

*

When Peg O'Connell arrived home that night, she related the story of Séadna almost verbatim to her son John and husband James, saying a very nice man at the 'Drama' society had explained it to a group of them.

That night John (Copper) O'Connell went to sleep feeling a lot better as at last he began to make some sense of the stuff that had been covered in the book so far.

CHAPTER 7

Ash Wednesday: 2nd March

8.00 AM Vera O'Brien, her husband and family were among the first of the day to be conferred with ashes. This was administered to the faithful as they knelt along the altar rails, similar to them receiving communion. As the priest came to each person, he stuck his thumb into a plate of ashes and then pasted this black ash, by way of a cross, onto the recipient's forehead. At the same time, the priest muttered in Latin. "Meménto, homo, quia pulvis es, et in púlverem revertéris." *(Remember, man, that thou art dust, and into dust thou shalt return).*

When the O'Brien family got back to their seats for a silent prayer in contemplation of their future deaths, the six children started giggling at how each looked with their black smears. This broke out into restrained laughter when three-year-old baby Nuala brushed her stained forehead, saying, "Dirty Poo!" Their father smiled with the kids and then took Nuala up on his knee, telling her she must not talk in the church.

"Why can I not be allowed to talk?" She loudly whispered and this made the rest of them even worse. Until Vera interrupted her contemplation with a stern. "Quiet!" to them all but whispering to husband Raymond. "Don't you be encouraging them!"

*

Young Seamus Hannigan and his pal Pat knelt at the altar rails awaiting their turn as the priest made his way toward them. He would reach Seamus first and then Pat. They were very interested in the process as it was different and only occurred once a year, so they looked attentively along as each person was branded. When it came to Seamus' turn, he automatically stuck out his tongue, as was his habit when kneeling at the altar rail. Fr McKenna ignored this mistake and crossed Seamus with the ash. However, Pat burst out laughing and Fr McKenna, realising why, punctuated his Latin verse with, "Behave, young man!"

The two, completely out of control, walked to the back seat and continued their hysterics when Pat said, "Jeez, I thought you were gona eat the ash!"

Once this hilarity had abated somewhat, they then sat there looking at the quality of each person's stain. Seamus noticed two local Legends,

Hairballs Finnegan, and Greasy Ryan. Seamus nudged Pat to make him aware the 'Lads' had arrived. Both these characters were sixteen or seventeen and well known for their amazing exploits. Hairballs, of course, got his name because he got hairs on his 'mickey' at the age of ten, way before any of his pals and even before most of the lads in the class above him. Because of this early blooming, it was put about that he was sex mad and was hung like a Johnson Mooney and O'Brien, bread-vendor's horse. The legend grew even in the last week when it was noticed that Hairballs had a bit of a limp. The story was, that he fell out of a tree one night while trying to see Masie Donnelly get ready for bed.

Greasy Ryan got his name due to the vast amount of 'Brylcreem' he used on his hair. He was also renowned for his own exploits, for example, when he was only ten, he had a fight with his sister and eventually pinned her to the ground. His mother caught them, and gave Greasy a clip around the ear, telling him that, "*that* was a terrible thing to do to your sister and you better tell that sin to the priest next Saturday in confession."

Greasy followed his mother's instruction and the next Saturday saw him in the queue for the confession box of the presumed deaf, Fr Crampton. Now the story has it that Greasy went into Crampton and in his confession, he said. "Bless me Father for I have sinned; I did a terrible thing to me sister!"

"What? Replied the priest, even louder than his penance volume.

"I did a terrible thing to me sister," repeated Greasy, and then for clarity added, "I did it with her on the floor."

"How old are you?" Shouted Crampton. "I'm ten and a half." Greasy trembled back.

"Sweet Jesus in Heaven!" screamed Crampton. "Say one 'Our Father' and forty-seven 'Hail Mary's! Now say, a good act of contrition and never go near your sister again!"

Some say Greasy peed his pants in the box, but all agree that when he came out, all those who had been waiting their turn had moved to another box or left the church.

Then there was the major scandal that occurred concerning Greasy with the hanging of a cat. It involved the house on the corner of Oaklands Park and Serpentine Ave Ballsbridge which boasted a huge walled garden and within, virtually on the corner itself, was a big oak tree. A large sign was nailed onto the top of the tree trunk, visible for all to see from outside, reading 'Trespassers will be prosecuted.' One morning, however, a dead cat was found hanging, with a rope by the neck from a branch, and the sign had been changed to read 'Trespassers will be executed.' Throughout Ballsbridge and Sandymount, the Gardaí, were spurred on by the cruelty people and indeed all good people to find the culprit or culprits. They never did. But the story was, that Greasy Ryan had found a dead cat on the side of the road that had been hit by a car, and he tied a rope round its neck, strung it up, and changed the word on the sign to executed from prosecuted.

The arrival of these two legends had temporarily stopped Seamus and Pat from their mirth, but it began again when Seamus whispered to Pat. "There'd be no point in Johnny Rags getting the ashes, as you'd never see them on his dirty face!"

*

Vera O'Brien's husband Raymond had just dropped the family back home from receiving their ashes when he commenced his long journey to Northern Ireland. He was a senior medical representative for his company, and apart from his main territory of northern Dublin and part of the north-east of the republic, Raymond also covered a specific territory in Northern Ireland that included Southern Belfast. He usually spent 5 days a month in the North to ensure full coverage. These five days consisted of two days one week and three days the next week away from home. This meant he was only away from helping Vera with the family three nights in any one month.

As a strong republican and member of the IRA Raymond played a very useful part, with the convenience of his job, in the so-called 'Border Campaign.' He had been approached several years before and asked if he was willing to help the cause, and without any hesitation he agreed. This had resulted in the boot of his car being remodeled to hide a secret compartment. This allowed small to medium arms and explosive devices or their parts, to be concealed, to be transported, over the border. In some cases, this cargo would be brought from the republic for a specific job and in other cases they would be taken out of the operation area to avoid detection.

The 'Border Campaign,' however, had recently been slowing down, so Raymond had found an additional use for his cargo hold. Originally, he had just brought the condoms, illegal in the republic, for his personal use. But then he realised that here was an opportunity to get extra cash for the needs of his large family. He had begun using the condoms with Vera two years previously and as she never really noticed him using them, he didn't have to listen about the sin of it all.

He certainly didn't want any more kids, as he felt he had contributed quite enough to Catholicism's membership by having sired six. Indeed, the extra cash he procured from selling the 'frenchies' was, often as not, spent on First communion or Confirmation clothes, so there was a little irony in that, he thought smiling to himself.

*

Thomas Masterson got ashes at about 8.15 AM and then continued on to work. His wife Nora went to the church at around 10.00 AM to fulfil her own duty and then went up to the village for the messages. As usual, she never made up her mind what they would have for their dinner until she went to the shops. Today, the pork chops looked very nice, and she bought two medium-sized ones for herself and Patricia and a large one for Thomas. Nora loved to see Patricia, her nearly teenage daughter, walk in the door from school with all the news of the girls in her class and the nice and not so nice nuns. Nora had never once regretted Patricia's arrival, and especially now with their two only other children, gone far away. Their second-eldest Sammy, to the army in the United States, and Tom Junior, the eldest, ordained only last year and away to the foreign missions in Africa. She worried about the two boys every day, what with the talk on the radio about the war in Vietnam and the possibility of Sammy having to go there. Then there was also trouble with the 'Mau-Mau' rebels close to Tom's mission settlement. Her husband, however, was proud as punch of Sammy in the army and as for Tom Junior, well on the day of his ordination Thomas was like a peacock walking around!

Thinking about her husband however, stimulated a little concern. She got the feeling of late that he was not quite himself, and she hoped he was not coming down with something. Anyway, she would make a nice dinner for him today with the chops, done in the oven as he liked and some nice cabbage and potatoes, all topped with gravy made from the juice of the chops and a little help from the 'Bisto Kids.'

Exiting Joseph Lawlor's butcher shop sometime later, Nora made her way to Lafayette and Fry general store for sugar, flour, salt, and mustard. She then dropped into McQuaid's greengrocer and purchased a quarter stone of potatoes and a nice head of cabbage. As she was paying for the vegetables, her attention was taken by small bunches of just slightly opened daffodils, and a little spurt of joy ran through her. Spring at last she thought, looking at the flowers that gave her the feeling of the end of winter. Without hesitation, she purchased a bunch, thinking of the satisfaction she would enjoy watching them reach full bloom like beautiful angels with their wings spread.

Arriving home, Nora put the daffodils temporarily into a cleaned-out jam jar with water and commenced the dinner preparation. Once she had peeled the potatoes, cut up the cabbage and placed the chops in the oven, it was 11.30 AM. She would light the oven around 12.15 PM, as Thomas and daughter Patricia would be home for dinner around 1.15 PM. She was then about to attend some other jobs such as collecting clothes for washing but remembered the daffs in the jam jar. So, thinking about a more appropriate vessel to place them, she remembered the dark green vase she'd given to Thomas, but now thought it would be a very nice receptacle for the matching green stems of the flowers. She would retrieve it from the shed, and Thomas could find something else in which to hold his wooden plugs. But then she realised the shed was locked and Thomas probably had the key with him. She was about to give up and wait until he came home, but, suddenly, remembered there was a box under the stairs full of odds and ends like a pair of her dead mother's glasses together with old keys and locks, pins, and tacks.

Having checked the padlock on the shed door she went back to the house to find the box and hopefully an appropriate key. This proved to be more difficult than expected as she firstly had to move three full bags of second-hand clothes which people gave to Thomas for the poor. Eventually, however, she got to the box and selected three keys that seemed the right size. The second one she tried, opened the shed lock and looking around she was unable to see the object she desired until she stood back, looked up at the high shelf, and glimpsed, almost out of sight, the green colour. There was nothing in the shed to stand on, so she went back to the kitchen and got a small stool and carefully managed to take the vase down and place it on Thomas' work bench. She turned it over and emptied all the plugs and looked inside to make sure they were all out.

What is that at the bottom? She thought as she pushed two fingers down to the bottom and extracted the knickers. She spread them out and thought, what, in God's name, is Thomas doing with a pair of my old knickers in the bottom of a jar? But then she thought, maybe he uses them as a wipe rag. And then she realised two separate things, firstly, they were not old, in fact, they looked new and unused and secondly, they were not hers as it was years since she had bought blue knickers. Then she got a bit panicky and thought they might belong to their daughter Patricia, but she knew Patricia's underwear well, and anyway they were far too big. Jesus Christ, she thought, is he having an affair? But who for God's sake would have an affair with him? Jesus, she thought again, an affair! And him so religious. Whoever it is, she must be a right hussy.

Nora knew what she would do, which was to confront him with them when their daughter was there to help give her strength. She headed back to the house, but before she got to the back door, another thought occurred to her. Maybe they belonged to Mrs Butler next door, they certainly looked as if they would fit her. Oh Jesus, she thought, he must have sneaked over the fence and stole them from her washing line. And God almighty, he probably intends to use them to do his thing into them. No, no, she thought, then what exactly would her favourite author do? Well, she concluded, Agatha Christie would probably have Miss Marple do a lot of sleuthing about, first by asking leading questions and perhaps some following of the suspect! So, it would be much better for Nora to find out what exactly was going on before she confronted him and whoever else was involved as, God forbid, it might even be a Garda matter. Indeed, her husband might be a 'Peeping Tom' and it's the right name for him too, as well as being a knicker robber.

She turned back on her heel and put the undergarment back into the vase with the wooden plugs and pushed the lot to the back on the shelf. Then she locked up the shed and went back to her kitchen to finish the dinner and await the sneaky shite-hawk.

Later, as she watched him eat his dinner, she silently hoped he'd choke on the chop, the dirty rotten hypocrite. But nothing, as far as she was concerned, was more definite in this world than the fact that she would keep an eye on the contents of the vase as well as her husband's movements until she had proof of his guilt. She felt a surge of confidence that within a few weeks she would have enough evidence to confront him with, and then see what cock-and-bull story he'd invent to cover his slimy secret.

As she looked at her daughter though, she knew that but for her husband, their daughter would have died, and they would not have been able to adopt her. She remembered very well that night he had walked in, from his stint at the St Vincent de Paul office, and told her that someone came into the office and said there was something going on at a certain address, and it needed to be looked into. In such circumstances, they would usually have called the police, who would, depending on their workload, attend immediately or within a few days. Thomas felt though, for some reason on that occasion, he should at least have a cursory look himself. Anyway, he had found the baby alone in the house with a note pinned to her giving her name as Patricia and date of birth 17/3/47. He immediately brought the child to Baggot Street hospital, had her examined and cleaned up, and advised the other relevant authorities. The next day he went to see what was happening. Two days later he arrived home with her, for a week, until the authorities could find a foster home, but within a day, the little girl, with the cute little dimple, had found a place in their hearts, and they fostered her immediately. Two weeks later, they had lodged the adoption application papers. No, they never had any regrets. But what, would this child think, Nora thought, when she realised her hero father was a bastard of the highest order.

Before he left to go back to work Thomas told Nora that the following night, Thursday, he would not be home until 9.00 to 9.30 PM as he had to work overtime, and the same again on the next Thursday the 11th. It had to do with them getting prepared for Easter, and it would mean extra money for Easter. He also mentioned that a colleague could probably get him a ticket for the Lansdowne Road rugby game between Wales and Ireland, to be held on Saturday, March 12th.

These announcements immediately triggered Nora's suspicion, especially the rugby game, as he had in all their years together never shown much interest in any sport except for the odd comment on horse racing when he occasionally had a little flutter. Then Nora asked him, would he not be attending the Thursday night novena session on the 11th, as therefore he wouldn't fulfil the Novena requirements? From the way, he answered that question the Miss Marple in her knew he was bluffing, particularly when he said that he would say the required rosary and novena prayer himself and might even make it to the benediction with luck. He also stated that he was quite sure St Francis would allow this slight interruption as his work involved the distribution of religious goods for the grace of many.

Nora nodded in agreement but in her heart, she thought she had never heard such a load of unadulterated shite in all her life.

*

At the usual time of 10.30 AM Raymond's wife Vera O'Brien sat down at the kitchen table to have her cup of tea before she tackled the bed-making and upstairs clean-up following the family's morning 'get-ready and out' ritual. As she took her first sip from her favourite China cup, she wondered if Jesus would appear to her today. Maybe today, she thought, His message might be revealed, and she would then be able to talk to Canon Skeffington firstly, about the visions and secondly, about the message. Although Vera preferred to make her weekly confession to Fr

McKenna, she thought the Canon would be the more experienced regarding dealing with visions.

For the moment, however, she would enjoy her brief period of relaxation with her cup of tea. Her thoughts wandered back to when her love of all things catholic began. She had been about three and a half when her mother told her she was a special girl as her name, Vera, which was short for Veronica. The name came from the kind and thoughtful St Veronica, who had wiped the face of Jesus with her veil as an act of kindness on His 'Way of the Cross.' For this loving deed, Jesus had rewarded Veronica with an image of his face on her veil. From that moment on, Vera tried to understand as much as she could about the teachings of the church, and to constantly try and perform acts of kindness like the saint for whom she had been named.

She remembered her first vision almost exactly three weeks ago, when she had been finishing off making the bed in hers and Ray's bedroom. She had just placed the eiderdown on top of the blankets when from the corner of her eye she saw a brightness behind her. With no feeling of anxiety, she turned around slowly to be confronted by a beautiful vision of the full-size and smiling Jesus the man. He held his hands out from his sides with open palms, displaying the bloody holes that had been made for his crucifixion. His whole presence emanated a bright but restful light. Vera had a complete sense of peace and holiness as she dropped to her knees and bowed her head, saying.

"My Lord and my God." When she looked again, expecting the vision to have vanished, she was again consumed with happiness that it was still present. She then without any fear or hesitation asked.

"What is it, Lord, you wish from me thy humble servant?" She received no reply except for the continued smile from her Lord and God, surrounded by his light. The vision lasted around ten minutes during which time she had prayed and again asked for a message or instructions but to no avail until the vision slowly faded away completely.

The vision of Jesus had come to her four or five times a week and on three of those visitations St Veronica had stood beside Jesus holding her veil which depicted His image. On each occasion, Vera was always calm and serene, but never failed to ask either of them for a message. All she received however were the beautiful, loving, and gentle smiles. She had also become aware that only she could see the visions, as on three separate occasions one or two of her children had entered the bedroom while the apparition was taking place, but the children showed not the slightest sign of seeing the miracle.

Following the first week of the bedroom visitations Vera had sat with her cup of tea and decided that she was certainly not mad in that everything else in her life was as normal as could be. It must be that she, although most unworthy, had been picked out for some reason that would eventually be revealed to her. Meanwhile, she should therefore be grateful to God for being so privileged. Indeed, the revelation she expected would now, she was convinced, more than likely occur with the completion of the novena.

*

"Sandymount Waves," said Patrick Foley, as he answered the telephone in the salon.

"Hello Patrick, Fr McKenna here. Look, I'm sorry but with everything going on, what with Lent and the novena, I really can't see you until Sunday afternoon the 13th. I really would like to catch up however but......Have you any ideas?"

"Well, I was thinking about your haircut. But firstly, are you hearing confessions tonight after the novena?

"No."

"Well then, why don't you come up here at about 9.15 PM, and I'll have the blinds pulled down and we'll have the place to ourselves, and I'll see to your hair."

"Wow!" Now, there is a good plan. I'll look forward to seeing you then."

"Me too Father." Said Patrick, as he replaced the receiver with a trembling hand.

*

At 4.00 PM Thomas Masterson, in a state of giddy excitement, decided he could not wait until tomorrow to try on some of his ladies' clothes, so he telephoned Nora to say that he was going to take a bus to Ranelagh and drop into his woodwork supplier shop and get a few items he required. Once this was done, he would take the number 18 bus directly from Ranelagh to Sandymount and be home by 8.00 PM.

The Novena

Nora said she would make him an omelette once he got in if he was hungry and then said goodbye. Once she put the phone down, though, she flipped the telephone number book beside the phone until she found the 'wood hobby' shop and rang the number. She found out the shop closed today at 6.00 PM, so it would be impossible for Thomas to get there in time, even if he left Shaws fifteen minutes early at 5.45 PM. No, she thought, he's going to see his hussy!

*

6.30 PM as Thomas was trying to open the door of the bed-sit on Sallymount Ave Ranelagh, a middle-aged man came out of the house next door he looked at Thomas and spoke.

"You must be Mr Masterson! Mick Mack told me you would be there for about three or four months. I'm Theo Blackmore, and you're welcome by the way. And anything you want to ask, just ask, okay?"

Initially, Thomas was shocked and felt like a child after being caught doing something really naughty. Quickly, however, he composed himself, thinking that this here neighbour, who knew his name, was someone he certainly did not want or need.

"Well," he replied, "what a nice welcome, Mr Blackmore, but I'm sure I'll manage with everything. Thank you." Thomas pushed the door open, wished Mr Blackmore a goodnight and closed the door quickly before anything else could be said.

He was excited and nervous at the same time. With hands shaking, he put the kettle on the gas in the small kitchenette to make a cup of tea to wet his dry mouth. He then went to the cupboard to retrieve the female garments he had put there. He placed these, together with the recently acquired others, on the bed before sitting down and caressing them with his fingers while he waited for the kettle to boil. Once he made the tea, he took off his coat, jacket, tie, and pulled down his brace's suspenders. He dropped his pants, took off his shirt, and then abandoned the idea of having tea. With growing excitement, instead, he quickly drank down a glass of cold water from the tap. Removing his underwear, he only then realised how cold he was completely naked, so he let up the gas fire set in the grate.

He first put on a white pair of knickers, and they reminded him of the pair he had hidden at home. However, he would deal with them tomorrow. Now he would enjoy his slow transformation. He felt enormous pleasure in the feel of the feminine garment on his body and then with quite a lot of difficulty managed to put on the bra which he stuffed with his male socks and two other pair of knickers. The excitement rushed even further when he pulled the silky pink slip over the bra and pants and had to fight hard not to look at himself in the three-quarter length mirror stuck to the wall.

He had promised himself not to look until he was completely dressed, with wig and make-up on. Next, he put on the suspender belt and the nylons he attached with some difficulty. He then took from his dress collection the blue floral belted dress and slipped it over his head, buttoned up the front top and buckled the belt. The shoes had only a slight heel, as he would have liked a really high heel, but he knew he would look like a giant and would probably fall over in them anyway. Then, from its box, he took out the blond wig that came with a fringe at the front to the top of his eyebrows and almost, but not quite, down to his collar. From his jewellery box, he put on a necklace of pearls and pearl earrings. He removed his male watch and replaced it with a small ladies' watch, and then slipped a small bracelet on the other wrist. It was only then that he realised he could not apply his make-up without looking in the mirror. So, he took a deep breath, stood up and went to the looking glass. Jesus Christ, he thought as he looked, and only saw his mother looking back at him. He quickly moved away and then slowly went back at the same time realising that of course it was only natural that he would look like his mother, but then thought that the make-up would probably help to glamourize the transformation.

He applied some rouge to redden his cheeks and then taking a powder puff, applied the powder lightly over his whole face. He then added the bright red lipstick in the way he had often observed Nora do. Then attempted to do what he had seen numerous women do when they put on their lipstick, he rubbed his bottom and top lips together. The result he achieved, however, was a complete mess, with the bright red covering his lips to be sure but also above below and on either side. There was even a smear on the bottom of his nose. He had to wipe it all off completely and then reapply some more powder, and over a period of about ten minutes finally got the lipstick only on his lips. Next came the eye-make up. He had some experience with this firstly by watching Nora again but also, he had read how to do it in 'Woman's Own' magazine which his wife purchased weekly and he secretly read cover to cover. So, on these instructions, he had had several practice sessions with his eyes.

He dabbed the little brush into the small container of Mascara and generously dabbed the stuff on his upper and lower eyelashes. Then, as per 'Woman's Own' he drew a line along the upper lash. Then, following a little plucking, applied the eyebrow pencil and finally the slightest hint of rouge as an eye shadow on his lids.

He stood back, twirled in front of the mirror and then standing still and looking straight at his image said out.

"You look good. I feel good. I am now eh. I am now Sadie. Yes, I am now Sadie, Sadie Masterson!" He flashed his eyes once or twice and thought he might even look a bit like Mae West and doing his best imitation sexy voice said. "Come up and see me sometime!"

He then walked around the room some more and looked at himself/herself a few more times and sat down, feeling the luxury of the feel of the clothes.

Then he thought he should do what many women would do and as he wished to do when he first arrived, he would have a cup of tea, only to discover he had no milk. But there was a shop just a five-minute walk away and while it was great to have the transformation in private, it would be even better to have it in public and be seen as a woman by people. So, he went back to the mirror and said, in what he thought was a female voice.

"A bottle of milk please?" However, it sounded more like broken French *E bittle uf milk pleus?*

He practiced some more until he felt confident and while he had not been planning to leave the flat as Sadie, now that he was her, he thought why not? She would only be out for seven to ten minutes at most.

"E bittle uf milk pleus? Sadie asked the middle-aged female shopkeeper.

The woman looked at Sadie for a bit and then asked.

"Have you got a bottle?"

"Uh no," said Sadie, just remembering it was usual to bring back a replacement bottle when milk was purchased in shops. His home milk, however, was delivered by the milkman and the empties were just placed outside every night for exchange with the full bottles delivered first thing in the morning.

"Pleus churge me fur the bittle." Said Sadie, handing the shopkeeper half a crown.

As she made her way back to the bed-sit Sadie was well pleased with the little excursion. Nonetheless, she would be happy to get back, have the cup of tea, change, and remove the make-up and then head for home. However, as she entered the garden gate to the flat, who should emerge from the house next door but Theo Blackmore. He stopped, looked Sadie up and down, and then saw the latchkey in her hand at the ready to open the bed-sit door.

"Oh," said Mr Blackmore, "you must be Mrs Masterson! I didn't realise Mr Masterson was married." Following this statement there was an awkward silence as Blackmore looked at Sadie curiously. Sadie quickly regained her composure.

"Uh, no, I um nut Mr Masterson's weife. No, I um his sister, Sadie!"

"Oh, Jaysis Miss, I'm sorry, yes, I can see that. Sure, aren't you the spittin image of him.

Blackmore gave her a big broad smile and flirtatiously continued.

"But of course, if I may be permitted, you are much prettier than himself. My name, by the way, is, Theo Blackmore and I'd be honoured if a lady like yourself called me Theo."

"Uh, thank you…eh…Theo…and you may call me Sadie. Now I must get Thomas his tea. Cheerie bye."

"Yea, and to you, too, Sadie. Sure, I'll see you again," said Theo, thinking, what a fine big strap of a mot.

*

David Williams walked in through his hall door from work at close to 6.30 PM. His wife's suitcase, together with a smaller leather carry bag, were situated beside the hall table, presumably for him to place in the car boot for their 20-minute drive to Dun Laoghaire. She had told him the night before that she wanted to leave not a minute after 7.30 so to make sure he was home well in time and not to expect any dinner.

"Hello darling, I'm home," he called, in his refined upper-class accent.

"Your half an hour late coming in!" was her greeting, "but now you've arrived take that case out to the car now, so we can just go at 7.30,"

David braced himself and gave her the news.

"I'm terribly sorry, my love, but the carburetor went completely on the way home and I had to get a tow to a garage in town."

"Oh, you bloody idiot, you should have known something would go wrong with that Morris Minor, I've told you, we need something more dependable like the jaguar daddy had!"

"Now, now, don't fret my lovely," he interjected, "I have called a taxi for 7.15, so you may go whenever you like after that. I'll leave your ticket for the boat and train together with the papers for the cabin and train sleeper. Also, like I promised, I got you a first-class cabin on 'A' deck."

"Good. Right." She replied, and then added. "Also, leave some taxi money and I hope you got me those travelers' cheques?"

"Of course, darling, but you should come down here now and sign them with your first signature, so they cannot be used if lost or stolen."

As she signed each cheque, he told her that Freddie, the colleague, who lived close by on Bath Ave, was coming around at 7.00 PM to attempt to fix the phone. Her lack of interest in this news was demonstrated by her packing her tickets, papers, traveler's cheques, and taxi money into her 'Beverley' leather handbag and walking off into the kitchen.

By 7.15 Freddie had still not appeared, but the taxi, however, did arrive on time, and Bronwyn was more than happy to start out her journey alone. As he kissed her on the cheek goodbye, David said he would ring Bethany's tomorrow night to see she had arrived safe and sound and get an update on Bethany's condition.

CHAPTER 8

Thursday 3rd March

At 10.00 AM Nora Masterson checked the vase in the shed and found that the knickers were still unsoiled and still at its bottom. So, at 2.00 PM following Thomas' departure for work Nora had been most anxious to check out the vase, as Thomas had made a visit to the shed just after he had finished his dinner and also before he left for work.

The knickers were gone. The bastard, she thought, he must be bringing them back to her. It was time, Nora thought, for her to take up the role of Miss Marple and prepare for her part.

*

Just before the Gaelic class began Copper and his pal Steeler were laughing at a joke Hennessy, sitting in front had told them *Why does Spence wear bathing togs when taking a shower? Because he doesn't like looking down on the unemployed.* Suddenly, there was a hush and Spence spoke from the top of the class.

"Copper," he said, "would you like to share the joke with the rest of us? For someone as limited as you, you seem to have little concern for your work!"

Copper's heart began to pound, but he never looked up. He knew there were several leather whacks in this, no matter what he said, and of course, the last thing he could say was the joke. So, with head still bowed and taking every ounce of courage, he ignored the question until once more, Spence said loudly.

"Copper, are you deaf as well as stupid? What is the joke?"

Slowly, Copper raised his head looked straight at Spence and spoke.

"Are you talking to me, sir?"

"Well, who else do you think I'm talking to? Amadán (fool)?"

"Well sir, my name is John O'Connell, not, Copper!"

The whole class held its breath, and Copper's heart was by then in his mouth as everyone awaited the hurricane from Spence. But it didn't happen. Well, not then. What happened then was that Spence said.

"Oh, I am sorry, Master John O'Connell, would you please share the joke with us?

"I'd prefer not to, sir."

"Right then, let us see what you have all learned from your homework last night?"

The class continued on, but twenty minutes in, Copper received the punishment he had expected in double measure for missing some simple question he just didn't understand.

*

A disguised Nora Masterson, wearing her mothers' old glasses and dressed in a long navy coat from the St Vincent de Paul bag, together with a blue headscarf her sister had given her for Christmas, but not yet worn. She stood outside the Carlton cinema looking straight across at Shaws. She was not in any way conspicuous, as where she stood was a well-known place where people often met in the city. She checked the time at 6.05 PM, and a few minutes later, Thomas appeared onto O'Connell Street. She was not sure where he would go but was completely shocked as he began to cross O'Connell Street towards her. She immediately turned to face the cinema but then realised he had not seen her and was walking quickly on her side of the street, towards the bridge. She followed at a safe distance and stopped when he went into Capp and Peterson on the corner. She remembered he went there for his 'Senior Service' cigarettes. Once out, he crossed the bridge to Westmoreland Street, unaware his wife was only yards behind. She saw, too, as he turned onto College Street, crossed over and stood at a bus stop, presumably to catch a bus but to where, was a mystery to her?

Nora tried to think where the buses from that stop would go and couldn't, yet she was quite sure they would be heading south. So, without hardly thinking about it, she slipped into a taxi on the taxi rank by the toilets on College Street and said to the driver that she wanted to follow a bus that would soon leave from the street.

"Jesus Misses," said the cabbie, "now that's a good one. For feck's sake. Oh, sorry. But I always thought someone might ask me to follow a car, but a double-decker bus now that beats all. Sure, don't you know they keep stopping at bus stops!"

"Look," said Nora, "I'll take another cab if you prefer not to do it, but there'll be a good tip plus the fare!"

"Oh, no Misses, you're grand, just tell me which bus, and I'm your man. But do you mind me askin who you're followin?"

"Yes, I do," said Nora, "it's none of your business all you have to do is keep behind the bus until I tell you the trip is finished. Then I'll pay the fare and give you a good tip."

Nora had by then taken out her make-up compact mirror and saw behind her that Thomas had got onto a number eleven bus that was just pulling out.

"That's it," she told the driver, "The number eleven."

The stop and go chase continued until the bus stopped on Sanford Road in Ranelagh where Thomas alighted. Nora quickly paid the taxi fare and followed Thomas who first went to a local shop to buy something and walked on to turn down Sallymount Ave, where he went in through a gate, took a key from his pocket, opened the door to the garden flat and went inside. Nora was astonished, and her astonishment had her literally stuck to the pavement. I've been married to that man for over 25 years, she thought, and he has another life that I know nothing about. She stood there for at least five minutes and at the same time began to lose her nerve about confronting him. Maybe, she thought, she would do it at home where she was more secure. Then she thought she might just wait a bit and see if he came out soon, but after another ten minutes there was no sign of him.

Meanwhile, Thomas, had dressed up in the same outfit he had the previous night and was walking around a bit before he decided to change into some of the other dresses, he had to check which he liked the best. While he was in the process of this, Nora walked up and down past the flat and could see the shape of a figure behind the blind. Then the shape who was obviously in a dress, his hussy, she thought, lifted the dress off over her head and Nora thought, the feckin 'bitch' she's stripping for him. This was too much, and she was about to go to the door and ring the bell, when out of the house next door came a man whom she would later find out was Theo Blackmore.

"Can I help you Misses," he asked, and continued, "I saw you walkin up and down and lookin in here."

"Well," said Nora, thinking quickly, "I'm searching for some friends, but I'm not sure where they live. Their name is Matthews."

"No," said Theo, "there's nobody of that name on this avenue, and I know them all. But the people next door has just moved in, Masterson is their name, Thomas, and his sister Sadie. Would that be who you are after?"

"His sister?" said Nora, surprised.

"Yes," said Theo, "they're the image of each other, I think they must be twins. Would those be who you're lookin for?"

"No," said Nora, "that's not them." But her mind was racing. His sister, she thought, Thomas had no sister as far as she knew, but life is strange, maybe she just showed up, and he was embarrassed about her, but then why would he have her knickers? Maybe, she thought, she had come out of an institution, and he had to buy her clothes, and he could certainly get clothes in Shaws. But then she thought, 'what a story,' Thomas had given his nosy neighbour. Clever it was, to say the woman you're having a bit on the side with is your sister and not just a whore.

"No," she repeated, again to Blackmore, "they are not the people. The ones I'm looking for are a married couple. Thank you, anyway, Mr Blackmore."

By then she had decided that there was just a small percentage of doubt, with the sister thing being thrown into the situation, and besides, she did not want any confrontation in front of snoopy Theo Blackmore. So, she turned on her heel and headed for the number eighteen bus, thinking, that following some 'Miss Marple' analysis of the case, she might be in a better position to decide the next move for Thursday evening the 10th.

*

The Short Drama meeting began as planned at 7.00 PM with only about 15 people attending including the committee members. They went through the agenda items again. Mikey O'Rourke said that he had sorted out the requirements for sound and lighting but would select specific necessities once he was able to see how the scenes were to be played out. When it came to the wardrobe and costume, Eve read out a note from David Williams saying he was away for a few days hiking and would give a full report on Friday 11th. After this, there was very little progress on other things, so it was all over by 7.30 PM.

Exiting the door together and intending to keep each other company on the way home the three ladies from Marine Drive, Joan Lawlor, Vera O'Brien, and Eileen Hannigan almost bumped into Mary Murphy, Peg O'Connell and Eve Roberts who seemed to be discussing something about catering and refreshments. Joan stopped and addressing them all said.

"Would any of you ladies like to drop into my house for a cup of tea before you go home?" They all readily agreed except for Peg O'Connell who said, her husband Richard, was picking her up, and they were going out for a drink. No sooner had she said these words than the man himself appeared beside his wife and spoke.

"Good evening, Ladies of Sandymount Drama, I trust you had a successful meeting?"

Peg smiled and spoke. "Ladies, please meet Richard, my husband, as you can see, he likes a bit of drama himself!" They all laughed, said hello, and Peg and Richard then left the women to make quiet comments about the Garda they had just met.

"I believe he's an inspector!" said Joan. "He has lovely hair!

I'd say he's a bit of gas, keep you on your toes." Said Eileen, "What do you think, Vera?"

Everyone looked at Vera, and she just threw her eyes back and spoke. "He's alright, I suppose, for a Garda!"

As this little backbiting was taking place, Cecilia Lombardi emerged from the hall and as she walked by said. "Goodnight, Ladies."

"Oh, Mrs Lombardi," said Joan, "we're going around to my house for a cup of tea, if you would like to join us?"

"How very kind," said Cecilia, I am a bit early for my appointment and a cup of tea would be lovely. Do you live nearby?"

"Five minutes," came the reply, and the five women began to walk. As they came to Miss Milligan's Hardware store, Mikey O'Rourke was standing there pretending to read the notices in the window. In fact, he was hoping Eve would branch off to Claremont Road, and he could accompany her home.

"Goodnight, Ladies," he said as they passed.

"Goodnight Mr O'Rourke," they replied, with Eve turning her head slightly to see his strong smile, a smile she thought was for her alone. When they had crossed the road and were passing the paper shop, Joan said.

"I suppose I should have asked Mr O'Rourke if he wanted a cup of tea. But he might have been a bit intimidated by a bunch of women."

"From the look of him," said Cecilia, "I don't think there is much that could intimidate him. But he might be more comfortable in the company of just one woman." She looked at Joan, and they both looked at Eve, who seemed to be off somewhere else in her thoughts.

With the ladies seated in her parlour Joan introduced her husband the butcher, whom all except Eve and Cecilia knew. Joseph looked at the flock and spoke. "You'll have to excuse me, ladies, but I need to discuss some Sandymount commerce with Mr O'Reilly. It was nice to meet you all, and goodnight."

When he was gone, Joan laughed and said he was off to the pub. She then introduced her eldest Peter, who was next door doing his homework and due for bed by nine.

At that point, Cecilia asked Joan if she might use the phone to arrange to get picked up from there later on. Joan showed her to the phone in the hall and returned to the parlour where Cecilia was heard by all to refer to the person she called as 'Dear,' and to pick her up at Joan's address. When she returned, Joan then excused herself, saying she would just check on the two youngest and then make the tea. Mary stood up immediately and spoke. "Please allow me to help you as I am, after all, the refreshment's manageress!" They all laugh as Joan and Mary headed out of the room.

"So," said Eileen to Eve, "have you got a family?

"No," Eve replied but then said. "Well, I have a sister with a husband and daughter living in London; otherwise, I'm on my own."

"Oh," said Vera, "do you not get lonely?"

"Sometimes," Eve replied, "but I have my work in an accountant's office and I visit my London relatives frequently and they visit me. In fact, next weekend my niece is coming over and she and I are very close."

Even then, wanting to shift the conversation away from her private life said to Eileen.

"Mrs Hannigan, I thought I saw you from the bus last Sunday with that Mr Williams, you know of 'Wardrobe and Costume,' walking along North Circular Road. It was you, wasn't it? Or was I seeing things?" Eileen could feel the redness rise from her chest to envelop her face.

"Eh, well, yes, I was over that side of the city on Sunday visiting my mother in hospital, but I was not with Mr Williams."

There was a silence in the room as everyone waited to see what would be said next by anyone.

It was finally broken by Cecilia, who asked.

"Is your mother very ill, Mrs Hannigan?"

"Well, yes," replied Eileen, thinking fast to save the situation, "my mother has a psychiatric illness, and it can be embarrassing for many to deal with."

"It certainly can," said Cecilia, "as most people don't realise that many of us get psychiatric diseases as well as physical diseases, but we tend to hide the psychiatric problems as many think they are a slur on the individual patient and also their family. But hopefully, that will change in the future."

Vera and Cecilia herself were content that it was the fact of her mother's mental illness had caused Eileen to flush with embarrassment. Vera, of course, suggested to Eileen that a prayer to St Dymphna would be of great assistance to her mother. Eve, on the other hand, said nothing but wondered why Eileen had lied.

The tea arrived with some biscuits and Vera reminded them all that the biscuits as such were not strictly allowed as Lent had begun only the day before. Joan apologised to all with a smile, regretting the fact that her forgetfulness had been a temptation to them all. Everyone laughed, but no-one took a biscuit.

The banter and talk about the Drama Society was in free flow until Cecilia decided to explain something of herself to the people who had kindly avoided asking her any direct questions regarding her personal life.

"I would dearly love to have a family," she said, "but unfortunately, my extremely handsome Italian husband psychologically abused me." Everyone looked at her in amazement, with Mary in particular wondering what exactly she meant. Cecilia then went on to give examples of her abuse to which those present, except for Mary, felt happier with their own circumstance.

"So now having separated from Antonio," she continued, "I find myself in a Limbo where I am stuck probably never to marry again due to my religion and the state laws and therefore never to have a child which is something I would dearly love. But, believe me, I am happier than I was in a bad marriage." Vera suggested that here was undoubtedly a hopeless case and the only person capable of solving it was St Jude. A brief awkward silence that followed this was quickly broken by Joan, who said.

"Did anyone see Kenneth Moore in that picture about the Titanic?"

"Yes," said Cecilia, 'A Night to Remember' it was called. I think I saw it in the Savoy last year."

"It was on in the Shack last week." Said Eve.

"Yes, Joseph and I saw it in the Shack on Saturday. I love Kenneth Moore, he's such a gentleman. They all nodded in agreement.

"I'd like to see the picture showing there at the moment, 'Some like it Hot' with Jack Lemmon, Tony Curtis, and Marilyn Monroe." Said Eve, continuing the theme.

"Oh yes," said Mary, "I just love Marilyn...Eh.... And Tony Curtis, of course. But it's about a year since I was at the pictures. I used to love to go!"

"I'll tell you what said, Eve. I have two complimentary passes I won in the Christmas raffle, why don't I give them to you, and you can go with your husband?"

"Oh, how kind," said Mary, more quietly, having lost her previous enthusiasm. "But my husband......" Joan and Eileen looked briefly at each other, both being aware of the Mary's domestic problems. So, Eileen quickly came to the rescue.

"Look Eve, you said you'd love to see the picture and Mary would also like to see it and there are two tickets available. Why not go together this Saturday?"

"No, they can't," said Vera, "on Saturday they have to attend the novena that I know they are both doing."

"Oh, for God's sake, Vera! Sure, can't they go to the Saturday morning session?"

"Well," Vera replied, "I thought those morning sessions were only if you couldn't go to the proper one in the evening?"

"No Vera. You can have a choice of going to one or the other. Or in your case, probably the two!"

"Oh. Well, I'm sorry I spoke. Go wherever or whenever you like, it's none of my business, obviously."

"Yes, the two of you go together. Now that's settled and that's the end of it," pushed Joan.

Eve and Mary smiled at each other, and Eve asked. "Can you get a babysitter for Saturday night, Mary?"

"I most certainly can." She replied, and not for the first time noticing that Eve had a most attractive smile.

Cecilia then stood up and looked out through the window curtains. "Oh, I see my lift has arrived. Thank you so much, Mrs Lawlor and all you ladies, for the tea and chat. I'll look forward to seeing you all, if you can make it, tomorrow week at 7.00. PM. Joan helped Cecelia on with her coat and saw her to the door, wishing her goodnight, and then returned to the parlour.

"Well," said Eileen, looking up at Joan as she entered, "what has you with the big grin?"

"You'd never guess who the 'Dear' was who picked Mrs Lombardi up!" She continued to grin like a Cheshire cat.

"Oh, come on then Joan, who was it?" asked Vera, who was bursting with curiosity.

"It was," said Joan, taking her time to wring the most out of her information, "none other than Dr James McNulty. Dear Robin, himself."

Eileen, Mary, and Vera literally gasped in surprise with giddy delight.

"Dr Robin," said Vera, "now isn't that something."

*

9.20 PM following the knock on the door Patrick admitted Fr McKenna to the salon.

"Good evening, Patrick, it is nice of you to take the time to do this for me. I must admit, though, I have never been in a Ladies' hairdressing salon before."

"Don't worry," said Patrick in an animated way, "only men here tonight!"

The priest smiled.

"Well, I certainly wouldn't be comfortable if women were here while you did my hair. But having said that, I wonder why that should be?"

"Well, take a seat there in front of the mirror and tell me what exactly you'd like me to do? Surely, you wouldn't want that natural curl of yours to be completely lobbed for a short back and sides?"

"Look, I'll put myself in your hands. Please decide what you think is best for me?"

"Oh, my God! Oh, my sweet Lord! What an offer!" Replied Patrick, his mind visiting the lowest depths of depravity and sensual fantasy. "However," he continued as he brushed his hand quickly through the priest's hair. "How about we start with a shampoo and trim, followed by a styled set?"

"That sounds wonderful, and I notice you have a really gentle touch."

The exchange of compliments continued through the whole operation but halfway through when Patrick began to message the cleric's scalp both men fell into silence as they each succumbed to almost enraptured pleasure.

Patrick tried to keep doing different things with the combs and brushes and managed to extend the job that should have taken no more than fifteen minutes to forty minutes.

"Now," said Patrick, "even if I say so myself, you are fit to meet the pope himself."

"Thank you, Patrick. I must say that that is the best haircut I have ever had in my life. Now, how much do I owe you, please?"

"You want to pay me! Please! It was my pleasure. But I would really like to do it again when your hair grows. Would that be alright?"

"Certainly, you have ruined me, I can never go to any other hairdresser again. But I would really not like to wait until my next haircut before we get together again. Would you like to meet up soon, you know, just the two of us?"

"Father McKenna, maybe I should not say this to you. But is the Pope a catholic?"

"I'll take that as a yes. And just one other thing, please call me Joe, when we are alone together."

"I will, Joe, and you, please call me, anytime!"

They wished each other goodnight and the priest set off for home while Patrick in a state of delight cleaned up for the night.

*

As he almost usually did at around 10.00 PM Johnny Rags O'Keeffe shunted along Tritonville Crescent, from the Sandymount Road end, and then turned left into the lane that led to the tennis courts. There was a large, locked metal ESB box measuring approximately four-foot square, containing, Johnny supposed, electrical paraphernalia. He was used to seeing the box as it had existed there for years but tonight, beside it, someone had dumped several flattened out cardboard boxes on top of each other. Johnny continued on a few more yards wondering about the square box and the cardboard when suddenly, Elvis burst into one line of a song, *well, you're so square and baby I don't care.* Then Johnny arrived at his back door.

The strong locked wooden door was set into a high, 'broken glass and barbed wire' topped wall that made entry difficult without a key. Johnny, however, had the key to fit the lock on a string around his neck. He entered the back garden and opened, with the same key, the red bricked shed which contained a bunk bed for two because sometimes, he liked the top and other times the bottom. He then replaced the stringed key around his neck and as usual, Elvis started, *Won't ya wear my ring around your neck and tell the world I'm yours by heck......*

In his parent's will, Johnny's siblings were left quite comfortable, but the house had been left to Johnny. He was happy with his sisters living there but would take no money from them and preferred to live in the shed and mostly never see or talk to them. When they realised, they couldn't change his insane wishes, they, gradually, made the shed into a comfortable, warm, dry, and safe refuge. In addition, there was an outside toilet and wash basin, the former, Johnny used when residing in the shed, the latter he used less often. The shed and facilities were cleaned and serviced daily. Sometimes, in the summer months, Johnny would sleep out, but he was sane enough to make sure he used the shed in winter. However, it was only for night-time, never during the day. His rule was that once he heard the angelus bell in the morning, he would be away shortly afterwards.

As Johnny made his way to the comfort of the top bunk, he fell asleep to the sound of the king singing, *"Well, please don't ask me what's on my mind, I'm a little mixed up but I'm feeling fine: I'm all shook up!"*

Johnny knew of course he was mad, but he was also intelligent having received a first in his 'Masters' from Oxford where he studied law and specialised in medical legalities. He knew that the voice that spoke to him, which he could clearly hear but not see, indicated that he was suffering from the psychiatric disorder of schizophrenia. So real in fact was the voice he almost always felt obliged to answer it, if required, in speech or else carry out the action recommended by the voice. Of course, no one except Johnny himself knew that the voice belonged to none other than Elvis.

Elvis first spoke to Johnny on his first confinement in the John of God hospital in 1956. With both his parents dying within days of each other and his girlfriend breaking off their engagement a week after the combined funeral, Johnny escalated his already heavy drinking to serious alcoholic levels. His sisters had managed somehow to get him into a help programme with the good brothers of John of God in Stillorgan County Dublin, and it was while he was drying out there, he first heard Elvis's sing 'Heartbreak Hotel.'

Well since my baby left me

I found a new place to dwell

It's down at the end of Lonely Street

It's called Heartbreak hotel

When the song finished, he clearly heard Elvis speak these words to him.

"Hay Johnny! Welcome to Heartbreak hotel"

Indeed, Elvis had explained to Johnny that he had to be aware of certain things called mysteries. One of these mysteries came from God, and it arose as follows: There were two groups of young people walking, now and then, up, or down Tritonville road in their holy war uniforms. The first being the Smiley's boys from the Church of Ireland orphanage, all in their grey battle uniforms and black hobnail boots. The second army was the Masonic boarding schoolgirls from Merrion Road, whom Johnny used to see pass his door on their way to and from the protestant church on Tritonville road. Their battle uniform was navy coats, navy stockings, black shoes, and navy bonnets.

The mystery Elvis told him was all about, who were they going to do battle with? The answer was, the Catholics, obviously because the two groups were Protestant. Yet, the Catholics and Protestants were all run from heaven by the same God. So, whose side would God be on? Now that was the mystery. But if you tried to solve it, you'd be looking for big trouble and Elvis would sing.

If you're looking for trouble

You came to the right place

If you're looking for trouble

Just look right in my face

I was born standing up

And talking back

My daddy was a green-eyed mountain Jack

Because I'm evil, my middle name is misery

I'm evil, so don't you mess around with me

Johnny slept and had no cares but the dream of a fine large bottle of Powers whiskey put a smile on his face.

*

As they finished dinner around 11.00 PM in the main restaurant of the Shelbourne Hotel on St Stephen's Green, Robin's hand crept across the table to land on hers.

"You look like an angel from heaven, my dear, what a pretty dress."

"Thank you, kind sir, and may I say you look...no, you are the handsomest man in the hotel."

"Ahem! Ahem!" came a voice at their table, interrupting their romantic moment. It was the hotel manager Paul Crothers, a big buddy of them both and a fellow member of Elm Park golf club.

"Good evening, Cecilia," he said, "looking lovely as usual."

"Thank you, Paul," she replied, at the same time rising from her chair and saying. "I'll just powder my nose. By the way, the chicken was lovely, Paul." And off she went.

"We'll just have the bill tonight, Paul, thank you," said Robin.

"So, you will not be requiring a key then tonight?"

"No, thank you, Paul, it is straight home tonight for both of us, but you are indeed a true friend and we both appreciate your discretion. But by the way, do you take on any trainees here for hotel management?"

"Well, yes, but we have a special process in recruiting them, and we also expect them to be quite bright. So, what I'm trying to say is, you are my friend and friendship is a great thing, but this is a business, and business is business!"

"Point taken Paul, and yes, it was a lovely meal. I'm already looking forward to next time."

CHAPTER 9

Friday 4th March

10.00 AM. With her husband gone to work and the kids to school Eileen Hannigan dragged the vacuum cleaner up from the closet under the stairs to the upstairs landing and plugged it in. She then went into her bedroom and lay on the bed, feeling a bit nauseous. Too much exertion, she thought, dragging that heavy contraption up the stairs. In future, she would get James to bring it up before he went to work. Her thoughts then drifted to her lover, and she immediately began to get an excited feeling in her breast.

She had noticed her lover, David Williams, on numerous occasions before they had ever spoken. David was a very noticeable man. He stood out from the crowd. He was, as her old school-friend Helen used to say a 'H and H' meaning a Head turner and a Hunk. And, indeed, if this was not enough, he had an easy listened to voice which exuded with a speech that simply not only charmed but seduced. There was no doubt, Eileen thought, she had been seduced. But not only that, she was sure she herself was also a seducer in the affair.

In the beginning, it was just a casual slight flirtation as she had noticed him looking at her when he thought she hadn't noticed. Just the same quick glances she gave to him. Then one day he didn't try to hide his look and turned it into an admiring smile. Instead of brushing it off, she found herself smiling back in such a way that indicated she liked it and liked him doing it. These smiles of mutual admiration continued for several weeks until one Sunday afternoon, as she waited alone for the bus to take her to visit her mother, his car pulled up, and he rolled the window down.

"Mrs Hannigan, may I offer you a lift into town?" He asked.

Eileen quickly looked around to see nobody paying any attention to what was occurring at the bus stop.

"Thank you for your kind offer, Mr Williams. But I'm fine with the bus and would not like to put you to the trouble."

"My dear Mrs Hannigan, not only would it be of any trouble, but it would be a great pleasure and indeed a privilege to be of assistance to you! In fact, as a gentleman, I insist you allow me to exercise good manners towards a lady in need of a carriage to town."

Eileen laughed at the elegant prose but was, nonetheless, hooked.

"Well then Sir, so that your good manners and kind thought are not compromised, I will be delighted for you to convey me to O'Connell Street in your fine carriage."

Within seconds, he had exited his side, ran around, and opened the passenger door. Then with a bow said.

"My dear lady, your carriage awaits." She stepped in, closed the door, and within minutes they were underway. Then, to break the ice, he said.

"So, Mrs Hannigan, do you like living in Sandymount?"

"Oh, I just love it. Nice people and close to everything. And do you like it?"

"Yes, I love its history and its connection with Yates and Joyce."

"Yes," she replied, "Yates was born on Sandymount Avenue, and he also had a connection with Sandymount castle."

"Right," he said, laughing, "I see you know your history."

"Well, I should, I used to be, or I suppose still am, a history teacher."

"Oh, I didn't know that." He replied, at the same time noticing they were passing the Star of the sea church. "And did you know that before writing Ulysses, James Joyce wrote to his aunt to ask her about the trees in the church grounds when viewed from the strand?"

"No Mr Williams," I didn't know that" she replied as they went by, on their left, the beautifully spired Presbyterian Church, fronted in its grounds, by a weeping willow.

"And over there on Newbridge Avenue," he said, from the same book commenced a funeral."

"Yes," that I did know that Mr Williams. It was Paddy Dignam's funeral, wasn't it?"

"Well, yes, Mrs Hannigan. I see you do know Joyce's novel," he said, "and isn't that a bonus," he laughed.

By then they had reached Irishtown.

"So," he said, "do you know how this Irishtown got its name?"

"No," she replied, now really enjoying the game.

"It was a little like how the 'Pale' was introduced, only I think it was a little earlier than that. Anyway, it was decided by some important lord or other that those of Irish birth, or uncouthness with speaking Gaelic, should be moved out of Dublin city centre to a place further out. So, lots of those evicted settled here, and the place then became known as Irishtown."

At which point, they had almost reached Ringsend, and he spoke.

"So, what famous person landed here, Mrs Hannigan?"

"Oh," she said laughing, one Mr Oliver Cromwell. And can you tell me the year he landed here?" David knew the answer, but he wanted her to win this one.

"1549." He answered.

"Well, you are nearly right," she laughed, "only a hundred years out."

"Oh," he said, "okay 1459 then."

"No, now you are being silly," she said laughing heartily, the other way silly ass, 1649!"

"Oh, I am sorry Teacher," he grinned, "I'm afraid you will have to smack me for that."

"I only smack naughty boys." She said teasingly.

"Oh," he said, "you can believe me when I say I am a very naughty boy."

"Well, I must say, Mr Williams, that really surprises me."

He then changed the subject and asked her if she was happy to be dropped at O'Connell Street or wanted to go elsewhere. She in turn had no wish to tell him about her mother's condition and insisted that O'Connell Street was perfect for her. She had later found out however that he knew exactly where she was going and indeed should have suspected it when on that same Sunday, as she was waiting for a bus to bring her into town, his car pulled up again. He had pushed open the passenger door, smiled and spoke.

"Well, Mrs Hannigan, what a lovely surprise! Fancy meeting you again today."

She was surprised certainly but also delighted and excited at seeing him again as while she was visiting her mother, he had been pervading her mind with her remembering his teeth when he smiled that lovely smile and the flicks of blond hair sliding now and then across his eyebrows and his hands that suggested a gentle and soothing touch.

"There is about half an hour of daylight left," he had said, "would you like a quick ten-minute jaunt to the park to see the deer?"

"That would be lovely," she replied.

Once in the park they parked in an isolated place with a view of the deer approximately 200 yards away. Neither of them had spoken for a while until he turned slowly, looked at her and spoke.

"You know I would be happy to drop you over here and back every Sunday if you wish?"

"Oh," she said, "not at all, Mr Williams. I would not want you to put yourself to such trouble."

"Look," he said, "firstly, please call me David and secondly, it would be my great pleasure as you are a most attractive lady and I really enjoy your company."

With this statement, he gently placed his hand on top of hers.

She quickly pulled her hand away and spoke. "Sorry, Mr Williams. No, eh yes, I am sorry if you got the wrong impression. In fact, I would be obliged if you would drop me off in town, and please do not come to the stop in Sandymount next week."

"Terribly sorry, Mrs Hannigan, I will keep to your wishes, but you cannot stop me thinking wonderful thoughts about you."

With that and in almost complete silence he drove to O'Connell Street where she caught her number 3 bus back home.

The following Sunday much to her disappointment he kept his promise, and she got her bus and visited her mother still unable to eject him from her thoughts. Following her visit, however, as she walked along North Circular Road toward her bus stop, he pulled up beside her and rolled the passenger window down.

"Please at least allow me to drop you into town?" He asked.

She opened the door, and slid in saying, "Please let us have a look at the deer first!" Having said this, she knew there and then, her life would change. Nonetheless, she wanted it to change.

Things moved slowly at first over the next few weeks but then their intimacy progressed to serious and passionate kissing and some fondling until the Sunday he announced that he'd taken a lease on a private flat on North Circular Road itself. He told her it was to be their secret place, and they could meet there in private. So, from then on, the affair developed into a weekly Sunday afternoon of passionate sex satisfying a need for them both. On numerous occasions, he had endeavoured to cajole her into meeting him there at other times but due to fear of being caught out in their unfaithfulness as well as guilt, she went from only Sunday to Sunday in a dream.

She had managed to control her guilt by simply confessing her sin every Saturday in confession, and then on the next day receiving holy communication, saying to God and herself that this week she would not, under any circumstances, get into the car when he pulled up. In addition, she had over the months of the love affair gone to each priest in four of the different parishes to confess her sin. This meant, she believed, there was no return to one to whom she had previously confessed and therefore none to question her 'firm purpose of amendment' which she believed she had each time she confessed. But, once Sunday afternoon came, the 'purpose of amendment' lost all its firmness with David's smile.

Now however, two separate things had arisen that would force her to act and cease her encounter of passionate fulfilment, satisfaction, excitement, and yes lustful adorable sex. On the one hand, there was the hope of grace for the strength to do the right thing from a participation in the novena and on the other hand, there was having been seen with David by that bloody Drama busy body Eve Roberts.

*

Around 10.00 AM with baby Nuala in her 'highchair,' eating a large slice of bread and butter covered with sugar, Vera O'Brien knelt down to say her morning prayers in front of the small table altar she had arranged under the kitchen window. The altar consisted of three statues, the Sacred Heart in the centre, flanked by the 'Blessed Virgin' and 'St Joseph.' On each side of this trinity was a small candlestick complete with candle. There were also two small vases, but today they were empty. As she was about to begin with 'The Morning Offering' it struck her that as today was the first day of the novena, it might be more holy to light the candles. However, upon retrieving the matches from the kitchen drawer, she spotted Raymond's spare car keys, which also had attached the key to the lock on his toolbox in the garage. Her mind began to race.

Within minutes, she had found three boxes of 'Durex' condoms, relocked the toolbox and was back in the kitchen seated beside Nuala who was covered in butter and sugar and gurgling gibberish. Vera was shocked, but it was really what she expected, as from the first-time Raymond had used them, she knew right well the difference she felt. The reality of having confronted it, however, was what had her flabbergasted. For, once there was a slight doubt, even though she knew the sin and confessed it, the whole thing was tolerable. But now she knew beyond doubt she had around 30 mortal sins sitting in the garage waiting to happen. What in God's name would Fr McKenna make of this development? She thought.

*

Fifteen minutes before evening surgery, the bell rang on the door of Dr James McNulty's Tritonville Road rooms. Mrs Byrne opened the door to the early patient, a priest. He bade her 'Good evening' and identified himself as Fr Horgan. He also stated that he knew he was early but needed to be back at the Star of the sea church by 7.45. Mrs Byrne didn't bother showing him into the waiting room, but instead ushered him directly into the doctor's office and asked him to take a seat. Two minutes later Robin entered, introduced himself, took the other chair in front of the desk at the same time turning it around and faced his patient. The priest then told Robin he was visiting from Gardiner Street to give the 'Novena og Grace' at the Star of the sea.

"Oh, yes," Robin replied, "that is something you will be doing for our parish, but now, what is it I can do for you Father? He inquired.

"Well," came the reply, I have been getting these splitting headaches for the past few weeks, and they appear to be getting worse instead of going away as such pains usually do."

Robin then asked him a series of questions that ruled out some conditions but left others doubtful. He then gave the priest a quick physical for coordination, breathing, blood pressure, hearing and sight and then sat back to say.

"In general, you are in good physical health, and I do think your headaches are probably due to tension, however, to be on the safe side I will arrange for you to have an x-ray next Wednesday the 9th at Baggot Street hospital, and I'll have the results the following Monday the 13th, I will convey these to you by phone as I expect you will have returned to Gardiner Street by then. Meanwhile, I'll give you some tablets to tide you over until tomorrow, when you may get the prescription filled that I am about to give you."

Robin then put two tablets into the priest's hand and handed him a bottle of 6 more samples tablets. Then from the sink got the patient a glass of water to wash down the two. With the medication taken and the samples in his pocket, the priest relaxed. While Robin sought, and found his prescription sheets and began to write, Fr Horgan saw on the desk a small bust with the name 'Aristotle' inscribed along the bottom. "I see you have an interest in philosophy doctor, you obviously like the works of Aristotle, are there others you also admire?"

"Well yes actually, two that would be extremely close to your cloth. One from the 13th century and one very recent! I am referring to Thomas Aquinas and Pierre Teilhard de Chardin!"

"Oh, my goodness, doctor! Have you actually read de Chardin's 'Phenomenon of Man'?"

"I have, Father, but I should say I have had to read it a few times before I began to see where he was going with it."

"Well, as I'm sure you are aware," said the priest, "it was not actually published in English until last year and while he completed it in the 1930s it was not published in his own French tongue until after his death, 'God rest his soul' in 1955. This was because, he thought our church might not have been comfortable with his views."

"Well, yes," replied Robin, "whatever his philosophy one could not dispute his wisdom." The priest smiled, appreciating the fact that he himself was in the company of a wise, and intelligent man.

"So, tell me, doctor, what particular philosophical notions do you admire in each of these men?"

"Put simply, it is their notions of consciousness. For example,

Aquinas believed that animals had a soul or let us say a consciousness. Teilhard de Chardin believed that some element of consciousness exists even in basic atoms. So, not alone is it in man and all other animals but also, in all matter, even trees, grass and rocks. If such is the case, then, in my opinion, much of our interaction with nature needs to be reassessed."

"How fascinating a discussion doctor, which has emanated from my simple headache," replied to the priest, looking at his watch, "unfortunately, I have a 'Novena' to give, but I really would love to discuss this further at a future date. Perhaps I could bring a bottle of nice Bordeaux some evening to your house, and we might continue this conversation?"

"Indeed, that would be delightful Father and I have an old bottle of Jamison that might also help the spirit of the conversation."

*

About four doors up from where Paddy Dignam's funeral commenced in James Joyce's epic, Sarah Brannigan put her, four-year old, only child Jimmy to bed at 8.00 PM. She then knelt on the floor beside the dying coal embers in the fire grate. The small glow from the embers plus a single lighted candle was the only light available for her to read the novena prayer. With the prayer completed, she put on a second cardigan and took a blanket from her bed to wrap herself in before she commenced 'The Rosary.' She would have loved to attend the novena in person at the church, but there was no one to mind Jimmy and besides, she was not allowed to leave the flat or there would be hell to pay. There would be hell to pay anyway, she thought, once her drink-soaked husband eventually came home.

When Sarah had heard the 'Parish priest' announce the novena, it gave her some hope for a solution to her own, and more important little Jimmy's life terror. Maybe, she thought, St Francis might have more luck with God than she herself had had in the last year. She'd prayed and prayed for her constant fear and punishment to be over, but it seemed as far as God was concerned, she was at the back of the queue. However, while she could not attend the novena, she believed that if she said the prayers and the Rosary each night and received Holy Communion as prescribed, she just might find peace for herself and her son.

She had almost got used to the beatings inflicted on her by the man she thought she once loved. But she would never get used to him hitting and squeezing little Jimmy's arm until he cried, just to punish her further. As if all this was not enough, her husband now restricted light and heat in the flat to only shine while he was home. Once he left the house, no more coal could be put on the fire, and she was lucky, he told her, to be allowed the one candle.

Sarah commenced the rosary, out loud, thinking if she did it the same as in the church maybe Jesus and his holy mother would look down on her little son, even if she herself was not worthy.

"Thou O Lord shalt open my lips

And my tongue shall announce they praise

Incline unto my aid O God

O Lord, make haste to help."

She continued the ritual to its end and then sat and awaited, the inevitable abuse from her returning drunk husband.

*

With the church, almost full on the first might of the 'Novena' at 8.00 PM, everyone stood as Fr Horgan walked out onto the altar genuflected in front of the tabernacle containing the Blessed Sacrament, whispered a silent prayer and then made his way to the pulpit.

Once there he began.

"In the name of the Father and of the Son and of the Holy Ghost, Amen. Please kneel, and we will recite the 'Novena' prayer." With all on their knees and most with a pamphlet, containing the printed prayer, the priest led the congregation.

O most kind and loving saint, in union with you, I adore the Divine Majesty. The remembrance of the favours with which God blessed you during life, and of your glory after death, fills me with joy; and I unite with you in offering to God my humble tribute of thanksgiving and praise.

I implore of you to secure for me, through your powerful intercession, the all-important blessing of living and dying in a state of grace. I also beseech you to obtain the favour I ask in this Novena, (At this point Fr Horgan told the congregation to take a minute in silence to request the favour they required, adding for all to remember 'The Lord works in Mysterious Ways') *but if what I ask is not for the glory of God or for the good of my soul, obtain for me what is most conducive to both. Amen.*

"Let us now begin the rosary," the priest intoned, but allowed a few seconds for rosary beads to be extracted from purses or pockets, and then he began.

"In the name of the Father and of the Son and of the Holy Ghost, Amen.

There followed then the familiar opening words of, "Thou O Lord shalt open my lips." The congregation answered the next line. Then with opening prayers completed, the priest announced the beginning of the 'Sorrowful Mysteries,' starting with, "The Agony in the garden.'

This Rosary, a medley of repeating shorter prayers to the 'Blessed Virgin' consisted of five decades, of 'Hail Marys' under each mystery and each decade bracketed by an 'Our Father' and a 'Glory be to the father' and when this repeating mantra was completed it ended with final summarising prayers.

When everyone was once again seated, the priest began by introducing himself, and then stating that the 'Novena of Grace' was about invoking, for all taking part, the help of Saint Francis Xavier to intercede on their behalf to have God's grace bestowed on them.

"Grace," he said, "is God's gift in direct help or the means to his assistance for our wants, provided they are good for our souls and not detrimental to others. St Francis," he continued, "was one of the founders of the 'Society of Jesus,' known as 'Jesuits'.""

The Jesuits, he told, had several houses in Dublin alone, himself being a member of the Gardiner Street house. He then went on to relate the story of the life of St Francis, together with the sacrifices and contribution this saint had made for the Glory of God.

With the lesson sermon ended, the priest retired to the sacristy for some minutes before emerging in the required vestments for 'Benediction.' He was led out onto the altar by an altar boy carrying a 'Thurible' containing the burning charcoal with incense. Then, once the sacred host had been placed in the monstrance on the altar, he and the whole congregation knelt in reverence to the exposition of the Eucharist and sang.

O salutaris Hostia

Quae coeli pandis ostium

Bella premunt hostilia

The Novena

Da robut, fer auxilium

Throughout, the altar boy swung the 'Thurible' to keep the charcoal alight. The ceremony followed the prescribed ritual as the priest incensed the monstrance with all singing the *Tantum Ergo*. The central element of the benediction itself was when the priest lifted the monstrance for adoration of and blessing with the Eucharist.

The ceremony finished with hymn 'Sweetheart of Jesus.'

There was no one the whole church, who sang the hymn with more enthusiasm and dedication than Vera O'Brien.

Sweetheart of Jesus, fount of love and mercy

Today we come, thy blessing, to implore.

O touch our hearts, so cold and so ungrateful

And make them, Lord, thine own for evermore

Sweetheart of Jesus, we implore

O make us love thee more and more.

*

9.00 PM Patrick Foley, having attended the first session of the Novena, caught the number 2 bus for town outside the church. He was still thinking about his acting role and how nice it had been to do Fr McKenna hair and his promise to meet up next week.

Once seated upstairs he lit up an 'Alpine minted filter' and thought about the night ahead. He was looking forward to the late night even though he had a pretty full day at work tomorrow as the senior stylist in 'Sandymount Waves' hair salon on Sandymount Road. In the salon, he was the manager even though the owner, Mrs Ridgeway, worked there on a part-time basis, he was, he thought, the King of the establishment even though he knew many would have thought of him more as its Queen. He really didn't mind this because in this hairdresser's Patrick never hid his 'gayness.' In fact, he often played to it, much to the appreciation of the clientele. However, outside, in the real, harsh, intolerant, and unforgiving world he tried his best to subdue and camouflage his real nature.

To be sure he had known since a very early age that he was homosexual and that people, behind his back called him Pansy. The reason for this he believed was that he displayed pansy mannerisms. These 'pansyisms' as he liked to call them were really a combination of the giddy mannerisms of young girls together with what might be referred to as the affectations of women in general. He was also aware that not all homosexuals displayed these 'pansyisms,' as he had often met men whom he had perceived to be 'normal' but had, nonetheless, propositioned him for a sexual encounter.

Tonight though, Patrick was on his way to a friendly pub for a drink and then on to a dance, featuring the 'Clipper Carlton' band at Metropole ballroom. He particularly liked the 'Clipper Carlton' because as well as playing the dance music they also put on a bit of a show. In fact, many of the other bands were taking their lead and now referring to themselves as 'Showbands.' Patrick loved the theatre of it all and being part of the whole show when participating in the various dances. Indeed, he would be up on the floor for nearly every set. In this regard, he liked to get his money's worth, as he had invested a fair bit in lessons at Barton's dance Academy in Lincoln place. He had in all attended tuition at least once, and often twice weekly, for the past six months and was now familiar with most of the ballroom dances. With this under his belt, he felt quite confident with most of the dance steps. By far, though, he excelled in the 'Waltz' and the "Quick Step."

Apart from the love of the dances and their often-flamboyant movements it was also his hope that if he held a woman in his arms long enough, he might overcome his homosexuality and change to 'normality.' His real dream, therefore, and his one desire was the hope, that the homosexuality of his nature would go away. He prayed so hard for this to happen, and now he hoped with all his might that the 'novena' would at last give him his heart's desire, provided of course it was for his own good. But how could it not be? He didn't want the 'condition', and neither did the church or the clergy didn't want it, and certainly God did not want it. So, he felt sure he would, at the end of the novena, be fully cured, once and for all.

With all this in mind he got off the bus at College Street and headed up to Bartley Dunne's for one gin and tonic and a few 'Babychams' before he began to trip the light fantastic with the 'Clipper Carlton.'

*

11.00 PM Emily Jones entered her bedroom and removed the box of coins from the her wardrobe and placed it on her bed. She had brought with her two 'Half-crowns' and three "Two-shilling' pieces to add to the box collection. Firstly, however, she got undressed, removed her prosthetic leg, and then put on her pajamas. Before she put the coins into the box, however, she removed, from the bottom drawer of her bedside bureau, a small 'bank weighing scales' together with a small 'ledger.' She weighed the box of coins and then, from that weight, deducted the tare weight of the box. When she saw the result, she knew beyond doubt that another two 'Half-crowns' had been taken by Mary to which she had not been entitled. She consulted her ledger and found out really what she already knew, which was that Mary Murphy had, since she began her stealing from the box, taken a total of five pounds and five shillings. In fact, each time Mary stole from the box Emily knew, simply because a 'Half-crown weighed around half an ounce and a two-shilling piece weighed two fifths of an ounce, so it was easy with the scales to know exactly what had been taken.

Emily was very much aware that she should have nipped this, stealing or even temptation, in the bud earlier, but somehow, she felt a strong bond with Mary. Her arrival to help had been a gift and allowed Emily to look on life a little more optimistically since her dear Helen had died.

The truth be told, Emily felt that Mary could be a kindred spirit, and she had begun to rely very much on her company. Nonetheless, the dishonesty had to be faced and resolved whatever the pain she would obviously cause Mary?

CHAPTER 10

Saturday 5th March

12.35 AM. Patrick Foley walked out through the exit of the ballroom. He was high-spirited having danced the night away and was even asked up for a 'Ladies Choice' for a great rendition of 'The Tennessee Waltz.' Unfortunately, he knew that the night had not changed his longing for male intimacy but perhaps within a fortnight, with the help of God, it might be different. As he moved onto O'Connell Street, he didn't even look at the bus stop for Sandymount as he knew the last bus had gone fifteen minutes earlier. This was not an unusual occurrence for him as, when dancing, the last thing on his mind was a CIE bus. The walk home to Ennis Grove would take only half an hour and while the night was cold enough the rain had held off.

While almost home having turned onto 'Londonbridge Road' he noticed three men, laughing and pushing each other about, right on the corner of his Ennis Grove turn. He suspected he knew them but, nonetheless, he became a little wary as there was no one else on the road. So, having lit up an 'Alpine' he approached. Then, giving them a wide berth, but still close, one of the trio, a thug-looking redhead, in a rough Dublin accent said.

"Ah, here Mister, ya wouldn't have a smoke there would ya?"

Patrick's mind was in overdrive, as these situations were not an unusual occurrence for him. Firstly, he realised he did not know them, so they were not local. Secondly, he thought to run, but he still lived a good bit away and such a move could trigger a chase and bash action. Thirdly, he could give then the whole box of 'Alpine' plus his matches and then walk on, as this might just be enough to satisfy them. He decided on the latter.

"Here take these" he said, to the red-headed protagonist, handing out the cigarettes and matches. The other two, Patrick noticed, had then blocked his forward path.

Redhead took the matches off the cigarette box and lifted up the almost full pack of 'Alpine.'

"What the fuck is these? These is not smokes! These is bleedin pansy pricks!" The two others burst out laughing.

"Oh, Jaysis Lads," said Redhead, looking Patrick up and down, "He

is a fuckin Pansy! He's the bleedin dregs of humanity! Shit dressed up!"
Then suddenly, he gave Patrick a full punch to the face and almost
immediately blood was everywhere, and Patrick was on the ground. He only
felt one kick to the head before he lost consciousness.

*

At a few minutes to 10.00 AM Father McKenna opened the sacristy
door an inch or two and peeped across to his confession box at the top
right-hand side of the church. There were five penitents waiting for him on
the right side and four at the left, but overall, he could expect between 25
and 50 before the 12.00 noon finish. The children and weekly penitents
would take just under two minutes each to absolve, but others with serious
problems and various questions could take up to four or even five minutes
each.

He quietly closed the door just as Fr Skeffington arrived, through
the Leahy terrace entrance, red of face and flustered.

"Cars parked everywhere around the church because of the match,"
said the Canon breathlessly, "I was lucky to the find a place down by the
strand."

"Do you think we'll win? McKenna asked, as he kissed his stole and
placed it around his neck, its ends hanging slightly below the waist of his
cassock.

"As you know, I'm more of a GAA man myself, but it's always nice
when the home team wins.

Both priests made their way to their respective confession boxes.

*

For the previous fifteen minutes Fr McKenna sat and listened to a
string of three or four children relate their 'disobedience,' 'talking in the
church,' and saying 'curse words' sins. He also heard how one woman
whom he knew to be Vera O'Brien had been 'uncharitable' to her
neighbour, as well as numerous other simple venial sins. In addition, she
told the same story as she did every week about an intimate part of her
marriage which she believed to be a sin, and he gave her the same weekly
reply that if it was not her intent to use the condoms, then she had not
sinned. On this occasion, however, she told him there were condoms stored
in her garage. He advised her that this was something for the police and not
a priest to consider, but she might not like to get her husband into trouble,

so better talk to him first before she considered reporting it. Joe Mc Kenna gave her absolution and she left as usual, not fully satisfied.

Then there was also a young man who had, in the last week, committed an evil act to himself no less than 25 times.

Finally, and against all the odds, a penitent with a 'common' Dublin accent, who confessed several more serious sins before he dropped a bombshell. This bombshell was a sin the priest thought he would never hear. But it was quite clear.

"Father, as well as dem sins, I also done murder two times!" and then there was silence. The priest was literally struck dumb until the voice broke the silence. "Did ya hear me? I said I done murder!"

After, Fr Joe McKenna got some control of himself, and he managed. "Are you sure?

"Not a bleedin doubt in the world," came the reply.

"Was this someone you knew?" asked Joe

"What does that matter, I done it! I thought I could get forgiven here?"

Joe was then even more flustered.

"Yes, you can, of course, be forgiven. Eh. Say a decade of the rosary, no, two decades for your penance, and now say a good act of contrition."

Joe McKenna gave his priestly absolution as the contrite act was recited. The penitent got up and left, and the priest moved to pull the curtain slightly to catch a glimpse of the killer. But then stopped himself. It was better not to see, as he could not break the seal of the confession, and so better to let the police work it out.

*

12.00 AM. Mrs Emily Jones heard the noon angelus bell ring as the familiar doorbell rang with her entering 'Sandymount Waves.' The junior girl, who was attending a client, turned to her, and said.

"Please take a seat Mrs Jones, we're running a bit late, but you'll be attended to, shortly."

Emily acknowledged this with a "Thank you" and sat down to read a copy of a 'Woman's Own' magazine she already had at home. Over the last many months, she had never known Patrick to be late but then thought, perhaps he had just gone to the Lavatory. By 12.10 however and still no sign of him, she wondered could he be sick? Yet, at the 'Drama' meeting in the Methodist Hall last Tuesday he was in fine fettle, displaying his theatrical affectations with gay abandon.

Then looking over at Patrick's workstation Emily could see clearly that his combs, brushes, scissors, clippers, and powder puffer were all lined up on the unit under the mirror in front of his coiffuring chair. It was so obvious how he prided himself on being the senior stylist in the salon.

Suddenly, the bell rang again, and Patrick limped in.

"My apologies, Mrs Jones," he said, "I've been in the wars a bit, but I'll be with you in just a minute."

Emily Jones was almost speechless by his appearance and just managed a weak.

"Alright, Patrick, whenever you are ready."

He then turned to the junior who was receiving payment from the client she had just finished and spoke.

"When you've finished there, Imelda, you can go to lunch." Two minutes later, with the client and Imelda gone, Patrick approached Emily Jones.

"Oh, my good Lord!" said Emily. "You, poor boy, are you well enough to be working? Whatever happened to you?"

With this obvious rush of sympathy, Patrick lost it and burst into tears. Emily put her arms around him and finally with the tears under control he told her of his beating and how he eventually got home, and his mother had cleaned him up, and in the morning how she had insisted he go to Irishtown Garda station and report it. He had telephoned the salon owner, and Imelda had taken his appointments up to the 12.00. noon.

He further explained that it was bad enough getting the hammering from the 'Louts' but he got no satisfaction from the Gardaí either. In fact, he got the feeling they believed his 'abnormal' manner had probably triggered the men's action and also that it was foolish for his 'type' to be out walking alone at that hour.

The Novena

*

Once they were seated in the expensive seats at the back of the Shack, Eve and Mary quietly chewed some sweets Mary had brought along. The documentary was a travel talk about somewhere in the Arctic and was boring, but they persevered until five or six smokers suddenly almost surrounded them.

"I don't mind people smoking," whispered Eve, as they moved to another seat, "I just don't want to smoke their smoke."

Mary laughed, thinking had she been alone she would have just put up with the smokers, but this Eve was not just a woman with an attractive smile, she also had a strong will. Once the documentary ended, there was a short interval.

"I love your cardigan," whispered Mary, "that blue really suits you."

"Thanks, but I really need to get my hair done, I don't feel anything looks well on me with my hair this way. What I need is a nice perm. Something like you have, now that looks really nice."

"This!" Said Mary, surprised but delighted, "My Catherine just put in a few rollers a couple of hours before I came out."

"Well, it looks really good." said Eve, thinking at the same time, is this what Lesbians do when they go out? It was pretty much the same as when she used to go out with Bridget. But of course, Mary was not like Bridget was then. Bridget was like Eve then and now, both single. Mary, on the other hand, was married, so there was no possibility of her being a Lesbian, which was a pity because it was enjoyable to be out with her and her hair was nice even if her face had a worried look about it.

The main picture, 'Some Like It Hot' soon started. It was a comedy or farce. It begins in Chicago in 1929 and is about how two musicians Joe (Tony Curtis) and Jerry (Jack Lemmon) who witness the St Valentine's Day massacre, or something similar, and need to get out of town and away from the gangsters fast. The best they can do to achieve this, is to dress up as women and join an all-female band travelling by train to Florida. Joe falls in love with Sugar Kane Kowalczyk (Marilyn Monroe). He must constantly change into men's clothes to woo her, while, at the same time, using information gained as her girlfriend when he's dressed as woman. Simultaneously, Jerry is pursued by a wealthy male millionaire who believes Jerry is a very attractive woman. In addition, both female impersonators are trying to avoid being caught by the gangsters.

Eve and Mary, when not in raptures of laughter along with the rest of the Shack's patrons quietly commented throughout on the fashions and clothes worn by the different characters.

Following the quiet stance at the end of the show for Irish national anthem the two women soon found themselves outside the cinema gates.

"Well now," said Eve, "That was really great, but I always feel a bit low after an enjoyable film if I haven't got anyone to talk to about it. So, as I only live a few doors up, why not come for a quick cup of tea, and we can relive some of the funny bits?"

"Some of the funny bits," replied Mary, "sure we'll be there all night! The whole lot was funny and thank you so much for bringing me. You have no idea how much I needed it. So, I'll let you get home."

"Oh, really, are you sure I can't twist your arm?"

"Oh, alright then, just a quick one."

Instead of tea they both opted for a cup of cocoa, with a generous helping of white sugar.

"I can see," said Mary, "what the men like about Marilyn, she full of…."

"Sex," said Eve, finishing the sentence, "and that Tony Curtis is so good-looking, if you like dark-haired men."

"And do you like dark-haired men?" asked Mary.

Eve looked at the woman across the table for a second and then said.

"Well, to be honest, I'm not really that keen on men at all. I had a horrific experience with them several years ago."

"Well, to be honest with you," said Mary, "I'm not very keen on them either as at the moment I'm having an awful time with my husband! He has us poor from his constant drinking."

The tears rolled slowly down Mary's cheeks, which she brushed away with the heel of her hand, but then she continued, "Oh, my God, Eve, I am so sorry for burdening you with my problem. We had a lovely night, and now I'm ruining it. I better get going."

"Don't you dare," said Eve, who got up from her chair and gave Mary a clean handkerchief from the sleeve of her cardigan.

"You just sit there and let it all out," Eve continued, "I'm flattered that you would confide in me. I'm well aware what it's like not to have someone close to tell your troubles to."

"Well," said Mary, in between her sobs, "You can tell me what your difficulties are? I won't be telling anyone, not with my shame, which I know I have brought on myself."

This invitation and the sight of Mary's upset triggered Eve's emotions, and she herself began to shed a tear.

"Well!" Eve commenced. "When I was fourteen, my two uncles molested me! I told my mother and while they never did it again because they were her brothers, it was all hushed up. And all my mother said was that I should keep away from men, as they were all the same! You know, Mary, I really have been an emotional wreck since then. In fact, I'm convinced the whole thing has turned me into a Lesbian."

"A Lesbian?" said Mary, her surprise putting an immediate stop to her tears.

"Oh Jesus," answered Eve, "Now you know, I am woman queer. It's terrible, please don't tell anyone, I'm so ashamed."

"Oh, Jesus is right!" Said Mary, "and, why would I tell anyone? Sure, I'm a Lesbian myself!"

"What?"

"I have refused to have relations with my husband. I don't want to have relations with a man, I'd like it better with a woman. My refusal has driven Stephen to the drink. He doesn't know why, but it's because I'm a Lesbian, or as you said, a woman queer!"

They both had stopped crying and were suddenly laughing hysterically.

CHAPTER 11

Sunday 6th March

It was announced at all Masses that an additional collection would be held on the following Sunday 13th March to assist with the bringing of the sick and lame on the parish's pilgrimage to Lourdes in May. Parishioners were urged to make sacrifices and give generously to this cause for people far worse off than themselves to seek a miracle in Lourdes, if, of course, it was for their own good and indeed the good of the church.

*

Around 12.45 PM with all the Sunday Masses finished Dermot Shaw, the clerk, had one more job to do before he lodged the collection money in the bank. This job consisted of a general tidy and fix up of the altars as well extinguishing all the ceremonial candles. Once this was completed, he would then firstly go down the Sandymount side and continue all around the church collecting the few coins, from the 'penny candle' offering display units. The whole exercise would take less than ten minutes.

Unfortunately, as he was leaning up to the candle on the right side of the high altar, he experienced an excruciating pain in his chest. The pain was so intense he lost consciousness, fell onto the top step, and rolled down the next two to the altar floor. Luckily for him, there was still one dedicated parishioner remaining in the church, kneeling, and praying at the grotto, displaying the head of the crucified Christ with the Crown of Thorns, in the back corner on the Sandymount side. This meant that she had her back to the altars and did not see the clerk collapse. However, she did hear him cry out in pain and roll down the steps.

An ambulance was summoned, and he was taken to St Vincent's Hospital, where it was touch and go for a few hours until the staff eventually stabilised him. Nonetheless, he was an extremely sick man and would need a lot of care.

*

David Williams sat in O'Reilly's pub having the first Sunday pint, of the two he would have, before he went home for a snack and then drove off for an afternoon of sexual bliss with the wonderful Eileen Hannigan. Over the previous few Sundays, however, he felt she was really beginning to feel the guilt of it all and with this bloody 'Novena,' he thought, the whole parish was getting a dose of the Veronica O'Brien insanity. Following his own well-planned action tomorrow though, he reminded himself, he hoped her mind would change and then, with luck, perhaps within a few months there would be bliss for the two of them.

*

As Inspector Richard O'Connell was just leaving his house and cursing the weather under his breath, he was thinking about his own son John, and worried he was having trouble with his Irish teacher. Being an excellent detective, it hadn't been difficult for him to work out the little whispers between John and his mother Peg, so he now believed it was time for him to become involved. He decided there and then that he would bring it all to a head after their tea tonight. With this thinking of his own young fella, Richard then noticed two slightly younger boys, oblivious to the heavy rain, strolling by his house. They were sauntering along on the strand side of the road towards the tower as if it was a sunny Sunday afternoon. The lads, however, were well rigged out for the day that was in it, both having school caps and scarves and long raincoats coming down beyond their Wellington boots. Richard, who was also in appropriate weather gear plus fishing waders, crossed the road just behind them. In addition to his weather gear, Richard carried a large Garda haversack for his fishing tackle and a bucket to hold whatever his long line baits had lured.

The two boys, Seamus Hannigan and his pal Pat strolled on at an easy pace pushing each other from time to time and laughing. They were on their way to the tower shop to buy, of all things on that winter's day, 'Patsi' ice pops.

At the Guildford Road, small opening, and steps down to the receding strand tide, the boys stopped and looked out at the man, with the haversack and bucket, following the tide out.

"Too feckin cold for Longline fishin today, Seamus, eh?"

"You're feckin right there, Pat, freeze the balls off a brass mackerel." said Seamus, laughing.

"I've never seen a feckin mackerel with balls, have you?"

"Of course, I have. The men mackerel have them. Your Ma probably only gets women Mackerel from McQuaid's."

"You're such a gobshite Seamus, everyone knows that fishes have no mickeys, so how can they have balls? Fishes are 'nuture'."

"What's feckin nuture anyway?" Asked Seamus.

"Never mind feckin nuture," replied Pat, "what's that feckin thing out there in the water?"

"You mean the longline man?" asked Seamus.

"Not the feckin man, ya gobshite, the feckin box thing over there to his right!" The two continued to look at 'the feckin box thing' till it was stranded from the outgoing tide about fifty yards from the wall.

Meanwhile, Richard O'Connell 200 yards from the wall and 100 yards to the left of 'the feckin box thing' had bucketed a small cod, three dabs, a couple of nice sized flats, and a small salmon bass. Happy with his catch and his gear all stacked in his haversack, he made his way back towards home. To his left, he recognised the two lads, he had seen earlier, make their way out from the wall towards a box of some sort.

"Jaysisss! It looks like a feckin suitcase," Seamus said, seeing the object on its side with its base facing them. He went up to it and gave it a kick with his Wellington boot.

"Oh, he said. It's feckin solid enough. I wonder what's in it. I bag anything good."

"Feck off, said Pat, "I seen it first."

"Okay" said Seamus, "pals share, right?"

"Right'" replied Pat, "pals share."

They moved around to the other side and saw the top was open and then bent and peered down and in.

"Holy Jaysis!" said Pat, "it's a dead dog and a woman's shoe.

"It's feckin alive," said Seamus, at the same time pushing Pat at it. He lost his balance and fell on top of it. Seamus roared with laughter and took off, with Pat in hot pursuit behind, in the direction of Richard who by then only about 30 yards away. In fact, the boys were nearly on top of him by the time Pat caught up and playfully grabbed Seamus.

"Calm down boys now, calm down," said Richard, "what's all the excitement about?"

"Ah, it's nothing, Sir," said Pat, "it's just there's a fancy suitcase over there with a big dead dog in it.''

"Yea," said Seamus, "and a woman's high-heeled shoe as well."

"Really?" said Richard, in disbelief, and then for fun said.

"Now you wouldn't lie to me, would you? You know I'm a detective from Irishtown station and no young boys lie to me!"

"We swear to God Sir, don't we Pat?" said Seamus, "there's a dead big dog and a woman's shoe in that box…eh. case over there."

"Very well then, boys, why don't we go and do a bit of detective investigation on it?"

The boys followed meekly behind as Richard led the way.

*

At the usual time, Eileen, once again, could not control her desires and slipped into David's car. He leaned over and kissed her on the cheek, and again she loved just the presence of him beside her.

When he stopped outside the flat, he gave her the key and told her to go on ahead as he had to get something out of the back to bring inside. Eileen did as she was told and then waited by the open door and watched as he took what looked like a toolbox and briefcase from the boot. As he came through, she said.

"What in God's name do you need those for here?"

"Well," he said, "firstly, the toolbox is to fix the shelf under the sink, not necessarily today as I have more important things to do. And secondly, the briefcase contains Thomas Cook traveller's cheques and I really cannot let them out of my sight as they are as good as cash."

Satisfied with this explanation, Eileen asked to be excused for five minutes to 'powder her nose' as she made off for the loo.

He moved quickly into the kitchen and removed the false bottom of the briefcase extracted the items therein and replaced them with a hammer from the toolbox before securing the false bottom again. He then placed the items he had taken from the briefcase at the bottom of the toolbox underneath a rag cloth, with all the other spanners and screwdrivers on top of the lot. He then closed and locked the box and placed it on the perfectly stable shelf under the sink. Leaving the briefcase on the kitchen table, he then went immediately to the bedroom, where Eileen was in the process of removing her dress.

With the major event of the afternoon completed to the participants' satisfaction, they lay on the bed in each other's arms.

"You know what I'd really like now?" Said Eileen smiling.

"I bet I can guess," Replied David, "a cup of tea. Correct?"

"Oh, you are a clever man. You read minds as well as bodies."

He smiled, slipped on his underpants and slacks, and headed for the kitchen.

"Oh shit," she heard him cry, "No bloody milk!"

"Don't worry," she shouted, "a glass of water will be fine." But he was back into the bedroom in seconds and pulling on the rest of his clothes, shoes, and socks.

"No, the lady wants tea," he said, "The lady gets tea. "I'll just slip down to the corner shop and be back in five minutes."

"No, really David. Oh, I feel awful, just a drink of water."

But he ignored her and was soon out the front door.

She really was thirsty, and water would have sufficed, so she thought she'd snatch a quick drink from the kitchen tap before he returned. She tossed down half a glass and was about to return to the bedroom when the briefcase got her attention. Without so much as a thought, she flipped open the top, looked in and was surprised to see it was empty. She closed it then and lifted it off the table. It seemed a bit heavier than expected, so for some reason she shook it a bit and could hear something inside move about. But upon checking again, found it was certainly empty. Again, she opened it wide and put her hand down to feel the bottom and pressing down found the bottom moved, leaving one end slightly raised and not completely flat. Her curiosity was now fully blown, so gently, she lifted the end to reveal the large carpenter's hammer underneath the false bottom. What? No, why? in the name of God, is that hidden in an obvious secret place? She thought, but fearing David's imminent return, quickly flattened the false bottom back in place, closed over the case top, but before she returned to the bed it struck her the toolbox was nowhere in sight. She quickly found it under the sink, sitting on a perfectly robust shelf.

There's something more to this man than meets the eye, thought Eileen, as he arrived in with the tea. And having thought this she suddenly felt, under her skin, that the 'something' was not necessarily very nice! However, her natural acting skills allowed her to carry on with their afternoon until it was time to go.

Before leaving and locking up, however, David collected the briefcase from the kitchen, saying he mustn't forget the Traveller's cheques. Eileen smiled, thinking; this man is a bloody liar. There must, she continued with her thoughts, be something unsavoury about that hidden hammer?

He dropped her back at the usual place in North Frederick Street to catch a bus home. But the latest revelation, of the hidden hammer, concerning her lover was, she thought, a little push by her Guardian Angel to disentangle herself from the affair before they were found out.

*

It was just past 4.00 PM and Raymond O'Brien was listening to a football match on the radio. This being of no interest to Vera she decided to go up to their bedroom and sort out some old clothes to parcel up for the St Vincent De Paul. However, no sooner had she taken three dresses she hadn't worn in months from the wardrobe and placed them on the bed, when the vision of Jesus alone appeared. As usual, a serene calmness enveloped her, and she fell to her knees. This was the first time He had appeared on a Sunday, and she wondered if that had some significance. She asked of course in her mind if He'd got a message, but as usual, all she got was that wonderful smile. She bowed her head and thanked Him for the great gift of seeing him and began a series of prayers she said during each apparition.

At a point in the middle of Vera's devotion, however, she noticed that the bedroom door opened, and Ray walked in. He looked at her on her knees, grunted something like a bad word and went around to the other side of the bed, presumably to get something from his bedside bureau. She paid him no attention, as he was used to seeing her pray at various times in the day, and she knew he could not see the vision of the magnificent Christ. But then her trance-like rapture was interrupted by him saying.

"Excuse me, Vera, love, but 'Wanton-Willie' wants to wander."

Vera's serenity had suddenly entirely changed to anticipated terror as she turned from the still smiling Jesus to see her grinning husband standing upright with his trousers down and shirt up, exposing his fully erect penis. Vera turned back immediately to face Jesus to see his probable disgusted reaction, but He was still smiling. She then thought that perhaps she had not actually seen what she thought she had seen. So, she turned again to see that Ray was actually holding it and flipping his thing from side to side as he half sang over and over, "Wanton-Willie wants to wander!"

The blood ran from Vera's head, and she collapsed in a faint onto the bedroom floor.

Five minutes later she awoke to find herself lying on the bed with her husband gently wiping her forehead with a wet facecloth.

"Jesus Mary and Joseph," he said, "are you alright love? You frightened the life out of me, I was only messin with you. Sure, you know I love you. Holy mother of God, it's not as if you hadn't seen my 'Wanton-Willie' before."

She looked at him remembering what had happened but realised that he didn't know Jesus was actually standing there, so, he really didn't do any wrong. But, she thought, thank God and all the angels and saints, that St Veronica wasn't there to see such a thing as him waving his 'thing' about.

"Let me go and get you a nice cup of tea, would you like that, love?" Ray asked.

"Please, that would be lovely Ray, I'm alright now, just felt a bit faint. I think it's because it's my time of the month."

He took off to get the tea, and she realised that the time had come to consult Canon Skeffington before something serious happened with these visions. Then she thought, maybe even sometime she and Ray might be having marital relations and suddenly Jesus and St Veronica could be in the room there with them and even worse again Ray might be wearing one of those rubber contraceptives. Oh, dear God and his Holy mother, the thought of it made her feel weak again. She decided, though, first thing tomorrow, she would try to see the parish priest.

*

At exactly the appointed time of 8.00 PM, Patrick Foley walked into the lounge of Wynns hotel in Abbey Street. He was dressed in a light blue rain mackintosh and a tartan scarf. The blue in scarf, exactly matching the 'Mack' colour. Joe McKenna, however, was confined to his clerical black suit and white priest collar.

The Novena

"Good evening, Fr McKenna," said Patrick, as he slipped off his coat to reveal an obvious hand tailored almost yellow suit. Underneath, he sported a deep wine shirt and a bright yellow bow tie. His tan kiltie tassel loafers finished of the flamboyant but stylish look.

"Wow, you look fantastic. I wish I could wear something like that!"

"Why thank you, Joe," Patrick whispered. Once you like it, I'm not concerned about all these drab people. Let's get some colour into the world." He finished and sat down.

The conversation went on non-stop, with both relating many aspects and occurrences in their lives to. And, at various times throughout the conversation, looking admiringly into the other's face. Joe completed his own story with the date, some years before, when he entered the seminary.

Then Patrick spoke of the point in time, where he had accepted his homosexuality, but even today still held out hope for a cure. He told Joe how he had grown up disgusted with himself and had sought answers in medical, religious, and philosophical books. In fact, when reading the 'existentialist' Sartre's 'Nausea,' he equated himself with its main character, Roquentin, who is continuously disgusted with his own existence. Patrick explained how he had even consulted Robin, whom he had asked for some sort of medical intervention, thinking that even castration might be better than his existing life of nausea with himself. But Robin had told him that such a solution was against medical ethics and also a sin against God, if he was a believer. Patrick had replied to Robin that such might be against medical ethics, but the church itself practiced it to give glory to God. When Robin had expressed doubts regarding the Catholic Church participating in such practices, Patrick had advised Robin of the 'castrati,' the boys the Vatican had castrated before puberty to sing, with a clearer but similar voice to that of a woman. In fact, Patrick believed there was probably one or two castrati till living, and only last year there was talk of yet another being prepared for the pope's listening enjoyment.

"When I told this to Robin, which is something you probably know anyway, do you know what he said to me?"

"Yes, I did know about the castrati," answered Joe, "but what did Robin say?"

"He asked me if I could sing! I mean, Jesus Christ, what a bitch!"

"And what did you say?" asked Joe, by then unable to control his own laughter.

"I said no! And, in answer to your next question, I'm not bloody thirteen years old either! After which, he and I laughed and laughed at how stupid the whole thing was."

"Robin is a wise man, and has a lot of experience, in fact, more than most." Said Joe.

"I know, he told me it would not be easy but to try and live my life being true to myself as homosexual, rather than trying to be something I am obviously not!"

"I agree with Robin on that." Replied Joe.

"But how can you? Surely, the church believes people like me choose to be queer for a perverse sexual desire. Whereas, although he never actually said it, I felt Robin thinks some men, and I suppose women are born with the preference of intimate desires for sex with their own gender."

"I certainly believe homosexuals, are born the way they are, just like some people are born with a big nose, others with a small one, and some with blue eyes and some with brown eyes."

"But how can you believe that being a priest?" Asked Patrick surprised.

"I believe it because it's the reason I am a priest!"

I don't know what you mean by that?" Said Patrick, by then completely confused.

"Okay," said Joe, lowering his voice to almost a whisper. "I believe some people are born as homosexuals because I was one of them," He stopped, so his words sank into Patrick's head. Patrick's surprised look was because Joe had 'come out' and told Patrick. It was not in itself any great news, as Patrick had recognised a fellow traveller almost from the first time, he had seen Fr McKenna saying mass.

"I suppose the reason I joined the priesthood," continued Joe, "was because, as a believer in God and his Holy Catholic Church, I saw a way to avoid the pressure of a loving relationship with a woman and a sinful relationship with a man. It was really, for me, a no-choice choice."

There was silence between them, while Joe wondered had he completely shocked Patrick?

But Patrick had two questions he desperately wished to ask Joe, the first being.

"So, tell me to mind my own business Joe, but have you ever or never been that way with a man?"

"I'd rather not say, at this point, if you don't mind, Patrick."

"No, that is alright, but I have to ask another question that is important for me to know. But again, it is none of my business, but anyway, do you think that, sometime in the future maybe, you might…. want to be with a man?"

"I have no doubt about it, Patrick. There will be many times in the future I will want to be with a man, but I have my vow of celibacy to think about."

"Right," said Patrick. "The unnatural option! I don't remember Jesus giving that instruction, do you?"

"Well, no Patrick. The vow of celibacy is of the church and of course the church itself of course is of Jesus. But having said all of that, I do have strong feelings for you Patrick firstly, as a friend but also maybe more. Before I could talk to you on these additional feelings, I need time, time to engage in prayer and with my conscience to reach a conclusion."

"I'm delighted to be your friend," Patrick replied and continued, "and of course would want to be even more close to you. I also understand your dilemma of conscience, so if there is anything I can do to assist the process during your time of reflection, which, I hope, will not be long, please just ask, and I'll come running."

"Thank you, Patrick," Joe replied, and his right-hand brushed Patrick's left. "There is one thing you can do for me tonight and that is you could give me a loan of Sartre's novel 'Nausea' because I too feel disgusted with myself but not because I'm queer but because I feel I'm a hypocrite."

As the priest and Patrick dismounted the bus at Irishtown, so Joe could walk Patrick to his Ennis Grove home and pick up the 'Nausea' book, the wind took up, and both men knotted their scarfs and buttoned their overcoats up to the necks. Proceeding down Londonbridge Road, however, they encountered three people in the distance approaching. It was only when the three were within 20 yards that Patrick stopped and spoke.

"Oh, sweet Jesus. It's them! The ones who beat me up!"

He grabbed Joe by the arm and said,

"Quick run now, quick, quick." But Joe not only held himself firm, but also held Patrick and turned him back to face the foe. Joe was then in control.

"Walk casually towards them," he said, "they won't touch a priest."

With his heart pounding, but taking confidence from Joe, Patrick did as he was told.

"Well for fuck's sake," said the red-headed thug, "it's the pansy prick from the other nite, and he's brung along his 'shirt liftin' lady boy!"

Joe immediately opened his overcoat and pulled down his scarf to show his collar. "Now, gentlemen," he said, "No need for such language, you should be ashamed. Please stand aside and we will leave you to be on your way."

"Jaysis lads, he's a puff priest. A fuckin pansy prick and a puff priest! Batman and bleedin Robin!"

The three were by then laughing their hearts out. When suddenly and without warning, the redhead went to throw a punch like before at Patrick's nose. Except on this occasion, the fist didn't reach its target. Instead, Joe caught it with his right hand, pulled it into his left and then in a swift bodily move, swung the arm over his head and down to his knee. The whole movement caused the redhead's shoulder joint to fracture, and his body end up prostrate on the ground, at which point Joe gave him a sharp heel just below the sternum, causing breathlessness and momentary loss of consciousness.

A second thug came at Joe but walked straight into a karate punch to the neck, dropping him also to the ground.

The third stuck up his fists in a boxing stance and spoke.

"Come on, ya bollicks. I have medals for boxin. I'll sort ya fuckin out."

Joe smiled, and swiftly and mightily kicked the boxer in the groin, causing him to scream and join his friends, in pain, on the ground.

Throughout, Patrick who had watched the performance in wonder, was standing open-mouthed looking at Joe.

Joe however, walked into a garden where a man had come to the door upon hearing all the commotion. "Excuse me sir," said Joe, "I am a priest from the Star of the Sea. Those three thugs have attacked a friend and I, could you please ring the Gardaí and ask them to send someone here as soon as possible?"

Within five minutes a squad-car arrived with two Gardaí, and soon behind them came two more on bicycles.

Once seated in Patrick's front room and awaiting the obligatory cup of tea from Patrick's mother, who was fussing about in the kitchen, Joe explained something to Patrick.

"When I was studying in Rome, I took up a Judo martial Arts course and liked it so much I kept it going, and before I came back to Ireland had actually gained 'black belt' status. Then, when I returned home last year, I couldn't find a club far enough away from the parish to keep it a secret. You see, I like to attend there as a civilian rather than a priest, as opponents don't like trying to beat and hurt priests. Anyway, the most convenient martial arts club I could find was in Bray, but it is a Karate club. However, over the last year, I have become quite proficient but still have a good way to go. So, when possible, I change out of my clerical black, in my sisters in Donnybrook, and take the bus out there as Joe McKenna."

"So, you don't have a brother after all?" Said Patrick.

"No, I told you that. Just two sisters."

"Just two sisters with their priest brother now, my hero," said Patrick, just as his mother arrived with the tea.

Heading home that night, Joe, with the book 'Nausea' secured in his pocket, realised he had some serious thinking to do.

CHAPTER 12

Monday 7ᵗʰ Mar

David Williams particularly needed this time to reflect on his current life story development, especially since he saw many similarities between his story and that of Séadna. Certainly, the similarities were not the same nor had they developed in the same sequence, nonetheless, and upon reflection, he did find in them an uncanny resemblance as he thought:

Firstly, he himself was the star of the story and therefore takes the part of Séadna.

Secondly, the part of the devil could be taken by his father who was, after all, a bit of a devil, what with his gambling, stealing money from his clients, and of course non-payment of debts. In addition, it was he who gave him the purse, so to speak, of money £4,850, so he could be independent and carry out various actions for his own satisfaction.

Thirdly, the two stories had a cobbler and leather worker in them that were essential for the plots.

Fourthly: There were several issues surrounding Séadna and marriage, as there was also concerning his own and other people's marriage.

Fifthly, there were three specific curses which had to be, in Séadna story, lifted, and in his own story, eliminated.

Finally, Séadna had managed to beat the sentence of hell by doing good works. David would also beat the sentence of hell by way of a religious rite.

These thoughts made him feel good and provided he remained aware of the importance of detailed planning, he felt he was almost invincible. And he was, within about an hour of eliminating his final curse. That curse being James Hannigan, the husband of his lover Eileen.

The plan David had hatched in his mind was that, with proper preparation he would arrange for Bronwyn to visit her sister in London, without the sister's knowledge, of course. He would murder his wife on the trip and dispose of her body. He would then continue on to London and murder the sister and dispose of her body. Once enquiries were made regarding their disappearance, he would sight evidence by way of a telegram and letter to show that both women had decided to take off to South America and leave their mundane lives including him behind forever.

David was enjoying sitting in his parked car on Wilfield Road going over, bit by bit, the details of how he had painstakingly implemented his plans. He was feeling very smug, but then why not? He prided himself on his attention to detail and his ability to commit any crime without the bog police force in Ireland or the Bent British Bobbies to ever catch him.

In fact, as he sat there in the car, remembering, he thought he himself could write the story Scéal David, under a pseudonym. Yes, he thought that would be fun to fantasise about, but maybe in the future sometime he might actually do! Indeed, he thought again, what a spiffing idea and the pseudonym he'd use would be Paddy Dignam.

So, how was it that Scéal David, thus far, developed and played out? Well, while he played the main part, other people, and circumstances, without David realising it, also had an input. There was no doubt that David's thoughts were developing, regarding his future life, way before he found his father's cash stash. But there is also no doubt that this event was the catalyst that allowed him to set it in motion. So, with this windfall he opened a bank account in his own name and address with all correspondence for the account going to a post office box number. It also helped that his hobby or leisure sport was that of a lone hiker/walker in the hills and mountains of Ireland, Wales, Scotland, and England. Such an activity allowed him to be absent without a soul being able to verify his whereabouts. So, he had secret money, access to cheap travel, and a lone pastime to assist him in his venture.

He sat thinking Paddy Dignam's story of David would be........

It probably began with the black moustache; he had found this at his father's house when clearing out his old room. He had acquired this for a part he had in H.M.S. Pinafore with the R and R Musical Society. He had stuck it on over his upper lip and with his father's dark-grey overcoat and dark-grey fedora hat he looked like a different person. He worked on this disguise by purchasing a pair of black horned-rimmed glasses, a Black male wig, the hair of which came down to the top of his eyebrows, and added to all by, ever so slightly trimming the moustache for a contemporary appearance. The result was, he believed, a complete metamorphosis. This same disguise had served him well, and now it sat behind him, on the car's back seat, in readiness for what he hoped would be its last assignment.

He had used this disguise first with the Cobbler Maguire when collecting his repaired shoes and ordering the false bottomed briefcase. This briefcase proved more than adequate to bring the gun and its additions into Ireland following the purchase in New York. He had been concerned about having to use his own passport for that trip but rationalised, that should it be necessary to justify the trip, he would simply say he went to the US to do some hiking around the upper Delaware River.

The next part of Scéal David saw him go back to the cobbler and acquire a suitcase of specific measurements and features. Once this was secured in the locked metal cabinet in his home garage, along with the briefcase all covered with hiking and camping gear, he realised the Cobbler Maguire had to go. The execution of the 'leather worker' proved simpler than expected, as the extremely drunken Maguire with the slightest push slipped into the cold water of the canal and hardly even struggled as he drowned. Following the Maguire execution, David had gone and confessed his sin to a most sympathetic priest in Clarendon Street church, where he received absolution from the sin, with the recitation of a decade of the rosary for penance.

To be sure his wife, 'Bullshit Bronwyn,' as he had once overheard her being called needed to be murdered, it being the only solution to his hatred for her. His own name for her though 'The Banshee bitch' he thought was more appropriate because of all her screaming for more, more and more. Well, he had thought, she got more than she bargained for.

Still though, he did have just a little difficulty in actually getting the nerve to carrying out the deed. And indeed, such was the case until that Sunday afternoon when he first picked up Eileen from the bus stop in Sandymount. This start and development of their relationship gave him the spurt he required to set his execution plans in motion. After all, he had the weapon already.

In this regard, David's first step was to get himself a simple false identity. He was unable to get e.g., a false passport or driving license, but he managed to secure a false library card from Ballsbridge library. The name he picked for his false identity was Michael Collins, after one of the leading people in the struggle for Irish Independence. David's vanity saw himself as 'The Big Fellow' the affectionate name many gave to their hero Collins.

Then with this identity he took out a lease on the flat on North Circular Road. This in turn enabled him to hide away certain items like his disguise, a second-hand typewriter, he purchased for special letters he would write, and the special briefcase and suitcase. With the flat at his disposal, he felt a greater security than having his secrets in the Marine Drive garage. Of course, the flat was also his 'pleasure pad' for liaisons with Eileen.

The next part of the Scéal was when he disconnected his home telephone, and he told Bronwyn was going to Belfast, but instead, he took a trip by plane to London, literally a flying day trip, in his 'dark-man' disguise. The purpose of which was simply to send the telegram, from Charing Cross 'post office' to his wife in Dublin, supposedly from Bethany asking Bronwyn to visit and help out due to the broken leg. He had even arranged, when at the post office around 12.00 noon, for the telegram to be sent around

5.30 PM, *advising them that no one would be at the receiver's address until after 6.30 PM. In reality, it was so it would be delivered almost at the same time he would arrive home. He had disconnected the phone just as a precaution, even though the telegram said not to call, and it seemed it was just as well he did. Then the next day he bought Bronwyn a first-class cabin ticket, through Thomas Cook, to travel that night the 2nd of Feb on the 'Mail boat' sailing. After he purchased her ticket, he organised to change into the person of the dark-man disguise. Then walking to the British rail office, in close-by Westmoreland Street, he bought himself a similar ticket, in the name of Mr Michael Collins, using a heavy Cork accent. As luck, would have it, he secured for himself alias Michael Collins the cabin next door to Bronwyn.*

When Bronwyn had taken off in the taxi for Dun Laoghaire he slipped out of the house and went to collect his car which he had parked 200 yards away on Farney Park. He drove the car home and into the garage where he first polished clean all his fingerprints from the case that was in his car boot and then putting on his woollen gloves, he loaded the boot with the suitcase, and within which was the briefcase containing the gun and accompaniments. He then drove himself to Dun Laoghaire and parked on Cumberland Street near the 'Purty Kitchen' pub. Adorning the dark man disguise along with his gloves, he took the suitcase with contents from the boot, locked the car, and walked to Old Dunleary Road and along to the mail boat dock for Holyhead. The special suitcase David carried, made by the cobbler Maguire, had specific measurements and, like the briefcase, it had a brass clasp, but it also had two leather straps over the top to be fixed onto buckles. These straps were extremely short and only just fit into the buckles. In addition, he had arranged for the prongs on the buckles to be removed. In this way, the small straps were not secured in the buckles, thus allowing the straps to open easily.

David didn't board the boat until the last minute and then made his way to the first-class cabins on 'A' deck. He was delighted to see that it had started to rain as he went past Bronwyn's cabin to get to his own. Confirming her presence there with a brief glance through the porthole, he entered his own cabin and placed the case on the lower berth bed. He then closed the curtain on his porthole and extracted the briefcase from the case.

With the boat, underway he soon had the gun loaded, and the silencer screwed on. One hour later, he went out on the deck and knocked on Bronwyn's cabin door, saying in a Welsh accent.

"Message for Mrs Bronwyn Williams." He had to repeat the knock and message again before she opened the door.

"Hello darling," he said, as he pushed her from the door and walked in, closing the door behind him. The only part of the disguise he wore was his father's overcoat with the collar turned up, as the heavy wind and rain would have blown off the hat and

perhaps even the wig. It took Bronwyn a few seconds to recognise him before she almost shouted.

"What the hell are you doing here?"

As she said, these words, she didn't notice him take the gun from his coat pocket and then answer her with two silent 'plop' shots into her heart. He immediately ran to her and lay her easily onto the floor before grabbing her 'Harrods' coat and putting it under her, so blood would not spread. He looked at her and when he was sure she was dead he looked around the cabin to make sure there was no blood spattered anywhere. Satisfied that he had carried out a clean execution, he went back to his own cabin and returned with the suitcase. He was pleased with himself when, bent at the knees and the waist, she fit snugly into the case along with one shoe on and one stuffed under her chin. He then with some difficulty stuffed the 'Harrods' coat into the small space between her shins and one of the corners before closing over the lid. He did not engage the brass clasp and only secured one strap into the non-pronged buckle. He then checked the outside deck to make sure it was clear and walked out to the deck rail with the case and slipped it, complete with Bronwyn, into the wind and rain swept Irish Sea.

With the major task complete he returned to her cabin, collected all her personal items, putting them into her suitcase and then returned to his own cabin with the lot. He sat on his berth bed and smiled, thinking to himself that it would be only a matter of maybe minutes before the body and other contents were worked free from then case and lost to perish in the sea. He congratulated himself on thinking of the suitcase use, as to try to carry a dead body onto the deck was too risky, whereas a suitcase on a boat trip was normal.

Oblivious to what would happen David had continued his journey, taking Bronwyn's suitcase as his own on the mail train from Holyhead in Wales to Euston station in London. Throughout the whole trip, he only took his gloves off to go to the toilet. At Euston, he had breakfast with three cups of hot tea to calm his nerves, and then at precisely 8.49 AM he hired a 1958 Morris Minor van using a broken English German accent and drove to a Marks and Spencer store where, using the same accent, he bought a woollen tartan car blanket. He had to take his gloves off only to get the cash from his wallet and take up the change from his purchase. On the way back to the van, he took the blanket out of the bag and discarded the bag in a rubbish bin. He popped the blanket into the back of the van and then drove to a hardware shop where, using a Yorkshire accent, he purchased a tape measure, small hand saw, gardening gloves, and three 2X3 foot plywood sheets together with a spade, shovel, and fork all of which he put into the back of the van.

Again, David's gloves were only removed for the cash transaction, after which he left the receipt on the counter knowing it would not be needed. His next stop was 'The Army and Navy' store, where he bought two hooded sleeping bags and an army rain cape. This time he used a 'Brummie' accent. He paid the assistant, who cashed up the purchases and handed him back the change and receipt. David handed the assistant the receipt back saying he did not require it and then asked for directions to the toilet, which he desperately needed due to his three breakfast teas. The assistant pointed out the direction, saying he would have the purchases bagged and ready to go, on Sir's return from the 'Gents.' Each sleeping bag came with its own cloth cover bag with a handle, and the assistant, out of habit, popped the receipt into a plain brown paper bag and placed the army cape in on top.

David returned to the van and placed the open cape around the passenger seat and on top of this, he placed the tartan car blanket making the seat very comfortable looking. He then set off for Colne Valley Regional Park, which was about an hour's drive away.

Colne Valley was an area he had often visited, in his last year at school, for hikes and canoeing, at weekends. The park itself, located only nine miles from Harrow, was easily reached. And more recently, at the end of October last, on the day following his attendance at an old boys Saturday night reunion dinner, he had hired a car and drove to the valley to reconnoitre a particular spot he remembered as being off the beaten track and quite isolated. This exact place was where Scéal David's plan called for an interment.

Upon arrival, he parked the van off the road in heavy brush, pasted the number plates with thick mud, took the plywood, tape and other tools from the boot and headed another 20 yards deeper into the wooded area to find his selected spot. He was still near enough to hear if a car stopped, or a walker was in the vicinity.

As fast as he could then, he dug a grave in the soft ground as deep as time would allow approximately 5-feet-long 2-feet-wide and 3-feet-deep with one end down to nearly four feet.

With it was completed, he covered the pit with the plywood sheets and these in turn with some clay. Then he spread the remaining extracted clay to a perimeter of about 4 yards out around the worked area. He finished off the job with an overall spread of twigs, leaves, and small branches. The whole operation took less than one and a half hours and while it would not stand up to heavy scrutiny, it was sufficient for his need.

He gathered the tools, gloves and tape into the van and set off for London.

Some hours later, as Bethany was walking back to the office from lunch, David pulled the van up to the kerb beside her and pushed open the passenger door and shouted.

"Bethany! Thank God. Get in quick, Bronwyn has had an accident. We need to get to her." Bethany stood for what seemed like minutes but more like a couple of seconds and eventually said.

"Oh. It is you, David. What? Why are you in a van? What are you doing here?"

"Get in now. It's Bronwyn! She needs you, been in an accident, hit by a car, accident, get in now," he said with force.

She slid in, and he leaned across and pull the door shut. White faced then Bethany asked.

"Is she bad? Why are you both in London? I wasn't expecting you. Her? Where is she?"

"She's in a doctor's surgery," he answered, "not far away. We'll go there now."

He pulled out into the traffic and began to talk to take her mind off the drive.

"We came as a surprise for you. I got tickets for 'My Fair Lady' at Drury Lane theatre! They are for the three of us for this Saturday night. They were bought a year ago, in a travel package which was cancelled. However, I snagged the theatre tickets. But now it looks like we won't make it. What happened was that Bronwyn got out of the van to go and buy some flowers for you, but she got hit by a car crossing the road. She was taken into a local doctor's surgery. The Ambulance is on the way!"

"Why didn't you stay with her?" Bethany asked.

"Well," he replied, "you know what she's like, she screamed at me to go and get you, and that is what I did!" He drove on, saying. "She looks bad, but maybe it's not as bad as it looks?"

Bethany then went on about how they should have told her they were coming over and this was a bloody mess and again saying he should have stayed with her. Her verbal outburst was silenced as he pulled into a car park at St James' Park, well away from other cars.

"Why have you stopped here?" she asked, surprised.

"I need to show you something important," he answered, as he leaned over and pulled a folded sleeping bag from the back, asked her to lean forward, which she did in her shocked state, and he placed it behind her. He then swiftly took the gun, complete with silencer, from under his seat and pointing it at her chest shot her twice through the heart. She conveniently slumped against the passenger door as if she was asleep. He quickly looked around to make sure this act had not been seen and then casually leaned over and pulled the folded sleeping bag from behind her to see that the two of the bullets had gone through her body and exited, close together, through the back of her coat. However, there was only one hole in the sleeping bag where one had entered, but no exit *holes on the other side. He immediately extracted this bullet from the bag and slipped it into his pocket. Then he quickly looked under her and around about the front for the second one, but to no avail, thinking he would find it later somewhere in the back.*

With the job of execution complete, he wrapped the blanket and the rain cape around her. He then got out the driver's door and went around the back. There, he climbed into the flat van back and dragged the body and covers there from the front seat. He closed the sleeping bag hood down over her face and fastened its remainder to completely conceal the body. Finally, he opened out the other sleeping bag and covered almost everything up in the van's rear.

With another look for the missing bullet but not finding it, he then realised he was pressed for time, so he got back into the driver's seat and headed back to Charing Cross. Once there, he found a parking spot, put on his 'dark-man disguise, took the keys for Beth's flat from her handbag, and put the bag into his briefcase. Ten minutes later, he had entered her flat and was in the process of looking for a phone number. This number, Bethany's boss, one James Newton, he found quickly in an address book on her telephone table.

David then sought and found a copy and details of Bethany's lease agreement and slipped it into his briefcase. He then packed a small weekend case with some of Bethany's clothes, make-up etc. locked up the flat, and again unseen left the premises and walked to the public telephone box in the Charing Cross post office.

Upon being connected to the civil servant, David, in his best upper-class British accent, said.

"Good afternoon, Mr Newton my name is Dr Jeremy Saunders, I'm ringing you on behalf of Miss Bethany Sheridan. She has asked me to contact you, as I have recommended for her not to try to speak for at least a week. You see, she consulted me about 30 minutes ago, and I have diagnosed her with Tetanus. You would probably be more aware of this condition by its common name of Lock jaw. So, therefore, you understand why she has not returned to work following her lunch."

"Oh, my goodness, me! Is there something we can do to help her out? Where is she now? Could we bring her home? Does she need medication? May I ask the prognosis?"

"Well firstly," replied to the pseudo doctor, "this is a most debilitating condition caused by an infection, but we have caught it, I believe, at an early stage. I have put her on a course of penicillin and treated some symptoms and sent her home in a taxi. Tetanus, while an infection, is not spread from person to person, but I believe contact with others is best avoided. I have, however, telephoned a friend of hers who will be with her within the hour and will take her to convalesce at her home in Hampstead. What she

needs is rest and quiet. I expect she will contact you early next week. She sends her sincere apologies for any inconvenience this will cause you."

"Oh, really Dr Saunders, the important thing is that Bethany recovers as soon as possible. We will, of course, manage without her, even though we do rely on her most competent contribution. Oh, and thank you most sincerely, doctor, for the call."

"My pleasure Mr Newton, replied to David, "and may you have a productive afternoon."

"And Good afternoon to you, doctor,"

Upon returning to the van David put his briefcase and Bethany's suitcase into the van beside her body and headed off for the Colne Valley Regional Park.

He parked in the same wooded spot as before and walked quickly to the grave and opened it up, ensuring no leaves, branches of clay fell in. He then pulled the sleeping bagged body from the car, and once again he checked to make sure there was only the one bullet hole in the bag itself. Satisfied that only one bullet had penetrated the bag and which he had retrieved, he then placed the body in the grave. He next took the empty brown paper bag that held the rain cape and emptied the contents of Bethany's weekend case into it. This he placed near the body's feet, at the grave's deeper end. When it was filled up almost to the top, he cut the plywood boards with the hand saw, so they would fit snugly on top and then put the few inches of clay cover on top of all to the level of the surrounding ground. As before, he used twigs, leaves, and broken branches as a final camouflage. He then drove a few miles to a deep water, secluded section of the Colne River. Once there he placed his tools and gloves etc. in the second sleeping bag and filled up Bethany's empty weekend case with rocks and then threw both, way out, into the dark deep water.

Almost done, David drove towards London but stopped on the way in a lay-by and for twenty minutes searched the car from top to bottom for the other bullet. Finally, he accepted that as it was nowhere to be seen by him, then it would also not be seen or found by anyone else. Also, he thought it could have fallen out of the car at any point during the whole operation, and should it be found, how could it be traced back to him anyway?

He returned the van to the car hire office and caught the evening mail train for Holyhead, eventually arriving in Dun Laoghaire next morning carrying his briefcase and its contents together with Bronwyn's suitcase as his own. He walked back to his car, changed out of his 'dark-man' disguise and into ordinary work clothes. He then drove straight into the city and parked near Grafton Street, and with an hour to spare before work he went into 'Bewley's' tea and coffee rooms for breakfast.

Feeling quite satisfied with his two kills. In fact, he considered if people knew what he had accomplished, they would consider him quite famous. And of course, he was in the right place, for the famous very often visited 'Bewley's' in Grafton Street. In fact, the very building in which Bewley's was situated was once a school attended by Arthur Wellesley, later to become the Duke of Wellington, who won the Battle of Waterloo in 1815..............

It was a good story so far, but it was not yet finished as David continued to wait for his next victim to arrive, he remembered he had to yet type two letters from Bethany with her forged signature. The first would be to her boss Mr James Newton which he would post on Friday. It would explain that there were complications with her illness and that she had returned to Ireland to convalesce with the help of her sister. In addition, the doctors in Ireland had told her that she would need a month or more before she could even consider returning to work. So, she had decided with sincere apologies to tender her resignation and requested, if possible, to have any personal items, she had left in the office posted on to the PO Box address given.

The second letter David would send as Bethany to her letting agents, advising them that she was giving them two months' notice of her intention to terminate her tenancy agreement. Also, enclosed in the letter would be a money order for rent up to termination.

In a months' time, then, when everything had settled down, David would arrange to have the flat cleared out and cleaned for vacant possession. With this complete, he would post the keys to the letting agent.

*

As usual on weekdays, James Hannigan left his house for work at precisely 8.20 AM for the ten-minute walk to Sandymount railway station on Sandymount Ave. James' preferred headgear was a cap, as he believed a fedora tended to look outsized on his diminutive height. This choice of hat ironically was to determine, partly, the intended method his executioner planned to use. But James was completely oblivious he was a murderer's target. He had other things of a more domestic nature occupying his mind.

As he walked on to his train, he stopped only to buy a copy of 'The Irish Times' from Maypotter's newsagent and was soon on his way again with the paper popped neatly in the outer pocket of his briefcase. Walking along the Avenue his thoughts strayed to two major worries he was currently experiencing, the first was his hope, and indeed almost expectation, of his promotion to the position of Town Clerk when old Robinson retired in a three weeks' time. For the previous year, Robinson, together with numerous councilors had indicated that he was, undoubtedly, the heir apparent, but in the last two weeks he had been getting the feeling that someone else, one Eamon Daly, was in the running. And if that was not enough, Daly, James had only just found out, was the brother-in-law of one very influential councillor. In addition, he had been told that Daly had only recently joined the political party to which the mayor himself belonged. Indeed, each day, his confidence in procuring the job lessoned. How, he thought, would Eileen react if he didn't get this promotion? She'd probably think he was an inadequate idiot. And that was his second worry, Eileen! It seemed to him that over the past few months she was very unhappy. He knew she missed her primary school teaching job, which she had left last year, but trying to do the job and look after the kids and house was too much. Perhaps it was his fault that he did not help her enough with the housework and the kids. Whatever it was, it certainly seemed to be really cutting her up, so much so, that he sometimes felt she had stopped loving him.

Arriving at the station platform James nodded a 'good morning' to the one other person who arrived just behind him. He was an odd-looking character with black moustache, brown horned rimmed glasses, and almost black fedora. The dark colours were quite a contrast to the light brown tan briefcase he carried. James had seen him catch this train before, at least once but perhaps twice, he was easy to remember. The train itself was almost always on time, arriving at the station between 8.30 and 8.35. As the council offices in which he worked, as an assistant Town Clerk, was close to the Dun Laoghaire station, this train would have him sitting at his desk by 9.00 AM on the dot.

The trains going in the opposite direction were usually packed with commuters heading into the city for work. By contrast, the train James would catch would be virtually empty and while he not only got a seat to himself, he was also mostly alone in the carriage. Also, only one or two other people caught his southward bound train from Sandymount. Today, however, as the train pulled into the station, there were only the two passengers to board. And James quickly climbed into an empty carriage and was only slightly surprised another passenger followed him in. It was not something he really cared about as he made his way toward a front seat facing the engine.

David Williams in his 'dark-man' disguise sat two seats behind facing James' back. David's Plan was simple and well-rehearsed. He had firstly driven his car to Wilfield Road off Sandymount Ave, parked a little way down, with the Avenue in sight, put on his disguise, and waited until he saw Hannigan pass for the station. Then he followed him onto the platform.

If he didn't get a carriage alone with Hannigan, he would try on other days until he did. The plan was that once the train left Blackrock station David would take the hammer and a hand towel from the false bottom of the case, smash in his lover's husband's head with one or two blows till he was at least unconscious, then cover his victim's head with the towel and bash again until death was assured, with the blood confined to the towel. He would then take off Hannigan's coat and jacket and prop him against the train seat until they reached just after the Dalkey station and below the Vico Road, where he would open the carriage door and fling the body out, hopefully over the cliff. He would then continue to Killiney station where he would change to the other side and get the next train back to Sandymount. Once there, he would change back to normal clothes and post a typed suicide note from James to Eileen. Everything completed, he would drive into his workplace in Grafton Street.

As The train pulled out from Blackrock station David took out the hammer and towel from the briefcase and quietly moved the few paces towards the sitting James. However, as he raised the hammer to take aim, James lifted the front page of the Irish Times to reveal its large headline clearly visible to David, which read. 'Body in Suitcase: Found on Sandymount Strand.'

David lowered the hammer and slumped back into his seat in shock, still though having the presence of mind to replace the weapon in his briefcase. Better, he thought, not complicate things further with another murder until he assessed this latest development. Perhaps it was not Bronwyn. But then realised such was just wishful thinking. The train stopped at Seapoint where David made his exit and James carried on to Dun Laoghaire, oblivious of his good fortune.

Of course, what David did not know regarding the case he put his wife in, was that the actual strap in the buckle would hold long enough for the body to begin to bloat and slightly expand due to the gases a corpse will produce. The same will not occur with tanned leather, and therefore Bronwyn's body already wedged in became increasingly stuck even when the strap became released. In addition, what David could never have anticipated was that Bronwyn's body, some four days after her murder, would turn up at, of all places, Sandymount strand. Her serendipitous arrival was uncannily occasioned by the interaction of wind and waves, together with the movement and snags, creating pulling and drags, by numerous sea vessels both commercial and military.

The Novena

*

It came as no surprise when the official orders were received around 11.00 AM at Irishtown Garda station that Inspector Richard O'Connell was put in charge of 'The body in the case' case. The two lads having drawn his attention to the case he had, with a little prodding, exposed that the suitcase contained a body. Without even telling this to the lads, he asked them to run as quick as they could to the Garda station and ask for Sargent Perkins and tell him that Inspector O'Connell requires a homicide team and equipment down on the strand as soon as possible. While he waited, Richard wondered, firstly, where the suitcase had entered the water. Had it just been dumped here on the strand? Had it gone in off the end of either of Dun-Laoghaire pies? Or off the South Wall at the Poolbeg lighthouse? Or any of the other piers from Howth to Greystones or even further afield? Then there was the possibility it came off a boat, the mail boat, a 'B and I' boat or some other vessel crossing the Irish Sea.

Since then, however, the time of death had been estimated at two to four days prior to the body being found.

*

At 11.00 AM sharp, Vera rang the bell on the door of Canon Skeffington's house on Leahy terrace. As she stood waiting for an answer, she noticed that his car was parked in front, so he was definitely in. It also occurred to her that the three-story house was large for just one person to live in. But then she thought, he was after all a Canon in the church and also had to have accommodation for his housekeeper, Mrs O'Sullivan. And it was Mrs O'Sullivan herself who eventually opened the door.

"I'd like to see the Canon, please, Mrs O'Sullivan." Vera asked.

"You don't have an appointment, as far as I know, Mrs O'Brien, do you?"

"No, I don't, Mrs O'Sullivan, but it's important that I speak to the Canon."

"Well, I'm afraid he is busy at the moment this being Lent and with the novena going on. But I'll make an appointment for you for maybe next week. I'll just go and get his diary."

"Well, if he is here Mrs O'Sullivan," said Vera, not being put off by Maggie O'Sullivan's self-importance, "he will want to hear what I have to say to him regarding a pressing matter for myself and the parish. So, I'll be obliged if you will just ask him to see me for a few minutes and when he hears what I have to say, I think he will want to talk to me for a lot longer."

"Well, like I said, Mrs O'Brien, he is very busy and cannot be disturbed. But if you would like to tell me the nature of your visit. I will be able to measure its importance and arrange for you to see him earlier than next week."

Vera looked at her and prayed not to have bad thoughts about pulling the old bit of wispy hair from O'Sullivan's scalp.

"Oh, certainly I can," said Vera, "it concerns a great mystery that is happening to me and will, when it becomes publicly known, cause hundreds if not thousands of people to visit this parish."

"And what might that mystery be, Mrs O'Brien?"

"It is a mystery that has to remain a mystery until I get guidance from the Canon."

Suddenly, the Canon came up behind Mrs O'Sullivan and asked.

"Now who might this lady be, Mrs O'Sullivan?"

"This is Mrs O'Brien from Marine Drive, Canon, I've been explaining to her that because of your busy schedule she needs to make an appointment to see you next week."

The Canon smiled at Vera and said, "Good morning to you Mrs O'Brien, I am indeed extremely busy this morning so if you would just give me an indication of what it is you want, we might be able to resolve it here and now."

"Thank you, Father, but it is a very private and personal matter I wish to discuss, and it will only take a few minutes of your time to hear it. But I believe you should know about it before I contact His Grace, Dr McQuaid, the Archbishop."

"Oh," replied the Canon, "whatever your problem is Mrs O'Brien, I'm sure there is no need to bother His Grace with it! Mrs O'Sullivan, please show Mrs O'Brien into the parlour, and I'll be along to hear her mystery in a few moments."

A very obviously annoyed Mrs O'Sullivan showed Vera into the parlour telling her not to sit in a certain chair as it was the Canon's favourite and then left her there, closing the door behind her with a thump. She then went straight to the Canon's study where she informed him that Vera O'Brien was well known in Sandymount as bordering on religious insanity, and the parish priest should see her off swiftly, or he would never get rid of her.

"Now," said the Canon, following his arrival and seated in his favourite armchair. "What can I do for you, Mrs O'Brien?"

"Well Canon, I'm having a visitation!"

"I know that Mrs O'Brien. Now, what is it I can do for you?"

"You know! How can you know? Sure, I haven't told anyone."

"Yes, Mrs O'Brien, I know you are having a visitation with me here and now."

"No, Canon, I'm having a visitation with Jesus. You know, an apparition."

"You're having an apparition with Jesus, here and now!"

"No, Canon, I have an apparition with Jesus in my bedroom!"

"Is this an impure apparition of Jesus in your bedroom? Do you want to receive the sacrament of penance, Mrs O'Brien?"

"What? I'm just having visitations that are apparitions every so often of Jesus, and they take place in my bedroom."

"Oh, so, you have a vision of Jesus when you are in your bedroom?"

"Yes Canon. Not all the time. Maybe four times a week but he just stands there, says nothing and smiles."

"And tell me, Mrs O'Brien, how do you know it is Jesus?"
"Well, he is dressed in a long white robe with sandals on his feet. He has a beard with long hair, and he has holes in the palms of his hands, and he looks like all the images of Jesus we see in the church! Canon, I know he is Jesus, he has light coming out of him all over."

The Canon looked at her, trying to see was there any physical sign from her that suggested she had gone completely mad, but he could find none and tried another approach.

"Perhaps he looks like Jesus even down to the wounded hands, but maybe it is just your husband, and the light is causing you to be confused, and you want to see him as Jesus?"

"No Canon, I assure you I am not confused. I thought about this long and hard before I came here because I know there was a lot of doubt about St Bernadette's vision at Lourdes and at first nobody believed her. But I have no doubt it is Jesus who is coming to me, and sure who else would have St Veronica standing beside him with His image on her veil?"

"St Veronica? Where, in the name of God, did she come from?"

"Wasn't it Jerusalem? She was there watching Jesus carrying the cross."

"Yes! I mean no! Actually, what I mean Mrs O'Brien is, does your vision also include St Veronica?

"Yes, but only sometimes. It's always Jesus just smiling, but sometimes he has St Veronica beside him with her veil and His image on it."

"And does St Veronica speak?"

"No, just smiles as well."

"And does anyone else see these apparitions, Mrs O'Brien?"

"No, not at all. On occasions, my husband and even my children have been in the room, but they have not seen the vision."

Again, the priest rubbed his chin trying to think how best to deal with this woman who was obviously suffering from religious hallucinations. After a few seconds, he thought he would appeal to her belief that she was rational and spoke.

"The mind plays numerous tricks on us, Mrs O'Brien, and sometimes we see things that are not really there or hear speech that is not spoken. I know that you are a very good Catholic and practice your religion better than most, but sometimes when we really want a special thing to happen, we make it happen in our heads, but it is not really happening at all."

"No Canon, I can see Jesus quite clearly and also St Veronica when she is there. I do not conjure them up for my own self-importance or wants, but I am happy to be selected to see them. Also, you would know the catechism says, *we can know God by our reason and by divine revelation."*

My God thought the Canon, she's quoting the catechism to me! And then he said.

"But as you mentioned Lourdes Mrs O'Brien, now wasn't St Bernadette spoken to by the Blessed Virgin as also did Our Lady speak to the three children when she appeared at Fatima. Yet, your vision hasn't spoken to you?"

"Neither did any of the 'Knock' apparition speak!"

The Canon looked at her and thought, this woman might not have her full faculties, but she knows her stuff. Then in a measured tone he said.

"If God is revealing himself to you, surely you must believe there is a reason! If not, then why is He doing it?"

Vera quoted again. *"There are some truths revealed by God that we cannot fully understand, these truths are called mysteries of religion: We believe mysteries of religion because they were made known to us by God, who can neither deceive nor be deceived."*

Frustrated then, the Canon, trying to bait her, said.

"Well, did you not even receive any secret messages?"

"No. Anyway, I cannot understand why secret messages were given to children when they cannot or do not reveal them?"

The Canon again looked at Vera, thinking he had often wondered the same thing himself. But also, realising he was not qualified to make a real assessment as to the mental condition of an obviously intelligent but perhaps religiously insane woman, another approach was necessary.

"Look, Mrs O'Brien, you would be well aware, with your knowledge of the apparitions that took place in Lourdes, Knock and Fatima, that before the church could, or would give them their backing, it required the visionaries to be assessed as to their truthfulness, beliefs and also their mental health. I am quite sure you understand the need for such assessment and therefore as an initial step, I would like you to pay a visit to Dr McNulty on Tritonville Road, and I'll give you a letter telling him what I would like him to do. I would also like you to give him permission to advise me on the outcome of his examination, only of course if, after it, you still wish to persist with the belief that you are receiving visitations from Jesus and eh, occasionally from St Veronica, in your bedroom. Are you willing to do that, Mrs O'Brien?"

"Well, I suppose it is necessary, but I can assure you that I don't tell lies, my faith is very strong and if I thought I was losing my mind I would have gone to the doctor in the first place."

"Quite so," said the Canon, as he scribbled a note, put it into a sealed envelope with Dr McNulty's name on it. He then stood up, indicating they were finished, and handed Vera the envelope saying.

"I will be most interested in hearing back from yourself or Dr McNulty at your convenience, Mrs O'Brien. May God go with you, and I'll remember you in my prayers."

On the walk home Vera considered what had just taken place. Well, she thought, what did she expect? Anyway, she thought, she would go to the Doctor and let him 'assess' her mental state as much as he liked, but she knew herself she was fine in that department. Besides, she had intended to go to the doctor because she believed she needed some glasses, so she'd kill two birds with the one stone!

*

Canon Skeffington walked up to the reception desk at St Vincent's hospital in Leeson Street Dublin. It was 5.45 PM and in between visiting hours, but this did not apply to a priest's collar that had access at any time or day. The Canon, upon receiving the answer to his question from the assistant at reception, set off to find Dermot Shaw, the clerk of his church.

"How do you feel?" The Canon asked the half dead Shaw.

The answer he received was a mutter he could not understand, but then said.

"Thank God you are on the mend anyway. Now would you like me to pray with you for a short while?" Again, he got another mutter, which of course he took for a "Yes," and then kneeling beside the bed, much to the distress of Shaw, the Canon began the rosary.

Luckily, the priest only said one decade, or the chances were that Shaw would have gone into cardiac arrest again.

*

The Novena

It was almost 6.10 PM when Mikey O'Rourke parked and locked his car in Henrietta Place. He pulled his hat down and collar up, and then walked down Bolton Street towards Dolly Fossets. As he passed Donovan's pub, one 'not drunk yet,' Stephen Murphy, sitting at a window with a pint almost finished and a small Power in waiting, immediately recognized him firstly as the fella he saw last week visiting Dolly's, but secondly, and more importantly he was also a fellow resident of Sandymount. Stephen immediately went to the pub's entrance and watched Mikey enter the Brothel. He then returned to his seat and smiled to himself as he finished the pint, downed the whiskey in one go, and ordered the same again.

A little under two hours later, having washed up from his meal, Mikey left the house to attend the novena. For sure, he felt like a hypocrite, but then he thought, if 'a just man falls ten times each day' a once-a-week sinner might find mercy and strength to desist eventually.

*

Peg O'Connell and Vera O'Brien left the church together following the Novena session. As they began their journey up Sandymount Road, Peg said. "Wasn't that a terrible thing with those kids finding the body in the case on the strand yesterday? I hope it wasn't any of your children Mrs O'Brien?"

"No," replied Vera, "but I heard it was Mrs Hannigan's son and his friend. You remember Eileen Hannigan, the auburn-haired glamorous one they picked to play 'Molly Byrne' in the play?" "Yes, I remember her, very attractive. Those kids thought it was a dog, you know. You see, my husband was out there fishing, and they thought the mink fur on the collar of her coat was doggy fur.

"Oh, my God, I didn't know that Mrs O'Connell, and to think I would have loved a coat like that myself, but now you have told me that I think I'll change my mind." They both gave a little nervous laugh. Then Peg said.

"Anyway, I could never afford something like that, so it won't be a worry."

"Me either," said Vera laughing, "but you know some people can afford those types of clothes like the likes of Mrs Williams! Do you know her?" Peg shook her head indicating she didn't, and Vera said.

"Well, you certainly know her husband, the gorgeous Mr David Williams. He, who gave you the translation of the 'Scéal Séadna' book! Well, his wife Bronwyn has a similar coat. But" she continued with a big smile, "I suppose I shouldn't say this, but some people call her, and I'll spell out the bad word, 'B: u: l:l:s:h:i:t Bronwyn' cause she's a bit stuck-up with her fancy clothes and handsome husband! You couldn't forget him now, could you? Tall, blond, talks with an English accent?"

"Oh, yes," replied Peg, "he's looking after the wardrobe and costume for the 'Drama' and didn't he want to play the part of the blacksmith opposite Mrs..eh. Hannigan."

"That's right," replied Vera and continued. "Anyway, 'B…. Bronwyn has a coat with a mink collar and, God forgive me, but I really envied her having it and would have loved one myself."

"Ah sure, I know Mrs O'Brien, sure we all want things we can't get." By then they had reached Marine Drive and after saying goodnight the two women went their separate ways.

*

As Peg was getting into bed that night her husband noticed a big smile on her face. He was glad to see this and had got over his disappointment in her refusing, for herself or the children, to eat any of the fish he had caught the previous day after he had told her in confidence that the body's face was unrecognisable due probably to being scavenged by fish. It was really his own fault, as he should have realised his faux paw before he said it.

"So, my dear," he said, "Are you smiling in anticipation of the sensual prowess of your lover?"

"Now you can just behave yourself tonight, Richard O'Connell, I'm just laughing to myself about Mrs O'Brien, on the one hand, she is a bit religious mad, but on the other she is quite funny."

"And why is that my love?"

"Well, we were talking about your suitcase case! Ha, Ha." She laughed. "Now, we only talked about it regarding what has been reported on the radio and in the papers. So, you don't have to worry, okay?"

"Okay, love, go on then. How was St Veronica funny?" "Well, we were talking about the mink collared coat, and she said she knew someone with one, a stuck-up bitch, she referred to as 'Bullshit Bronwyn,' but she couldn't say 'Bullshit' she had to spell it out."

He looked at his wife quite seriously for a few seconds before saying. "Maybe it was 'Bullshit Bronwyn' in the case?"

"Oh, don't be silly Mr Detective, from the way St Veronica was talking 'Bullshit Bronwyn' is very much alive and kicking."

CHAPTER 13

Tuesday 8ᵗʰ March

Detective Inspector O'Connell was just coming out through the O'Brien front gate as Vera arrived home from 10'clock mass.

"May I help you?" She asked, recognising Peg O'Connell, husband.

"Yes," he replied, "You are Mrs Vera O'Brien? My name is Detective Inspector Richard O'Connell, I believe I met you briefly on Thursday night?" Vera turned white, thinking he must he here about the condoms she found in the garage.

"Oh yes," she managed, at the same time putting her hand on the wall to steady herself. They looked at each other and Richard knew that when he introduced himself officially, as he had just done, it often frightened some people because they didn't usually have anything to do with the Gardaí. Or sometimes some people had something to hide, in most cases something small. Also, some people were skeptical of the detective's bone fides until they saw an identification. So, Richard produced his 'warrant card,' opened it out, so Vera could inspect it and asked.

"May I speak to you for a few minutes, Mrs O'Brien, probably inside would be better out of the gaze of neighbours?"

"Inside!" She repeated, and then asked quietly and nervously.

"Do you mean inside in the garage?"

"Well," answered Richard, a little confused, "we can go into the garage if you like, but perhaps the house might be better?"

"Oh yes, right, the house." She said flustered but then opened the Front door and showed him into her Living Room.

"May I sit?" He asked.

"Of course," she replied, "I'm just not used to Policemen." He sat on one of the Lounge chairs while she sat facing him on the sofa.

"Now, Mrs O'Brien, you are aware we are trying to identify the body of the woman found on the strand on Sunday. She was wearing a tan coat with a mink fur collar. My wife told me that you know of someone with a similar coat. I would therefore be obliged if you would tell me her name and where I might find her? You see, we want to find out where she bought it, as the victim may have bought hers from the same place."

"Oh, I see," said Vera, noticeably more relaxed and went on, "you are here about the body in the case. Yes, I see now. Oh, and I've forgotten my manners. Would you like a cup of tea or......Well, only tea? I've no coffee."

"No, nothing thanks you," said Richard, "just the woman's name and where she lives?"

"Well, that's easy," came the reply, "she lives next door, Mrs Bronwyn Williams and the coat was bought in Harrods in London. Well, that's what she told me. She said her sister who lives there bought it for her."

"Oh, that is great. Thank you, Mrs O'Brien, you have been very helpful. In fact, I'll just pop in to see her now."

"Well, I'm afraid she's not there and won't be back for about two or three weeks. But if you need help to find out who the body in the case is? Try St Anthony, he can find anything, put a penny in his box, just ask, and your prayer will be answered!"

"Thanks, Mrs O'Brien."

As the Inspector walked out the gate hearing O'Brien's door close, he also noticed the Rubbish bin lorry making its way down toward him, slowly collecting the rubbish on the way.

The dust bin for the Williams house was out on the path, like the others, ready for emptying into the lorry. The Inspector, out of intuition, picked it up and brought it back into the garden, so it would be missed by the corporation men, and he then lifted the lid. Inside he found the usual household rubbish as well as an unusual piece of leather, but he was only interested in the array of unused female make-up items such as, lipsticks, compacts, eye brushes and even a pink toothbrush. He picked them all out with his gloved hand and placed the lot in a brown paper envelope he had in his pocket and placed the lot into his overcoat inside pocket. He then waited to make sure the rubbish lorry missed collecting Williams' rubbish, and then he headed off to the station. Once there he instructed a Garda to take the contents of his envelope and get the fingerprints on the items checked, if possible, for a match with the body in the case.

Two hours later it was confirmed to Detective O'Connell that the fingerprints belonging to the murder victim matched the fingerprints on the cosmetic items taken from the Williams' dust bin on Marine Drive. In addition, identification was confirmed with dental records from the dentist on Sandymount Road. The post-mortem had also revealed that the body was dead before it entered the water, and death had occurred from the two bullets removed from her heart. Armed with this information, Detective O'Connell and a colleague went to the Thomas Cook travel agency in Grafton Street to convey the sad news to David Williams that the body in the case, found on the strand, was almost certainly that of his wife. Mr Williams, as was expected, showed firstly shock and then a sadness which manifested itself in tears for a minute or two until he asked.

"How can you be sure it is my wife?"

"We have evidence that points strongly that it is her," replied O'Connell, "but we do need you to accompany us now to the morgue for confirmation."

"What is the evidence that makes you think it is Bronwyn?" pushed David.

"There are a few things," answered the evasive O'Connell, "but of course once you identify her, we will be sure."

At the morgue, David, could see immediately that there was little doubt it was Bronwyn. However, he hesitated, to confirm it was her, wondering was there anyone else whom he thought could identify her? The first who came to mind was that mental case next door, Veronica O'Brien. So, he then said.

"Yes, that is my beautiful Bronwyn. Oh, God!! This is terrible."

"One more thing before you go," said O'Connell, as he walked David into an adjoining room that had the suitcase, in which the body was found, displayed.

"Would you confirm that this is your wife's suitcase?" he asked David.

"No sir. Well, not to my knowledge. I have never seen it before."

The two Gardaí then thanked David for his time, gave him their sympathy for his loss, and before they parted Detective O'Connell asked him to call into the station first thing in the morning 8.30 AM if possible as he needed to ask him some questions to help find the person who had caused such a dreadful act. As David walked out from the morgue, Richard O'Connell immediately remembered seeing him and the wife every Sunday morning walk up the church. Something at the back of Richard's mind told him that that memory was important, as indeed was David Williams' hesitation before he made the identification of his wife. Because Richard thought, God forbid, despite the state of the body, if it was his own wife Peg, he'd recognise her immediately!

*

From around 3.00 PM Mikey O'Rourke began to feel a slight itch in his groin area. It was only mildly irritating, and a discrete scratch every 45 minutes gave sufficient relief. At 5.30, however, as he was preparing to go home, he went into the 'Gents' and examined the itchy area to discover he had a mild rash there. He dropped into a nearby chemist before it closed and purchased a bottle of 'Calamine Lotion.' This he applied immediately he got home, and again before he went to bed.

*

The evening papers again led with the 'case in the case' and it now also gave the body's identification as being that of a local woman, Bronwyn Williams. It also displayed photos of the suitcase itself, which the Garda had released, requesting any information on its origin. In addition, the 6.00 PM news on Radio Éireann said the body had been identified as that of Mrs Bronwyn Williams of Marine Drive in Sandymount. The announcement also made a request from the Gardaí to all citizens who might have any information, no matter how trivial they thought it to be, concerning the deceased, or her movements over the last week, or the circumstances under which she was found, to contact the authorities with same. This information could be given confidentially and even anonymously, and would, of course, be treated with complete discretion. A similar request was printed in the newspapers.

CHAPTER 14

Wednesday 9ᵗʰ March

Richard O'Connell showed David Williams into the interview room at Irishtown Garda station.

"Why did your wife decide to take a trip to the UK at this time of year?" was the first question Richard asked.

"She got a telegram from her sister, who had broken her leg, and needed some help while it was getting better."

"Do you still have this telegram?"

"Yes, I have it with me. I thought it might be important." Said David, handing it over, while all the time exuding confidence and basking in his own cleverness.

"You, purchased the ticket for your wife at your Employer, Thomas Cook, is that correct?"

"Yes, sir, which is correct."

"Just call me Inspector, please."

"Very well, Inspector."

"Have you had any contact with your sister-in-law since your wife's body was found?"

"I tried to contact her at her home but got no reply, and yesterday I contacted her employer. But they just told me she was out of the office ill."

"Were you at home on the night your wife sailed for Holyhead?"

"Yes."

"You did not go into work the next day, last Thursday the 3ʳᵈ and also didn't show up at the Drama meeting which I believe you are part of, so, please tell me where you spent the day and the evening?"

"These questions Inspector! Surely, you don't think I had anything to do with the death of my beloved Bronwyn?"

"Mr Williams, I need to explore all possibilities so, as an expression of cooperation, I request you to answer the question?"

"Certainly, Inspector, I have nothing to hide. I had the day off on Thursday and I spent it in walking the Wicklow mountains. I carry a small one-man tent in my car, so I camped out for the night, as I often do when my wife is away."

"I suppose you camped out in an isolated place where no one could verify your story?"

"Unfortunately, that is probably the case."

"Did you recognise the suitcase in which your wife's body was found?"

"No, Inspector, I have never seen it before."

"Thank you for your cooperation, Mr Williams. We will keep in touch with you regarding developments. Meanwhile, please do not leave the country, as we may need to get in touch with you urgently. Oh, and there is just one more thing, we will need to check your movements, as a matter of routine only, so we will be calling on your employer to verify dates you have been on leave, sickness, and travel etc."

"That is quite alright Inspector, I understand fully, and I appreciate thoroughness."

David then, being on compassionate leave, headed home to just sit and think about what he had just been through. He recognised in O'Connell a smartness that was just kept under the surface, and it was something David needed to constantly be aware of. He also knew now that some of the letters he'd intended to write were now not appropriate.

As he went in through his front gate, he noticed the dust bin and went to bring it out into the back. He was more than surprised to see it had not been emptied. He thought it was odd but at the same time, maybe it was good because he took out a piece of leather that was probably better discarded in a rubbish bin in town, rather than the chance of it being found in his bin. The gun and its accompaniments had yesterday been flung into Dublin Bay from the end of the pier in Dun Laoghaire. So, all in all, following a cup of tea he felt he needed to drive out to Glencullen, park the car, and do a ten-mile hike to think how best to proceed from this point on. One thing was for sure in his mind, though, all contact with Eileen should be avoided until well after Bronwyn's funeral.

*

The Novena

As Canon Skeffington had arranged with his two curates, each of the priests of the parish would visit Dermot Shaw in hospital on different days to avoid two or even the three of them arriving at the same time. Saturday coming was allocated to Fr McKenna, but today it was the turn of Fr Crampton.

Arriving at Shaw's bedside Fr Crampton made his greeting and then announced his intention to give the clerk Holy Communion. Shaw, who had improved considerably, agreed immediately, his speaking voice returned, if somewhat weak. The priest kissed his 'stole,' placed it around his neck and then produced a 'pyx' from his pocket which held the 'Blessed sacrament' host. The ritualistic prayers followed, and Shaw's tongue received the body of Christ. Following the clerk's prayers of thanksgiving, they continued a somewhat difficult general discussion, with the volume of Shaw's voice not helping the hearing-impaired priest.

Finally, they said their goodbyes but just as the priest had moved slightly away, Shaw call him back and spoke.

"Don't forget. Place the collection-money in the Sandymount bank parish account!"

However, what, slightly deaf, Fr Crampton heard was.

"Don't forget. Please collect honey in Sandymount, thanks, it is paramount."

To get clarification, the priest asked. "Which shop?"

There being only one bank in Sandymount Shaw wondered what the priest meant but said.

"The one near Lafayette and Fry!" Of course, the only thing the priest picked up was Lafayette and Fry, the name of the large grocery store on the corner by the Green.

"Certainly, Dermot," replied the priest, "it will be a pleasure. I'll deal with that." And as he was leaving, he thought that he could have Fr McKenna bring the honey with him on his Saturday visit.

*

At 9.30 AM Inspector O'Connell was sifting through some twenty odd calls that had come into the station relating to the Bronwyn Williams case. Two in particular caught his eye. The first one was from an anonymous male caller who reported having seen the husband of the victim go into a wig shop, opposite 'The Old Stand' in Exchequer Street, about a year or so ago and come out with a parcel under his arm.

The second caller was a leather worker and cobbler who had a shop in Trinity Street. He thought he recognised the suitcase.

While Richard was pondering these, a young woman rang in to speak to him regarding the case. She would not give her name, and Richard got the distinct impression that she was attempting to disguise her voice.

"Detective O'Connell, you are in charge of the Bronwyn Williams case. Is that correct?"

"Yes, Madam, or is it, Miss?"

The caller almost answered Miss but stopped at M.

"That is not relevant, and I told the Garda who answered first I did not wish to be identified as I really feel badly about doing this, but I also feel it is my duty. You see, this may all be quite innocent, but the papers said, anything at all that might be relevant to the case should be reported."

"Yes," replied Richard, "please tell us what you know?"

"I have seen some weeks ago, at around 5.00 PM, Mr David Williams together with Mrs Eileen Hannigan also of Marine Drive in Sandymount appearing to act in an intimate way on the North Circular Road near where the cattle market is held." There was then a silence which Richard felt he had to break.

"Yes," he said, thank you for that. Is there anything else?"

"Well, yes, you see anytime I have seen them in proximity since, they seem to make it a point that they hardly know each other!"

"Oh, I see." Said Richard, thinking, now, that is interesting.

Before leaving the station, Richard received a call from Inspector Simon Lawrence of Scotland Yard. The call was answering the call Richard had made to him the previous day, asking if he would check up on a Miss Bethany Sheridan at an address in Charing Cross, and who worked at the 'Foreign Office.' Lawrence had had an officer make the checks, and he reported to Richard how she was supposed to be in Ireland with her sister recuperating from lockjaw. On hearing this, Richard expressed his concern for Bethany's safety, telling Lawrence that her brother-in-law, the husband of her murdered sister, was of particular interest in the case. It was therefore in Richard's interest and now, in the interest of Lawrence, to try to establish if David Williams had been on board the mail boat and perhaps continued to London, where he had a hand in the disappearance of Bethany. So, Richard suggested that Lawrence make a check of car-hire outlets near Euston station to see did if a David Williams hired a vehicle on the morning of Thursday 3rd March. A bona fide driving license would be required for the hiring. Also, having now the telegram received earlier from Williams, he asked Lawrence to check if it had been sent from the Charing Cross post office on Tuesday 1st March by Bethany Sheridan.

*

Richard's first call along with Sargent Boyle was to the 'Timothy Maguire' cobbler's shop in Trinity Street Dublin. When Richard had introduced them to the man behind the counter, he inquired.

"We are looking for Mr Michael Maguire."

"I'm your man." Answered the big man with the big hands.

"You contacted us regarding the suitcase in which the body was found. That is correct, isn't it?"

"Correct," replied Maguire, and continued. You see, I'm nearly sure my brother made it some time ago for a big country man. If it's the one I'm thinking of, he also made a briefcase for the same man, and your Coppers will like this! The briefcase was made with a false bottom."

Richard looked at Boyle and they both smiled.

"I'd have to see the suitcase, mind you, not that I've seen it before, but I'd have a good idea of my brother's work. But apart from that, on some part of everything Tim made he always put his initials. Very discretely, you'd really have to be looking for them but if he made it, it'll be there. TFM for Timothy Francis Maguire, just like an artist signing his work and sure that's what he was."

"When you say was, does that mean he is ……"

"Oh no, sorry, he died just last year. It was a tragedy."

"Well, please accept our sincere sympathy, Mr Maguire. But please, what was the tragedy?"

"Well, I suppose it was his own fault. Jaysis, he loved the jar. He got himself pissed and fell into the canal on the way home one night. An awful loss of a great craftsman."

*

Inspector O'Connell looked around at the various wigs and hair pieces on display before he rang the bell and the assistant almost danced out with a flare.

"How may I help Sir?" he said, giving Richard his best smile.

"I'm Garda Inspector Richard O'Connell." Richard said, holding out his identification badge. "I need a list of every male who bought a male or female wig or hair piece from January to April 1959?"

The assistant produced his receipt dockets covering the period, handed them to Richard and said.

"Our clientele is mostly females. Our customer numbers are four female clients to one male. Now, I'm afraid I've just not got the time, Sir, to pick out the men from the women but be my guest."

Only two male clients stood out as interesting for Richard and they both had bought wigs on the same day; one was a Thomas Masterson on Sandymount Road, and the other was a Michael Collins of some address in Blanchardstown. The Blanchardstown gentleman was only of interest to Richard because his name was that of one of his hero's, 'The Big Fella' of the 1916 Irish rising against the British.

The Thomas Masterson of Sandymount, however, was at least a connection.

Richard asked the assistant if he remembered the customer.

"You should be so lucky, I should think!" He said firstly, but then said. "Actually, I think I do remember him, he was buying a woman's wig! You know what I mean, I think it was for himself. He was very nervous and very good-looking except for a little scar on his lip. Well now there! I amaze myself!"

"Thank you for your help." Said Richard, having noted down Masterson's and Collins' addresses.

*

3.00 PM, Nora Masterson checked out her disguise clothes for her confrontation with Thomas the next day. Then it occurred to her that if she was going to confront him, a disguise would not be necessary. She was really still in a quandary about the whole thing. At one point, she had even thought about ignoring her husband's indiscretion completely, as she knew, that once he knew that she knew, nothing in their lives would be the same again. Then she wondered how she could keep up such a subterfuge. Well, she thought, it did not seem to bother Thomas. Then she wondered, for the first time, how long had this been going on. Was it just a recent thing? Or had it been going on for years? No, she decided, this needed to be brought to a head, and she would do just that tomorrow night, but something told her it would be best to wear her disguise, as once she was in plain view, there was no going back.

*

Eileen Hannigan answered her doorbell at approximately 4.30 PM. She immediately recognised Peg O'Connell's husband, accompanied by obviously another Garda in plain clothes.

"Good afternoon, Mrs Hannigan, you might remember me from the other night. Richard O'Connell, Garda Inspector, and this is Sargent Boyle."

"Of course, I remember you, Inspector. How can I help you?"

"Well, would you mind if we came in for a few minutes, I need to ask you a few questions?"

With this last sentence, Eileen felt her world begin to disintegrate around her. She could see in her mind, James' face, with an incredulous look, on hearing she'd been having an affair with the dead woman's husband.

"Of course," she said, stepping aside and opening the door to the living room for them to enter. Once the three were seated facing each other, the Inspector said.

"I'll come straight to the point Mrs Hannigan, we have received information, that you and Mr Williams the murder victim's husband were seen together, acting in a very friendly way, on one Sunday recently on the North Circular Road. Now, before you confirm or deny this, I need to caution you Mrs Hannigan that you should be careful how you answer, as we are investigating a murder here."

"Who said they saw me….us?"

"We are not at liberty to say, but please be assured that as far as possible and if it is possible, your name will not be brought into any proceedings unless you are involved or, indeed, it is necessary. In other words, if you were in a relationship with Mr Williams, we would not tell anyone unless it became necessary. That also, by the way, includes not telling your husband."

Richard used the last sentence as a veiled threat. Eileen thought maybe she should offer then a cup of tea, but then thought, perhaps it was better to just tell the truth and pray and hope for the best.

Before Richard and Sargent Boyle left the Hannigan household, they had discovered that Eileen and David Williams had indeed been involved in a romantic affair and the address of the flat on North Circular Road was where the liaisons had taken place. She also told them about the briefcase with the false bottom concealing a hammer, together with the lie about the perfectly good shelf under the shelf that needed to be repaired. Richard had also requested her to give a signed statement down at the station and to avoid further meetings with herself and Williams, if possible. In addition, she should, as he expected she would, not mention a word of what she had told them to anyone else, including of course, Williams.

*

The doorbell on Thomas and Nora Masterson's house rang at about 9.20 PM. Nora went out and answered. The elder of the two men spoke.

"My name is Inspector O'Connell, and this is Sargent Boyle, does a Mr Thomas Masterson live here." Asked Richard, tired now after a long day. It had taken three door knocks from the original address to finally track down Masterson.

Nora, almost lost control of her bladder. Jesus Christ, she thought, it's the knickers! He had robbed them off the line next door and somebody has seen him.

"What did he do?" She asked, her voice quivering.

"Well, nothing, as far as we know," answered Richard, "we just want to see him for a few minutes, if he lives here?"

"Thomas," she called, "the police are here to see you!"

Thomas showed them into the front sitting room and once all were seated, he asked how he could help them. At the same time, Richard noted the slight scar on Thomas' upper lip.

"We would like to talk to you alone, Mr Masterson, on a confidential matter." Said Richard, while at the same time looking at Nora.

"Oh, Nora love, would you mind making a cup of tea for these gentlemen? It'll warm them up on a cold night like this." Requested the Thomas.

Nora looked at her husband like she was ready to kill him.

"Yes, love, of course." She managed to reply with some credibility.

"Oh, and would you mind closing the door behind you as you go out, please? Said Thomas. His wife obliged by slamming the door as she headed for the kitchen, thinking, what was she missing?

Richard kept his voice very low and decided to unsettle Thomas from the start.

"Mr Masterson," he said, "we are aware that you purchased a female wig about a year ago, may we ask you the reason for your purchase?

The blood literally drained from Thomas' face, and he thought he was going to pass out.

"It was for myself…. Eh…" He stammered.

Richard, having succeeded in producing the desired reaction then said.

"Well, that is your own affair, but are you able to tell us anything about the murder of Mrs Bronwyn Williams. Her body was found on the strand, out there," he said, nodding towards the window, "on Sunday last?"

"Look," said Thomas, slightly relieved but still concerned, "I telephoned the station this morning and told your people that I saw the husband go into the wig shop on the same day that I was there. I was just on the other side of the road in the pub. He went in and ten or twenty minutes later he came out with a parcel under his arm. I can only suppose it was a wig."

"You are sure it was Mr Williams?"

"Yes, I am certain, no doubt."

"Very well, Mr Masterson. That will be all for now. However, you will need in the next day or so to come to the station and give us a signed statement about your sighting of Mr Williams."

"Certainly, Inspector, I'll be in tomorrow."

Almost on cue Nora arrived with the tea. She poured it out, gave them all a cup, and made her exit, a little quieter than before. The policemen only took a couple of sips, out of politeness, and were soon gone, but not before Thomas had been informed to keep what he had told them completely confidential.

"What, in the name of God, was that all about?" "Not allowing your wife to know what you, my husband, did?" Nora confronted Thomas.

"Look, I'm not at liberty to say, but between you and me it has to do with the St Vincent de Paul and some clothes handed in that they think belonged to the dead woman on the strand." Thomas quickly invented.

"Oh, my, Jesus, save us!" Nora said, firstly because of the murdered woman's clothes being given to charity and secondly because it had not been about robbing knickers off the neighbour's line.

*

Copper O'Connell climbed into bed at 11.00 PM, he turned out the light and allowed his thoughts to wander to Rosie O'Neill and was pleased to remind himself, that she was still number one in his 'A' division list of females. Long ago, he couldn't remember exactly when, he had divided girls into two divisions. Division 'A' were the girls he loved and had a crush on but wouldn't do anything to them that his religion defined as 'dirty' or 'impure.' Division 'B' on the other hand, consisted of virtually any other girl or even female whom he would like to do 'impure' stuff with. Liking to do this 'impure' stuff consisted of thinking about it when it came into your head. It seemed it would be put into your head by no one less than the devil himself. This fallen angel worked overtime on Copper with little or no let-up. However, once these impure' thoughts arrived, courtesy of old 'Nick' himself, and unless you got rid of them by thinking of something else you were committing a 'mortaler.' So, dwelling on such thoughts represented a mortal sin, punishable, should you die in such a state, by the fires of hell for all eternity.

This situation had been inculcated into Copper's brain since he could remember. The Christian Brothers did offer help in this regard and while never referring to what exactly 'impure' thoughts were, they advised that the best thing to do, when the devious demonic devil put them in your head, was to think of a football match. Not a 'foreign' football match like soccer or rugby, but a Gaelic football or Hurley GAA match. Somehow though, this diversion never worked for Copper, as his whole body, geared up no doubt by the devil, seemed to have a driven urge for sex. This same sexuality that was, as far as he knew, somewhat okay in marriage regarding having babies, but without marriage was not okay at all. So, what it boiled down to about sex was, that nothing in your head, nothing with yourself, and nothing with anybody else, was allowed if weren't married. The Pope himself, down to the bishops and Priests, and the brothers and sisters in religious orders all practiced this nothing. Therefore, it was quite all right and acceptable and completely necessary for everyone else to practice it until they were married.

It was not that the devil did not try to get Copper to have 'impure' thoughts about his division 'A' girls because he certainly did, but because they were 'special' he tried harder to think about a football game when this occurred. It seemed, though, that the older he got, the more influence the devil was having, and sometimes, in Copper's thoughts, division 'A' and 'B' were merged, and all Gaelic and Hurley games abandoned.

Copper soon was asleep, and nature played its part with the 'impure thoughts,' begrudgingly tolerated in dreams by the church, releasing his adolescent male drives.

CHAPTER 15

Thursday 10ᵗʰ Mar

12.05 AM, Stephen Murphy, noisily and drunk, tumbled through the front door of his house on Seaforth Avenue. His wife Mary lay still in their bed, even though the noise had awoken young Stevie, who had begun to whimper. Stumbling up the stairs, Stephen swung open their bedroom door and loudly said to his wife. "Your baby is crying! Can you not be a mother at least, even if you can't be a wife?" Unable to control her own tears any longer, Mary pleaded.

"Please, Stephen, you'll wake the other kids too. Just come to bed." She ignored the curses he mumbled under his breath as he pulled off his clothes, flung them all over the room and slid in beside her completely naked.

"Right, Mrs!" he said, pulling her over against him, "it's time you did your duty."

With all her strength Mary managed to release herself, got out of the bed and out onto the landing where Catherine, young Breda and baby Stevie stood with tears and fear on their faces. Without thinking, she turned and closed the bedroom door just as her husband began to shout and rage, the likes of which she had never encountered from him. Then the smashing of the room began with mirrors, chairs, pictures and what sounded like her dressing table drawers being flung about in mad abandon.

In the deepest stress, but remaining protective of her children, she told Catherine to immediately take the two younger one's downstairs, sit on the settee, and she would be with them in a minute. She then gathered their pillows and some blankets and quickly joined them in the front room, where she wedged the back of a chair against the door handle. The noise upstairs seemed suddenly to stop as she settled Catherine and Breda on the settee and tucking them in. She then settled herself, with Stevie on her lap, on a lounge chair.

*

Copper O'Connell's beautiful and fulfilling dreams he had had going to sleep, by morning, turned to a nightmare. This nightmare, of course, featured Christian Brother Spence, who in a dreamlike state called him into a dark room that appeared to be a torture chamber. Inside the room was the savage dog Henry, chained to the wall, growling and dribbling.

"What is the story of 'Scéal Séadna'?" Spence asked him.

"It's about a boot maker, Sir."

"Well, upon my religious and somewhat stained soul, you amadán you are correct. And tell me O'Connell amadán, what else do you know about the Scéal Séadna?"

"It's about a deal the boot maker makes with a dark man."

"Again, correct O'Connell. But tell me, who is the dark man?"

"Is he the devil, Sir?"

"No, amadán, it is me. I am the dark man and I have a deal for you. I will give you all the money you could wish for, but you must never have anything to do with impurity or ever get married. You must be pure, like me, forever and only think about football matches in which you are not good enough to play. Now, if you don't agree to the deal, you will be punished every day by 20 leather lashes from hell. Do we have a deal, amadán?"

"But Sir, I love Rosie O'Neill."

"You love filth, filth, filth, amadán, amadán, amadán. Put your hand out for hell!!"

With no other choice, John O'Connell held his hands out for his punishment, after which he put each hand under the opposite armpit to give some relief from the stinging pain.

"Oh, it hurts, does it?" Laughed Spence and then added, "I have a remedy for that. Give me your hand here!" With that, he grabbed John's hand and dragged him towards the dog, saying.

"Just allow Henry here to lick each of your palms and the pain will completely disappear." He then pushed John's hand to the open mouth of the dog, and the mongrel snapped its jaws over the hand up to the wrist.

"No, no, no!" the sixteen-year-old screamed.

"Wake up John love," said his mother, Peg, "poor lad. You were having a nightmare. There now, son, it's alright."

"Oh, Thanks Ma. Eh, what's for breakfast?"

*

9.45 AM, precisely John O'Connell's father called into Thomas Cook's in Grafton Street. The manager referred Richard to Freddie Conway, who would check the 'Leave and Absence' log for the confirmation information on David Williams. Once all these dates were confirmed, Richard casually asked Freddie.

"Do you and Mr Williams work the same job?"

"Yes. Well, to be honest, he is a senior clerk, more like a supervisor."

"And is he a hard task master?"

"No, but he's not a slacker either. You know we all like him here. He's a great laugh with his antics."

"His antics?"

"Yes, he's a brilliant mimic, he can take off any county accent even though he has a natural English accent. Jezzz, you'd want to hear him do James Stewart with the drawl. Or Humphry Bogart! Sure, he can do them all."

"Sounds as if he has many talents?" Said Richard, as he bade farewell to Freddie.

"Talents like you wouldn't believe." Answered Freddie, as Richard walked out.

*

Mikey O'Rourke, very sheepishly, entered Robin's Evening surgery. His itch had gotten worse and was now a full-blown rash. He had convinced himself that he had gotten syphilis from Sabrina at Dolly's.

Twenty minutes later in answer to Robin's question as to why he was there, Mikey said he had a rash in his groin area, and he had tried using Calamine lotion on it, but it seemed to be getting worse. He then told Robin that he feared it might be a venereal infection.

"Why would you think it could be a venereal infection?" Asked Robin.

"I just thought that it might be." Came the evasive reply.

"Have you been careful with your sexual behaviour, especially with hygiene?"

"I think so, doctor."

"Alright Mr O'Rourke. Let us take a look. Please stand up and drop your pants and underpants to your ankles."

"Take everything right down to the floor?" Said Mikey, feeling embarrassed at the thought.

"Well," said Robin, as he fixed the forehead reflector light round his head and donned rubber gloves. "I'm not Superman, no x-ray vision to see through your trousers!"

"Sorry. Yes, of course." Mikey said, standing, and eventually having Robin, complete with magnifying glass, examine with eyes and fingers his penis and scrotum and immediate surrounding area. Never in his whole life had Mikey felt so humiliated. Due to his physique and agile intelligent mind no one had ever intimated him but standing there in the surgery he knew he was the cause of his own humiliation and vowed to address his wayward pursuits.

"Alright Mr O'Rourke. Please be assured you do not have a venereal disease. So, you may get yourself dressed. You have what is now commonly called 'jock rash.' I'll give you a prescription for an antifungal cream, and it should see you right."

"Oh, thank you so much, Dr McNulty, you've taken a lot from my mind."

"My pleasure, Mr O'Rourke. And if I might suggest, you should be extremely careful regarding hygiene when taking your own pleasure! That way, such a visit will not be required in the future.

"Thank you again, doctor."

*

Copper O'Connell sat in the Irish class, avoiding eye contact with Spence hoping he would not be asked a question on the story of Séadna so far. This was the procedure Spence followed, at least once a week, by way of revision. However, Copper's hope was in vain as he heard his name called and then the question.

"Sean O Conaill, Cén mhargadh raibh Séadna dhéanamh leis and fear dubh?" *What bargain did Séadna make with the Black man (devil)?)*

Copper knew that the 'fear dubh' was the devil but had no idea what 'mhargadh' meant. So, he tried to think quickly back to the story his mother had gotten from the 'Drama' man. At first, he didn't reply at all to Spencer, hoping against hope that he would just move on and ask someone else. But of course, Spencer smelt blood and repeated the question.

Copper then using the information his mother had given him attempted to answer in his bad Irish. "Suig and fear dubh sa chathaoir agus ansin chuaigh se go dti an áit na tine." *The Black man (devil) sat in the chair and then went to the place of fire.*

"Céard é sin? Céard é sin? Amadán léann tú an deireadh an leabhair. Anois fhios ag gach duine an deireadh!" Scairt Spencer.

"What's that? What's that? Fool, you have read the end of the book. Now everyone knows the end!" Shouted Spence.

As Spence spoke, he moved up to Copper and smacked him full across the head with his open palm and the shouted. "Coinnigh do lámh amach!" *"Hold your hand out!"* as he, like a gunslinger, slipped the 'leather from his pocket. Copper took the four hard ones on each hand, trying to show as little pain as possible, but such was extremely difficult. His hands ached for hours afterwards.

*

6.30 PM as Nora Masterson stood in a shop doorway in Ranelagh, some twenty yards from the bus stop where her husband would get off. She didn't have to wait long, and soon she was trailing him as he made his way towards the Sallymount Avenue turn-off. She didn't follow him down the Avenue because she didn't want 'Nosy Theo' catching a glimpse of her. Instead, she stood at the corner and saw him go through the gate and then the door into the flat.

As before, she had thought she might give her wayward husband and the hussy about fifteen minutes to get down to business before she banged on the door and window and screamed for him to come out and face her. She had even thought that 'Nosy Theo' would be out for a look at some of this action, but she would soon put that 'shite-hawk' in his place. It was bitterly cold, but a clear night. She looked at her watch and when the fifteen minutes were up, she found that her nerve was beginning to go and convinced herself that another ten minutes' wait would be best. She waited the extra ten minutes and then slowly began to walk down the Avenue on the opposite side to the flat. She had, however, only gone a few yards when the door opened and out walked a woman. Nora had to force herself to keep walking and as the width of the road was but ten yards across, she had a clear view of her rival, especially as she walked under the streetlight. Jesus Christ, she thought, she is the image of Thomas. There was no doubt in her mind it was his sister and yes, 'Nosy Theo' had been right, the likeness was so much it looked as if they were identical twins. Oh Christ, she thought, I'm glad now I didn't go banging on the door. With this thought, she waited until the Twin had turned out of the Avenue and then went off herself to get the number eighteen home.

As Nora sat on the bus, a million things went through her head, not the least being why would his sister take her dress off in front of him? But perhaps, she thought, maybe Thomas had looked the other way, or maybe he was in the toilet or not there. But the biggest question of all was, why was it a secret? Did Thomas' mother give one of them up at birth? Or even, was the mother Thomas had, his real mother? All these thoughts ran through Nora's head on the way home and for the next two days. Yet still, she had the thought, it might be a mistress, who just happened to look the image of him.

However, unable to take it any longer she decided, it had to be flushed out this Saturday afternoon, when she knew that instead of rugby he would instead be participating in his shenanigans, whatever they might be, in the Ranelagh flat?

*

As Fr Horgan was giving out the third mystery of the rosary at approximately 8.12 PM Stephen Murphy, in a drunken state, entered the church looking for his wife. Following his night of screaming, he managed to make it into work the next morning and actually teach two classes. He was then free until 3.00 PM. He had needed a drink very badly but had only coppers in his pocket, so he decided that maybe they might give him a pint on tick in the pub. However, as he was getting his overcoat from the men's locker room, he realised he was alone, due to the male staff either in the administration offices or teaching. So, almost without thinking, he began to check if any of the lockers were open. He found two, but each had nothing worth taking. But as the seed had been sown, he quickly crossed the corridor and peeped into the ladies' locker room. Again, this was empty but there he struck gold, collecting almost £3 in notes and coin from four handbags.

Of course, he didn't make it to his 3.00 PM class and partied all day until he had only his bus fare home. But as the bus was passing the Star of the Sea church, he realised that Mary would be in there at the novena carry-on, so, almost falling down the stairs of the bus, he made his way to get the money for a few more jars.

He stood swaying at the back, until he saw her about halfway up on the right centre. As best, he could, he walked quietly up to her seat and half pushed his way in beside her. The majority of the congregation from Mary's seat back, on both sides of the nave, while muttering the 'Holy Marys' responses to Father Horgan's 'Hail Mary's,' were instead focusing all attention on the Murphy's.

"I need ten bobs." Stephen said to Mary, quietly enough."

"I'll be out in half an hour, please Stephen, don't make a show of me."

"Well then," he replied, "give me the ten bob and I'll be out of this fuckin mumbo jumbo!"

Mary quickly opened her bag and rummaged around until she found a single half-crown, which she handed to her husband.

"That's all I have," she said, "now please go, and I'll see you at home."

"I know you've more," he said, loud enough for most around them to hear, but stood up and pushed his way out. The onlookers quickly looked away then, as Mary pulled a handkerchief from her bag to smother her tears.

When Mikey O'Rourke turned away, he noticed Eve for the first time, up a few pews on the Sandymount side, and his heart gave a little flutter. He smiled to himself, thinking he was growing quite fond of this young lady.

With the evening novena session finished, Mikey timed it so that he arrived out the door at the same time as Eve.

"Hello," he simply said to her.

"Oh, Hello Mikey," she replied, giving him a lovely friendly smile. They just kept looking at each other until their mutual gaze was interrupted by Joan, the butcher's wife.

"Goodnight Eve," she said, "are you walking home up Sandymount Road or Tritonville Road tonight? If you're going my way, sure we can walk together."

Eve looked from Joan to Mikey, wanting to walk with Mikey alone, but also not wanting to miss an opportunity to chat with her new friend Joan.

"Oh yes, Sandymount Road, she replied, "and nice to have your company."

Mikey hung back behind them, but then heard an alarmed exclamation beside him.

"Oh, God no!" Mary Murphy muttered, looking straight ahead at her husband swaying drunkenly just inside the church gate. He suddenly saw his wife and shouted.

"Yoo hoo darling, I've come to meet you!" He then started pushing up against those trying to exit as he tried to reach her. Then as the drunken Stephen and the mortified Mary met almost halfway between the church doors and gate, everyone around them, sensing trouble, gave them a wide berth. Stephen grabbed his wife by the shoulders and while shaking her he screamed.

"Give me the fucking money, you, miserable bitch!"

Eve and Joan, who were two of the closest by-standers, stared open-mouthed at the scene with fear and horror on their faces.

At that point Mary was trembling and weeping openly, seeming to be struck dumb. Stephen then began to try and pull her handbag from her arm. His attempt was stopped, however, by the large hand of Mikey O'Rourke, who grabbed Stephen's arm in a vice-like grip and spoke.

"Just hold it there, man, and show the woman a bit of respect."

"You fuck off, ya big country mug, and mind your own business! This fuckin whore's my so-called Missus and my business alone."

Mikey swung him around and lifted him with one hand, almost until their faces were six inches apart.

"No wife deserves to be called that name," he said to Stephen, and then marched him through the parted parishioners to the path outside the gate, where he pushed him further away.

"Go home and get yourself sober, and then apologise to this lady for the embarrassment you've caused her."

Stephen was shaken himself by the strength and power of the man who had pushed him about. However, at the same time, he began to realise that he had seen him before and not just around the neighbourhood.

"Hay ya big bog man," he shouted at Mikey for all to hear, "you should know about whores, sure aren't you a regular yourself at Dolly Fossett's!" And then in a shout continued, "Oh yes indeed ladies and gentlemen of Sandymount this holy fuckin Joe, coming out of the church, is one of Dolly Fossett's' best customers. Go on, deny it, ya bastard?"

Mikey was completely taken by surprise, and the blood drained from his face. He looked over at Eve, Joan and several others who had questioning looks on their own faces. Then he got control again, went right up to Stephen and in a whisper said.

"Say one more word, and I'll break both your hands and arms, and you'll be lucky to ever lift a drink again, you are fucking excuse for a man. Now get yourself home before I kick your arse to kingdom come."

Stephen smirked and knowing he had inflicted the most hurt, slinked off up Sandymount Road.

Mikey turned in the direction of Irishtown where he intended to drown his own embarrassed sorrows in Clarke's public house.

Mary's neighbour Mrs Ryan took Mary back into the church saying, loud enough for Joan and Eve to hear.

"Come on, love, back inside, and we'll clean up your tearful face." They then walked back inside.

Not knowing Mrs Ryan was Mary's neighbour, Joan and Eve decided to wait for a few minutes outside in case Mary needed some support on the way home. So, while they were waiting, Eve asked Joan.

"What are Dolly Follies?"

Joan burst out laughing. "It's Dolly Fossett's, and it's a house of ill repute, a brothel."

"Oh, my God," said Eve, "do you think Mikey O'Rourke frequents a place like that?"

Over the brief time Joan had known Eve, and for that matter, Mikey, Joan had noticed a spark of budding romance between them. So, quickly thinking, not to allow it to be blown out, she replied.

"Who knows what a single man gets up to? Sure, it's his own business if he has no woman in his life to answer to, but he is certainly a fine big strap of a man and a bit of a hero tonight. Don't you think?"

"Yes," grinned Eve, "a bit like John Wayne in 'The Quiet Man.'"

"Exactly," said Joan in reply, as Mary and her companion emerged from the church.

Eve, being now a soul mate of Mary, felt an obligation to protect her.

"Mary," said Eve, "I'm walking... I mean, Joan and I will walk you back home to make sure you're alright going into the house."

"Oh, good, said Mrs Ryan. I actually live next door to Mrs Murphy, "I'm Mrs Ryan. You see, I told my sister I'd drop in on her in Cranfield Place after the novena."

"Thank you all," said Mary, "you are all so good."

"Sure, you'd do it for us." Said Joan.

As Mrs Ryan went towards her sisters' house the three others walked up Sandymount Road with Eve and Joan on either side linking Mary. When they reached Marine Drive, Mary insisted that there was no need for the two to accompany her the rest of the way home. Her two companions, however, insisted on seeing her into the house.

Once inside Mary asked Eve to put the kettle on for a cup of tea and then went to check on the younger kids and Catherine. On returning, she said the little ones were fast asleep and Catherine was in her room studying.

As they sipped the tea Joan asked. "Have you ever thought of leaving him, Mary?"

"All the time."

"And why don't you? Asked Eve.

"Two simple reasons. The first is. How do I support the kids? The second is. Where do I go?"

"Would you not at least come home with me tonight? Asked Eve, "I'm afraid for you. He was so aggressive and didn't care who saw or heard him. Only for Mikey…Eh …. Mr O'Rourke, God knows what might have happened. There'll be no one here to protect you once we're gone."

"I know, actually, I have never seen him as bad as he was last night or tonight."

"What happened last night? Asked Joan.

"Screaming and shouting and breaking up furniture in the bedroom. Me and the kids put a chair up to the door in here to keep him away. But it was very frightening not just for me but the kids, including Catherine, were petrified."

"This is awful," said Eve, looking at Joan, "Is there not a place for women in her predicament to go?"

"Not that I know of. I think the only place to turn to is the police or the convent. I really don't know."

"That's it!" Said Eve, "You and the kids are coming home with me tonight. I can make up beds. We can make ado, at least for tonight."

Before Mary could reply there a sudden loud ring on the front doorbell which made the three women jump.

"Jesus!" Said Mary, it's him, he must have lost his key. You two better get out fast before he starts."

"We're staying with you," said Joan, looking at Eve for support and receiving it.

They went to the door together and fearfully Mary opened it. Emily Jones, complete with walking stick, smiled at Mary.

"I have come to take you home," she said. "I know you are having harassment from your bothersome hubby, so you will need a temporary refuge."

The four women were all bunched together in the hall as Emily explained that she had known of Mary's peril for some time, from her own intuition and some things Mary had said. Also, she had alerted the neighbour Mrs Ryan to keep her informed and updated on the situation. They had both concluded it was now time for affirmative action.

Emily explained that her four-bedroom house had been ready for some time to accommodate Mary and children, if and when it became necessary, and now was the time. Arrangements were then made for Joan to go home and bring back the car to take Mary and her off springs to the safer place. So, with Catherine brought up to date, bags were quietly and efficiently packed. Then Joan drove Emily together with Mary and the two little ones to Emily's house. Eve and Catherine followed on foot, arriving there seven minutes later.

With Catherine tucked up in one room and the little ones in another, all with hot water bottles, Mary for the tenth-time thanked Emily and went to the bedroom allocated for herself.

Sleep would not come, as her mind raced with, on the one hand, relief of being safe, but on the other, of being worried about the future. Her nerves finally gave her no choice but to make yet another trip to the toilet, however, on her way back she noticed the light was still on in Emily's room. Almost in a trance, she tapped the door and heard a whispered.

"Come in."

Emily's sympathetic lovely smile lifted her heart as she walked over to kiss the forehead of her saviour and tell her, before she returned to her own bed, what a wonderful person she was. Instead, Emily pulled the covers back beside her and patted the bed for Mary to get in. The two simply and naturally moved into each other's arms, and within minutes their relaxed contentment and closeness induced the peace of a beautiful sleep.

*

While all the commotion was going on outside the church with Mary and Stephen Murphy, Fr McKenna had been rostered to hear confessions along with Fr Horgan.

One female penitent having received absolution and their penance said.

"Father, I need to talk to you about a matter that I'm afraid to do anything about, but I think you would be the man for the job!" The priest secretly sighed to himself, hating this kind of opening, especially in confession, where he just knew it was going to be something he would not like.

"How can I help you?" He asked.

"Well, Father I live over a flat on Newbridge Avenue and below me in the basement live the Brannigan family, a husband and wife and a little boy of four years old. The problem is that the husband beats them up on a regular basis. Also, when he leaves the house, I found out, he won't allow her to put on the lights, and she cannot put any more coal on the fire until he comes back home. This is usually when the pub is closed, and it's mostly then he starts hitting them. It would break your heart, Father, particularly to hear the little one crying."

"Have you informed the Garda? Or the Prevention of Cruelty to children, people?"

"No, Father. I'm afraid he'd know it's me, and then maybe he'd give me a belt! Sure, I wouldn't put it passed him."

"Are you married?"

"Yes Father."

"What does your husband say about it?"

"He says I should mind my own business. What goes on in a marriage, he says, is between husband and wife and should be no concern to anyone else. But Father, I'm afraid he'll kill her, and the damage he's doing to his own little child is pitiful!"

"I'm not certain," said the priest, "that I could do a lot myself, but give me the address, and I'll call on the flat."

She gave him the number and at first, he thought he would leave it till next day to confront the situation, but then thought maybe the mother and child would be dead by then.

It was 9.20 PM by the time Fr McKenna got to ring the Brannigan's door. A few seconds later, a feeble female voice answered through the still-locked door.

"Who's there?"

"It's Father McKenna from 'The Star of the Sea.' Could you open the door, I'd like to talk to you for a minute or two?"

The door opened only very slightly. The woman held her head down and away, but not far enough to conceal the bruises on her face.

"Look, Mrs Brannigan," said the priest, "if you are in trouble in your family situation, which I am informed you are, then you can get help. You may be prepared to put up with it yourself, but I believe you have a child who is an innocent and might need attention."

"I'm afraid to do anything, Father. I've a sister in London working on the busses, and she has a small flat. She said she would take us, but I'm afraid to leave in case he'll find us. And sure, I've not even a penny to my own name."

"Look, Mrs Brannigan, do you want me to help?"

"Yes Father," she replied, now crying, "I need someone to help me and little Jimmy. We are so afraid."

"Look," said the priest, "I'll have to make some short-term arrangement, and then we can work out something more permanent. But will you be alright tonight? As it is too late now to do anything unless you want to get Jimmy and stay at my home tonight. That's all I can think to do at present."

She was about to answer when an approaching drunken male voice said.

"What the fuck do you want with my wife?" Are ya here to give us some of all the wealth, you shower of bastards, keep collecting from the poor?"

"I was just making a parish call on your home. Mr Brannigan. Is it?"

"I don't want any talk with you bastards, I'm just back for me cigarettes!" "And you," he said to his wife, "keep that door closed, and I'll deal with you when I get back."

Fr McKenna hid down the lane by the A.O.H hall and waited till Brannigan went by on his way back to 'Clarkes' in Irishtown. Then he waited another five minutes to make sure he was gone. The priest then went home immediately and made two telephone calls. The first was to the police, who said they would get someone there as soon as possible, and the second one was to a couple who lived on Thorncastle Street in Ringsend. Then he went immediately back to the Brannigan flat but got no reply but kept trying until a Garda arrived, on his bicycle.

"I'm not getting any answer," the priest said to the Garda. But then from the upstairs hall door a woman appeared and addressed them both.

"That poor woman and the child have gone about ten minutes ago; I don't know where, but wherever it is she'll be better off."

"Which direction did she go?" asked the Garda.

"I'm sorry, but I didn't notice that. My husband told me to close the curtain and mind my own business."

"Well," said Fr McKenna to the Garda, "I didn't see them going in the direction of Sandymount! Did you see a woman and child go towards Irishtown? The Garda replied that he had not, so both men took off towards Landsdowne Road and Herbert Road and further on for about half an hour but all to no avail. The Garda said he would tell his colleagues to be on the lookout for them, and Fr McKenna thanked him and went home hoping and praying they would both be okay.

*

Around 10.00 PM as usual, Johnny Rags turned into the lane off Tritonville Crescent. Once he was alongside the big square ESB metal box, Elvis began again, *you're so square and baby, I don't care.* But then Johnny noticed that the cardboard boxes were put up at a 45-degree angle to the side of it and another in front. He was not particularly interested until he heard a little whimper. It must be a cat or even a rat, he thought, and he gave the cardboard a kick. He jumped back shouting, "Beelzebub you bastard be gone!

The poor Mrs Brannigan and Jimmy screamed in fear from the sight and sound of the madman Johnny Rags, until he started to sing quietly, *Now that's alright my mama that's alright with you that's alright my mama anything will do.* And then Johnny said quietly and gently.

"Now that's alright. What are you doing here with a child on this cold night?" But the only answer the woman could give was.

"I've nowhere else to go!"

Elvis began to sing again, *He's a poor boy, poor boy, poor boy, and he is lonesome, and he is blue, but he'll never be a poor boy if he had a daddy like you.*

CHAPTER 16

Friday 11ᵗʰ March

Having heard the Angelis bell, Johnny Rags O'Keefe cautiously peeped over the side of the top bunk and quietly gasped when he realised, he had not dreamt meeting the woman and child last night. The two were cosily tucked up, fast asleep in the bunk below him. *Well, blessa my soul what's wrong with me, I'm itching like a man on a fuzzy tree. I'm all shuck up!*

*

Mrs Ryan knocked on Mrs Jones' Claremont Park door at 9.30 AM. Emily showed her into the sitting room and told her she'd get Mary in to see her.

"How are you today, Mrs Murphy?" she asked Mary.

"I'm much improved," Mary replied, "and I believe much of it, I have to thank you for! Everyone has been so nice."

"Ara stops, will ye." Replied Mrs Ryan and continued. "I have here a letter from Dr McNulty it was delivered by his housekeeper Mrs Byrne to me, when she found out you were not there. I told her I'd give it to you, and I didn't tell her anything else. She said it was important that you got it before 11.00 AM today."

Mary took the envelope, which was addressed to herself and her daughter Catherine. Inside, the message simply said that if Catherine was interested in a hotel management traineeship at the Shelbourne hotel on St Stephen's Green, she should report there at 4.00 PM today for an interview with the hotel manager, Mr Paul Crothers. She should also be aware that, if successful, she would be required to 'live-in' from this Monday coming 14ᵗʰ March and would also be required to continue her course at Rathmines. If, however, Catherine was not interested in the position, Mr Crothers should be informed, and the interview cancelled.

Mary handed the note to Mrs Ryan to read and sat back thinking, God is good and so is Robin.

*

A call came into the station for Inspector O'Connell from his counterpart Inspector Lawrence of the 'Yard.'

"Hello Richard, I hope your weather is a little better in Dublin than it is here. The rain is pouring down!"

"Simon," said Richard, "you can believe me while it is not raining here at present we get so much of it, it is only a matter of time before it starts."

"Well, I suppose that is why you have such a beautiful, lush green country. But to business! Firstly, there is no record of a telegram sent from Charing Cross post office on Tuesday, March 1st by a Miss Bethany Sheridan. So, I'm afraid that is a dead end. Secondly, we have checked, on your request, about the five car-hire companies within a radius of three miles from Euston station, but no one by the name of Williams leased a vehicle on that day. There were several Smiths and even one Jones together with the usual foreign tourists from France and Germany etc. but even these would have needed a valid driving license. So, you may be sure he didn't hire a car from the immediate vicinity of the station."

"Look, thank you so much for your help, Simon, I owe you a pint. Nonetheless, please keep me posted on any progress you have finding Bethany Sheridan."

"Most certainly, Richard, and I'll look forward to that pint sometime. Cheers."

"Goodbye and thanks."

*

Having waited for nearly 30 minutes, Vera O'Brien was shown into Robin's surgery by Mrs Byrne at approximately 10.00 AM. Vera, said. "Good morning" to the doctor, and handed him the unopened envelope from The Canon, and continued with a smile.

"You need to see if I've lost my marbles?"

Robin, with raised eyebrows, looked at her in return and then opened the envelope and read the note:

Dear James,

I would be obliged if you might examine Mrs O'Brien for 'Delusions' and 'Religious mania.'

She claims she is having apparitions (in her bedroom). It seems Jesus himself is a regular visitor, while on occasions, St Veronica accompanies him. Other people have been present during these apparitions but do not see them. In addition, there is no conversation between Mrs O'Brien and those who appear to her.

Mrs O'Brien presents as quite rational and well versed in matters surrounding revelations and apparitions.

She has given me her permission for you to report her mental state back to me. You, of course, may confirm this.

Sincerely,

Michael Skeffington PP

"Well," began Robin, "tell me Mrs O'Brien how is your general health today? Is all well with your tummy and your water works?"

"All fine in both departments, thank you, doctor."

"And your menstrual cycle, all, okay?"

"All okay."

"That's great Mrs O'Brien and I will give you a full physical in a few minutes, but firstly tell me if there is anything else on the physical side that is bothering you?"

"My eyes. I seem to be finding it hard to read, and I expect I need some reading glasses."

"Quiet," said Robin, "not an uncommon happening as we get older. "Firstly, however, I need to ask you several questions regarding your apparitions."

Then, based on his knowledge of various manifestations produced by mental disorders from shell shock to delusional states and numerous instances of mania and depression, Robin began his questions. He smiled at Vera when he finished and spoke.

"Well, Mrs O'Brien, my diagnosis is that there is nothing whatsoever wrong with your sanity. So now, let us see how your health stands up to a physical examination. Robin then did the usual checks on her blood pressure, breathing, heart rate etc. and finally, he spent quite a long time checking out her eyes, which apart from looking into them with a lighted instrument also entailed having her read different size letters from a chart on the wall. He then went back with the lighted instrument and looked into her eyes again.

Well," he said, "apart from your eyes, Mrs O'Brien, you are in excellent health. But unfortunately, you have developed cataracts on both eyes, but these can be removed with a simple enough operation which of course will improve your sight. So, I will arrange for you to see an ophthalmologist, and we will set that procedure up most lightly in the Eye and Ear hospital on Adelaide Road. I should also tell you now that there is every likelihood that the visions you are experiencing, are a result of your impaired vision, caused by the cataracts. It is my belief that you are suffering from a condition that was first described by a gentleman called Charles Bonnet in the second half of the last century. Simply put, your impaired sight is causing you to hallucinate and because of your religious, shall we say, dedication, these hallucinations are religious in nature."

Robin then looked straight into Vera's face to see her reaction.

"Oh, thank God." she said, "To be honest doctor I did not feel in any way mad, but at the back of my mind I was worried. Thank you so much. I can tell you it is a difficult thing to think that Jesus is visiting you in your bedroom."

"Yes, indeed it must be," replied Robin, turning away quickly to avoid her see him stifle a smile.

*

Following the Friday Novena session, Mary, Joan, and Eve walked together up Sandymount Road. They were unaware that Mikey O'Rourke was walking behind them at a distance of about 30 yards. Mary told the two others that she had gone back home at 11.00 AM thinking Stephen had gone to work but found him still in the house. He had apologised profusely for frightening and embarrassing her and the children and begged her not to leave him. However, he had then gone off to work, knowing that it was payday, and the whiskey and stout would flow later on. But Mary was hoping that giving him, yet another chance might temporarily give her some little time to decide her future.

Joan and Eve looked at each other, not convinced of this strategy but resigned themselves to avoid interfering where they were not wanted.

"So," said Joan to Eve, "what plans does a free and single young lady like you have for the weekend?"

The Novena

"Well actually, I have a bit of parenting to do, as my niece, Samantha, who is also my godchild, arrives from London at around 12.00 tomorrow and following a quick lunch I have to bring her to the Mansion House where she is entered in an Irish dancing competition."

"Oh, my God," said Joan, "did you know that Joseph and I are big into Irish set dancing. Do you do Irish dancing yourself? And does your niece learn it in London? And how is she in the competition in Dublin? And….." Joan stopped and they all laughed at her enthusiasm.

"Well, let me see," said Eve. "First, no, I didn't know you were an Irish dancer, and no, I don't, nor did I ever do Irish dancing, but my sister Edwina, Samantha's mother, who lives in London, won several medals and cups before she went off and married her Englishman with a GP practice in Hampstead. So, my sister wanted her only daughter, to be proficient in the jigs and reels. The result is, she attends a good Irish dancing school in London and last month won a place to compete to dance in the parade here on St Patrick's Day. If she's successful, she'll stay with me until next Thursday, but if not, she'll go back on Sunday afternoon."

"What are her chances?" asked Joan, but also thinking, couples who cannot have children usually adopt, so they have at least one child to complete their idea of an ideal family.

"Not great really, but she loves coming over here. But you never know? Anyway, it saved me having to go over there for her birthday on tomorrow week! I can make a fuss of her this weekend instead."

"Ah, God help her," said Mary, "sure, we'll all say a prayer for her to win. And tell me, Eve, does your sister in England have any other children?"

"No," replied Eve, and then lowering her voice, she confided to the other two. "Edwina couldn't conceive, despite all the natural and medical assistance processes she tried, so her and her husband Roger Penrose decided to adopt Samantha, whom we all see as a great gift from God. Now Samantha knows she is adopted, but we never talk about it, and I'd be obliged if this goes no further."

The other two nodded conspiratorially, but Joan's heart began to race.

"How old will she be on her birthday?" asked Joan.

"Thirteen," replied Eve, with this answer Joan felt the blood drain from her head. But it was only temporary, as she then realised that 'tomorrow week,' as Eve had said, was the 19th and Joan's excitement waned, and she spoke. "Yes, we will all say a prayer for her."

*

Having wished goodnight to the two-other women, Eve progressed onto Claremont Road towards Serpentine Avenue. By the time, she reached the hockey pitch about halfway, Mickey had caught up with her.

"Do you mind if I accompany you to your home?" He asked, surprising her, as she had not realised, he was walking behind.

"Well," she said, quite gruffly after gaining her composure, "it's a free country I suppose."

"Oh dear," he said, "You don't seem your usual self. Has something happened to you today to upset you?"

"Not me. You!" She said, blurting it out without meaning to.

"Me! What have I done?"

"Oh, sorry, it's none of my business."

"What? Please, Eve? If I have done something to upset you, at least tell me what it is?"

"I'm sorry, Mr O'Rourke. You are none of my business, and I am none of yours. So, it is best left at that."

"Well, it is not best left at that for me. Also, I thought we had gone beyond the Mister and the Miss names. So, please tell me what it is I have done that has you upset?"

She stopped walking, turned, looked at him and quietly said.

"What that man said about you outside the church last night, I thought you would have been above that type of thing!"

"What type of thing are you actually talking about?" Mikey asked, knowing full well what she meant and feeling disgusted with himself that she should be even remotely aware of his bad habit.

"I am not going to put it into words, but I am sure you remember what he said about you. You see, I thought you were a nice man but

192

someone who…" she couldn't finish the sentence and instead said.

"Please, I'm sorry. It is none of my business. May I please walk home alone?"

"Okay, Miss Roberts, you certainly can. You are right, it is none of your business. I'm sorry that you believe what a drunk had to say about me. I'm sorry that you heard it. And now I want you to know that I have no intention of confirming or denying it because it is my own affair. It's not as if we are married, engaged, or even going out together as a couple, then you could take me to task on what anyone says about me. You see, I thought we were good friends getting to know each other, but obviously, I was wrong. It's a shame really because I do like you, and I'm sorry you are upset. Goodnight Miss, Roberts."

Eve went home and cried into her pillow, thinking what an idiot she had been. He was right, she had a cheek accusing him, even if he did visit that Dolly place. Men, she thought, were different from women in their approach to sex. So, with this in mind, she eventually went to sleep glad she was a lesbian.

*

While Cecilia Lombardi was drying her hair at around 8.00 PM, a knock came to her front door. It was a telegram delivery boy. With much curiosity but also trepidation, she read the message while standing at the door. It was from Antonio's father, telling her that her husband had been in a serious accident, and she needed to come to the Salvador Mundi Hospital in Rome post-haste.

Once she had thanked the telegram boy and closed the door, she immediately called Robin, who had just arrived back, obviously tired, from his evening house calls.

"Oh James, I'm so confused, and I know you're tired, but I just got this telegram!"

She then read it out to him, and his reaction was that she obviously needed to get to Rome, as soon as possible, as it appeared serious. He then asked her to get her bags packed for about a week's stay, and he would get onto the airport tonight or first thing tomorrow and organise the first available flight to get her to Rome.

It had been a mad rush what with having to inform her employer, cancel a dental appointment and a golf game with three other women and of course the Drama group. Then there were the decisions about what to bring and what to leave out. But it was only really when she was seated on the plane and awaiting take-off that she wondered just how bad Antonio was.

Unfortunately, when she finally arrived at the hospital, she was only minutes late for his final breath. Arriving at his private room, she met his mother and father, who were both understandably extremely upset. Also, present was a female cousin who introduced herself saying, she had met Cecilia before at the wedding. Cecilia, however, had no recollection of meeting her but was grateful for the cousin's English language ability which enabled communication between daughter-in-law and Antonio's parents. There was no animosity on their part regarding the separation between their son and his wife, they were just understandably grief stricken by their loss.

Cecilia stayed and attended the funeral and was told that the 'will' would be read within two weeks. She advised his parents that she neither expected nor wished anything but hoped in time their pain would heal.

As she sat on the plane heading back to Dublin, she thought about the irony of the whole episode of Antonio's death. It seemed that, as part of his job with the tourist ministry in Rome, he was making a trip to New York to promote the great attractions of the eternal city. Tragically, he was travelling on the Alitalia flight Roma-Shannon-New York route, when the Douglas DC-7C aircraft crashed on Friday 26th March shortly after taking off from Shannon Airport. Cecilia vividly remembered seeing the crash headlines in all the newspapers.

As chance, would have it, Antonio survived the crash with just a broken leg and some minor cuts and bruises. He had then cancelled the New York trip and returned to Rome to recuperate. Then on the morning of the day Cecilia received the telegram, Antonia was trying to cross a busy street in Rome and unable to move quickly enough, due to the encumbrance of his plaster of Paris enclosed leg, he was hit by a speeding bus. The impact was so severe he never actually regained consciousness.

*

Following the evening novena session, Thomas Masterson decided to go to confession rather than wait until tomorrow's hearings. He noted that there was a large body of people waiting outside the confession box allocated to Fr Horgan, but not too many in the queue for Fr Crampton's.

Making his way quickly then to Crampton's box, he knelt down, and began to examine his conscience.

He was, in his mind, confessing the 'Thomas' sins and not the 'Sadie' sins, so he must remember not to get confused. He was convinced in his mind that Sadie 'dressed up' was nothing to do with Thomas. But then it occurred to him that there was a period when he was a bit of Thomas and a bit of Sadie. This short period was obviously when he was putting on the women clothes. Such particular time period might be a sin because it was not 'appropriate' for a man to put on women's clothing. So, it might be just as well to confess to that small period. The changing back, though, was fine, as he was changing back to men's clothes, which of course were most appropriate for him being Thomas.

When the hatch was slid back, Thomas said the opening prayers and confessed, in a low voice, his usual ordinary sins. Then, in an even lower voice, he said.

"And father, I sinned as I was dressing inappropriately as Sadie Masterson." But what the hearing-deficient priest heard was.

"And further, I sinned when I was dressing inappropriately as sadomasochism." Fr Crampton coughed and after muttering 'Dear Jesus' to himself asked.

"Do you think it is right to inflict pain on people or have pain inflicted on yourself when wearing studded leather collars and chains and the like?"

"No, Father," replied the completely surprised Thomas.

"Good man, and do you promise that in the future you will not subject others to physical pain or ask others to cause you physical pain?"

"Yes, certainly Father, I promise," replied the even more confused penitent.

"Very well then, for your penance say, One Our Father and seven Hail Marys and now say a good act of contrition.

As Thomas was saying his penance, however, a part of him was already looking forward to tomorrow afternoon, when he intended to take Sadie outside for a proper walk around the shops in Ranelagh.

CHAPTER 17

Saturday 12th March

Fr McKenna walked in the main entrance of St Vincent's hospital at precisely 8.45 AM. He was carrying a small paper bag, which Fr Crampton had told him was the honey Dermot Shaw had requested. Fr Crampton had thought it was a strange request, nonetheless, he was happy to oblige. It was the least of his concerns, as he had other, more pressing things on his mind. Firstly, there was the fact that he had to be back at the church for confessions at 10.00 AM. Secondly, he had to sort out something more permanent for Sarah Brannigan. As a last resort, he thought, he could give her the money he had saved, from his meagre priestly salary, for a week's holiday to the Isle of Man. This would help pay her and the child's fare over to her sister in London. Thirdly, he really needed to make some big decisions about his life in general and about his life and his friendship with Patrick.

Arriving at the ward door, he was met by Dermot being wheeled out in a wheelchair.

"Oh, Dermot," said the priest, "are you off somewhere?"

"Yes. Hello Fr Mc Kenna. I must go for some tests. I think I'll be at least an hour, but if they work out, I'll be home on Monday or Tuesday."

"That's great news, Dermot. Look, I'm sorry I can't stay. I have confessions at ten, but here is your honey from Fr Crampton." Dermot, a little confused, took the honey and put it on his lap.

"Thank you for coming Father, and don't bother coming again as I'll probably be home on Monday."

"Well, I hope so," replied the relieved priest, as he made his farewell and headed back to Sandymount to consider, as far as he was concerned, much bigger issues.

*

Saturday morning Confessions ran from 10.00-1200 noon and as it was the last day of the novena many penitents queued at the box designated to the facilitator Fr Horgan. It seemed everyone wanted to confess to him. Vera was of course the first in the queue, on the altar side. She had a serious sin to confess apart from her usual serious sins. This serious sin had occurred with Raymond making off for the North on his second monthly trip last Wednesday. She knew in her heart that he would probably, in the holy time of Lent, be bringing more of those sinful frenchies into her home. So, on Thursday, she had called the operator and asked to be connected to the customs office in Newry County, Down. Once connected, she informed the officers of the number plate of Raymond's Austin A40 car and that the driver, Raymond O'Brien, would be attempting to carry restricted goods from the North over the border to the South.

Veronica O'Brien began her confession.

"Bless me father for I have sinned, it is a week since my last confession. I had bad thoughts about my neighbour's husband. I spoke a bad word when I hit my hand. Not only that, but I took the name of the Lord in vain. And I told the Police and Customs in the North that my husband was bringing illegal goods over the border, and all I thought was that they were sinful contraceptives, but they found guns, and he was arrested, and I'm sorry, and I want to tell him I'm sorry. But when I do, he might leave me, and the kids and the IRA might kill me for telling. For these and all the sins of my whole life, I am truly sorry!"

There was silence for a second, and then the priest said. Do you know exactly what the sacrament of penance is?"

Vera quoted from her memorised catechism. *"Penance is the sacrament by which sins are forgiven which are committed after Baptism."*

Very good," came the reply and continued. "And how does the priest exercise the power to forgive sins?

The priest grants absolution from their sins to those who are rightly disposed.

"Correct," said the priest, at the same time wondering what he had started, but pressed on anyway.

"And what must a sinner do to dispose himself or herself to obtain pardon in the sacrament of Penance?"

Vera gave the answer she knew well. *"To obtain pardon in the sacrament of Penance, a person must have true contrition for his sins, confess them to a priest, and accept the satisfaction or penance imposed on him."*

"Excellent." Replied the priest. "Now," he continued, "for your penance I want you to say three Hail Mary's and remember that for absolution you must accept the penance I impose on you and that penance is that you must not tell your husband or anyone else in this world, that you told the Police and Customs up North about his illegal activities. Now, do you make a promise to God to forever carry out your penance until death?"

"I do, Father, yes I do."

"Good, my child, now say a good act of contrition."

He then said the words of Absolution, finishing with, "In the name of the Father the Son and the Holy Ghost."

*

There was a hive of activity around Sandymount on each Saturday an international rugby match was played in Landsdowne Road. The ground being a fifteen-minute walk from Sandymount Green. This Saturday Ireland were hosting Wales. The Welsh fans with their red and white scarves, were a very jolly bunch always in good humour and ready to burst into song. The Irish fans, of course, were hoping for a win as so far this season their results were, to say the least, poor.

Thomas had told Nora that his boss had given him the afternoon off from 2.00 PM to see the match as Thomas had rarely asked for time-off, and they were not expecting a lot of the Welsh fans to be buying religious objects that afternoon.

So, at the appropriate time, Nora, once again, got on the number eighteen bus for Ranelagh, giving herself a little extra time for the trip due to the match traffic. When she alighted at the Sanford Road stop and began, with head bowed, to walk towards Sallymount Avenue, a voice behind her said.

"Good afternoon, Madam, I hope you found your friends!"

Of course, it was 'Nosy Theo,' who was obviously wanting to get some information out of her.

"Yes, thank you," said Nora curtly, as she moved on quickly. She could feel his eyes on her back and therefore purposely did not hang around the corner of Sallymount and Sanford but kept on walking on in the direction of the canal. Finally, after about a quarter of a mile, she stopped and pretended to look in a window but checked instead to make sure 'Nosy Theo' was not following her or anywhere in sight. Satisfied, she had lost him, she walked on up to the canal and then back again before she went into a tearoom for a pot of tea and cake.

With these consumed, she noted the time was almost 3.30 PM and thought, it's now or never, and walked to the door of the tearoom and almost bumped into Sadie who was on the way in. Nora's heart jumped and she blurted.

"Excuse me, but I am the wife of Thomas Masterson!"

But as she was looking into Sadie's face, she realised it was not a woman at all, but it was Thomas! He in turn realised it was Nora. They both just stared at each other in complete amazement until another woman trying to get into the tearoom said.

"Excuse me, may I get in?"

They moved aside and then almost simultaneously husband and wife burst into tears of anguish, sorrow, embarrassment, and pity. Nora put her arms up around his head, pulled it down to her shoulder, and still weeping whispered in his ear.

"It's alright love. I love you. We will work this out."

Together, then, in a state of weakness from the shock each had experienced, they walked back to the bed-sit. But just as they were about to put the key in the door, 'Nosy Theo' came out his door and spoke.

"Well now. So, what's going on here, then?"

Nora, opened the flat door, pushed Thomas in, turned to Theo and saying.

.   "None of your fucking Nosy business, you pest. You're like a rat, always looking for dirt, so feck off back into your hole."

With that, she went inside and slammed the door behind her.

CHAPTER 18

Sunday 13ᵗʰ March.

Following the first collection of the 8.00 AM mass, the substitute clerk, Michael, emptied the plate money content into the bank cloth moneybags. He had been informed, by the Canon, on the banking process. With this knowledge, he then took the key from behind the statue of the 'Blessed Virgin' and opened the press to lock up the cash. To his surprise, there was a large bag of money already there. Soon, however, he realised that with all the confusion that followed Dermot's heart attack, last week's collection had not been banked. So, he knew then that today, he would deposit twice the amount as was usual. But then he thought it would be even more as he was expecting to deposit another large amount from the additional Lourdes collection to a separate account, of course.

*

As Joan Lawlor and two of her three children were about to enter the church gates for the ten o'clock mass, she noticed Eve Roberts accompanied by a blond and curly haired, awkward young girl with a limp.

"Eve." Joan called, to catch them before they went into the church. The two turned with Eve smiling when she recognised Joan.

"I was just wondering how you got on yesterday at the Mansion House?" Said Joan with a smile, and thinking, as she looked at the young girl, Patricia probably looks exactly like her.

"Oh," said Eve, "Unfortunately, just at the beginning of Samantha's set, she somehow managed to twist her ankle, and we have decided that if that had not happened, she would have got first place. So, those are the breaks!" And with that, Eve and her young companion burst into laughter, obviously enjoying a private joke. Joan was enraptured when the young girl's laugh had turned to a lovely smile. In fact, Joan had to try to stop staring at her. So, quickly she said.

"You must be Samantha; you are a lovely girl. I'm Joan these are two of my lovely lot. Peter and Nuala.

"How do you do?" said Samantha, in a very posh London accent, to which the other two kids burst into laughter.

"We are very well," said Joan, but some of us need to remember our manners. Samantha smiled again that lovely smile.

"I'm sorry about your ankle," said Joan, but anyway, we better go inside, and we'll catch up after mass."

Joan sent Peter and Nuala up to the children's section and sat herself, two seats behind Eve and Samantha. Throughout the Mass, Joan found it neigh on impossible to take her eyes off the back of Samantha's head. She is so close to Patricia's age, she thought and again fantasised, this is probably just how she looks. Please, God, let me some day see her again before I die!

Thirty-five minutes later Joan, along with her kids came out of the church, almost the same time as Mikey O'Rourke, and recognising him, she said.

"Good morning, Mr O'Rourke of 'light and sound,' I hope you said a prayer for a successful production?"

"Oh yes" he replied laughing, "I said, 'Let there be light, and I heard the sound of trumpets playing!"

Joan laughed, and at the same time saw Eve and Samantha just exiting the gate. She immediately called them over, telling Mikey the young girl was Eve's niece visiting from London. Eve, however, seeing Mikey, half hesitated but then, along with Samantha, joined them.

"Have you got a bandage on that ankle love?" Joan asked Samantha.

"No," she has not," said Eve, answering for her. "I told her she needs to have it strapped up."

"Yes, you certainly do, my girl," said Joan, "you can't walk around with that ankle not bandaged until you get onto the aeroplane this afternoon. Besides, what would your father and mother think of us over here in Ireland, sending you home without even a little care to your dancing foot?"

"Where would I get a bandage today," said Eve, "the chemists are all closed on Sunday."?

"Don't you worry about that at all," said Joan, "Nurse Lawlor has plenty of bandages at home and years of training and experience in putting them on. So, come along with me, and we'll have you sorted out in no time."

"Hold on there now for just a second, Mrs, sorry, Nurse Lawlor," intervened Mikey. "I would never neglect a damsel in distress. My car is parked just here, and I insist you allow me, not only to drive this young lady for her treatment now, but also, I request to be permitted to drive her and her very nice and capable aunt to the airport this afternoon."

Eve turned scarlet. Joan's mouth opened in a surprised grin, and Samantha replied.

"Thank you, Sir. That is most kind."

Surprised again, Joan, Eve and Mikey were taken aback by the sophisticated answer from young Samantha. But Joan didn't hesitate, and she quickly went over to Mikey's car and bundled herself and two children into the back, while calling Samantha over to join her. This left only the front seat for Eve to take beside Mikey.

As they motored up Sandymount Road, Eve said to Mikey.

"This is very kind of you, but we will not impose on you this afternoon. I intend to order a taxi to take us to the airport, her flight leaves at 4 PM, and I'll take the bus home."

"Oh, don't be silly Eve," said Joan, "Mr O'Rourke is delighted to take you."

When she said this, she nudged Samantha with her elbow who quickly added. "Yes, let's go with Mr O'Rourke."

"It will be my great pleasure to have the opportunity to assist two damsels in one day." Said Mikey, as he turned into Marine Drive. A minute later, on Joan's instruction he pulled up outside her house.

"I'll wait here and read my paper till the operation is completed on the young lady," he said, "and then drop you both home, and you can tell me what time you wish to be picked up this afternoon."

"That will be great," said Joan, answering for Eve, "it will take me only ten minutes, and you can be on your lucky way with two lovely women."

Eve was pretty much speechless by it all happening around her but felt unable to change the arrangements, and within minutes Joan, the kids, and she and Samantha were sitting in Joan's front room.

"That man," said Joan to Samantha, "really likes your aunt you know."

"Yes, I think he does Aunt Eve," Replied Samantha, to Eve, "he kept looking at you with a stupid grin on his face."

The three of them burst out laughing and Joan went off to find the bandage, leaving young Nuala alone with Eve and Samantha.

As Joan rummaged in her first aid kit and knowing Samantha had twisted her right foot, Joan wondered how she might check to see was there a birthmark under the inside left ankle. She knew she was clutching at straws and life did not conjure up such coincidences, but she had to hope. So, returning with the bandage, she asked Samantha to put both feet up on a stool in front of her. Quickly then, before the child could protest, she pulled the stocking of her left foot down below the ankle. Just as quickly, though, Samantha pulled her foot away and the stocking slid back above the ankle.

"That's the wrong foot," she said, laughing.

"Oh, so sorry," replied Joan, "what a 'lu-la' I am," she continued, not showing her disappointment as she had seen, in that brief part of a second, that there was no birthmark below the left ankle. Anyway, she thought, what did she expect? The child's name was wrong, as well as her birthdate.

Thanking Joan and about to leave, Eve asked to use the toilet and when she was gone, Joan took the opportunity to wish Samantha a very happy birthday, to which the child replied quietly in case Eve might hear,

"Thank you, Mrs Lawlor. Yes, but it would be nice if my god-mother Aunt Eve was going to be there, but at least my godfather, Uncle Dicky, said he will definitely make it back from his skiing trip. I thought he would be away, but he must be back for a meeting on Tuesday, so he'll be there. He's really funny. He makes me laugh," she continued, smiling. "Before he went, he said to me. Snow going to the snow and Snow coming back from the snow!"

"I'm sorry," said Joan, "I don't get it?"

"Oh," laughed Samantha, "you see his name is Snow, Dicky Snow, and he went to the snow to ski. Get it?"

"Oh yes, now I do" replied Joan as Eve, arrived back from the toilet.

Walking out the door, however, Joan whispered to Eve.

"I'll give you a ring tonight to see how you got on." Saying this, Joan nodded towards Mikey's car and winked. Eve just shook her head and smiled.

Once Joan had closed the door behind them, however, she leaned her back against it and thought, Dicky Snow, well, is the name Dicky Snow not short for Richard Snow? The very name of the man who had fathered Patricia. This, she thought, is really strange.

Before Mikey dropped Eve and Samantha off in Serpentine Avenue, he arranged to pick them up again at 1.30 PM and so have plenty of time to spare. As they were walking to the door, and due to his window being down, he heard Samantha say to Eve.

"He is really nice. I think he would like to be your boyfriend Aunty Eve!"

"Oh shush," was all Mikey heard Eve reply before she closed the door behind them. What she continued to say once inside however was.

"I know he's nice, but I'm not interested."

She was not about to explain to her niece that she was a lesbian, or for that matter, that there was a good chance Mikey visited prostitutes.

*

Six-year-old Nuala came into the kitchen as Joan was basting the brisket of beef for the dinner.

"Mammy," said the child, "why is Peter so bad?"

"He's not bad. He just teases you. He really loves you just like Mammy and Daddy do."

"He is bad Mammy. He said I was ugly, just like that girl Smansra."

"Samantha is her name, and she and you also, are beautiful. Now skedaddle and let me get on with the dinner."

"Okay Mammy. But what is a teenjar?"

"A teenjar? I don't know. Where did you get that?

"Samantha said she would be a teenjar on St Patricks' day."

"Oh, I see what you mean love. What you mean is 'teenager.' Samantha will be a teenager not on St Patricks' day but next Saturday."

"Well, I told her I was six, and she said, she would be a teenager on St Patricks' day."

Not for the first time on this day did Joan's pulse quicken.

*

At 12.40 PM, precisely the church was empty except for the one lady who had heard Dermot Shaw having the heart attack. She was placed, as she had been the previous Sunday, praying devoutly at the 'Crown of Thorns' grotto.

In this position, she did not see Johnny Rags enter, as quiet as a mouse, into the church through the Irishtown side door. He moved quickly up the side aisle until he slipped into the second pew from the top in front of St Joseph's altar.

He then lay down on the kneeler completely out of sight. Everything was quiet except in Johnny's head Elvis began to sing.

The warden threw a party in the county jail
The prison band was there, and they began to wail
The band was jumpin,' and the joint began to swing
You should've heard them knocked-out jailbirds sing

Despite this great song, Johnny could see the substitute clerk come out the vestry door with the candle extinguisher in hand. He first extinguished the candles on St Joseph's altar. Next, he did the candles on the high altar. Then he turned right to head for the Blessed Virgin's altar, and Elvis sang.

Let's rock everybody, let's rock
Everybody in the whole cell block
Was dancin' to the Jailhouse Rock

On cue, Johnny slid like a snake with the speed of a python over the two pews, the altar rail, and into vestry, taking up a concealed position behind the door as Elvis continued.

Spider Murphy played the tenor saxophone
Little Joe was blowin' on the slide trombone
The drummer boy from Illinois went crash, boom, bang
The whole rhythm section was the Purple Gang

Remembering the vestry from his time as an altar boy, Johnny noted no change had occurred over the years. From his pocket, he produced a cloth shopping bag. He then moved with speed again to the fast rhythm of Elvis.

Let's rock everybody, let's rock
Everybody in the whole cell block
Was dancin' to the Jailhouse Rock

He quickly took the key from behind the statue and opened the press and was momentarily shocked to find three money bags instead of the expected one. So, the gift horse by three was immediately secured into the shopping bag, with Elvis showing his appreciation.

Number forty-seven said to number three
"You're the cutest jailbird I ever did see
I sure would be delighted with your company
Come on and do the Jailhouse Rock with me"

Johnny then made his exit through the vestry grounds' door and over a period of four minutes he travelled unnoticed down Tritonville Crescent and into the tennis court lane to finally arrive in his sleeping shed, for the first time ever during the day. As he closed the door behind him, Elvis finished up.

Let's rock everybody, let's rock
Everybody in the whole cell block
Was dancin' to the Jailhouse Rock

*

While Eve was preparing some sandwiches for lunch and Samantha was finishing off her packing the telephone rang.

"Hello?"

"Oh, Hello Eve, Joan here, I just wanted to wish you luck with Mr O'Rourke today. He seems really keen."

"Hello Joan, thank you for ringing but, to be honest, I'm really a bit worried."

"Sure, what is there to worry about love, isn't he is a great catch and obviously, he's mad about you."

"No, I really am worried Joan. I'd really like to confide in you about something before this gets out of hand. Could I?"

"Of course, love, we can arrange that." Both had various things to do what with the 'Drama' society, step dancing, Friends of the Zoo, and children's schools, so it was finally agreed that the coming Thursday they would meet in the evening at Joan's house for a chat.

"Thank you, that is perfect," said Eve, "I'll look forward to catching up then." Before she could hang up, however, Joan said.

"By the way, could you give me Samantha's address, I'd like to send her a card for her birthday, so it gets there before next Saturday the 19th?"

"Oh, that is nice of you Joan, but you'll need to send it pretty soon as her birthday is Thursday the 17th of March, St Patricks' day."

"But I thought you said it was Saturday?"

"No, her birthday party is Saturday, her actual birthday is 17th of March."

"Oh. Okay. And one other thing Eve," pushed Joan, while at the same time trying to control her breathing, "Samantha's godfather, I think I might have known him when I trained in England. Did she say his name was Peter Snow from Bromley Road Hospital?"

"No, his name is Richard or Dicky Snow, and he's at Great Ormond Street."

"Okay," lied Joan, the wrong Snow. Anyway, good luck with your chauffeur this afternoon! Bye."

*

1.30 PM on the dot, Mikey knocked on the door of Eve's Serpentine Avenue home for the trip to the airport. Samantha insisted that Eve sit in the front with Mikey and then, in a child's way, attempted to play cupid by singing Eve's praises to Mikey. She told him of Eve's achievements, good nature, respect for the old, great with children and animals, and she even sponsors a giraffe at the Zoo. And, as he would know, she is an expert on Drama and stage production. Throughout this testimonial, Eve made several attempts to close Samantha off, while Mikey encouraged and egged her on. In the end, Eve just acquiesced in embarrassment, believing she wouldn't have anything more, on the social side, to do with Mr O'Rourke anyway, once this afternoon was over.

At the airport, Mikey parked the car and carrying Samantha's case walked the two females to the departure area. There, he wished Samantha a safe trip home, telling her it had been a pleasure to meet such a pleasant, attractive, and smart young lady. Samantha blushed red from her forehead to the top of her chest but was delighted by the compliment. Mikey then told Eve to take as long as she liked with her goodbyes, but whatever time she came out of the terminal, he would be waiting for her. Just as he turned around to go, however, he nearly bumped into Joan and the husband, the butcher.

"Hello," said Joan to all. "I just caught a glimpse of you from the far door and thought we'd wish Samantha 'Bon voyage'."

"Oh, thank you, Mrs Lawlor. I feel I'm getting quite a send-off."

"Our pleasure." Replied Joan, and then to all. This is Joseph my husband he was just seeing off his cousin from Donnybrook going to New York."

Joseph looked at his wife with his eyes open and jaws dropped, until Joan said to him.

"Well, say Hello, Joseph."

"Hello," he said, wondering why he had allowed his wife to drag him to the airport believing she had found her lost child, and then fibbing as to why they were there. Anyway, nobody seemed to notice or care and Mikey O'Rourke, whom he's seen in his butcher's shop, shook his hand.

*

An hour after Mikey had left them Eve emerged and got into the car.

"I'm delighted to have the opportunity to say how sorry I am for walking off like a naughty child on Friday night." He said sheepishly.

"No," she replied, "It's me who was in the wrong. It was none of my business, and I do appreciate the time you've taken to bring us to the airport. Don't you usually go to the 'Rovers' football on Sunday afternoons?"

"Well, sometimes there can be more important things to do."

"That is a very nice thing to say, Mr O'Rourke, but I'm afraid you may have taken my responses to you in the wrong way."

"Oh, please Eve. I thought we had gone beyond the Mr and Miss?"

"Okay then…Mr Mikey." She said with a smile.

"You know you have a lovely smile," he said, and continued, "and no, I don't think I took up your responses in the wrong way. I am old enough to know that my, shall we say, advances were met with a certain acceptance. Well, enough to give me encouragement."

"Well then, I'm sorry. It is my fault; I have obviously given you the wrong message. Please believe me it is probably because I really don't have much, or to be honest, any experience with men. Sorry again, but I should have said, no experience with a nice man."

"You see," he said, on the one hand you say I'm getting the wrong message but on the other you classify me as a nice man! I'm getting confused. If you want me to just leave you alone I will, but I really don't want to, as underneath I get the impression you don't want me to either."

"Look Mikey, to be honest, I like your company, and you are a handsome man and were a hero the other night at the church. We thought you were like John Wayne in the 'Quiet man,' but I am not interested in men. Now I've said it so…"

They drove on in silence for twenty minutes until Eve said. "I hope we can still be friends."

"Oh Jesus," Said Mikey, "Okay, let's be friends."

For the remainder of the trip Mikey asked her about her connection with the Zoo, her niece, her sister, and her probable new job in the Irish Sweep stakes.

"Thank you so much for the lift," she said, when he finally drove up outside her door.

"Your very welcome," he replied, and added. "Any chance of a cup of tea for a friend?"

"Of course," she said with a smile and a feeling of great relief in her tummy.

Once inside and seated in her front room with a hearty fire and a cup of tea, he said.

"Look, just one question, please tell me, as a friend, why is it that a lovely woman like you is not interested in men?" This question was followed by a long silence until she said.

"If I tell you as a friend, do you promise never to tell anyone?"

"Of course, you have my word."

"Well, I was molested by my mother's two brothers when I was fourteen and since then, I have kept away from all males, only to talk to them. So, I now have become a lesbian, and I'm only really interested in women!"

"Sweet mother of Jesus! You poor girl. Isn't that a dreadful thing to happen to a young colleen? So, you've never even kissed a boy or a man?"

"No, never."

"But you have had like intimate feelings or affections with women?"

"No, of course not, never."

"But then how do you know you're a lesbian?"

"I feel more comfortable in woman's company and want to go out with them and not want to have the same sort of friendship with a man. So, it must follow, there is no doubt, I am a lesbian."

"So, how do you feel in my company? Are you uncomfortable?"

"No, not at all but you're different. You're very nice."

Mikey knew this was a most delicate situation and the wrong word or move could ruin his chances with the woman he had come to love.

"So, tell me Eve would you have any objection if I touched your hand, just for a second, it is such a nice hand?"

"Well….I suppose that would be fine, but you're not going to try anything on. I'm trusting you?"

He slowly leaned over and placed his hand on hers and left it there for a bit. At the same time, he smiled into her face saying.

"It is so lovely to actually touch you." He then took his hand away and sat back.

"Would you please come out with me to dinner one night and perhaps also we might catch a film. It would be strictly as friends only?"

"Yes, just as friends. That would be nice."

"Fine I'll ring you tomorrow and make the arrangements. Alright then. I'd better go while I'm ahead."

"Okay and thank you again for the lift and the hand touch. Would you touch my hand again, it was nice!"

He took her hand and quickly raised it to his lips kissing it briefly.

"Goodnight, dear Eve, I look forward to speaking to you tomorrow."

Eve spent the remainder of the night before falling asleep, taking quick glances at the spot on her hand where he kissed.

*

A preparatory meeting was being held at Maynooth College for the up-coming 1961 Patrician year, a celebration in recognition of 1500 years of devotion to St Patrick in Ireland. This meeting was the first to be held with representatives of the various religious communities around the country. Fr Horgan SJ was one of the speakers, and he advised those present that he would be coordinating many of the religious ceremonies around the country.

Also, attending this meeting was Brother Spencer from Westland Row, who was delighted to meet up with his old friend Padraig. They had met while at the noviciate, St Helen's in Booterstown. Of course, Spence was not aware that the boys in Artane industrial school, where Padraig was a teaching brother, called him Mickey Mouse.

Padraig got this name because, like Spence, he inflicted pain, on the innocent children in his charge. Unlike Spence however, who enjoyed inflicting only physical pain, Mickey Mouse enjoyed inflicting both physical and mental pain but not necessarily with the leather. Mickey Mouse inflicted pain by abusing the boys sexually. He was a cruel and repeating abuser who constantly had an evil, dirty grin on his face. He usually had a harem of four boys going simultaneously. The irony was, of course, that he had himself invented his own nickname. This came about when he was in the process of grooming a boy. He would start by touching the boy's genitals over a period of days, until eventually, he would introduce his own genitals to them by asking them to meet 'Mickey Mouse.' Once this introduction was made, the child's life was hell on earth for up to sometimes two years, until that child was dropped, and a new innocent was brought into the harem.

The Maynooth meeting lasted from 2.00 to 6.00 with a break for afternoon tea where the attendees mingled with each other. During this break, Fr Horgan mingled with as many as he could and stopped at one point to speak to Mickey Mouse and Spence. The conversation briefly covered the use of older secondary schoolboys to act as stewards at the major event of the congress to be held at Croke Park.

Before moving on from this conversation, however, Fr Horgan had found out that they both were from schools in Dublin and had come by train. On hearing this, Fr Horgan told them to meet him at the door once the meeting was over, and he would give them a lift back to Dublin in his car. The brothers were delighted with this offer as it meant, apart from getting back earlier than expected, they could go to a café and have a good chat before they got back for evening devotions.

At precisely 6.20 PM, with Mickey Mouse beside him and Spence sitting in the back directly behind him, Fr Horgan was travelling at a good speed on the main road and enjoying the chat and company. Suddenly, he got a piercing stab of pain in his head. At the same time, an oncoming truck's lights seemed to exacerbate the pain. One second later, Fr Horgan lost consciousness and as he slumped forward onto the steering wheel, his foot increased the pressure on the accelerator and the car veered into the path of the truck at about 80 miles per hour. The impact on the right side of the car was the worst and resulted in priest and Spence dying instantly. The twists, turns, and rolls of the car from the collision amazingly caused the top of the gear lever to break off, leaving just a steel rod still connected to the gear mechanics. The convoluted twists of his body together with the impact contortions resulted in Mickey Mouse ending up with the gear's steel rod lodged firmly through his scrotum and up the shaft of his penis. Throughout this intricate operation of fate and its excruciating pain the Christian Brother had somehow remained in a conscious state for 30 minutes and as he was being moved into the ambulance he succumbed to the peace of death. Others, however, particularly those who believed in an after-life, might take satisfaction that the pain he suffered in his last hours was but a sample of the ongoing suffering he would endure in his final destination.

CHAPTER 19

Monday 14ᵗʰ March

Copper O'Connell had just cycled by Newgrove Avenue, enroute to school. He anticipated, with a bit of good luck, passing Rosie, but with bad luck having to deal with the fuckin dog.

Sure, enough in the distance he saw Rosie walking towards him along the path on his left. In between them however was the hound from hell waiting to attack. As the three actors in the play came together the dog went for Copper, barking, snapping, and snarling. Copper though was ready to implement his counterattack. So, just as he and the dog approached each other Copper swung his left foot back and then forward with a hard kick to the dog's jaw, the momentum of the kick being increased by the forward motion of the bike. The impact echoed with the loud crack sound. The dog was literally lifted off the ground and the fallback hit the ground with a smack. On looking back, John saw the whimpering injured animal slink onto the path beside Rosie who was looking down at it.

Copper felt like Kirk Douglas in the film 'Spartacus' a hero who took on the most difficult of enemy and succeeded. Not only that, but Rosie had seen it all so, not only was he a hero for defeating the dog, but he would also be her hero. Things, he thought, could not get better. However, on that score he was both right and wrong.

Arriving in school, even before he had spoken to anyone, Copper had a feeling there was something going on. Then, from two different boys he heard a rumour that Spence was dead.

"I don't believe you," he said to the first boy, but hoping against hope it might be true, and then asked.

"So, what did he die from then?"

"I'm not sure," came the reply, "I suppose it was TB or cancer!"

"A car crash," said someone else, "that's what I heard anyway."

Stealer had the full story when Copper slipped into the desk beside him.

"Two Christian Brothers and a priest crashed into a lorry. The three wise men all dead. We might get a day off!"

That afternoon, after Spence and the other two holy men were prayed and prayed for, and the class got off early because of the tragedy. Before they left, however, they were told that they would, in fact, get a morning off to attend the funeral mass, but then it would be back to school.

"I knew he wasn't even worth a fuckin day off," said Steeler to Copper, as they got their bikes from the shed. Copper nodded his agreement but was thinking because he was early, he'd be able to see Rosie on the way home.

Sure enough, as he was passing the infants school on Beach Road, he saw her walking home from Roslyn Park towards him. She was about one hundred yards up the road. So, buoyed by his earlier heroic dog deed he thought he might now speak to her. He dismounted, took the bike onto the path, and pretended to be fixing the chain until she reached him.

"Hi Babe," he said, trying desperately to emulate the stance and voice of James Dean in 'Rebel without a Cause.' But she made no reply.

"Hi Babe," he said again, only this time his voice broke a little.

"Poor Henry," she said, "you know you nearly killed him?"

"Henry? Oh, the dog! That animal was trying to kill me!"

"You should be ashamed of yourself, the poor little doggie."

She walked off with a stern look on her face.

*

4.30 PM Detective Inspector O'Connell telephoned Inspector Lawrence at Scotland Yard, advising him that he would be travelling to London next day, and perhaps they could meet for lunch or that pint. He also asked for permission, as a courtesy and not official, to call on the Charing Cross post office, stating that he might just uncover something a local constable had missed. He again conveyed to the Yard's Inspector that he now suspected Bronwyn's sister may also have been murdered. Simon Lawrence said that as far as he was concerned, he would trust Richard to tread carefully. But, as an Irish police officer, he would not have authority to act, as such, in the greater London area. However, the Met would afford Richard their full cooperation and the Garda would be met by a squad car and driver for his use throughout the day.

CHAPTER 20

Tuesday 15ᵗʰ March

Detective Inspector Richard O'Connell boarded the 8.00 AM flight for London. He placed his briefcase in the overhead locker and sat down on the aisle seat, third row. Just as he began to open his copy of 'The Irish Times' another passenger who had just entered the aircraft tapped him on the shoulder.

"Well, you never know who you are going to bump into on this flying lark!" said Joan Lawlor, with a big smile on her face.

"Oh, Hello," replied Richard, immediately recognising her as one of the women he had met outside the Drama thing. But which one? He just couldn't recall.

Joan, realising his dilemma, smiled, and said. "

"Joan Lawlor. I'm the butcher's wife, I met you the other night with your wife."

"Of course," replied Richard. I do remember, but I didn't know you were Joseph's husband. I sometimes have a pint with him in O'Reilly's."

With that, two more people were trying to get to seats further back. Richard nodded for Joan to move on, saying he'd see her when they arrived at London airport.

Joan waited for her small case to be unloaded, picked it up and not seeing Mr O'Connell anywhere made her way through the customs. Upon arriving out the other side, she saw him waving to her as he stood by a small coffee and tea shop.

"May I buy Mrs Lawlor a cup of coffee before she begins her journey into the big and beautiful City of London?"

"Oh, I'd love a cup of coffee, Mr O'Connell, but do you not have to get on with your business?"

"No, I'm waiting for a police car to pick me up and bring me to Scotland Yard. They'll call me over the loudspeaker when it arrives, but I don't expect it for about twenty minutes."

"Then a cup of coffee would be great. I get a very dry mouth when flying. I know it's because I'm so nervous."

When Richard arrived with the coffee and placed the cup with saucers onto the green Formica tabletop, he sat opposite Joan and asked.

"So, what brings you to this big smoke, at this time of the year?"

Joan had been expecting this question since seeing the Garda on the plane and gave him her well-prepared and almost truthful answer.

"About ten years ago, I did my nurse training over here, and so I know this place well. I also have a sister living outside London, but before seeing her I hope to catch up with some of the people I knew during my training. Joseph surprised me with the ticket, as it's a special time of the year for me, so I was delighted with his present and here I am! But you. I suppose you are here for some super-secret police work?"

"Well, yes, but not all that secret to you, as I'm still investigating the death of your neighbour Mrs Bronwyn Williams."

"So, no major breakthroughs yet? Oh, sorry, I suppose you can't talk about it. I should mind my own business. But I really feel sorry for the husband, David. What that man has had to go through. I doubt if I could manage to carry on if Joseph was found under such circumstances."

"And Mrs Lawlor," probed Richard, "did you know Mr Williams well?"

"Only as a neighbour. You know. Good morning and Good afternoon. But he surprised us all that night with the Irish story."

"The Irish story?"

"The Scéal Séadna story. Sure, it was to your wife he told it to! Did she not tell you?"

"Yes, you're right, she did tell me. But she didn't say it was told to her by David Williams. You also wouldn't expect him to be versed in the Gaelic, what with his accent."

"That's exactly what we all said at the time. You never know what some people have in them."

"You're right, Mrs Lawlor. You never know?"

'Attention please, could Detective Inspector Richard O'Connell please go directly to the *main exit where a car is waiting for him.'*

Richard stood up and said he would have to go and thanked Joan for the chat. He then asked if she would like a lift into the city. This, she declined, saying his destination was not in her direction. She thanked him and they wished each other goodbye.

As Joan sat on the train for the first part of her journey that would eventually take her to Russell Square tube station, she thought through the conversation she had on Sunday night with husband Joseph, after the kids had gone to bed.

For the second time, or was it the third, she had gone over all the happenings of Samantha's birthday, and the Richard Snow from Great Ormond Street hospital. Plus of course that Samantha was adopted. But Joseph had cautioned her to remember there was no birthmark? This, she had to admit, was the only glitch in the almost perfect fit. But when he had said this, she had burst into tears yet again. He then took the role she loved about him, and that was his simple and easy but non-wavering way of taking affirmative action when she was floundering in all directions.

"First thing in the morning we will buy you a plane ticket and on Tuesday you can fly over to London and confront Mr feckin Snow and find out the truth! Now that is it,." he said.

And that was it, and here she was. She thought she might have been nervous about confronting Richard after all these years but if he had managed to have access to their child while she could not, then she not only wanted to know why? But Jesus Christ, she was entitled to know why?

She entered the post office and handed in the birthday card addressed to Miss Samantha Penrose and paid the extra in express post to ensure its delivery next day. With that happy chore complete, she set about her desired task.

Upon entering the hospital, Joan went directly to the female toilet and produced a white coat, which she immediately put on. She then placed a stethoscope into the right pocket of the coat, making sure one earpiece was sticking out. She then pinned a makeshift identification tag to the lapel. This would not stand up to scrutiny but would suffice. Finally, she pinned her upright watch to her blue dress and while she neither looked like a doctor nor a nurse, she appeared to be in an appropriate place.

Then, with the confidence and experience of a professional, she found out that Richard was now a consultant surgeon and would be attending a clinical budget meeting in the 2nd floor conference room at 2.00 PM. This meeting was due to finish no later than 3.30 PM.

Joan made her way to the second floor at precisely 1.45 PM and walked past the opened door meeting room, outside of which was an unoccupied desk and chair. She turned around intending to pop her head in on the way back, but from the lift she had just used appeared Richard and another man, both of whom began walking towards her. She held her head confidently high, looking straight at the father of her first child. He in turn was doing the same and now had a smile, albeit surprised smile, on his face.

"Well, I'll be," he said, stopping in front of her. "Joan, how are you? Lovely to see you. What are you doing here, for goodness' sake?"

"It's lovely to see you too, Richard. Well, as you ask, I'm her to discuss Samantha and her prognosis. I won't take up less than ten minutes of your time. Perhaps when your meeting is finished, over a cup of coffee in the canteen?"

Richard's colleague had moved on into the conference room, so only Joan heard his reply.

"I'm not sure what you are after Joan, but I hope for your…and my child you are not going to cause trouble?"

"Nothing like that, I promise. But I think I deserve some explanation of how you have managed to have ongoing access, while me, her mother, was sent to hell!"

"Alright Joan. Calm down. I really must put in a show at this meeting. I'll see you in the canteen at 3.15 PM."

"Make sure you're there." Said Joan, not trying to hide the threat.

"I understand Joan." He said and was gone.

Not trusting him, Joan made her way again up to the second floor at 3.05 PM to make sure he didn't make a run for it. But at 3.07 precisely he came out and, seeing her, nodded a hello. She moved closer and heard him tell the secretary now at the desk, to advise reception that he was being picked up by a Dr Roger Penrose at 3.30 PM but had to meet a staff member in the canteen and might be a few minutes late. With this arranged, he turned to Joan and gently taking her arm steered her toward to lift.

"Well now," he said, "life has been kind to you. You are still a most attractive woman."

"And" she replied, "I can see you have lost none of your charm, or was it always bullshit. I was never really sure?"

"Oh, Joan, I love that Irish directness. That great fire. But let us see if we can sort out this whole thing."

When they were seated with their coffee, he began.

"So, you obviously know the child's name is Samantha and you believe I have access. Is that correct?"

"That is correct. Uncle Dicky!"

"You have met our beautiful girl?"

"Yes, and at least on this we agree. She is beautiful."

"May I ask, how you have met her? And then I promise I will tell you of my connection."

"A neighbour Evelyn Roberts is a sister of Edwina who adopted Samantha. She…Samantha has even been to my house. I even checked to find the birthmark under her ankle. But I have worked that out now, what with her god-daddy being a plastic surgeon. And from what I saw, if only for the briefest second, quite a good one."

"Well, thank you for all that. Now I suppose you deserve to know what happened. I should add that a lot of it was down to my parents but at the same time, selfishly, I was happy to have the opportunity to have access to my daughter. I must stress that Samantha Penrose knows she is adopted, and neither she nor her adoptive parents are aware that I am the father."

"So, Richard, what happened?"

"Well, what happened was the 'Knights of Columba.' In the year 1919, in Scotland, the 'Knights of St Columba' as a society of social catholic doctrine was formed. You would know that St Columba originally came as a missionary from Ireland to the island of Iona in Scotland."

"Yes, I am aware of that. But what it has to do with Samantha, I have no idea?"

"Well, my father and Roger's father were great friends and very catholic. They were also medical colleagues, and both became early life members of the St Columba society. They both strictly adhered to its principles of 'Charity, Unity and fraternity.' So, my father being aware of Roger and Edwina's non-productive plight, had a few words with Roger's father and they both went to the archbishop, who in turn, gave instructions to the nuns in the adoption home as to who was to receive the child.

It was agreed that Roger, Edwina, and I should not be privy to the arranged adoption, as was the case with the birth mother, you, of course. However, the irony was that Roger asked me to be godfather saying they would christen her again ceremonially giving her their own choice of name Samantha. However, upon seeing the child at the christening, I swear even before I saw the birthmark, I felt she was our Patricia. But then, once I saw it, plain enough as it was, I went to my father and confronted him. I just wanted the truth and if I didn't get it from him, I threatened to cause consternation at the home etc. etc. Eventually, he explained all, and said that it was God's will that I have the opportunity to see her grow up and be close to her."

Joan sat back thinking, there was no doubt that a story like that would be hard to make up, in the hour or so he had in the meeting. So, she thought she would take it as fact. Anyway, she had received confirmation that her darling Patricia was her darling Samantha, and for the moment she was happy to leave things as they were. Better not to upset the applecart and maybe upset the child in it.

"Thank you, Richard. It is nice to know she loves you anyway, and perhaps in time with the few times I get to see her she will get to like me too."

"Excuse me," said, a tall man with grey hair but about the same age as Richard. "Sorry to interrupt," he continued, "but take as much time as you like, don't rush, I'm just reading the newspaper in the reception area, I just came in for a cup of tea."

"Oh, Roger! I'm just coming. This is Mrs Joan Corrigan," he said, using her maiden name, as he could see she was married but didn't know her married name. "We are old, well not her, work colleagues from over ten years back, just catching up!"

"Nice to meet you Mrs Corrigan, I'm Roger Penrose, sorry to have interrupted."

"Nice to meet you too, Dr Penrose. I'm in a rush anyway to catch a plane."

"Goodbye then."

"Yes, goodbye."

*

The Post mistress at Charing Cross post office, Miss Smithers, told Detective Inspector O'Connell that she had already told the Bobby who had called before, that on the day in question there was no telegram sent by a Miss Bethany Sheridan. Richard thanked her but asked if she would mind showing him the record list of those people who did send a telegram on that day.

Richard's usual calmness shifted to low-key excitement when he saw that none other than a Mr Michael Collins had requested a telegram for remittance that day at 12.15 PM.

"Do you know which of your staff sent the message for the Michael Collins listed here?"

"That would be, Jonathan," she said.

Upon Richard asking Jonathan if he remembered anything about the Michael Collins gentleman or the telegram, the postal clerk smiled and said.

"Oh, yes, Sir, I certainly do. He was a strange-looking bloke, big, with a black moustache. I remember him well because," at that point Jonathan's voice dropped to a whisper, and he continued, "he slipped me five bob to hold it, and not send it till I was going home at five o'clock. He said the person it was going to would not be at home until the evening!"

"You never mentioned you took a telegram on that day for Ireland to the constable who called here on last Thursday?"

"Last Thursday and Friday, I was off with the flu."

Richard obtained a copy of all the details from the post office and had his driver then go in the direction of the first of four car-hire outlets close to Euston station he intended to visit.

Sitting in the back of the squad-car and rustling some papers so as not to have to talk to the driver, Richard took out a large paper pad and began to write.

1. Suspect David Williams, believed to have murdered wife Bronwyn and be involved in the disappearance of her sister Bethany.

2. The suitcase in which the body found has barely readable initials TFM Maguire on the inside bottom.

3. Bullets found in victim's body ballistics show from same gun, but no gun found so far.

4. Michael Collins is name of man who purchased wig last year and sent telegram to Bronwyn.

5. Michael Collins is the name of the man who purchased the ticket in Westmoreland Street and occupied the cabin next to Bronwyn.

6. Description of telegram sender somewhat like man with black moustache exiting plane when awaiting criminal Tony Turner. And on reflection had the same walk as Williams walking up church at mass. Now, with him in London at the post office, it ties him coming back that evening.

7. Believe suspect wears a wig and false moustache.

8. Believe Suspect Williams and Collins one and the same.

9. The Affair with Hannigan is motivation. Briefcase with false bottom concealing hammer not found. The suspect said he had no briefcase when asked, as it might contain the Maguire initials. A briefcase case might be in the Flat on North Circular Road.

10. 24-hour watch on suspect himself and on suspect's home and the flat.

11. No doctors in the Charing Cross area telephoned Bethany's place of employment.

12. Telephone call traced to post office.

13. All evidence circumstantial to date

14. Need to find, (a) gun (b) wig and moustache (c) Briefcase with false bottom.

15. Warrant to search suspect's 'house' and 'Flat' available 8.AM tomorrow.

16. Now believe that piece of leather originally in suspect's rubbish bin but now missing was part of the briefcase, perhaps the false bottom.

17. What was the hammer for?

18. What really happened to Maguire?

17 Where is Bethany?

19. Most pressing of all is for hard evidence that Suspect travelled on mail-boat 2nd Mar and mail train 3rd to London Euston.

With help from what the butcher's wife had told him, Richard had sought and received permission from his counterpart in the Yard to revisit the car-hire outlets around Euston station. It was not until he called on the third on his list that he found what he was looking for.

CHAPTER 21

Wednesday 16ᵗʰ March 1960

8.00 AM, a warrant is served on David Williams to search his house on Marine Drive in Sandymount. The arrogant and confident Williams simply said to Inspector.

"Oh, please, you did not need a warrant, all you had to do was ask, and I'd have given you permission."

The colour on his face changed to white, however, when Richard replied.

"And how would you have reacted if I asked to search your flat on the North Circular Road?"

"I'm not saying another word until I consult my solicitor." Replied the murderer.

Later on, that morning in the North Circular Road Flat, leased for a Michael Collins, the hat, coat, glasses, wig, moustache, and briefcase without the false bottom, but with the Maguire TMF initials on the inside, near the bottom, were found. The briefcase was later identified by Eileen Hannigan as the one she had seen with the false bottom concealing a hammer. Also, Inspector O'Connell was certain that the piece of leather he had seen in the Suspect's bin was the false bottom itself.

When all this evidence was put together with the information surrounding the telegram sent to Bronwyn, all was needed was one final piece of evidence, and Richard found it in London.

The suspect had purchased the ticket 2ⁿᵈ March for Dun Laoghaire-Holyhead-London in the name of Michael Collins. The records showed that the cabin was taken up by a gentleman. So, David Williams, as Collins, was on the boat the night of the murder. In addition, Richard had made checks and confirmed with all ports and airports that no one by the name of David Williams had journeyed on their transportation from Ireland to London on the relevant date.

However, while looking to see did a Michael Collins hire a car in London 3ʳᵈ March, presumably with a false driving license, Richard found something else he had suspected from what Joan Lawlor had said at their coffee stop. He discovered that a 1958 Morris Minor van was hired with a driving license in the name of Dáithí MacUilliam of Céide na Mara,

Dumhach Thrá, Baile Átha Cliath (David Williams of Marine Drive, Sandymount, Dublin).

When making the arrest, the first thing Richard did was to secure the driving license to ensure the murderer, Williams, didn't discard it and claim it got lost.

In Ireland, a driving license may be issued in Gaelic or English and the London Bobby upon fist checking the car-hire outlets did not, of course, realise that David William's name in Gaelic was Dáithí MacUilliam.

Afterword

The Year of Our Lord, 1961

Saturday 11th February

2.00 PM London Time: Novena participant, Patrick Foley, fussed about his client's hair and joked that he had made her so beautiful that when she got home her husband would forget about the football and ravish her instead! At the same time, Patrick's partner, former priest Joe McKenna, was preparing the evening meal of 'Shepard's Pie' for the two of them. This culinary activity was taking place in the kitchen of a beautiful two bedroomed flat in London's Charing Cross.

They got the flat under a very reasonable lease six months before, as it had been vacant for several months before due, the landlord told them, to a legal issue regarding the previous female tenant.

Joe was following, to the letter, the recipe his partner and lover Patrick had given him that morning as he left for work. Patrick usually did all the cooking, but he was encouraging Joe to get involved. Also, should Joe have any questions, all he had to do was go across the road to the hair salon, where Patrick was employed as a senior stylist. As he worked away, Joe was singing with Elvis on the radio a song he thought was very appropriate, 'It's now or never.'

Joe had never been as happy as he was having made the decision, under a year ago, to tell Patrick he loved him and wanted to go to bed with him and live with him together forever. Patrick had reacted by becoming even more flamboyant than usual in excitement.

"But you're a priest! He said. "It's a sin what you're saying! Oh, Jesus, I'd love it but....It would be wrong?"

Joe remembered well his reply. "Patrick," he'd said, "the God you and me both know and love is a God of Love. He made us the way we are and obviously wants us to be that way because we also know that he doesn't make mistakes! As well as that, he tells us that above everything and anything else, we are to love one another. And what better way is there for us, his children, to express it than to be with each other?"

Patrick had looked at him and said.

"You mean I don't have to try and not be homosexual?"

"I think," you could be anything you liked, according to God, provided you harmed no one, and you helped as many unfortunates as you can. But I love you the way you are. I don't want you to change in any way, except, of course, to put the top back on your hair dye when you're finished with it."

That evening, while on their way to a gay bar in Soho, the 'Clippy' came upstairs to collect their fares. But before asking for the fares she looked Joe straight in the face and blurted out.

"Oh, goodness me, I'm sorry, I thought you were someone I knew in Dublin."

"Sarah Brannigan!" said Joe, immediately recognising the woman from Newbridge Ave who had been abused.

"Oh, it is you, Father. I saw the clothes and thought I must be mistaken."

"It's lovely to see you, Sarah. So, did everything work out alright for you?"

"Yes, it certainly did. I'm living with my sister now, in a bigger flat, with little Jimmy who is now in school, and all is safe and well. And it is thanks to you Father and also Johnny…O'Keefe, who turned out to be a fairy godfather."

"Oh, forget about me, but yes, Johnny was good to put you up that night, and you obviously got the bag I dropped into Ringsend for you. He had asked me specifically to make sure you got it."

"Oh, I did father, and did you know that under the few things I had managed to grab before I left Newbridge Avenue, Johnny had left three bags of money for me! He must have saved it up over the years from beggin and people must have liked him as there were loads of notes in there as well. But in his kindness, he gave it all to me."

Things were clicking in Joe's head, regarding stolen collection money, but his thoughts were interrupted by Patrick digging him in the side.

"Oh, sorry Sarah, this is my friend from Dublin you may know him, Patrick Foley."

"Yes, I think I do from the hairdressers?"

The Novena

"That's right," said Patrick. "Nice to meet you, Sarah."

Sarah took the fares and gave out the tickets, and when she returned downstairs, Joe whispered to Patrick.

"When we get to the bar, have I got a story for you.

"Oh, God, I hate you! Tell me now or I'll burst."

Joe managed to hold off until they got off the bus, and then related the church-collection robbery saga that until then had unsolved. Patrick's reaction was to begin to scream and scream with delight, but neither cared about the attention it drew from people around.

*

2.30 PM Dublin time: Novena participant, Dr James (Robin) McNulty, and his wife Cecilia had taken their seats for the Ireland vs England rugby match at Lansdowne Road. They smiled at each other like newly-weds, but in fact had been married for nearly eight months,

"Are you sure you are comfortable enough? Please wrap my rug also around you, we don't want you catching a cold now, do we?" said Robin, eying her pregnant bump of seven months.

"I'm not an invalid, James," she replied, "and I'm very cozy, so just relax and enjoy the atmosphere."

Robin sat back, smiled, and thought back on the year gone by. They had been married within a month of Cecilia returning from Antonio's funeral in Rome, and she became pregnant almost immediately. Unfortunately, he never got to have his discussion with Fr Horgan on the notions of consciousness etc. from the 'Phenomenon of Man.' But he did have to attend the inquest on the accident in which he gave evidence to the effect that it exonerated the lorry driver, as Horgan, according to the x-ray results, had an inoperable brain tumour that more than likely, due to its position, probably caused loss of coordination and/or convulsions which resulted in the crash.

*

2.45 PM Belfast time: Novena participant, Veronica O'Brien' waited with her six children in the in-mates waiting room of Crumlin Road prison for her husband Raymond to be brought in.

Raymond got 18 months for the discovery of two hand pistols found in a concealed compartment of his car boot. He had claimed that he had no idea who put the guns there. This part was actually true as he was supposed to park the car, at a certain time outside a certain pub off the Falls Road, and once he finished a pint, he would return and drive away with whatever some unknown person had secreted in the boot.

When the case was heard shortly after his arrest. There had been much laughter in court when the prosecutor explained that these arms were bundled up in ten boxes of condoms. This hilarity was soon quashed, however, once the judge called for order.

After his conviction, Raymond, had told Vera that she was to take her housekeeping money out of the bank and that his friends in the republican movement would keep the bank account topped up, so she would not go short while he was away. He also said that his job would not be there when he got out, but another job would be waiting for him, courtesy of those friends again.

A short time later Vera was delighted to hear in a letter from Raymond that this would be her last visit as he was getting out earlier for good behaviour and would be home by the beginning of March. She put this down to her constant prayers to St Leonard, the patron saint of political prisoners. The novena had also sorted out her problem of Raymond using those 'Frenchies.' It was probably a miracle she thought, as when she went to Dr McNulty regarding her hit-and-miss periods, he had told her to try to relax and asked when she was next due? Upon hearing this, he told her to come back to him two weeks after that date to report whether she had menstruated. On her return, she advised him that she had 'no-show' at all, but lately was beginning to get a lot of sweating. He advised her that she was at the start of a relatively early menopause and would experience probably quite a lot of 'hot flushes' and sweating for a while.

She had weathered the menopause sweats and all with no more periods for the previous seven months, so when Raymond came home, he would not need to use any contraceptives at all.

*

3.00 PM Sydney time: Novena participant, Eileen Hannigan, together with her husband James, sat with their backs to the wall on that glorious sun filed day watching Thomas, Tilly and Paul run play and splash in the rock pool on Bronte Beach, close to, but not as crowded as Bondi.

Their son Seamus was surfing further up the beach and no doubt looking forward to his pal from Ireland Pat, who was coming to stay with them in two days' time for a month's holiday.

With James, not getting his promotion because of favouritism, they had sold up, took the plunge, and emigrated from Dublin to Sydney. He got a job with Waverley council at the same level he had in Dun Laoghaire, but a higher salary, while Eileen to her amazement got a teaching post at Paddington State School teaching both boys and girls.

Selling up and moving to Australia because of James not getting the promotion was, however, only the secondary reason for the shift. The primary reason was to make a new start to their marriage, which had been rocked when Eileen had to give evidence for the prosecution at David Williams' trial. The defense council had, under cross-examination, exposed to all and that she had been in a relationship with the accused.

Initially, James had moved out of their house, but with a lot of help from both Joan and Joseph Lawlor together with Fr McKenna, a delicate reconciliation was achieved. Sydney was as far as they could get away from Sandymount, which was necessary for their future life together. It was difficult, but every day their relationship improved.

*

4.00 PM Dublin Time: Novena participant, Thomas Masterson, while half listening to the rugby match was of two minds as to get changed before he went out to his shed to do some woodworking or continue to mess about the house in his ladies' attire. He would have to change in thirty minutes anyway, as soon after his daughter Patricia would be home from the afternoon matinée at the 'Shack.'

Apart from his ladies' underwear, today he was adorned in a lovely light blue taffeta dress with a darker blue angora cardigan. He checked that the seams on his nylons were straight as he looked down at his new court shoes.

"That is really a lovely outfit you're wearing today, Sadie," said his wife, Nora.

"Why thank you, Nora, for the compliment, and may I say you are looking quite well yourself. Oh. And thank you so much for lending me your powder puff, I'd be obliged if you would buy me one for myself next week."

"Yes, I'll pick one up in McAuliffe's Chemist with your lipstick on Monday," came Nora's reply as she went to the kitchen to prepare the tea.

Nora, a practical woman, had almost completely come to terms with her husband's transvestite need. It had taken all her practicality, tolerance, and will power, from the moment she had been confronted with it, on that ominous day in Ranelagh last year. She had gone back to the bed-sit with him, feeling at any moment she would vomit, but managed to keep it down as she watched how wretchedly pathetic and embarrassed, he was as he took off his ladies' knickers and put on his big Y-fronts. Then she felt a huge sadness for him, thinking, how would any man go to so much trouble unless there was within him a great need? They talked and talked in the bed-sit and talked and talked on the way home, and when they got home, they talked and talked again.

So out of love for him, little by little she allowed him, when they were alone, to dress up and just walk around the house. Also, they had gone away for two weekends when she and he in his transformed state had gone out together for a bite to eat. Indeed, the big plan was that when they went to the Isle of Man, in the coming August for a week's holiday, he would spend most of the time as Sadie and in fact she was almost enjoying buying clothes for him for the adventure.

She knew that many other women would have left him, but he was not a drunk, he did not beat her, they still had marital relations in bed, he was a good provider, and she still loved him. But he had a need that was not acceptable in society, and she was contented to deal with it. After all, if he was struck with TB or some other compliant, she'd have to deal with that. So, all was okay in the Masterson home and getting better every day.

*

5.00 PM Dublin time: In the O'Connell household Peg, has had her pains relieved by at least 25% and some days by as much as 50% due firstly to some surgery performed by Robin and secondly Robin has got her onto a clinical trial of a new drug called ibuprofen. Richard had moved on from longline fishing to fishing off the pier at Bullock harbour. He did, however, get a commendation for his work in the arrest and imprisonment of David Williams and also a special mention from the London met. Williams was convicted on the following evidence.

1. It was shown beyond doubt that he had taken the false disguise of Michael Collins at the 'Flat' address on North Circular Road in Dublin. This false identity was enhanced by the wig and moustache disguise found in the

'Flat.'

2. With this identity, Williams had sent the telegram from Charing Cross inveigling his wife to take the mail boat on Wednesday 2nd March, the night of the murder.

3. He had also used the identity to purchase the ticket for the cabin next to her on the evening of the crossing.

4. It was shown that he, as his alias, made the crossing and continued to London where he hired a van shortly after the Irish mail train arrived in Euston.

5 He had claimed the suitcase in which the body was found was not his wife's, and he had never seen it before her death. However, Michael Maguire, the brother of the man who made the suitcase, gave evidence that the suitcase and the briefcase found at the 'Flat' were purchased by the same man.

6. Maguire also made a similar leather false bottom, as one missing, to show how it had fit to hide the hammer and perhaps a weapon.

7. The motivation for the murder was due to his affair with Eileen Hannigan and the desire to be free of his wife.

There was a further development in the William's saga, and Richard was expecting a phone call in that regard from London early next week. He was optimistic he would receive good news.

Richard will be sitting his exams in a few months for 'Superintendent' and is expected to get them.

John (Copper) O'Connell had a successful result for his Inter Cert and is getting on alright with Brother Delaney, not because his Irish studies had improved, but Delaney was in charge of the senior football team and Copper was a stalwart of the team. This was evidenced when Delaney had put a sheet up on the notice board, listing the team members for next week's final. Besides each name, Delaney had identified each player's ability and skills with a specific number of stars. Four players received the top 4 stars, and Copper was one of the top four.

On the romantic front, Copper, had long got over his crush on Rosie O'Neill and was now concentrating on Heather Fleming from Claremont Road. She had in the last month bloomed into a 'peach.' And, not only that, but she also didn't fit into either category of 'A' or 'B' girls because as far as Copper was concerned, she was the whole alphabet.

Richard and Copper listened to the Ireland vs England rugby game on Radio Eireann and when Ireland won 11 points to 8, they were both delighted and proud.

*

5.00 PM London time: Inspector Simon Lawrence of the Yard was disappointed that England lost the rugby game to Ireland, but his thoughts of rugby soon went when he thought of the news, he would give to Richard O'Connell first thing on Monday.

The news stemmed from what had been discovered the previous Saturday, by a man walking his dog, in Colne Valley Regional Park. The man and dog were walking in an extremely isolated area of the Park when the dog, a dachshund, notorious for digging, stopped at a particular spot, and having sniffed for a few seconds began to dig furiously. The man ignored this usual behaviour and walked on. After several minutes with no sign of the dog following him, he retraced his steps and sternly called the animal to come to heel. Still, the dog continued to dig. Approaching the deep hole already made, the man was about to pull the dog away by the collar, when he saw part of an exposed piece of plywood. Further investigation had him contact the police, and the body was fully revealed a short time later. From that point on, the following had occurred.

1. The body was identified thanks to dental records as that of Bethany Sheridan.

2. Within the sleeping bag a single bullet hole was found, and further investigation showed that while there were two holes from which the bullets had exited the body, by some freak happening both had entered the sleeping bag through the same entry point before going on their own trajectory path. One bullet was retrieved while the other was missing.

3. Ballistics would show that the retrieved bullet was fired from the same gun as the bullets that had killed the victim's sister.

4. A receipt was found from an Army and Navy store at the bottom of a bag buried with the victim. It was dated the same day the victim went missing. A finger and thumbprint revealed it belonged to the victim's brother-in-law, who was three months into serving a life sentence for murdering his wife, the victim's sister.

5. At whatever future date David Williams is released from Mountjoy Jail,

he is to be extradited to the UK to stand trial for the murder of Bethany Sheridan.

Inspector Lawrence had only received confirmation from the Yard's ballistics department on the bullet late on Friday and decided to make Richard O'Connell's Monday morning a happy one.

*

6.30 PM: Novena participant, Mary Murphy, was finishing up drying the dishes after tea. She loved the modern kitchen in Emily's house, and she loved everything else about her move, with her two youngest, into the Claremont Park abode. With daughter Catherine now living in her traineeship in the Shelbourne hotel, it was an easy move for Mary and the other children, following the sale of their family house on Seaforth Avenue.

Mary was still in a state of shocked happiness at what had happened to her life since the day following Raymond's ructions and embarrassing performance outside the church.

The next day, which was a Friday, his pay day, he had apologised to her for all the embarrassment he had caused and went off to work. She just acknowledged his apology, as usual, but believed once he got paid, he would arrive home drunk, as was the habit. This was not the case, however, in fact, instead of going to the pub he had gone for a walk and later attended an 'Alcoholics Anonymous' meeting, at the AOH hall on Newbridge Ave. To his credit, he had not touched a drop since.

With the result of this, they had then been able to talk about their marital difficulties, and it was mutually agreed that they would sell the house, separate, and make their own lives. It was also agreed, that while she kept the two younger children, he would have access to them on an ongoing basis.

Shortly after Raymond had gone on the dry, Emily confronted Mary about the shoebox shortages. However, Emily told her that it was partly her own fault for putting temptation her way. She also told Mary that she had not been very honest herself. She confessed that the woman who had lived with her was not her sister and that neither of them had, in fact, ever been married. The two had been in a loving relationship. Emily had then asked Mary if she understood what that meant? Mary smilingly told her that she understood very well what Emily was talking about and detailed her own similar life preferences in that regard.

Mary then related her plight from her first night in the wedding bed, through the still-born deaths of her babies and finally, her discussion with Robin.

Following these confessions, they both expressed their growing love for each other, and even before moving in, Mary had spent numerous nights of intimate love in Emily's bed. With the move, their relationship blossomed with Mary having, at last, an honest love, and Emily lovingly adjusting to the parenting process.

Catherine was doing extremely well in the 'Shelbourne' and had confided to Mary that she had seen her Dad one evening walking along Grafton Street with a lady on his arm.

*

7.00 PM: Novena participants. Evelyn and Mikey O'Rourke, enjoying their honeymoon, were just leaving the room at the Waldorf Astoria hotel in New York's Manhattan. They were on their way to see the Broadway production of 'Becket' at the Royal Theatre. Earlier, they had taken the boat tour out to the 'Statue of Liberty' but tonight was Mikey's special honeymoon present to the theatre loving Eve.

Their relationship, since he had kissed her hand, seemed to remove all notions in her head that she was a lesbian. And in fact, once he got around to kissing her on the lips, for her, there was never going to be any going back.

They had made an agreement that they would never talk about the abuse she had endured as a child, or the accusations made about him by Raymond Murphy. Rather, they would start their relationship as two virgins and look only to each other for their future love, friendship, and intimate satisfaction.

It turned out that Eve never needed to get the Sweepstake job or to have the arranged talk with Joan about her concerns, as her hero, John (Mikey) Wayne, remedied all her emotional worries and concerns. The wedding had been a happy celebration in Galway, with Samantha as bridesmaid and Edwina and Roger attending, as well as Mary and Emily, Joan, Joseph, and Vera who of course gave them a blessing from the patron saint of love, St Valentine.

*

9.00 PM, Samantha was staying in Joan's house for a few days after Eve and Mikey got married. It had been arranged that she would attend, with Joan and Joseph, a set-dancing session on Sunday afternoon, after which they would put her on the plane for London.

The kids had gone to bed and the butcher had gone to discuss commerce with Mr O'Reilly.

"Where do you keep the shoe polish, Mrs Lawlor?" Samantha asked Joan. "

"It's in a cardboard box in the garage and by the way Samantha, don't you think it's time you started calling me Aunty Joan instead of Mrs Lawlor, it sounds so formal."

"Well," replied Samantha. "How about instead of calling you Aunty Joan, I actually started calling you 'Mom'?"

Joan's heart skipped a beat.

"What did you say, Samantha?"

"How about I call you Mom, in private when no one else is around?"

Almost winded, Joan asked.

"Why, love, would you call me Mom?"

"Well, because you are my real mother. Is that, not, right?"

Joan didn't want to betray the trust she had given, nor wanted to say or do anything that might stop her being able to see Samantha on the times she had managed to do so.

"Sweetheart," she said, "I love you, but you have a mother in London, so just let's leave it at Aunty Joan."

"But you are my real mother. I know."

"How could you know that?"

"By simple deduction. It was elementary, my dear Watson. You know I love Sherlock Holmes and his deductive powers, and I also like Hercule Poirot books from Agatha Christie. So, after I read about three detective books when I was ten, I decided to gather clues to try and find my real Mom and Dad. I wanted to know who they were because I wanted to know where I came from. I really do love my adoptive Mom and Dad, they give me everything, and I'd die if they were not there, and I'd never hurt them by saying I wanted to find my birth parents!"

"Of course, you love them and of course they love you, and no, you should never hurt them." Said Joan, the tears seeping from her eyes.

"I suppose the first thing I used to think about," said Samantha, "was, who would I like to have as my real Mom and Dad? The first person who jumped into my head was Uncle Dicky for my Dad and the more I thought about it the more real it became so; with all the little and big things he'd do for me. But nobody fitted the place for my real mother, until you changed my bandage. I liked you before, but when you checked for my birthmark, I got the heebie jeebies in my tummy."

"Birthmark? Whatever do you mean?" Lied Joan.

"Just let me continue with all the clues, and then you can say I'm wrong?"

Joan nodded her reluctant consent.

"The clue was the telephone call you made on that Sunday, which I overheard Aunty Eve giving you my date of birth and something about Uncle Dicky. Then you came to the airport, and I was so delighted, I hoped you came to see me. Next, I got the birthday card from you, and it was posted in London on the day my Love dad, Roger, told Mom he thought he had met an old girlfriend of Uncle Dicky. And he said her name was Joan Corrigan. Then, when I got the opportunity here in Dublin, I asked Nuala what her Mommy's name was before she was married, and she said it was, Joan Mary Corrigan! So, when we are alone, may I call you Mom?"

God works in mysterious ways

God moves in a mysterious way
His wonders to perform
He plants His footsteps in the sea
And rides upon the storm.

Judge not the Lord by feeble sense
But trust Him for His grace;
Behind a frowning providence
He hides a smiling face.

William Cowper (Hymn) 1774

Character Profiles

Name	Occupation	Family	Address	Situation
Brannigan Sarah (Mrs) Age 27	Housewife (abused)	Husband: Brannigan + Child Jimmy	Newbridge Ave Sandymount	Seeking help for abuse
Crampton Peter (Fr) Age 59	Priest	N/A	Leahy Terrace	Curate with impaired hearing
Foley Patrick (Pansy) (Mr) Age 27	Hairdresser	Mother	Ennis Grove	Seeking a cure for his homosexuality
Hannigan Eileen (Mrs) Age 37 Very attractive Looks younger than age	Housewife Ex Teacher	James: husband Seamus 14 Twins Thomas and Tilly 11 Paul 4	Marine Drive	Bored with domestic life. Has a great secret.
Hannigan James (Mr) Age 40 Small, thin and good looking with good personality	Assistant Town Clerk	Eileen: Wife Children (above)	Marine Drive	Wants promotion to impress wife
Horgan John (Fr)	Priest (SJ)	N/A	Gardner Street Dublin	Facilitator and presenter of Novena
Jones Emily (Mrs) Age 45	House widow	N/A	Claremont Park	English comfortable war widow and Invalid.
Lawlor Joan (Mrs) Age 32	Butcher's wife Ex Nurse	Husband Joseph Peter 9 Nuala 6 Jack 2	Marine Drive	Contented wife and mother but her mother's instinct aches for fulfilment.

Name	Occupation	Family	Address	Situation
Lawlor Joseph (Joe) (Mr) Age 32	Butcher	Joan: Wife Children (above)	Marine Drive	Aware of wife's wish
Lombardi Cecelia (Mrs)	Radiographer	Antonio: Husband	Merrion Road	In bad marriage but cannot get a divorce.
Masterson Nora (Mrs) Age 55	Housewife	Thomas: Husband Tom 24 Sammy 20 Patricia 12	Beach Road	Worries about her sons being overseas and her husband acting strange.
Masterson Thomas (Mr) Age 56	Supervisor Shaws Store Religious Dept.	Nora: Wife Children (above)	Beach Road	Desired a transformation frowned on by society
McKenna Joseph (Fr) Age 29	Priest curate	N/A	Leahy Terrace	Has a desire and an activity that his parishioners would not be, at all, happy with.
McNulty James (Robin) (Dr) Age 46	Doctor	N/A	Tritonville Road	GP and Specialises in women's health.
Murphy Mary (Mrs) Age 38	Housewife	Stephen: Husband Catherine 17 Rory 6 Bertie 4	Seaforth Avenue	Difficulties having intimate relations
Murphy Stephen (Mr) Age 38	Teacher	Mary Wife Children (above)	Seaforth Avenue	Frustrated with wife and heavy drinker.

Name	Occupation	Family	Address	Situation
O'Brien Raymond (Ray) (Mr) Age 42	Medical Representative	Veronica: Wife Pat 14 Sarah 13 Peter 11 Larry 8 Jill 5 Nan 3	Marine Drive	Member of the IRA. Uses artificial contraceptives and thinks his wife does not know.
O'Brien Veronica (Vera) Mrs Age 38	Housewife	Raymond: Husband Children (above)	Marine Drive	Bordering on religious insanity.
O'Connell John (Copper) Age 16	Schoolboy	Son of Peg and Richard Siblings: Monica 14 Eamon 5 Rose 2	Strand Road	Physically and mentally abused in school. Has a major crush on a local girl.
O'Connell Peg (Mrs) Age 42	Housewife	Richard: Husband John 16 Monica 14 Eamon 5 Rose 2	Strand Toad	Suffering pain and effects of Symphysiotomy procedure. Concerns re son's school.
O'Connell Richard (Garda Inspector) Age 49	(Garda) Policeman	Peg: Wife Children (above)	Strand Road	Longline fishing on Sandymount strand
O'Keeffe Johnny (Rags) (Mr)	Beggar man	N/A	Tritonville Road and the Streets.	Schizophrenic and alcoholic.
O'Rourke Mikey (Mr) Age 30	Engineer	Parents and siblings. N/A	Claremont Road	Has an antisocial habit.

Name	Occupation	Family	Address	Situation
Roberts Evelyn (Miss) Age 28	Secretary	Married sister Edwina with husband Roger and daughter Samantha living in London	Serpentine Avenue	Due to assault when young she believes herself a Lesbian but only seeks friendship. .
Shillitoe Roger (Rev) Age 55	Vicar	N/A	Sandymount Green	Vicar of the Methodist Church and Drama committee member.
Skeffington Michael (Fr) Age 65	Priest	N/A	Leahy Terrace	Canon and Parish priest.
Williams Bronwyn (Mrs) Age 38	Housewife	David: Husband	Marine Drive	Snob and social climber. Despises her husband.
Williams David (Mr) Age 40	Senior Travel Clerk	Bronwyn: Wife	Marine Drive	Good looking man who desires to make his life better.

ABOUT THE AUTHOR

John Francis Hopkins (Jack) was born in Dublin where he attended Primary and Secondary school.

In 1972 he moved to Australia, on assisted passage, for a different life. There he received a Bachelor of Arts degree (Economics/Philosophy) from the University of Sydney and later completed post graduate Marketing qualifications at Charles Sturt University NSW where he graduated Valedictorian.

He worked in the Pharmaceutical Industry for over 35 years commencing as a Medical Representative eventually progressing to Senior Management (director level).

In addition, he has lectured in Marketing and Senior Sales Management and for leisure plays a five-string banjo and button accordion. He currently lives back in Dublin with his wife Christina.

He has also, in 2016, published with *AMAZON* an economic proposition for a new form of *Capitalism* based on *Quantum Physics,* titled "Brilliantbranes".

Printed in Great Britain
by Amazon

21224124R00142